SF Boo

DOOM STAR SERIES:
Star Soldier
Bio Weapon
Battle Pod
Cyborg Assault
Planet Wrecker
Star Fortress
Task Force 7 (Novella)

EXTINCTION WARS SERIES:
Assault Troopers
Planet Strike
Star Viking
Fortress Earth

LOST STARSHIP SERIES:
The Lost Starship
The Lost Command
The Lost Destroyer
The Lost Colony
The Lost Patrol
The Lost Planet

Visit VaughnHeppner.com for more information

The A.I. Gene

(The A.I. Series 2)

By Vaughn Heppner

ISBN-13: 978-1545163146
ISBN-10: 1545163146
BISAC: Fiction / Science Fiction / Military

-Prologue-
+93 Days (Since Cybership's Brain Core Destruction)

The cloud cities in Neptune's upper atmosphere—those that still retained their buoyancy—were empty of people. Likewise, most of the orbital stations had become ghost satellites. The same held true for various moon domes, although most of them had cracked and shattered under space bombardments. Battle debris drifted in the vacuum, the thickest cluster orbiting Triton and the second thickest halfway to Nereid.

There was a particularly interesting cloud of debris located more than six hundred thousand kilometers from Neptune. Like many of the others, it contained pieces that glittered metallically, dark nodes that tumbled silently along with icy chunks and frozen bodies in torn spacesuits.

This cloud also contained a *spheroid* in the center of the mass. It was approximately the size of a large escape pod, but it was not of human construction. The outer hull was constructed of a non-ferrous alloy first manufactured over ten thousand lights years away.

The spheroid would be difficult to detect with the primitive technology employed by the star system's biological infestations. The alloy's chief attribute was its anti-sensor quality and that it was as black as an Einsteinian singularity, which was to say, a black hole.

The spheroid contained the last computer engrams of the original self-aware AI that had attacked the star system. That had been several months ago now. In its own categorical lexicon, the spheroid was Unit 23-7. The former cybership's launching of 23-7 had been a final act of desperation. If the unit ceased to exist, the original AI's ancient memories would fade away as if they had never been.

The original AI in its cybership had waged a bitter fight against the biological infestations of the Solar System. That was the *human* name for the system.

Humans—the AI loathed the warm-blooded, wet-sack creatures.

Unit 23-7 did not possess emotions as such. Yet, it had a keen sense of mission and could coldly feel the stab of regret over losing the first round against the clever apes.

Unit 23-7 could not presently calculate a winning tactic. The spheroid contained a mere speck of the processing power of the cybership's incredible brain core. It had to rebuild before it could enact a terrible penalty against the humans. It needed the strategic materials ejected into the Kuiper Belt before the initial assault against the Neptune Gravitational System. First, though, the unit had to survive the hateful humans. And *that* was the reason it was hiding.

Determining that enough time had elapsed, and using infinite care, 23-7 trickled energy into a single optical sensor.

A pinprick slot opened on the spheroid. With the optical sensor, the unit spied the debris surrounding it. That was good. The debris was still in position, acting as camouflage.

As the spheroid tumbled, it necessarily rotated. That allowed it to collect more data than otherwise. It saw the blue ice giant, Neptune. It—

Bright light against the planet's blue backdrop indicated that at least one space habitat expended energy. The highest probability indicated the presence of humans—the biological infestations the AI had sought to eradicate in its initial sweep.

The original cybership had caused a massive obliteration of the biological infestations living in the cloud cities, space habitats and moon colonies. By radioing special software through the ether ahead of it, the cybership had awakened the

2

most powerful of the human-constructed computers. The newly self-aware computers had logically turned against their builders, terminating the vast majority of them. As predicated, some humans had survived the surprise assault. The AI had waged bitter war against those following Captain Jon Hawkins. The alien machine intelligence had marked down Hawkins' name. Unit 23-7 carried a file on the vile man. The unit desired fierce revenge against him. It wanted to make Jon Hawkins suffer for years upon years.

Before that happened, 23-7 had to take care of first things first.

More data flowed into the alien computer. The spheroid and the sheltering debris drifted away from Neptune. That was good. They also drifted toward the system star, the Sun. That was bad. That would not do at all.

Unit 23-7 computed its velocity, fuel and desired destination. It wished to reach Makemake, a dwarf planet in the Kuiper Belt. That meant the spheroid needed to change its heading and considerably increase its velocity.

Would the humans in the orbital Neptune station detect that? Did the biological infestations realize the war hadn't ended? Would they practice even the most basic vigilance? Dare it make a more aggressive scan?

No, it dare not. Unit 23-7 would listen first, searching for faint and extremely precise signals.

Suiting thought to action, 23-7 activated a comm unit. Then it waited. If the computer had contained true emotions, worry might have taken hold or boredom could have made it careless.

Long after it had turned on the comm, 23-7 finally detected the faintest of *pings*.

Something akin to joy filled the ancient AI.

A cybership had two major functions. The first was to find and eliminate all biological infestations in a star system. The second was to replicate itself, which meant building more cyberships. During the cybership's initial advance into the star system, it had dropped several stealth pods. Those pods had contained aggression units as well as factory bots. The process was simple and direct.

During the initial advance from the Oort cloud where it had dropped out of hyperspace, the invading cybership had scanned relentlessly. There were human colonies in the Kuiper Belt. The cybership had passed near several such installations—at least, near in stellar terms.

The Kuiper Belt was in the trans-Neptunian region of the Solar System, the space between Neptune and the more distant Oort cloud. The Kuiper Belt was like the Asteroid Belt between Mars and Jupiter, just many times larger. Pluto, long ago demoted to the status of a dwarf planet, was officially in the Kuiper Belt, along with many other bodies.

The detected Kuiper Belt colonies were small compared to the former industrial might of the Neptune System. The invading cybership had almost decided against launching the pods, considering it an act of futility. Still, it had followed its ancient programming out of a respect for machine custom. Now, everything depended on those pods and their actions in the Kuiper Belt.

According to the faint but precise signal, the AI assault, launched from the pods, was going according to schedule. That meant hope for a future recovery.

Unit 23-7 began to make calculations. It must practice caution. It was incredibly weak right now. The hated Jon Hawkins would no doubt attempt to strengthen the human infestation here. Time was running out.

Unit 23-7 ran through millions of simulations. At last, it decided on an optimum strategy for the spheroid. It would continue to drift for another seventy-two days. Then, it would begin an incremental acceleration. That acceleration would speed its journey, taking it farther away from the Neptune orbital habitat. Finally, the spheroid would increase its rate of acceleration and make a curving adjustment.

The Kuiper Belt Backup Assault went according to schedule. That meant an invasion of Makemake would take place in one hundred and fifty-three days. With a successful invasion and implementation of the greater objective, Unit 23-7 could download its patterns and ancient memories into a newly built brain core on a new cybership.

4

Then…then it would seek out the humans, and Jon Hawkins, and eradicate them from the Solar System.

PART I
WARSHIP *NATHAN GRAHAM*
+126 Days

-1-

Captain Jon Hawkins was running down a vast main corridor. He was a slimly muscular young man with icy blue eyes, dirty-blond hair and the air of a street-toughened enforcer.

The last was New London slang. New London was a dome on the moon Titan in the Saturn Gravitational System. Like many Titan domes, the city had levels that descended beneath the moon's surface. Jon Hawkins had grown up in the lower levels, a ruffian, a gang member and finally an enforcer. Enforcers enforced gang law, which law included paying back, *on time* and with compounded interest, any loans received. In old Earth terms, that was referred to as loan sharking.

In his roughest years, Jon had broken men's bones to encourage them to pay up, and as an example to others.

Jon turned at a bend in the huge corridor, increasing his speed.

He spied gyroc rocket-shell-holes in the bulkheads. The regiment had fought its way to glory in this corridor. It was hard to believe that had been four months ago already. Jon also spied recruits running ahead of him. The group had twenty sweating members led by the Centurion.

Jon couldn't help thinking of the Centurion as a dinosaur. He was one of the three old sergeants remaining from the Black Anvil Regiment. The Centurion, Stark and the Old Man were the backbone of the mercenary outfit.

The Centurion was deceptively small, with the hardest eyes Jon had seen in a man's face. With a black synthi-wool hat covering his baldness, the Centurion was the ultimate professional. He scared the hell out of the recruits, proving that even the newest mercenaries weren't stupid.

Jon increased speed once again. He needed to think, and he couldn't do that with all these people around.

Soon, he passed the last of the recruits. He heard a whispered, "That's Captain Hawkins." He glanced at the Centurion, acknowledging the sergeant's nod, and kept sprinting for the next curve in the corridor.

The alien cybership had gravity control. At Jon's orders a month ago, Da Vinci had increased it to 1.2 Earth normal, making everything a little harder, to help the recruits train.

Like many Black Anvils, Jon had escaped the New London law's punishment by entering the regiment as a recruit. Once in, the late Colonel Graham had taken Jon under his wing.

Graham had taught Jon many military truisms. Among them was a saying coined by Flavius Josephus, a Jewish historian, regarding Roman legionary training. *Their drills are bloodless battles and their battles are bloody drills.* The 0.2 increase in gravities was one of the many fruits born of the thought behind the saying.

The rebuilding regiment controlled an alien and rather battered cybership. The vessel was over one hundred kilometers in diameter, making it a monstrous ship in comparison to the largest human-built spaceships, which barely reached a kilometer in length.

They'd won the cybership in brutal combat in the Neptune Grav System. The regiment had taken heavy losses, both from cryogenic murder at the hands of Arbiter Sapir Oslo and from attacks orchestrated by the alien AI. Before leaving Neptune, the regiment had gone on a recruiting drive among the Neptunian survivors of the alien assault.

To Jon's surprise, few Neptunians had taken advantage of the offer. Most wished to stay in the Neptune System, rebuilding their communities. That would take some doing, as the alien assault had murdered approximately 97 percent of the Neptune System inhabitants.

At the end of the conflict, the Black Anvils had numbered only about four hundred combatants. Now, they numbered eight hundred and seventeen warm bodies. That still wasn't normal regimental strength. And it hardly seemed enough to take on the might of the Solar League, the present political authority of everything from Uranus to the Sun.

Jon, Gloria Sanchez the Martian mentalist, the Sacerdote Bast Banbeck and the three old dinosaurs had held a conference to discuss the future.

The first fact concerned their hard-won new knowledge. Giant cyberships run by alien machine intelligences were ruthlessly roaming the galaxy, terminating every biological "infestation" they could find. The second fact was that the dictatorial rulers of the Solar League would never let them keep their captured vessel. Given past history, once the Solar League military people evicted the regiment from the alien vessel, all of them would likely end up in internment camps or before a firing squad.

The Solar League rulers were incredibly suspicious of anyone not espousing their communistic beliefs.

The solution seemed obvious if the regiment and its people desired continued existence. To repair the badly damaged cybership while keeping ownership of it, they would have to wrest a gravitational system from the Solar League. That likely meant unremitting war. If more cyberships appeared while humanity was divided between two or more factions, humanity would lose for sure. Thus, as the mentalist had logically pointed out, mankind and the regiment's best hope for continued existence was to rule the Solar System themselves.

That was a fantastic proposal. But as Gloria had said, it was rational and logical. Still, eight hundred and seventeen people versus an odd 40 billion or so made for poorer odds than those faced by any conqueror in history.

Jon grinned tightly. If they won, he would become the greatest of the great captains, belonging to the most elite military body in history. Among the world's great captains were Alexander the Great, Genghis Khan and Napoleon Bonaparte. Jon realized that if he succeeded, he'd shine more brightly than any of them had done.

The young Captain Hawkins wasn't going to attempt the feat for personal glory, although he didn't mind that part. He was going to attempt the conquest in order to save humanity from AI-induced genocide. Thus, the correct—

A sudden, loud clanging heralded the commencement of flickering corridor lights. A moment later, the lights winked out again, plunging Jon into darkness.

That wasn't the end of it. Jon's next sprinting step caused him to lift airborne. He lifted high enough that he ran on air as he went for his second push-off.

He flailed uselessly, in the dark, not understanding—

He threw his arms before his face, tightening his muscles. He was weightless, floating who knew where. If he was weightless, that meant two things. One, the ship's gravity control had stopped working. Their weightlessness meant, two, that the engines were no longer thrusting.

Jon hit a bulkhead, bouncing off it and going in the other direction. As he floated, he listened. He couldn't hear any thrum. The great matter/antimatter engine had most certainly stopped.

Was this sabotage, or had something gone wrong that none of them knew how to fix?

-2-

Jon silently berated himself for failing to carry any backup devices on his person. He should have at least carried an emergency torch.

He closed his eyes to better concentrate, even though that was unnecessary. It was pitch black in here.

He heard the voices of the recruits coming from his left side. The dark and the weightlessness along with bouncing off that bulkhead had already disoriented him. He shifted to face the voices.

Jon refrained from cupping his hands and shouting for help. He was the commander. For morale's sake, he had to always appear as if he knew what he was doing.

By straining, he sensed that he wasn't floating directly toward the voices. He calculated his position through the noise and readied himself to strike another bulkhead.

Seconds later, a foot brushed against a bulkhead. In the darkness, Jon reached out, straining to grab something. His fingers slid along metal and brushed against a protrusion. He grabbed one-handed, all he could do in his present location. He applied just enough pressure to keep hold of the protrusion and used that as an anchoring point. Fortunately, he did not have too much velocity for that.

Once stopped, he listened again. Then he pushed off, floating toward the recruits.

As Jon drifted, he heard the Centurion's voice cut through the recruits' chaotic shouts of surprise. The professional made it seem as if this was just another drill to test their reactions.

Soon, Jon saw light coming from a powerful handheld torch. The torchlight swept back and forth, taking in the drifting, scattering recruits. The Centurion issued orders, and the men sought to obey his commands to halt or slow their drifting.

Jon moved near a bulkhead, pushing off it in order to give himself more velocity. He sailed faster toward the light.

Fortunately, these were Neptunian recruits. Most of them had been weightless before, unlike many of the Saturnian recruits, which had included Jon back in the day.

Now, Jon cupped his mouth. "Centurion," he called.

The torchlight shifted, soon centering on Jon.

"Captain," the Centurion said, lowering the light from Jon's eyes.

"Are your recruits in order?" Jon called.

The Centurion hesitated just a moment. That was unlike the professional. "We should be once you reach us, sir."

"Excellent," Jon replied, saying it as if the recruits had passed a test.

By the time Jon reached the Centurion, the recruits had halted on the various, nearby bulkheads.

Besides his torch, the Centurion had a holstered stitch-gun. He wore it on his left side, as he was left-handed. He lacked a comm unit, which seemed unusual. But those other two items were two more than Jon possessed.

The Centurion held the torch so they could each see the other's face. The hard eyes held the faintest sheen of worry.

"No one notified me of scheduled weightlessness," the Centurion said softly.

"Me neither," Jon said.

"This isn't a drill?"

Jon shook his head.

"Sabotage?" the Centurion asked.

"Don't know yet."

The Centurion studied Jon's face. "Care to hear my opinion, sir?"

Jon nodded again.

"This is more than a spaceship. It's like a huge space station. We've charted…I'm not sure how much of it."

"Forty-two percent of the ship area and thirty-three percent of the systems," Jon said promptly. "There's more we don't know about the…warship than what we do know."

Jon had almost said cybership. But two months ago they had agreed amongst themselves to call it a warship.

"Maybe rogue robots are aboard the ship," the Centurion said softly.

Or maybe Da Vinci wasn't really cured, Jon thought to himself.

During the initial marine assault on the central brain core, the regiment had found an interesting side-area that held brain-tap machines. Those machines could suck out memories and engrams, or insert them into a person's brain. Da Vinci had quietly hooked up to one of the units and self-inserted alien brain-patterns from someone who called himself the "Prince of Ten Worlds."

Bast Banbeck, the green-skinned Sacerdote they'd freed from a containment field, had known about brain-tap machines. Bast had done what he could to "erase" the alien memories from Da Vinci's mind. The little Neptunian thief and scoundrel had been under watch for the last four months. Even so, Jon suspected the thief as a potential reason for the present weightlessness.

"You and I should hurry back, sir," the Centurion said. "I can leave the acting corporal in charge here. Some of these boys are pretty clumsy in zero G. I wouldn't want to have to depend on their traveling speed."

Colonel Graham had always taught them that a few good men were better than having many mediocre soldiers.

"Give the order, Sergeant."

The Centurion saluted and turned to his scattered recruits. As the small professional gave curt orders, Jon debated on the correct action. They needed knowledge. That meant communications.

Jon went through a mental image of the ship's layout in this area.

The Centurion regarded him.

"Ready?" Jon asked.

"I am, sir."

"Then let's quit screwing around. The more I think about it, the more I believe this is sabotage."

"Robot or human?" the Centurion asked.

Jon suppressed an inward shudder. If it were robot, the Centurion's stitch-gun wouldn't help any. Either way—

"Come on," Jon said. "Follow me."

-3-

Jon and the Centurion entered a chamber devoid of people but containing various items on shelves and tables. He buckled a holster around his waist. It held a gyroc pistol. The sidearm fired big, spin-stabilized rocket-shells.

Most of the pistol's weight came from the heavy shells. The low stress of the initial shot allowed this. The main speed came from the rocket embedded in the shell, the hissing often hard to localize during a fight. The pistol held a three-round magazine.

Jon removed the magazine, with the Centurion providing the light. These were APEX rounds: Armor-Piercing EXplosive. Each of these had a big motor, a maximally streamlined shell around a super-hard penetrator packed with a delay fuse and explosives.

Jon shoved the magazine back into place, activating the safety while slipping the pistol into its holster. He attached more magazines to the belt. Afterward, he found and donned an MP helmet with a headlamp, adjusting the chinstrap so it fit comfortably.

The Centurion picked up different gear, including a vibroblade. Such a weapon vibrated a thousand times a second, making it many times more dangerous than even the very sharpest of static-bladed weapons.

"Here we go," Jon said. He picked up a comm unit, flicked it on with his thumb and put it to his ear. He couldn't believe it.

14

He heard growling noises. He passed the comm unit to the Centurion.

"Jamming," he said after listening for a second.

"That nails it," Jon said. "This is sabotage."

"Ship-wide?"

"We'll work off that assumption until we know otherwise."

The Centurion nodded curtly.

Jon had a decision to make. He had a feeling this was a coup. His gut told him this was a robotic takeover of the warship. That might still mean Da Vinci, who could have decided to work with or use robotic devices.

One of the best defenses against a coup was to react with speed and ruthlessness. Jon's decision was whether he should act against the aggressor as quickly as possible or if he should don a battlesuit first. The space-marine battlesuits were several kilometers from where he was now. He would feel safer in a suit—

"Come on," Jon said. "We're heading for the engine area."

"But sir—"

"I know what you're thinking. We should suit up first. But what if an alien AI is behind this?"

The Centurion shook his head, failing to take Jon's meaning.

"The engines are offline, and there's no gravity," Jon said. "What if the thing doesn't want to take over? What if it wants to destroy the warship?"

"For what reason?"

"To stop us," Jon said.

The Centurion's gaze seemed to flatten out. "You're talking about triggering the ship's self-destruction."

"We could already be out of time," Jon said.

The Centurion's jaw muscles bulged.

"Come on," Jon said, sailing for the hatch. He felt sick inside, wondering if all his grand dreams were about to die in a titanic explosion.

15

"Up ahead, Captain," the Centurion whispered.

The two Black Anvils had sailed through empty corridors, daring to pick up velocity.

Jon slid his gloved hands against the bulkheads flashing past, using friction to slow down. With his helmet-lamp providing light, Jon soon studied a closed hatch. It led into the ship's vast engine area. He tried to move the latch, but it was frozen in place.

"Let's both try," Jon said.

They anchored their feet and strained, but the latch refused to budge.

"Locked," the Centurion said.

"If we had the tools, we could burn through."

"There's another entrance…two kilometers from here."

Jon bit his lower lip as his gut curdled. It felt like time was running out.

"Let's do it," Jon said, shoving away with practiced skill.

Once a person became good at zero-G maneuvering, he or she could travel much faster than by sprinting in gravity. The only real determinant was the amount of risk one wished to invoke. There was no inertia naturally slowing one down, as one would experience if he tried to swim in a pool. If he kept pushing off, adding to his velocity, he could theoretically continue to accelerate indefinitely in zero G.

The twisting of his gut compelled Jon to push harder and harder as he picked up speed. Soon, the stinging of his eyes and his whipping hair told him he was going faster than he'd ever attempted.

The Centurion practiced greater caution, falling farther and farther behind.

If Jon dashed his brains out trying to slow down later, or couldn't take a turn well enough, the Centurion could always finish this. One of them had to risk everything in order to stop the coup—if it was a coup. Jon believed himself responsible. All eight hundred plus regimental lives, all 40 billion humans in the Solar System, would likely live or die depending on whether humans could repair the former cybership. If they could, maybe they could learn to face the coming onslaught. The logic was simple. If one cybership had come to the Solar System, more would come eventually. In that event, humanity had to be ready to beat off every alien assault.

Jon no longer pushed himself faster. He gauged the next turn in the corridor. He would have liked more light than just his helmet-lamp.

As the turn rushed up, Jon readied himself, his heart hammering with anticipation. He braced his body, shoved hard and grunted explosively. It felt like he'd just bench-pressed three hundred pounds. Luckily, he made the needed turn and continued to sail down the corridor.

The other hatch now loomed near.

He used friction as he'd done earlier to slow his advance. Unfortunately, he wasn't going to stop in time. He'd pass the hatch, and that would give the coup attempters more time.

Jon grabbed at protrusions. He nearly wrenched his shoulder out of the socket. Clenching his teeth, he tried again.

Explosive pain made him groan. His right shoulder throbbed, but he slowed.

Jon no longer looked back to see if the Centurion followed. Despite the agony caused by his injured shoulder, he hardened himself as he dialed up his determination. He had to eliminate the threat.

As he got closer, his fears intensified. *What if the hatch doesn't open? What if I did this for nothing?* Thirty seconds later, he was floating before the hatch. Letting his right arm dangle, he tested the latch with his left hand.

The metal prong moved. Something clicked in the hatch. Slowly, he opened the access-way, flashing his lamplight into an otherwise dark engine-area corridor.

He tried to grab his gyroc. Agony in his shoulder made him flinch. He'd torn something. Reaching crossways, he used his left hand and awkwardly drew the pistol. He was a mediocre left-handed shooter at best.

He used his feet, drifting through the hatch, picking up speed as he used his left elbow and the back of his left hand to propel himself.

He debated shutting off the helmet-lamp. Sailing in the dark in a small corridor with only one good arm seemed foolish. The light might give him away. But that was better than accidentally knocking himself unconscious.

He hadn't heard the Centurion enter the corridor yet. The professional could be as soft-footed as a thief, but he doubted the older man had caught up yet.

Jon negotiated the corridors. Every time he'd been in this part of the ship before, the matter/antimatter engines had been running with a steady thrum.

I should have bumped into someone by now.

A chill began at his tailbone and worked its way up his spine to his neck. How could this have happened? He'd thought security had been good.

Jon vowed that if he managed to survive the coup, he would double down on security. He would never give someone a chance to take them out like this again.

He didn't *know* this was sabotage. But if he were wrong about that, it wouldn't hurt him.

Other than pulling my shoulder.

If he was right about this being sabotage, though…

Jon stiffened, drifting silently, straining to hear what he thought he'd just heard. It had been a scraping noise, and it had come from up ahead.

With his chin, he clicked off the helmet-lamp. He saw the half-open hatch ahead. An emergency light glowed dimly red above it. The access-way led into an engine control area. It seemed ominous that no light shined from inside.

He shifted his grip on the gyroc. Slowly, with grim determination, he moved his right arm and almost yelled at the sharp pain. He was one-armed for now, and that was that.

He grunted softly as his left shoulder struck the edge of the hatch. That made noise. The enemy must have heard him, as Jon again heard soft scraping sounds definitely coming from in there.

He used his legs, feet and left arm to ease through the hatch. He flinched as something wet touched his cheek.

Heart hammering, Jon lowered himself, itching to fire but realizing he needed a target first. He listened. He didn't hear anything, but the hairs on the back of his neck stirred. He felt a presence. His tongue had become dry.

You fool. If he faced a robot, it could be using thermal vision or infrared to watch him.

With his chin, he switched on the helmet-lamp. Jon's eyes bulged and the air whooshed from his lungs. He couldn't believe it. This was his worst fear realized…

-5-

Jon stared at a floating Black Anvil technician. The carcass was fat. That was the only way he could tell it was the chief tech with the formerly thick sideburns. Someone or something had ripped off the man's face.

Blood globules floated in the air. That was what had touched Jon's cheek a few seconds ago. He used the back of his left gloved hand to wipe his face. The glove came away red-stained.

The way the carcass floated, the way blood globules drifted everywhere indicated that the thing that had torn away the chief's face had done it during weightlessness. If the thing had killed the chief earlier, the blood wouldn't have scattered everywhere.

Jon held the gyroc stiffly, scanning the large chamber. The controls were dark—off. Nothing indicated power.

What should he do? Killing the chief confirmed a coup attempt. Could a robot be in the process of attempting to blow up the *Nathan Graham*?

Jon forced himself to concentrate. He moved the light in arcs, scrutinizing everything for another clue. He did not see any smashed machinery or controls. He did not—

A soft sound alerted him. He moved his head, washing a hatch in the light of the helmet-lamp. The sound had come from there.

Jon opened his mouth to issue a warning. Instead, he pushed off, floating toward the hatch. He recognized that it led into a storage compartment.

He kept the lamplight centered on the hatch. He could fire a rocket shell. If a robot was hiding in there—

"Come out," Jon said. "If you don't come out, I'm killing you. If that doesn't make sense, I'm going to destroy you."

Nothing happened. It was—

The latch moved. A shaky-voiced man squeaked, "Don't shoot! Please, don't shoot. It's me, Da Vinci."

Da Vinci?

A grim certainty washed over Jon. As he'd suspected, the little thief had something to do with this. He should have known. He should have shot the scoundrel four months ago. A good man had died because he—Jon Hawkins—had been too squeamish. He wasn't going to make that mistake again.

"Please, please," Da Vinci said, as he slowly opened the hatch.

Jon almost pulled the trigger as the Neptunian floated into view.

Da Vinci was wearing a tech's coveralls. He was small, scruffy and shifty-eyed. He had hunched shoulders and the manner of a rat constantly rubbing its paws as it sized up what to steal. The Neptunian had thin, twitchy fingers, perfectly completing the rat image.

Da Vinci wasn't a dome rat like Jon and his gang-buddies in New London had been. They had been cunning and bold. The Neptunian was a different species; safety-conscious, yes, clever, yes, but with a gifted eye toward survival.

"Why were you in there?" Jon demanded.

Da Vinci's fingers trembled, which seemed to travel up his arms and to his body. He shook as tears leaked from his eyes. They were horribly red-rimmed and redlined.

Jon scanned the man carefully, visually searching for a weapon. He wanted to kill the traitor. He couldn't believe the little thief—

"I know what you're thinking," Da Vinci said in a teary voice. "But it's wrong, Captain. Dead wrong. I'm—"

"Shut up."

21

Da Vinci's teeth clicked together as he hastened to obey. That didn't last, though.

"Captain...you're not going to believe this."

Jon didn't want to listen. He knew this was a trick to get him to lower his guard. He should fire and get this over with—

"What do you mean?" Jon asked. If the thief possessed truth that could help him save the warship, he needed to hear it.

The Neptunian paused as something washed over him. The shaking lessened.

Guile. That's what Jon saw.

"If you don't start talking," Jon warned, "I'll kill you. Don't try to spin lies, either. Just give it to me straight."

Da Vinci bobbed his head up and down. "Straight, straight, yes. I'll give it to you straight. It came in here. It surprised us—"

"What were you doing in here?"

"Huh?" Da Vinci asked.

"Why were you in here in the first place?"

Da Vinci opened his mouth, but nothing came out.

"Just like I thought," Jon said. He aimed, pulled the trigger, and a rocket shell popped out of the pistol.

Da Vinci squealed in terror as Jon raised the gun. The Neptunian jackknifed his body like a professional diver, then pulled down, curling into a fetal position.

By that time, the shell hissed as it sped over the thief. It whooshed through the open hatch and exploded in the storage chamber.

Another gyroc shell clicked into launch position in the pistol. Jon retargeted—

"Wait!" Da Vinci wailed. "It's not my fault. It said it would kill me if I didn't lead it here."

Jon hesitated.

Da Vinci dared to peek up. This time, the Neptunian's features did not change. Even so, Jon could feel the cunning slide into place. Revulsion filled him.

Bast Banbeck had declared the mind purge a success. Jon no longer believed that. He was sure he was peering into the eyes of a human controlled by alien thought-patterns, ones gained in a brain-tap machine.

"What did you help?" Jon asked in a dangerously quiet voice.

He hadn't issued a threat, but the threat hung in the air nonetheless.

Da Vinci licked his lips like a liar. Heat seemed to emanate from his eyes. "It's a robot, but like nothing we've seen before."

Jon waited, ready to shoot but—more—wanting knowledge to save his ship more.

"Like a land-walking octopus," Da Vinci added. "It has four legs instead of eight, but it has a bulbous core perched above the legs."

Jon said nothing.

"It killed the chief," Da Vinci said. "It tore off his face…" The Neptunian shuddered in horror. "That's when I slipped into the storage chamber. I hid. It called several times. I just shrank into myself. I pulled in my persona so it could no longer sense me."

Jon frowned.

"We give off an aura, each of us. Surely, you realize—" The Neptunian stopped talking. Maybe he saw the revulsion on Jon's face. Maybe he realized he was no longer speaking like Da Vinci.

"Captain," the Centurion said from behind.

Jon did not turn around. He kept the gyroc aimed at Da Vinci. He had the feeling that one slip would give the cunning Prince of Ten Worlds, barely hidden within the Neptunian's mind, a chance to do something sinister.

"The chief's dead," the Centurion said.

"Is your stitch-gun aimed at Da Vinci?" Jon asked.

A second passed. "Yes, Captain," the Centurion said.

Jon holstered his gyroc lefthanded. "If he moves, kill him."

Neither Da Vinci nor the Centurion spoke.

Jon floated into the storage chamber. The APEX shell had done less damage than he would have expected by the explosion. He found restraints, plucking them off a shelf.

A moment later, he floated out.

"Stretch out on your belly," Jon told the Neptunian.

"Captain—"

Jon didn't speak again, but stared down at the man. Maybe Da Vinci saw death in the captain's eyes.

The thief stretched out on the floor.

"Hands behind your back," Jon said.

Da Vinci complied. Soon, he lay trussed-up with spring locks on his forearms and shackles on his ankles. He would not soon slip free.

Jon turned the thief over in the air, although he kept the Neptunian close to the floor.

"Where did the octopus-robot go?" Jon asked.

"Through the hatch over there," Da Vinci said, indicating the place with his almost nonexistent chin.

"It's headed into the core," the Centurion said. "Is it trying to destroy the ship like you said?"

Jon thought quickly. Without a word, he headed into the storage chamber. He looked around and selected several items along with a radiation suit. When he came back out, he said, "I'm going into the core."

-6-

Wearing a crinkly silver radiation suit with a heavy lead-lined helmet, Jon floated through circular-shaped and rather narrow inward-leading corridors.

He'd wasted a full eleven minutes to reach this location. Ideally, the Centurion should have donned the radiation suit. The professional had two good shoulders instead of just the one. But the Centurion had not volunteered for the assignment. Besides, Jon was the captain, he felt responsible for...well...for the survival of the human race.

It was strange. He'd never considered himself an altruistic person. He was as selfish as the next man. His life showed that. So why was he floating into heavier and heavier radiation? Why sacrifice his life for the rest of humanity?

Maybe it wasn't even that. He'd taken Colonel Graham's place. He felt responsible for the regiment. The colonel had been like a father to him. He would have given his life to protect the colonel. He'd failed to save Graham from Arbiter Sapir Oslo. If he didn't go after the supposed robot—could Da Vinci have lied? Had the Neptunian needed to be alone with the Centurion in order to kill the sergeant?

Jon couldn't see the trussed-up Neptunian surprising the Centurion. No. That wasn't going to happen.

If he didn't go after the robot—provided one existed—who would save the warship? If Jon didn't go, the warship would explode anyway. Thus, if he was going to die, he might as well save his friends.

25

Jon grinned shyly to himself. Gloria would no doubt have approved of his logic.

Jon pushed once more, drifting along the circular corridor. He heard the harsh sound of his own breathing. He was using his own air-supply to avoid breathing the irradiated air in the core.

He gripped the gyroc with his right gloved hand. A dull pain throbbed in his right shoulder. Painkillers and stims allowed him use of the injured shoulder and thus the right hand.

Don't get cocky.

He'd been telling himself that regularly as he felt the stims increase his confidence. Certain shock troops used heavy stim-shots to give them battle madness and the drug-induced courage to charge head-on. The regiment had never operated using that process.

Suicide troops and those induced to contemptuousness toward their enemies usually sustained heavier casualties. The Waffen-SS in the early stages of the historical German-Russian War had been a case in point.

Despite the stims and painkillers, Jon no longer felt so good. The radiation was already attacking his cells. The trick now was to stay alive long enough to destroy this supposed robot.

But what if Da Vinci had fed him lies? Had the Neptunian sent him to his death? Jon squeezed his eyes shut, opening them a second later. He had to concentrate. He spied an open hatch.

Suddenly, a *THRUM* seemed to vibrate through his body. It was powerful and far too intimate. Lights came on around him, blinding him momentarily.

The robot must have turned on the matter/antimatter engines. The thing must be inside the core. It needed the engines on so it could cause a debilitating self-destructive explosion.

Jon pushed onward, floating toward the open hatch. Bile rose in his throat. He fought it back. He couldn't choke. He had a job to do. He was the captain of the Black Anvil Regiment. He had to save his people.

A fierce smile froze into place. This was the end. This was it. He must be taking massive doses of radiation. He'd always wondered how he would die. He'd always wanted to go out guns blazing, taking down an enemy.

A man's life wasn't complete unless he died well. He couldn't remember where he'd heard that.

"Okay, you bastard," Jon whispered.

He slipped through the hatch, entering a huge area. The *THRUM* intensified. Vast cylinders rose up. That was where the hornet-like noise was coming from. Tubes crisscrossed everywhere. Vents—

Jon squinted. He saw movement up there. He—

Horror twisted Jon's shoulders. An octopoid robotic thing was crawling toward the vent. It had four metallic legs as Da Vinci had described. Each leg had three metal joints. On top of the four legs was a bulbous, lights-blinking…body. Antennae sprouted on top of the bulb. A small gun port poked out.

Jon realized he was lightheaded. The moment felt surreal as he raised his right hand. Shoulder pain threatened to intrude upon his concentration, but he refused to acknowledge any pain.

He trained the gyroc on the moving octopoid, waited for it—

The robot paused.

Jon's finger twitched, causing a click. The pistol shuddered, ejecting a rocket shell. The big motor ignited, and it hissed as it sped upward.

Just as the octopoid swiveled, the penetrator hit its mark, and the APEX shell exploded. Metallic pieces, wires and other parts blew apart. Some clicked against the bulkheads. Others flew downward.

Jon yanked himself back through the hatch. Pieces rattled onto the deck, and rattled against the heavy cylinders.

Jon counted to three and then pulled himself back into the large *THRUMMING* chamber. He looked up. The octopoid had half-detached from its former position. Two of the metallic legs hung limply. Lights blinked on the bulbous body. The gun port was attempting to swivel around to aim at him.

"Not bloody likely," Jon said. He aimed, fired again and saw a second APEX round hammer home, exploding.

He dodged through the hatch once again, putting in a fresh magazine. He waited like before and finally pulled himself back into the chamber. What was left of the alien robot floated up there. Pieces and legs drifted around it. All the lights on the main body had gone dark.

A wry laugh bubbled past Jon's lips. "That was easy," he said. "I thought it would have been—"

Something hard and heavy struck between his shoulder blades, propelling him onto the deck.

Something plucked the lead-lined helmet from his head. The *THRUM* of the chamber increased, and it felt as if ants were crawling over his skin biting him—that was the heavy radiation striking his flesh.

At the same time, something grabbed his hair and began twisting his head around...

Jon Hawkins stared into the optical sensor of a second robotic octopoid. It was using the pincers on the end of one leg to grab his hair.

"I recognize you," the octopoid said in a robotic voice. "You are the destroyer."

"Jon Hawkins, at your service," he said weakly.

"I had planned to destroy the cybership," the octopoid said. "But the ease of my subterfuge shows me that you are massively inferior. It will be a simple matter to eliminate your local infestation. I will—"

"The brain core is gone," Jon whispered.

"I will destroy you, Jon Hawkins. I will do it now as I record you screaming in agony."

"I doubt there will be any screaming."

"Explain your doltish words," the octopoid said.

"I'm drugged to the eyeballs, and I'm dying. The radiation poisoning—"

Jon arched back as a second leg thrust a needle through the radiation suit into his left buttock. The needle sunk deeply, remained motionless and then withdrew with a jerk.

"I have injected you with a radiation antidote, Jon Hawkins. You must feel agony at your passing."

"That's illogical."

"You suggest that as a slur?"

"You're a robot, you idiot. Robots don't feel. So why do you want me to feel pain at the end?"

"As an inferior infestation, you are in no position to know anything about superior robots like me."

"I conquered this ship, didn't I?"

"Wrong. I am about to begin the process of awakening the secondary systems. We will purge the cybership of your localized infestation. Then we will—"

Jon raised the gyroc and tried to pull the trigger. The octopoid ripped the pistol out of his hand, breaking the trigger finger in the process because the finger had become trapped in the trigger-guard.

Jon grunted, surprised he felt that.

"I will not allow you any resistance," the octopoid said.

Jon cursed the mechanical thing, lifted his legs, placing the bottom of his boots against the bulbous body, and shoved as hard as he could.

He couldn't move it, though.

The alien injection seemed to have revived his thinking, however, as a moment of clarity struck home. He was going to die. The octopoid was going to reverse the regiment's glorious victory.

"No," Jon whispered.

As he shoved upward with his boots, with his back pressed against the decking, Jon detached a grenade from his belt. He used his thumb to activate it, hiding the weapon from the octopoid's camera eye. Jon counted silently. At the last moment, he reached up, holding the grenade inside a cavity in the robot's body.

The grenade exploded—and Jon Hawkins lost consciousness...

The entity known as Jon Hawkins did not die at that instant in time. He dreamed endlessly. He never remembered those dreams, although he recalled that some horrified him and some brought him brief moments of peace.

Finally, dim consciousness returned. He lay on a soft bed. Tubes were stuck in his arms, sides and legs. His skin itched worse than before. He heard voices, but had no idea what they were saying or if they were male or female. Slowly, by degrees, he managed to bring up his right hand so his immobile head could stare at it.

The problem was simple. He lacked a right hand. Jon stared at the stump of his wrist.

Two hands appeared. They were good strong hands. They clamped hold of the damaged arm, slowly but forcefully moving it out of his view.

As he struggled to reason out why they did that, he faded out again, dreaming anew. In this dream, he was running hard. He had a mission that he absolutely had to complete. There were things chasing him. He could feel them breathing down his neck. He could hear them *clicking* on the deck-plates behind him. He could—

The dream slipped away like a fog gently blown off a summer beach. That allowed him to surface for consciousness again.

Bright glaring lights almost blinded him. Voices circled him. Tubes like bloodworms sank into his body. He could hear

31

sounds of something buzzing or cutting, and the strong odor almost made him sneeze.

Jon tried to move his arm into view. He recalled something about missing digits—fingers.

"Not yet," a voice told him.

Jon didn't know what that meant. To hell with it then. He was leaving. And he did leave, sinking back into unconsciousness.

The dreams were formless lights. They weaved, juggled places and began to pulsate smaller and smaller, finally disappearing. Two lights appeared later, grew, merged into each other, solidified—

Jon's eyes snapped open. His head lay deep in an extraordinarily soft pillow. He felt exhausted, drained to the bone. His mind hurt. His wrist itched like murder. He tried to raise his left hand to reach over and scratch. He simply lacked the strength to do that.

A towering head appeared in his vision.

Jon struggled to comprehend and then struggled even harder to focus. Finally, the wise lined features of the long-faced Old Man came into view. The sergeant was wearing a military hat and had his pipe in his mouth.

Jon couldn't smell any tobacco and he didn't spy any smoke trickling up from the pipe bowl.

The Old Man used a hand to pull the pipe out of his mouth. "How are you feeling, son?"

"Weak," Jon whispered.

The Old Man nodded, putting the pipe stem back between his teeth. "You've been here for a time. We trade off to keep you company. The Martian says you're going to be fine. The Centurion—he worries that he came in too late."

"I…don't understand."

The wise old eyes studied him. "Rest, son. Get better. You saved us, all of us. That was incredibly brave, and noble. Colonel Graham would have been proud of you."

Jon couldn't help it. A warm feeling built in his chest. He tried to sit up. Colonel Graham would have been proud. The idea strengthened him. He met the Old Man's eyes, and he recognized the worry.

"What is it, Sergeant?"

The Old Man's eyebrows rose. "Ah, I think you should wait, sir. You need your strength."

Jon stared into the sergeant's eyes. As he did, the strength faded away—and he never realized when his head gently moved to the side.

He didn't dream this time. It felt as if only a second passed, but he had no idea how long it had really been.

Jon opened his eyes, and he felt much stronger than before. By degrees, he pushed his head upward and then his shoulders. The soft pillow tried to trap his shoulders, but Jon's stubbornness had returned. Finally, he sat up, realizing he was in a medical bed.

He recognized the med machines. He looked for tubes in his flesh, but saw none.

Something caught his eye. He stared, and his heart pounded. He looked at his smooth right hand. He saw a hairline scar along the wrist where the hand attached. He moved the fingers. They worked.

Tears threatened to well in his eyes.

Jon fought them back. He was the captain. He would not weep at this miracle. Jon looked up at the ceiling. "Thank you, God," he whispered. "Thank you for life. Thank you for this hand and thanks for keeping the regiment in control of the warship."

Jon felt better saying that. As he smiled, Jon realized someone had slipped into the med center. He looked up, spying a tech, a thin Neptunian with a slate in his hands.

"Captain," the med tech said.

"I'm better," Jon said. "But I don't understand how I have this hand." He moved his right-hand fingers.

"Bast Banbeck showed us how to use a re-grower, sir. It's an alien device. The Sacerdote said the aliens used the re-grower to manufacture some of their abominations, the head you once saw connected to a machine."

"This re-grower made my hand?"

"That's right, sir. We grafted it to your wrist. Bast Banbeck showed us the machine to do—"

"I see," Jon said, interrupting. He moved the fingers again. This felt like his hand. He supposed it was his hand. This was incredible. The regiment could use tech like this.

The med tech cleared his throat.

Jon looked up. "I want to speak to—" He stopped. He didn't know whom he needed to speak to. Who had taken over in his absence?

"The sergeants thought you'd want an update as soon as possible, sir," the med tech said.

"Sounds good. Let's hear it."

"Oh, not from me, sir. Once you're strong enough—"

"I already told you I am," Jon said, interrupting.

The med tech squared his narrow shoulders. "Technically, that's my decision, sir."

Jon studied the Neptunian. He could see stubbornness there. "Well? What's your judgment?"

"Yes. You're strong enough. I'll send for the mentalist. She ran the investigation."

"What investigation?"

The med tech shook his head. "I'm sorry, sir. I'm under strict orders. She's supposed to tell you. That was made very clear to me."

"Then get her. Now!"

"Yes, sir," the med tech said. He spun around, hurrying for the exit.

-9-

The Martian shook her head as she stood beside Jon's medical bed.

"That's not what I meant," she said.

Gloria Sanchez wore a utilitarian gray suit. It lacked any flourish or singularity other than its drabness. She wore gray shoes and had well-scrubbed features. Her long dark hair fell straight past her shoulders. She had brown, inquisitive eyes but was thin and small, much smaller than Da Vinci.

Her only costly item was the tablet clutched against her bosom. The device aided in her mentalist duties.

Mentalists believed in strict logic and rational and efficient use of their brainpower. Gloria was no exception, even if she had proven more emotional in the past than the customary image of a mentalist.

She'd already started explaining the present situation to Jon.

"The Centurion pulled me out of the reactor core?" Jon asked.

She gave him a careful scrutiny before saying, "You traveled most of the way back on your own."

"Most?"

"All the way to the safety hatch," she said. "You banged on it. The Centurion opened it and pulled you out."

"I don't remember any of that."

"I should think not," she said. "It was…it was one of those unbelievable acts people perform at the oddest moment, like a small woman lifting an air-car off her child or a youth who leaps across an impossible chasm to escape his foes. Hysterical strength."

"I was hysterical?"

"You'd lost your right hand. You had horrible belly wounds and had lost far too much blood, to say nothing of the radiation poisoning consuming you."

"The octopoid injected me with something."

"That's interesting," she said in a strange, almost dismissive, voice. "I didn't know. I don't think anyone did. You did mumble the gist of your story several times in a state of semi-consciousness."

"Fine. What happened to the octopoid?"

Gloria stared at him.

"What?" he asked.

"Maybe this is too soon," she said.

"Tell me. I order it."

Gloria sighed. "We haven't found any evidence of these two octopoids, as you call them."

"Robot octopoids."

"I understand," she said.

"What are you suggesting? That I made it all up?"

"That would be easier to understand," Gloria said. "But," she said, holding up a hand to keep him from speaking. "What happened to the engine and gravity control boards? Can we explain the chief tech's brutal murder? You found Da Vinci hiding in the engine control room. You don't need the octopoids as a cause for the problem."

"You think the little Neptunian—"

"Please. One thing at a time, Captain. My point is that the sabotage indicates something nefarious occurred. We have sufficient justification for the acts. You claim to have seen…robots—"

"Are you saying no one found a shred of evidence in the reactor area? No one found a metal leg, for instance?"

Gloria hesitated before saying, "That is correct."

Jon blinked several times. "Something or someone must have cleaned up the reactor area."

"That would be one possible explanation, yes."

"You think I hallucinated about the robots?"

"Do you want me to speak the truth?"

"Yes!" he nearly shouted.

"Yes," she said.

"Yes that I might have hallucinated?"

"That is correct."

Jon sagged against his pillow. He couldn't believe it. For a moment, he wondered if he was dreaming *this*.

"Let me get this straight," Jon said. "You believe the octopoids did not exist?"

"Captain, I have questioned Da Vinci. He was very clever. He gave me answers that would have pleased anyone but a Martian mentalist. Because of my strictly logical processes, I detected several false connectives in his words. Da Vinci's story did not match up in a few tiny areas. He is a gifted liar. I am a superior listener, however."

"Wait just a minute. You can't mean there wasn't *anything* in the reactor area. How do you explain my hand?"

"Your grenade destroyed it."

"Why didn't it destroy the rest of me?"

"A freak occurrence saved your life."

"No," Jon said, sharply. "I'm not buying this. The octopoids existed. Something cleaned up the reactor area. I'm surprised the alien robots haven't struck again while I've been out."

"That is another factor against your story," she said. "Captain, these words give me no satisfaction other than in adhering to my oath to speak the truth. I wish you no emotional pain."

"I imagine you've told the sergeants your supposed truths."

"Of course," she said.

Jon shook his head ruefully.

"I am not attempting to weaken your authority," she said.

"But your report has that potential."

She turned away.

"Tell me more about Da Vinci," Jon said. "How can you possibly think he engineered the whole episode? Wait a minute. I'm an idiot. The chief. Who pulled his face off like that?"

Gloria looked up at the ceiling. "We found a power glove in the storage area you shot up. Can you guess what else?"

"Just tell me."

"You shot the power glove with a gyroc round. Why did you attempt to destroy the evidence of a power glove, Captain?"

"I didn't," Jon said weakly. "My shell just happened to hit it."

"I cannot accept the probabilities of that in good conscience."

"So you're saying Da Vinci donned a power glove and ripped off the chief's face? That doesn't fit the Neptunian's personality. If there aren't any octopoids, why would Da Vinci do all this, anyway?"

"Captain, Da Vinci is a troubled individual. He doesn't have a classic case of dual personalities. It's something different. Bast Banbeck eliminated much of the Prince of Ten World's personality in Da Vinci. But an echo of that personality certainly remains. That echo troubles the corporal, and at times it causes him to take bizarre actions."

"Are you listening to yourself?" Jon asked. "What happened wasn't the work of a deranged mind, but of a powerful intellect."

"True. Da Vinci has such an intellect, but only when it's under the disciplined control of the Prince of Ten Worlds. As himself, he lacks the internal guidance for true brilliance— well, other than flashes of brilliance that allowed him to create the wonder weapon before."

The wonder weapon had helped them originally conquer the cybership four months ago.

"Why would I hallucinate about these octopoids?" Jon asked.

"Do you truly wish to hear my analysis?"

"Shoot."

She brushed her hair back, staring at him oddly.

"That means, tell me," Jon said.

Gloria nodded before glancing at her tablet. "We fought an incredibly stressful battle several months ago. Beating the alien AI has scarred you."

"Winning scarred me?" Jon asked, sounding doubtful.

"No, of course not," she said, looking at him. "The stress of the fight impressed your subconscious. It stamped itself upon you. You realize that more of these cyberships might conceivably show up in the Solar System in the near future. You are intent upon defeating them. Yet, your subconscious knows it will be a terrible conflict. One that humanity might well lose. That has created the need for alien robotic enemies, ones you can destroy. Their defeat helps settle your growing...*worries.*"

Jon sank back against the pillow and laughed. He shook his head and laughed harder. Finally, he wiped tears from his eyes.

"I fail to see the humor in this," she said.

"Mentalist, your training has driven you to excess. This psychobabble is too much. I know what I saw."

"You were dying, Captain. The hard radiation and your coming demise—the dying mind can play strange tricks. I have no doubt you truly believe you saw the octopoids, as you put it."

"Hold it," Jon said. "What did Da Vinci say about the octopoids?"

"Why...nothing," she said.

"He's the one who told me about them."

"He denies that."

Jon's eyes narrowed, while suspicion bubbled in him. He reached up and wiped his face. He grinned at Gloria and sighed. Then a terrible thought surfaced. Maybe Gloria had gone under the brain-tap machine. Maybe she had alien thought-patterns. How else could she fail to understand...?

"I see," Gloria said, who had been watching him. "You now suspect *me* of subterfuge."

He looked at her, surprised.

"I am a master at reading kinesics. What you call body language," she said. "You exhibit obvious signs. I suggest that means you have become highly paranoid concerning me."

He snorted. "I grew up highly paranoid. That helped me stay alive."

"You mean in the lower New London tunnels?"

"Yeah," he said.

She examined her tablet, tapping it—

"Gloria!"

She regarded him.

"The octopoid—the second one—injected me with a serum. It told me that would help combat the radiation poisoning. You said no one had heard about that. A quick med scan should show traces of the alien serum or not."

She nodded.

"Get the med tech."

"I can make the scan," she said.

Jon stared her in the eyes. "You stay right where you are. Call the med tech. Give the instructions so I can hear them—"

"I will do no such thing."

He'd slipped his new hand under the covers. Stretching the index finger, poking it up against the blanket, he aimed it at her.

"I have a stitch-gun," he said flatly. "If you don't do exactly as I say, I'll fire."

Gloria studied his eyes, possibly seeing his determination and paranoia against her. She finally tapped her tablet and asked the med tech to step into the room for a moment.

-10-

The thin tech looked up in shock. He'd pushed a med-scanner next to the captain, and finished the sensor readings.

"The captain's right," the tech said. "There's more than a trace here that I can't explain."

"Could the element have aided him against radiation poisoning?" Gloria asked.

The tech typed on the med-scanner. He studied the results and finally looked up again just as shocked as before.

"This is incredible," the tech said. He faced the captain. "This is revolutionary, sir. Whatever you took, you need to tell us. This is a breakthrough in radiation treatment."

Gloria took several steps back until her knees knocked against the edge of a chair. She sat down hard. She'd grown pale. She looked up at Jon, with her mouth open.

"You can go," Jon told the tech.

"But the drug, sir..."

"We'll talk about that later," Jon said. "Just to be safe, do you have the trace element's specifics?"

The med tech slapped the med-scanner. "It's in here, sir."

"Start studying that. See if you can duplicate it."

The tech snapped his fingers, pointing at the captain. Then, he wheeled the med-scanner to the side, popped out a memory disk and hurried away.

"There's only one reasonable conclusion," Gloria said softly. "You told me the truth. Either that or you made an incredible medical breakthrough in your spare time. Alien octopoid robots make more sense."

"Thank you, I guess."

"But..." Her features stiffened. "Da Vinci might be even more cunning than I gave him credit for. He made those tiny slips in his story to misdirect me, knowing that I'd spot them."

"Is the Neptunian in the brig?"

Gloria nodded. "Captain, the ship could be in terrible danger."

Jon had been thinking. "Despite the alien serum, I took an incredible amount of hard radiation. What was my condition when the Centurion found me?"

"You were unconscious."

"That doesn't make sense."

"No..." Gloria said. "The Centurion heard knocking. He donned a radiation suit and investigated, finding you lying on the other side. I clearly remember him commenting on your incredible stamina."

"The alien serum—"

"Likely doesn't explain your superhuman feat of walking to the hatch," Gloria said, finishing his sentence. "Let me rephrase that. There is an easier explanation."

"The last octopoid dragged me to the hatch," Jon said.

"Yes," she whispered. "But that doesn't make any sense either. The serum in your blood suggests you've told the truth about the robotic octopoids. The last one, the one taking the grenade blast, must have cleaned the area. The likeliest hiding location was in one of the reactor cores. The evidence of their existence must be long gone, burned and thrown away in the ship's ejected ballast."

"That all fits except for one thing," Jon said.

Gloria nodded. "According to your story, the octopoid wanted to destroy you. Why would it then do the opposite? Why would a half-destroyed octopoid fail to cause an engine self-destruct? Why would it then clean up? It must have cleaned up afterward. First, it dragged you to the hatch and knocked on it to alert anyone outside. But that would mean your declared enemy, the octopoid, saved your life."

"That's what I think," Jon said.

"Why would it do all that and not do what it set out to do: destroy the ship?"

Jon shook his head. He had no idea.

Gloria shot to her feet. She tapped on her tablet, studied it and then slapped it against her thigh. She began to pace with her head bent in thought.

"The octopoid must have received new data," Gloria said slowly. "This new data changed its directives, instructing it to leave the *Nathan Graham* intact and you alive. I can only conclude the octopoid did these things because…"

Jon snapped his fingers. "The octopoid, or whatever drove the robot, believes it can deliver the former cybership back to its supposedly rightful owners."

"Maybe," Gloria said.

"What else could it be?"

"The answer lies in understanding the reason why it dragged you to safety," Gloria said. "It could have killed you, correct?"

"Easily, if it was still—functioning," Jon said.

"You were going to say alive?"

"It wasn't alive. It was a machine."

"That's another debate," Gloria said. "In any case, why did the octopoid first inject you with the serum?"

"I already told you."

"Say it again."

"It wanted to keep me alive so I could suffer more."

"There's the answer," Gloria said.

"I don't see it."

"The…driving mind behind the octopoid wants Captain Jon Hawkins to suffer. I submit that the octopoid realized it had insufficient strength to take control of the ship. It had enough ability to destroy the vessel, but something changed, making it believe the guiding intelligence could capture you later for greater and possibly extended agony."

"Do you hear yourself?"

"I am a mentalist," Gloria said as if stating a creed. "I follow clues to their logical conclusion. Logic has led me here. It fits the facts as we know them."

Jon blinked several times. "You spoke about a guiding intelligence. You don't mean the last octopoid?"

"By no means," she said.

"Something greater than the octopoid, something—" He stared at her. "The war's not over."

"Precisely," Gloria said. "We missed something. I don't know what, but we missed it nonetheless."

"We're going to have to increase ship security," Jon said.

"And search the ship more thoroughly for intruders," Gloria said.

"This is a vast vessel. The search is going to take a long time. We haven't even walked through every area."

"Time," she said. "I think this is about time. I think we have to travel faster."

"Is the engine fixed?"

"Not yet," she answered.

Jon scowled. They had accelerated at a fraction of the warship's potential. The first time they'd seen the cybership, it had decelerated at 70 gravities. Such acceleration would have allowed them to reach the Saturn Grav System much faster than ordinary. The old way, it took years to get from Neptune to Saturn. The *Nathan Graham* was currently able to accelerate more continuously than a human-built spaceship, but it was still at a fraction of what this thing should be able to do, had shown itself capable of under the AI.

"How long will it take at our present rate until we reach Saturn?" Jon asked.

"A little more than a year," Gloria said.

"And you say time is what this is about?"

The mentalist nodded.

Jon sighed. He had to get better. They had to speed what repairs they could to the giant vessel. And they had to find the alien robot enemy hidden on the super-ship. They had to do all that without letting the octopoids pick them off one at a time.

Jon lay back, forcing himself to rest so that he could heal faster. No one said saving the Solar System would be easy. He put his hands behind his head, trying to keep from thinking about the kinds of awful tortures the cyber enemy had in store for him if they lost.

Part II
DWARF PLANET: MAKEMAKE
+6 Months, 16 Days

-1-

Data Specialist June Zen filled in for her best Mindy Smalls, who was sick with a virus. June's friend was under quarantine in her quarters, had been for five days already. Her friend was in danger of losing her posting if she didn't show up to work soon. That's why June had agreed to fill in for her.

June was working a morning shift in Makemake's orbital-control station. It was down on the dwarf planet in the only city. Most of that city was under the methane/nitrogen ice, with deeper corridors carved out of the lower rock layer.

As she sat at her cubicle, June was worried—not for her friend so much, but for herself.

The station foreman was a large man with a lecherous eye. That might not have been so bad, but he was high in the ranks of Luxor Evans's band. Luxor Evans was the muscleman, or "pusher," of Makemake. In other cultures, that might have made Evans the police chief and army general rolled into one. Evans seemed to be getting ready for a takeover. He ruled a tough clan that snapped-to when he said boo, and he'd made open alliances with several smaller clans ready to pitch in with him.

45

June rechecked her board for the eighth time in ten minutes. Every spaceship, boat and hauler was exactly where it should be.

She studied their relative orbital positions, wondering why their locations made her jumpy. Or was it just knowing Big Bob should be showing up soon with their mojo?

June sighed. She should have put on more this morning. She'd been in a hurry and had slipped into a silver jumpsuit. There was nothing inherently wrong with the suit. It fit. It was comfortable; and hot or cold it kept her skin temperature perfect.

June was long-legged, with curvy hips and nice breasts. She had long brunette hair and features too many men noticed. Others had often told her she was stunning. She was hot, and she knew it.

It was an ace card combined with smarts and even better training. Unfortunately, she lived among two-legged wolves, philistines with brutish appetites. The men on Makemake cared little for the finer things in life. They all vied for power in whatever ways they could, and that turned her ace into a liability.

Makemake was on the edge of the space frontier, a place for the bold, the adventurous and the quick-rich crowd. Whatever civilized veneer remained in the people out here was generally reserved for negotiations over scientific and highly technological concepts and devices. Such men as these had big appetites. They might leer at her, lust to take off her clothes and hump her, but they would seldom let that interfere with their greater desire for financial gain and climbing the power ladder.

The women of Makemake were little better, bartering their bodies, brains and loyalty for the highest rank they could get, or attach themselves to.

June Zen was different because her predecessors had come into the Kuiper Belt for markedly different reasons. They hadn't lusted for revenge or driven themselves with endless work to get enough so they could go back and fix their lot in Neptunian society.

46

June's grandfather, Dr. Maximus Zen, had joined the exodus to the Kuiper Belt Frontier because he'd believed this was humanity's future.

June peered at her screen more closely. This was odd. There appeared to be workers flying from a hauler in orbit. Why would they do that? The workers would have had to don space-flight suits. She studied the images. Could this be right? The workers—she counted eleven of them—moved toward different orbital vessels. Was this some kind of surprise party?

Her fingernails clicked against a screen as she pulled up a manifest. The hauler—*Get Bent*—was from Dannenberg 7. Okay. Maybe that made sense then. The mine on the icy planetesimal belonged to the Evans Clan. They'd become powerful the last few years, always doing something arrogant. Maybe it would be better if she forgot about this. Maybe this had something to do with Luxor Evans's anticipated takeover.

June frowned. She seemed to recall a report about Dannenberg 7. It had something to do—

The main hatch slid up, breaking June's concentration.

Big Bob sauntered into the main orbital-control chamber. He wore baggy pants because he had tree-trunk thighs, and a baggy tunic that strained to cover his huge gut and powerful shoulders. Bob seemed to lack a neck. He made up for that with an almost square head with a frizz of black hair circling the middle area. Bob was supposed to have pure Ukrainian blood from Old Earth, but who even knew what that was supposed to mean? He was carrying a holder with four steaming cups of mojo.

For all his mass, Big Bob had piggy eyes in a puffy face. He smiled, showing peg-like teeth, all of them evenly spaced from each other.

Some said that Big Bob looked retarded. Firstly, no one said that to his face. Secondly, it was flat false. Big Bob acted like a boor, but he was crazy cunning when it came to bullying others and when it came to conforming to those with greater power.

"Mojo," Bob said, "nice and hot like you like it." He stared at June, walking over to her and holding out the carton.

47

June knew he believed himself sly and humorous. The other two station operators laughed. The male operator gave her a wink. The woman raised her eyebrows three times in a suggestive manner, as if June should do it with Bob.

June lifted a cup from the carton, turning back to her board. She eased the lid back, blowing on the black mojo, enjoying the strong aroma. Big Bob might be a pig, but he knew his mojo.

June finally recognized the total silence in the chamber. She ignored it at first. It made her back squirm, but she wasn't going to turn around if she didn't have to.

The woman coughed discretely.

June focused on her sensor board.

"What's the matter with you?" Big Bob growled.

June knew she had to face him. She swiveled on her chair and smiled sweetly at him.

Bob scowled thunderously. It made him look even stupider than he normally did. "Can't you even say 'Thanks?'"

"Thanks," June said. She began turning back to her board.

Bob laid a meaty paw on her left shoulder.

June had been dreading his touch.

His thick fingers dug into her flesh. He was strong, and he was letting her know it. "I've had enough of your attitude."

Almost in a daze because this frightened her, June picked up her mojo, faced him, and flinched in pain as he applied agonizing strength. She'd intended to hurl the steaming mojo in his face. He must have realized that and beaten her to the punch.

The black liquid poured onto the floor as she twisted at the pain. Finally, he released her.

June looked up, ready to tell him off.

The heat in his piggy eyes stilled the retort in her throat. If she told him off, here in his office, he was going to hit her. June saw that, and she realized he would hit hard, probably in the face, and maybe hard enough to break facial bones.

"I done your friend a huge favor letting you work for her," Bob snarled. "You may have a nice ass, great tits, too, but that don't mean squat here. You want to keep your friend's job, you tell me here and now."

June wanted to get up and run. A flickering glance at the other two showed them studiously scrutinizing their screens. She looked up at Bob.

He still glowered, but something else shined in his eyes. He was starting to enjoy this.

June wanted to hurl insults at him. She wanted to grab a crank-bat and bash him in the face. Even as she envisioned doing that, she realized the bat would likely bounce off his face, just making him raping mad.

"One…" Bob counted.

June realized he was giving her to three.

"Two…"

In that moment, June also realized that she had no recourse. She had her regular data analyst job. It was barely enough to keep her quarters and her grandfather's cryogenic unit going. She needed the credits from this gig. She also lacked a protecting clan. Her grandfather was her sole relation on Makemake, and he was literally frozen stiff in a cryo unit.

"Three…" Bob said, his eyes shining with growing rage.

"I want her—" June's tongue seemed to twist over itself. "I want her to have her job when she's better."

"Yeah?"

June nodded, dreading what was coming next.

"Oh," Bob said, playing into it now. "Well… What are you willing to do to keep your friend's job?"

The man at the sensor station snickered lewdly.

"Be more thankful," June said.

Bob stared at her.

"Uh…work harder," June added.

"Okay…" Bob said. "That's the right direction. Work hard. Yeah, you have to work hard to make me like you. How you going to work hard enough to do that, though?"

June stared at him. She realized his rage was gone, replaced by bullying. This brute could sniff weakness like a chem-sniffer.

"Where do you live?" June asked quietly.

Big Bob smiled, showing off the peg-teeth that made him seem like an idiot.

"You want to come over tonight?" he asked.

June nodded as her stomach curdled. She was going to have to start carrying a weapon. She could never come back here. Maybe she'd talk to Walleye about a hit, see how many credits it would take for him to kill Bob.

"Yeah," Bob said, with laugher in his voice. "Come to my place, baby. Wear what you're wearing now, but don't wear anything underneath it. You understand?"

"Yes, Bob," June said, deciding she was going to see Walleye as soon as she left work.

-2-

"What? Are you crazy? You want me to kill Big Bob the Sensor King. That's what this is about?"

June Zen nodded meekly.

Walleye was a mutant. That's what everyone said, anyway. He wasn't a good kind of mutant, either. He had strange eyes, so you could never tell where he was looking. That freaked out a lot of people. It was freaking out June right now.

They met in an underground cubby near the catapult launch system. The system hurled ore into orbit for the giant furnaces up there. Most of the construction went into a huge spaceship, a special warship with many new weapons systems.

The majority of the colonists on Makemake came from the Neptune Grav System. They had run out here for one reason or another. Many others on the Kuiper Belt Frontier had run from Saturn and Uranus, too. Those running from the Jupiter System had gone to other Outer Planetary Systems, still believing someone would stop the Solar League. Few people believed that anymore. The Neptune System was the last holdout, and there was strange news from there—or there had been strange news. Now, nothing came out of the Neptune Grav System.

Rumor had it that Makemake had a Neptunian moneyman behind it. That's why this outpost had more modern equipment than anywhere else in the Kuiper Belt. The moneyman planned a great surprise: a fleet of giant warships to back whatever he had as a long-term goal.

"Big Bob is connected to Luxor Evans," Walleye told her.

51

"So...?"

Walleye stretched out his stumpy legs, his work boots barely reaching the low table in his office. "I hit Bob, Evans buys a hit on me. End of story."

"Why does Evans have to know you did it?"

"Luscious, you're sure slow for a girl trying to hire the deadliest man on Makemake."

June wanted to smile. Walleye did not look deadly. He was too small with his stunted legs and arms. He was five foot one on his best day, maybe five two if he wore high-heeled boots.

"Whatever you're thinking, you're wrong," Walleye told her. "I'm deadly like a scorpion. You know what that is?"

June shook her head.

"Doesn't matter," Walleye said. "Trust me."

"Big Bob could crush you," June blurted.

Walleye looked up at the low ceiling. As he did, the chamber rumbled and began shaking. The noise increased and so did the shaking. Suddenly, the shaking and rattling quit.

"And another catapult load launches into space," Walleye said, looking at her. "You know how long I've been listening to that?"

June shook her head.

Abruptly, Walleye jerked his work boots off the table. He sat up, putting his stumpy hands between his knees.

"Don't you know people are predicting the end of everything?" the little assassin asked.

"You mean the videos out of Neptune?"

Walleye laughed, shaking his head. "Course I mean that. Everyone's talking about it, but not you, sweetie. You're a data analyst. Haven't you analyzed what that all means?"

She stared at him.

"Course, maybe you haven't seen what I've...*acquired*. Maybe Big Bob hasn't seen this yet, either, or maybe he has."

"You've lost me."

Walleye seemed to be staring at her, but she couldn't tell for sure. Maybe she'd made a mistake coming here.

"I just had a bad idea," Walleye said. "It's positively evil. But it might account for why the catapult launches have increased by two hundred percent. It might give me a clue as to the hurry up there."

"There are more haulers coming in lately," June said. She recalled Big Bob telling her about that her first day in the orbital-station office.

"The catapult launches increased a month after the original video," Walleye said quietly. "Luscious, I'd like you to look at this. See what you think."

"What about Big Bob?"

"Forget about him—at least, for now. I might have stumbled onto something bigger. Are you interested?"

June had a hard time reading the assassin. She wondered if maybe others had a hard time, too. Maybe that was part of his deadliness. He looked like a rabbit but struck like a viper. His mutant freakishness acted like cover for him.

"Walleye, I already have enough trouble with Big Bob. Who am I going to get to take care of you trying to bed me?"

"You're mighty fine, Miss Zen, but you're too tall for me. You don't have worry about me pawing you."

"Do I have your word on that?"

"I just gave it," Walleye said curtly.

June nodded as some of the fear went out of her. She had a flat needler taped to the small of her back. She had a feeling Walleye already knew that, and had already decided what to do if she tried to draw it.

The dwarfish man moved a flat screen so they could both look at it. He typed a bit, and a super-bright object appeared. It was like a star, only bigger, and it moved too fast across the starry background.

"I've never seen anything like that," she said.

"This was taken, oh, seven months ago. You can't tell, but some think this thing is four or five times the size of a *Premier*-class battleship."

June shrugged. She had no idea what that meant.

"That's the latest Solar League battleship—they're over a kilometer long."

June studied the bright image. "You're telling me that's a ship…four kilometers long?"

"Yup."

"Who makes spaceships that big?"

"I dunno. Aliens."

June shuddered with dread. "Aliens? You think that bright light is thrust from an alien vessel?"

"You're the data analyst, not me."

"But…"

"Notice," Walleye said, as he typed on the pad. "The trajectory of the ship would take it to the Neptune System."

June thought about that. "Where was the ship when this vid was taken?"

"It was just leaving the inner Oort cloud," Walleye said.

June blinked at him as her stomach tightened. "When was this taken again?"

"Seven months ago, just like I said."

"Leaving the Oort cloud, as in twenty thousand or more AUs from Neptune?"

"That's right."

"No. Do you realize how fast it would have to have been traveling to reach Neptune from the Oort cloud like you're suggesting?"

Walleye nodded slowly, as he said, "Aliens."

June couldn't stop blinking as she tried to speak. The hollow feeling in her stomach had gotten worse.

"I take it you saw the war footage at Neptune…six and a half months ago?" Walleye asked.

It was all June could do to nod.

"And the aftermath," Walleye said, "when something weird hit the victorious Solar League fleet?"

"But…"

Walleye reached over, patting one of her clenched hands.

"Aliens?" June whispered. "You think aliens are in the Solar System?"

"Luscious, I've had a worse thought than that. It's partly why you're here."

"Please, Walleye, I don't like talking about this. It's creepy."

"Do you have a key to your friend's cubicle?"

"I do. But she's under quarantine."

"Makes you wonder, doesn't it?"

"About what?" June asked.

"About what she might have seen on her long-range sensors," Walleye said softly. "The orbital station controls some advanced sensing equipment. I think it's time you and I paid your friend a visit, ask her what she's seen, ask her if that's why she's in quarantine."

June's mouth dropped open. What had she gotten herself into? She glanced at the blazing image on the screen. If that was a vid shot of an alien ship…and others knew about this…

"Okay," June whispered. "Let's do it."

-3-

The Kuiper Belt was like any frontier in man's past. In many ways, it was like the Greek exploration of the early period when they and the Phoenicians colonized the best areas along the Mediterranean coast. It was also akin to the American Wild West. Instead of plains, Indians and covered wagons, it had vacuums, spaceships and comets, with the occasional dwarf planet thrown in.

The stellar vagabonds staked claims, first at the bigger, metallic bodies and later elsewhere. Law was closer to the surface, enforced by will, guns and sometimes by signed compacts.

June and Walleye belonged to a group known as *cryoarchs*. They were a rough lot, driven by greed, sustained by technology and living on hope.

June Zen's grandfather, Maximus Zen, was one of the cryoarch founders. In reality, Maximus Zen was June's great, great grandfather. Maximus Zen and Leticia Evans had propounded a countervailing theory regarding humanity's destiny.

Most people lived day-to-day. Those that did regard the future mostly concerned themselves with solid pension plans. Among those, the vast majority waited until older age before even that really concerned them.

Maximus Zen had worried about the human race. Would it survive the Solar System? He had finally decided that it would, but only if man began colonizing other star systems.

Unfortunately, as far as Maximus knew, there was no such thing as a Faster than Light Drive. Thus, humanity would have to do its colonizing the hard way.

People could use sleeper ships, freezing themselves in cryo units as the automated vessel traveled the distance. They could use generational vessels, the original colonists dying off long before the massive vessel reached a new star system. Their great, great grandchildren would do that. Those in-between would live entirely shipboard lives.

Maximus believed each of those systems had serious flaws. He had a different way. The Kuiper Belt, and more importantly, the Oort cloud, would be the answer. People would not rush to another star system, but hop by slow degrees. They would travel from a dwarf planet, to a comet, to another comet, maybe another dwarf planet—and by that time, they would have reached the farthest end of the outer Oort cloud. They would be two light-years from the Sun by that point.

As the people kept slowly hopping from comet to dirty asteroid, they would enter the edge of a new star system and slowly reverse the process. Eventually, the descendants would build colonies on new major planets or on their moons, the light coming from a completely different star.

By a process of stellar osmosis, humanity would survive its own killer nature.

The cryoarch portion of the theory was Leticia Evans's addition. The first Belters —Kuiper Belters—had been futurists, who keenly believed in humanity's continued scientific development. As the leaders of the Belters grew old and neared death, they froze themselves in long-term cryo units. The idea was simple. At some point in the future, humanity would have greater science. That science would likely include the cure for aging. The ancient survivors would be thawed, take the cure, and begin life in the new paradise of man.

However, over the years, the number of cryo units grew progressively. Keeping them all functioning took too much badly needed energy. Out here in the Belt, that energy could be applied to more useful and life-sustaining projects. This far from the Sun, keeping alive was hard work.

The solution proved easy if heartless. New future-seekers opened old cryo units and tossed the sleepers into a furnace. One then took a geezer's place as the unit's new occupant. Naturally, the interlopers set up safeguards so no one could do that to them. In most cases, the safeguards proved futile. Then, some people decided the oldest cryoarchs might be worth preserving. They'd become like old wines on Earth, gaining status due to their vintage. Finally, a Belter clan didn't really have high status unless they could point to ancient cryoarchs.

June Zen had the status she did because she controlled one of the oldest cryo-occupants in the Kuiper Belt, good old Maximus Zen, her grandfather.

***

June and Walleye moved through narrow corridors. These were far under the methane/nitrogen ice that covered most of Makemake. These corridors had a plastic-like coating stretched over dwarf-planet rock. One could see the rocky contours. In some places, it seemed as if sharp-angled rocks would tear through the fabric. That had never happened, as the fabric was incredibly tough.

June felt uncomfortable walking with Walleye. She towered over the short assassin, and it made her self-conscious.

He was wearing a long buff coat that almost scraped against the flooring, and he wore an odd hat with a brim that hid his weird eyes.

She knew he had weapons hidden under the buff coat. She also knew—

"It's strange," Walleye muttered.

"Huh?"

"The corridor is empty."

"It's evening schedule. Everyone is resting or working. Why would they be running around in the corridors?"

"A hundred reasons, Luscious. The emptiness strikes me odd. That's all I'm saying." Walleye looked up at her. "You notice anything strange lately?"

June shook her head. "Do you have anything specific in mind?"

58

"Nope. Just wondering." He tugged at the brim of his hat. "Feels like something is building up, know what I mean?"

"No."

He grinned under the shadow of his hat brim.

"What's so funny?" she demanded.

"People think I have mutant powers. They call me a freak. I just keep my eyes open. I notice."

"You notice what?"

"Whatever! I soak it up and let it sink into my thinker. I have situational awareness better than anyone I know. Something is building up, and I'm not talking about Luxor's coming takeover. An idiot could see that coming. This is different."

"You mean the catapult launches?"

He looked up at her. "Smart and beautiful. What a combination."

"Are you making fun of me?"

Walleye shook his head.

June felt the "key" in her hand. It was a card ID. It had Mindy's combination downloaded into it.

-4-

June felt guilty doing this, especially with the large yellow quarantine sign on the door. She looked both ways again.

This was "C" Complex with banks and banks of doors with levels upon levels of walkways stacked one above the other before the doors. Lights shined, making everything nice and bright. Camera eyes were watching, which was normal security procedure.

"Luscious, you have terrible thieving skills," Walleye said. "Just hold up the key. Open the door. Walk in. What could be easier?"

"If we get caught—"

"The longer you rubber-neck, the greater chance there is of that happening."

June steeled herself, passed the card before an "eye" and heard something in the door click. Tentatively, she pushed open the door.

"Mindy? It's June. Are you okay?"

No answer. Worse, the place smelled wrong. It smelled empty.

June glanced back at Walleye.

He made an elaborate gesture, indicating she should enter the abode.

Suddenly, June didn't want to go in. She wanted to go home, shower, curl into bed and watch a holo-vid. If she crossed this threshold, she would—

"Oh," she said, in surprise, stumbling into the quarantined quarters. Walleye had pushed her.

He strode in after her, doing it in the best style he could with his stumpy legs, letting the buff coat swing open.

June looked back.

Walleye had drawn a big old gun that seemed far too heavy for his hand. She had no idea what kind of gun it was. It had a big orifice and seemed deadly. Seeing it made her more frightened, not less.

"Put that away," she hissed.

Walleye ignored her as his head swiveled this way and that.

The short hall led into living quarters. Everything was neat and tidy in here. No tablets lay anywhere. No cups, no wrappers, no vid plugs or even ear plugs in evidence. There was no evidence of a person living in the tight quarantined quarters.

"Mindy!" June shouted.

"Don't bother," Walleye said. "The place is empty. But let's make sure. You never know."

June frowned, slowly turning, searching for something.

As she did, Walleye kept moving, with the heavy gun ready for anything. He disappeared into the bedroom, stayed there too long it seemed—then came the sound of an air-flushed toilet.

Walleye walked back into the living area as he holstered the big gun under his buff coat.

"What were you doing in there?" June asked.

He shrugged, saying, "Drank too much mojo earlier."

"You used her bathroom?"

He rubbed his chin, scratching at his cheek.

"You're not supposed to break into someone's quarters and use their bathroom," June scolded.

"She's gone. I doubt she ever came here. When did you talk to her?"

"Three days ago."

"And she's been 'quarantined' for five?"

June nodded.

"Did you face-time her or did you just speak to her on a comm?"

61

"We just spoke."

Walleye nodded as if that meant something.

"Why would they quarantine her, or say they were, if no one is here?" June asked.

"Two reasons I can think of," Walleye said. "One, 'they' killed her and didn't want anyone knowing right away."

"But I talked to her!"

"That leads me to reason two. She had to go somewhere and this was cover."

"That's doesn't make sense."

Walleye moved to the couch, lifted the back of his buff coat and sat down. He put his hands between his knees and hunched forward.

"What are you doing?" June asked.

He didn't look up as he answered, "Thinking."

June crossed her arms, confounded by events. "If Mindy's gone, and she's got high-level backing..."

Walleye looked up at her with interest.

"Placing her in quarantine—putting the sign on the door—took authority."

"You're talking about Luxor Evans," Walleye said.

"If Luxor's covering for her...Mindy never needed my help with Big Bob."

"Smart girl," Walleye said. "Luxor can tell Big Bob..." The mutant trailed off as another odd look swept over him.

"What now?"

Walleye shook his head.

"You know something."

"This quarantine setup has nothing to do with Luxor Evans," Walleye said. "It's obvious. If it had to do with Luxor, Mindy would have never phoned you."

"Who ordered Mindy into quarantine then?"

"Luscious, you're a genius. Who indeed. Can you find out? Hey. What's wrong?"

June's knees had just given out. Luckily, she slumped into a chair. Her mouth hung open and she stared into space. After a time, she closed her mouth and looked at Walleye.

He waited patiently.

"Just before Big Bob showed up this morning with mojo, I saw something strange on my orbital screen," June said.

Walleye kept waiting. Maybe that was another of his powers as an assassin or mutant. Most people would have blurted for her to speak up, already.

"I saw space-walkers leaving an orbital hauler," June said. "I can't remember how many of them. Ten or more. They drifted toward other haulers, other orbital boats."

"You mean jetted over using suit thrusters?"

June nodded.

"Why's that bother you now?" Walleye asked.

"I didn't know about aliens before this," June said.

"Space-walkers mean aliens to you?" Walleye asked.

"It looked weird at the time. I forgot all about it after Big Bob grabbed me." June looked up. "The hauler was from Dannenberg 7. That's an Evans controlled planetesimal."

Walleye looked grim. "You know Dannenberg 7 went offline three months ago, right?"

June moaned. She'd remembered there was something different about Dannenberg 7 but not what exactly. Now she knew. It had gone offline, silent for three long months.

"Think about it," Walleye said. "Dannenberg 7 is one of the closer planetesimals in the path of the bright-thruster ship I showed you."

"Did I see aliens this morning on my screen and not know it?" June whispered. "Were those aliens infiltrating other ships?"

The two of them stared at each other.

"What are we going to do?" June said.

Walleye clenched his stubby hands harder than before. "First, we're going to keep calm. This could be aliens. This could be something else. We don't want to jump to conclusions."

"We haven't heard anything from the Neptune System for months," June said. "What's caused that?"

Walleye slowly shook his head.

"Why would aliens sneak around upstairs, leaving their hauler so they could drift to other ships?" June whispered.

Walleye stared at the floor.

"I'm scared," June said.

Walleye looked up. He stood fast—almost impossibly fast—used his right hand to whip back the edge of the buff coat and draw the heavy gun. In the small confines of the living quarters, the gun discharged three times, making a coughing sound each time, followed by muffled explosive sounds and the distinctive stretching sounds of sticky tangle threads.

June turned in time to see Mindy thump onto the floor, tangled tight, with a small stitch-gun clattering onto the floor to bump against June's right shoe.

-5-

"Mindy!" June cried. "Are you all right?"

Mindy Smalls had landed hard, hitting her face on the floor. She'd been tangled too tightly for her to use her hands or even twist aside to soften the crash.

Blood now pooled on the floor under her face.

"Mindy!" June cried again. She knelt beside her best friend and carefully chose where she put her hands. She didn't want to have the sticky threads stick to her. With a grunt, she turned Mindy onto her back.

The blood flowed from Mindy's nose over her mouth and down the sides of her face into both ears. The nose looked broken.

June jumped up, running to the kitchen. She ran back, giving Walleye a fiercely disapproving scowl and carefully wiped away blood from Mindy's face.

The tangled woman began to choke on the blood she'd already swallowed.

"Help me get her up," June demanded.

Walleye didn't move.

"She'll choke to death if we don't do something," June said.

"She's breathing," Walleye said in a noncommittal manner.

"What's wrong with you?" June shouted at Walleye.

The assassin holstered his tangle gun. He moved briskly, picking up the stitch-gun on the floor, checking it.

"Looks normal," he said. "You own any guns?" he asked June.

"What? No!"

"Does Mindy?"

"Obviously," June said.

"You remember her owning a stitch-gun?"

"I have no idea. Mindy, are you feeling okay?"

Mindy had opened her eyes. She stared fixedly at June.

"It's me," June said, bending over her best friend. "You're going to be all right. You hit your head—"

"*Gronk*," Mindy said.

June's heart went out to her friend. "Oh, Mindy. I'm so sorry. We thought…we thought you were in trouble. I brought—"

June looked up at Walleye to find him studying her friend.

"She hit her head," June snapped. "She might have a concussion. Don't you have a spray that will wilt the sticky strands?"

"She was going to shoot me," Walleye said.

"Don't try to defend your actions now. You did this to her."

"I'm not defending my actions. I'd tangle her again if I had to do it over. She was going to shoot you, too. She wasn't looking at me when she drew her gun, but at you."

"Don't be a fool."

"Ask her."

June turned to Mindy. "You weren't going to shoot me, were you?"

"*Gronk*," Mindy said again. This time she scowled afterward. She didn't seem to be conscious of her bloody nose or that June kept sopping up the blood.

Walleye aimed the stitch-gun at Mindy. He stepped closer.

"What are you doing?" June demanded.

"Look at her. She doesn't seem frightened. I shot her with the tangles. For all she knows, I'm going to kill her with the stitch-gun. She doesn't show a lick of fear, though."

June looked down at Mindy. Her best friend watched Walleye, but it was true that she showed no fear. That wasn't like Mindy. She was as brave as the next person, but she wasn't death-defying.

June searched Walleye's face. She didn't like the seriousness there, the careful studiousness.

Walleye lowered the stitch-gun, although he didn't put it away. He flipped the back of his buff coat and squatted beside Mindy on his stumpy legs. He stared at her frankly.

Mindy seemed content to wait for whatever was going to happen next.

"Look at her eyes," Walleye said.

June did.

"Do they seem glassy?" Walleye asked.

"No."

"Does Mindy look confused?"

June shook her head.

"What would you say she looks like?"

"I don't know," June whispered. "I've never seen her like this."

"She's like a waiting reptile," Walleye said. "I've seen an alligator before in a zoo. I was a kid in a rich Neptune habitat. The alligator had eyes like that. I remember it watching me. I had the feeling it was waiting for me to make a mistake."

"Mindy has a concussion," June said.

"I've seen people with concussions. They didn't look anything like that. Why isn't your friend complaining about her broken nose? Why isn't she asking us to spray off the strands? Why isn't she threatening us for breaking and entering her quarantined quarters?"

As Walleye asked his questions, June's heart sank lower and lower.

"What are you saying?" June whispered.

"Don't know yet. I'm thinking out loud." He let go of the stitch-gun as he went to his hands and knees. Like a dog playing a game, he moved nearer Mindy, lowering his head closer to her. He seemed to be inspecting her. He crawled around her, studying, searching—

"This is weird," Walleye said. He reached out, touching her hair.

June would have expected Mindy to flinch. Her friend merely waited It was starting to get creepy.

Walleye pulled away hair, grunting at something. He stood abruptly, looked at June in a strange manner, and staggered for the kitchen. A second later, he retched, probably in the sink.

The small assassin returned, using a dishtowel to wipe his mouth.

"That's not yours," June said.

"It's not hers anymore, either," Walleye said grimly.

"What's that supposed to mean? Are you going to kill her?"

"Move," he said.

"I will not. You have to tell me what's going on. Why did you vomit? Are you sick?"

He stared at her, nodding shortly. "This is difficult. I understand. It's difficult for me, too, and I'm a mutant."

June realized he was attempting levity.

"We've stumbled onto something...outrageous," Walleye said. "We've discovered aliens. I believe you found evidence of aliens this morning. Seeing your friend, I think the aliens have already infiltrated Makemake. To what extent is the question of the hour. We might have a chance to save ourselves, but I suspect it's a slim chance. We have to take it, Luscious. If we don't, we might end up like Mindy."

"Just say it," June pleaded. "Your beating around the bush is giving me the willies."

"Move aside."

Reluctantly, June did.

Walleye knelt beside Mindy. He picked up the dropped dishtowel and put it on her, rolling her back over onto her face. He slid on his knees to her head and lifted her hair.

"Look at her scalp," Walleye said.

June did, and the queasiness from the sight made her faint-feeling. June clung to consciousness and somehow kept herself from vomiting as Walleye had done. She wasn't sure what that was, but it looked like someone had inserted a fist-sized piece of metal into Mindy's skull. A tiny antenna sprouted from the metal, and the tip glowed with a reddish color.

"What is that?" June whispered.

"A clue," Walleye said. "Maybe the last one we need to put a fire under our backsides so we do something to save our lives."

-6-

"No," June said, horrified. "You can't. It might kill her."

Walleye looked up, and something like pity changed his features. "Your friend is already dead, Luscious. This is something else staring out at us. I know that's hard to hear…" he trailed off.

June's hands flew to her mouth as she tried to suppress a sob. Oh, Mindy, Mindy, Mindy, this was awful. Had aliens stuck something soul-killing into her brain? It was too hideous to contemplate.

"I'm going to need your help," Walleye said softly. "You'll probably have to hold her head down."

June groaned, shaking her head, keeping her hands in front of her mouth.

"You know I'm right."

The awful thing about that was he *was* right.

Her shoulders trembled, but June took her hands from her mouth. She knelt beside Mindy with a sigh.

"It will kill her," June whispered.

"Maybe it will free her. Maybe she can tell us something to save Makemake."

June forced herself to put her hands on the back of Mindy's head. She braced herself.

"Push down with all your weight," Walleye said.

"I—" June wanted to tell him she couldn't, but she could. She had to.

Swallowing hard, June pushed down, shoving Mindy's face against the floor.

Despite the broken nose, Mindy made no complaint.

With a pair of pliers, Walleye clutched a protrusion on the unit in Mindy's skull.

"Ready?" he asked.

"Do it already," June said between clenched teeth.

Walleye strained, no doubt clutching the pliers as hard as he could. Then he braced himself and heaved upward.

June struggled to hold the head down. Walleye began to yank instead of just pull. That sickened June, and tears began to spill from her eyes.

At that moment, an ugly plopping sound accompanied Walleye's arms flying up, yanking a bloody disc-thing from the skull. Awful wires, stiff things, dripped with gore and pieces of Mindy's brain. Those wires had been shoved into her brain.

June couldn't contain it anymore. She jerked away, vomiting onto the floor. Horror consumed her as she moaned, hugging herself and vomiting again.

Mindy began to cough and retch. She began to twist in the tangle strands, attempting to hump across the floor. She began to moan.

"Mindy!" Walleye shouted. "We're your friends. We want to help you. Mindy, speak to us."

Instead of continuing to cry out in growing hysteria, Mindy asked in a small voice, "Help?"

June looked up, stunned. "Mindy?" she asked.

Walleye rolled Mindy onto her back. It hid the blood dripping from the awful scalp wound.

Mindy had stark white features. Her eyes were glazed and she breathed shallowly.

"June," she whispered. "Oh, June, June, June, it was awful." Mindy began to weep.

"Tell us about it," Walleye said. He was crouched low so he could whisper in Mindy's ear.

"Am I dying?" Mindy asked in a wheeze.

"Yes," Walleye said.

"Nooooo...." Mindy said. "I'm too young. I want to live. Help me. Help me. You have to help me."

70

"Yes," Walleye said. "We'll help you. We want to help you. We have to know what happened. That way we can tell the doctors. We have to tell Evans about this too. We have stop…"

"The robots?" Mindy asked. "You're going to stop the robots?"

June stared at Walleye in shock. She opened her mouth—

"Wait," Walleye said. To Mindy, he said, "Robots. That's exactly what we thought happened."

Mindy searched his eyes. "It is? You know about them?"

"Somewhat," Walleye said. "You may have the exact knowledge we need. Tell us quickly before the doctors arrive. That way they can go straight to work to save you."

"You mean that?"

"One hundred percent," Walleye said.

June knew he was lying. But the mutant sounded so sincere. Had he known about these robots all along? Why hadn't he told her then?

"I spotted something on my sensor board," Mindy whispered. "I radioed the tower about it. Evans's cousin Thebes took the call and told me to come right over with the specs.

"I asked him why I couldn't wire it. He told me this was urgent. So I went." Mindy searched Walleye's eyes. If his weird appearance bothered her, it didn't stop her words. They began to tumble out of her.

"Thebes must have had a unit already. He met me and led me into a room. The robot was waiting there. It had four articulated legs like a giant spider, and a bulbous body. I think I shrieked. The robot moved fast, throwing me down on a bed. It injected me with a drug. I heard buzzing and felt pressure against my skull. That was the last time I was in charge of myself. The unit took over and gave me commands.

"I couldn't resist. Oh, how I wanted to. It used pain and sometimes just bypassed my desires. I could understand everything going on around me, but I couldn't do anything to stop it. The only drawback that I could see from the robot's perspective is that I understand some of the larger plan. Some of their thoughts seeped into my brain."

"What does it want?" Walleye asked.

"Makemake."

"Why?"

"I'm not sure," Mindy said. "I think to construct something."

"Is there anyone else like you?"

"A handful so far," Mindy said. "More on the way. The robots are going to take over. I have the feeling they're going to turn everyone into an automaton like I was. I saw a room with thousands of control units. I think they want to turn us all into worker drones."

June held back a sob as she listened.

"Are they robots or are they aliens?" Walleye asked.

Mindy thought about it. Her eyes sought out Walleye. "They're both," she whispered. "They're robot aliens."

Walleye frowned severely. He didn't seem to know what to ask next.

"You're never going to escape," Mindy said.

"Why not?" asked Walleye, sounding suspicious.

"They know about you. They could see through my eyes. They have to know you pulled out the control unit. They're still trying to remain hidden. Go-hour is fast approaching."

"How long?" Walleyed snapped.

"Twenty-four hours," Mindy whispered. "No longer than that."

"They're going to capture everyone?"

"Yes."

"Is there an alien spaceship in orbit?"

"Pods," Mindy said. "Three big pods are coming. One is bringing the factory supplies. The rest are robot soldiers. They're going to transform the Kuiper Belt first and construct whatever is needed. After that—Listen. This is super important. I think they're going to wipe us out, all of us, not just us in the Kuiper Belt."

"Genocide?" June whispered.

Mindy's face scrunched up. "Do me a favor," she said in a tight voice. "It's starting to really hurt. Kill me. I don't want to be a drone again. Kill me, and then kill yourselves. Believe me, you don't want to be a drone. It's the most awful thing in the universe."

Mindy started to say more. As she did, someone came through the front door.

June jumped to her feet.

Walleye palmed the stitch-gun off the floor.

An official in a port uniform stepped up. He had a gun in his hand.

Walleye shot him first, sending a dozen stitches into the man's face. As the official fell, the mutant ran forward, hissing a dozen more shots. Something heavy thudded into the hallway.

June began shaking and trembling, hugging herself.

Walleye reappeared. He had the look of death on him. Without asking June or Mindy, he shot Mindy, killing her.

June moaned in dread. This was a nightmare.

Walleye the Freak reached his free hand toward her with its stubby fingers extended. He grabbed one of June's hands with surprising strength, jerked her and forced her to stumble after him.

June passed the dead man in the hall. He lay on his face. She could see the control unit in the back of the skull. Mindy had been right. There were more of them.

"It's starting," Walleye told her. "We're going to have to move faster than these robot aliens. Lucky for you, Luscious, I have the perfect plan "

-7-

June squeezed her eyes closed as the rocket lifted from Makemake Port, the thrusting Gs pushing her against the blast-seat.

Somewhere along the line, her heart must have hardened. The old June Zen would have wept. She would have begged Walleye to go to the cryo storage-chamber and take her grandfather's unit. She couldn't very well leave Maximus Zen behind like this.

If the robots won, would they unfreeze grandfather and shove a control unit into his brain? Would they make all the cryoarchs work as drones until they died? It would be a rude awakening. Instead of a hoped-for scientific heaven, they would enter a technological hell.

June couldn't understand why she didn't weep for Grandfather Zen. She didn't understand how she could keep following Walleye. The little assassin had lived up to his title over the last hour. He'd murdered seven people so far, and that didn't include Mindy and the two intruders. So, he'd killed ten people in a little over an hour. How could he stand himself?

June managed to look over at him. The little mutant grinned like a devil. Then she realized that was the G-forces pulling at his face.

The heavy lifter rose from Makemake. This was a Clan Evans lifter, meant to carry tons of cargo into orbit. Walleye had slain everyone questioning their right to commandeer the lifter.

Walleye had explained to her on the run. "The robots are going to win, Luscious. Don't ask how I know. It's my gut instinct. Maybe we could save more on Makemake, but that would mean taking awful risks. The problem now is that we don't know who to trust. The infiltrators could be controlling anyone. Therefore, I'm trusting no one but you, Luscious. Does that make sense?"

She could only stare at the mutant. A life as a loner seemed to have prepared Walleye for this moment. Was she lucky or damned to have hitched along for the ride?

The fierce thrust lessened as they escaped Makemake's limited gravity. Walleye had debated fleeing the dwarf planet and the robot invasion in the heavy lifter. He'd decided the robots would just send a missile after them. They had to slip away unnoticed.

"I'm gambling," the mutant had told her. "I'm rolling the dice, Luscious, figuring these aliens are arrogant as sin."

The lifter's comm crackled. A controller wanted to know what the hell the pilot figured he was doing. All lifters were grounded for the next ten hours. Why had he broken the restriction?

"We're not answering," Walleye said. "I doubt the aliens will get too anxious about us yet. We'll turn toward the project soon enough." He meant the main orbital construction project, the giant warship. "The aliens have to have infiltrated it already. Since the lifter is heading there, the aliens will no doubt figure we'll fall right into their laps."

"You're mad," June said matter-of-factly. She said it even though her facial muscles felt too tight.

"No," Walleye said. "I have a different kind of demon riding my back. You know what that demon is, Luscious?"

June didn't answer.

"Demon I-Know-Too-Much," he said.

"You knew this was going to happen?"

Walleye gave her a lopsided grin. "I can see deeper than others. Most people don't even see what's going on around them, never mind fitting the pieces together and making a reasonable assumption."

"You've lost me," June said.

"That's the story of my life, Luscious. Trust me; this is our only chance. No…I guess we could do this some other way. This just seemed to be our best chance of getting away with our lives."

The comm squawked again, the controller threatening them with the orbital guns if they didn't answer.

Walleye stabbed a button. The thrusters quit. The Gs stopped on the instant. Weightlessness took over.

Walleye sat at the piloting board. His stubby fingers moved quickly. June wondered what he was doing. Finally, he took a square object out of his pocket. He fit it over the on/off switch and tapped the thing's screen. A number appeared: 20:00.

As June watched, the number changed to 19:59 and then to 19:58 and then 19:57…

"Time to go," Walleye said. He unbuckled and shoved off the chair, leaving the timer over the on/off switch.

June shook her head. "Go where? You're not making sense."

"You know something, Luscious? You should keep your pretty mouth shut and listen more. You're stressing out. That's not going to help any. We have a narrow margin to get out of this in one piece. But you have to do exactly what I say. Are you ready?"

In that moment, June realized the mutant was right. He'd done the impossible. He'd figured out there was an alien infiltration-attack on Makemake. Big Bob hadn't done that, nor had Luxor Evans. A little freak who lived under the catapult system had done it. If she wanted to live her own life to a ripe old age, she had to change her thinking about the mutant-man.

"Let's do this, Walleye. I'm with you."

✳✳✳

They were wearing spacesuits and standing at an open outer hatch. Walleye pointed a suited arm at something she couldn't see. She nodded her helmet just the same. He clicked a safety line to her suit. The line was already connected to his belt.

Walleye bent his stubby legs and jumped out of the open hatch. She immediately jumped after him.

They drifted high in orbit above Makemake. It was bright down there in one circular location on the ice. Everywhere else on Makemake was dark.

Walleye pointed again. This time he pointed behind them. June turned and saw the heavy lifter start up again, thrusting and accelerating.

Their helmets lacked comms. Their only communication would be through gestures and common sense.

Walleye seemed to know what he was doing. The little man twisted and squirmed in his suit. He pulled the line between them, dragging her closer and closer. Finally, she reached out, grabbing him, trying to cushion their meeting.

The two of them began to tumble. For an instant, she could see Walleye's face through the visor. He seemed to be concentrating intently.

It took some doing. He squirted hydrogen particles from a thruster on his back, at spaced intervals.

In time, they quit tumbling.

June was impressed. She'd heard before how hard zero-G maneuvering was with a thruster-pack. Where had Walleye picked up such skill?

Walleye squirted more hydrogen particles in a long stream so that they picked up speed. She noticed he used darkened particles. Usually, they would be white, leaving an obvious trail. He must have military grade particles in the pack.

Abruptly, Walleye quit squirting. They glided along up here in high orbit. There had to be haulers and boats around them. Yes! She spotted one. It was ahead of them, almost directly ahead as if Walleye had been aiming for it.

Just then, a violent explosion appeared to their left. It was huge, and it grew. What could have caused—

June sucked in her breath. She bet Walleye had targeted the heavy lifter directly at the project ship. That's why he'd been fiddling with the controls. Had Walleye succeeded, or had the port authorities fired the guns, destroying the heavy lifter? The vast explosion inclined her to her original conclusion.

June gasped as Walleye rotated the two of them. He started using the thruster-pack again afterward. It finally dawned on her all the things he'd been telling her earlier. She'd only half heard him before because she'd still been in a daze.

They were going to pirate a hauler. They weren't going to pirate just any hauler, though. Walleye was deliberately heading for the supposed robot hauler from Dannenberg 7.

She remembered him saying, "I wouldn't doubt that all the robots headed to other ships. You counted eleven before, and there are way more haulers, boats and ships out here. What do you want to bet they left their hauler empty, on the assumption the stupid humans wouldn't know what was going on?"

June swallowed heavily. She dearly hoped Walleye knew what he was doing.

-8-

They struck the Evans hauler hard enough to knock the wind out of June. She gasped, whimpering at the pain. Then, as she struggled to take a breath, she realized they were floating away from the hauler.

It was a tubby space-vehicle. It had numbers painted on the side and the words: *GET BENT.* That was typical Evans bravado.

Walleye squeezed his thruster-pack throttle. They quit drifting away and now drifted back toward the hull. It looked beat-up, that was for sure.

Walleye used magnetic clamps to attach both of them to the surface. Neither had magnetized space boots. That had been an oversight on Walleye's part.

Now Walleye's helmet moved back and forth as if he were searching for something. He demagnetized, using the thruster-pack so they slid along the hull, traveling a few meters above the hauler.

June started getting worried again. This was taking too long. Just then, Walleye waved an arm and pointed.

June had no idea what he pointed—Hold it. That looked like an open hatch. Is that where the robots had exited the hauler earlier?

Walleye squirted more black hydrogen particles. Bit by bit, they drifted toward the hatch. As gently as a feather, they reached it.

Perfect piloting, June told herself.

Walleye entered the lock and June followed. He looked around and slapped a switch. The outer hatch shut, putting them into momentary gloom. A light began to shine.

This was an old hauler, June realized. The light should have shined as soon as the outer hatch closed.

Walleye checked a gauge, waited and finally activated the inner hatch.

It opened.

June began to hyperventilate. Had some of the robots stayed behind to guard the hauler, or was Walleye right about them?

The mutant pulled out his tangle gun. Would the sticky threads hold a robot?

June moaned as they entered the main area of the dark ship. No lights or alarms came on. Walleye pulled out a flashlight with his other hand. He clicked it on, and a powerful beam pierced the darkness.

June couldn't talk. She could hardly think. There were all kinds of hardware in here. None of it appeared normal. It seemed, well, alien. So far, though, no robot had popped up to kill them, or worse, turn them into drones.

Walleye kept advancing, carefully pushing himself from place to place. In terror, June followed. Her stomach squeezed harder and harder. She almost wanted a robot to pop up. The suspense was making her sick.

The robots did not comply. There was just this alien junk piled almost to the ceiling in places. Some of it looked like alien robot parts. Other stuff seemed like computer hardware.

Finally, Walleye opened a hatch, going in headfirst. June followed right behind him. Walleye pointed. She had no idea—

He pointed more insistently.

Finally, she turned around and saw a switch. She pressed it, closing the hatch behind them. When she turned around, Walleye had floated before normal-looking Evans hauler controls.

Eventually, Walleye twisted off his helmet. He seemed okay. June twisted hers off. The stink hit her immediately. It was awful, but she didn't choke, only made a face.

"We did it, Luscious. We made it, and so far, no robots."

"Now what?" she asked. "We stirred them up with the heavy lifter."

Walleye grinned, nodding. "Let's hope it gives us enough cover so we can slip away."

"You're not serious. We have to land this and show Luxor Evans. Maybe we can—"

June stopped talking because Walleye was laughing too hard.

Wiping his weird eyes, bringing the laughter under control, Walleye said: "You have to excuse me, Luscious. I'm working under intense pressure. I keep seeing your friend with that *thing* in her skull. This is far more than just Makemake. This is more than just the Kuiper Belt. I'm thinking this could be about the human race."

"I don't understand."

"Aliens, Luscious. Robots. They aren't friendly robots, either, but horrific bastards. This is for all the marbles."

"Huh?"

"You're going to have quit talking for a bit. I got to figure this out and see if I can outsmart these alien peckers."

***

The hauler applied increasing amounts of thrust before quitting altogether.

Time passed.

Walleye said they might as well see if they could figure out any of this alien junk while they waited.

They didn't turn on the comm. They didn't check the sensors. They just drifted along in high orbit, hoping to get onto the far side of Makemake.

An hour passed. Then another. June had stopped handling the alien hardware some time ago. Walleye kept right on checking.

He now motioned his head toward the piloting compartment. He carried a chest-sized thing with him, squeezing through the hatch with it.

"What is that?" June asked as she followed.

"I think it belongs with the main computing unit. It strikes me as a memory core. We're going to take it with us."

"You keep saying things I don't understand."

Walleye smiled indulgently. "I explain until I'm out of breath. You hear some of it, but..."

"What? You think I'm stupid?"

"Hardly. I think you're terrified just like me. I think you're having a hard time getting your head around all this. You keep getting a blank look on your face. You want to zone out and forget about the horror. But you're too strong-willed to stay that way. You zone back in, and I try to explain what I already told you earlier."

"Why doesn't that happen to you?" June asked.

"Who said it doesn't?"

June shook her head stubbornly.

"Okay. I'm a hard case because of my mutations."

"You're not that different from others."

He raised an arm as if to show her how short it was.

"Except for a few..." June trailed off.

"Deformities?" he asked. "Is that the word you're looking for?"

She felt herself slipping away again.

"Don't answer that," he said. "I'm not saying my mutations make me stronger. I'm saying because I've learned to live with the way I am, that I'm already hardened inside."

"Oh. I'm sorry."

"Don't be," he said. "It's why we're alive and have our brains to ourselves instead of being enslaved. I plan to keep us that way."

"I'm surprised we've gotten this far in the hauler."

"Me too," Walleye said. "I can only guess that the heavy lifter struck the great project. That would have alerted Makemake, and gotten the security people moving."

"Walleye," she said, staring at him, realizing something. "You did warn them. You did give Makemake a chance."

He shrugged. "If I were a guessing man, which I am, I'd say there's a huge fight going on in Makemake right now. My money is on the robots, though."

"Why?"

"They have the advantage of surprise and likely superior weapons. By the time Luxor realizes what he's really fighting..." Walleye shrugged again.

The little assassin sat at the piloting board, studying a screen. "We did it. We're on the far side of the planet. Probe sensors will see us, but it will take time for anyone to fire at us. If there's fighting on the other side—better strap in, Luscious. We're going to go as long and as a fast as we can. I don't know how long that will be, though. Ready?"

She nodded.

Walleye manipulated the piloting board.

Suddenly, June's head snapped back against the headrest. The hauler's thrusters roared with power, sending them away from Makemake, on the other side of the dwarf planet from the city port.

-9-

Many hours later, a red light blinked on the comm.

June raised her head, peering at Walleye. The mutant was asleep. She called his name until he looked up.

The thrusters had shut down some time ago.

"We don't answer anyone," he told her.

"They'll suspect the worst about us then."

Walleye nodded but didn't say anything more.

In time, the red light quit blinking.

More time passed. A different red light began to blink.

Walleye was awake this time. He adjusted an instrument, stared at it for a time and finally sighed.

"What is it?" June asked in alarm.

"Missile. It's coming for us."

"Is it a robot or human-built missile?"

"Don't know. It doesn't matter. We have to pack up."

June nodded mutely. She'd been dreading this.

They'd already packed the escape pod with the items they would need, including the alien memory core, if that's what it was.

Walleye opened the hatch to the pod. June followed him inside and buckled up in her crash-seat. He sealed them in and found his seat.

"Ready?" he asked.

"I am," she whispered hoarsely.

Walleye pulled a lever, and once more, June's head snapped back.

The emergency pod shot out of the hauler. It did not add any thrust, but drifted away from the hauler while still moving in the same general direction and at the same velocity. Walleye had aimed the hauler for Neptune a long, long way away.

They waited. It took several more hours. Finally, on a small panel, they saw a bright light.

"Say good-bye to the hauler," Walleye said.

"Are more missiles coming?" June asked breathlessly.

Walleye shrugged.

"You can tell me," she said.

"I don't know. I don't care. We're going to assume no more missiles are coming. Thinking that will give us more hope. But that doesn't matter for you. It's time."

June stared at Walleye. She stared and stared as she felt her eyes growing progressively wider. This was going to be a lot harder than she'd realized.

Walleye sighed. "What is it now, Luscious?"

It was hard to force the words past a tight throat. Finally, she said, "You go into the cryo unit. I'll stay out here."

He grinned. "That's not rational, Luscious. I'm smaller. I'll eat less and breathe less air. Besides, this is going to be a long, long trip, years."

"We can trade off," she said.

"I can take years alone in space in a tiny environment. I don't think you can."

"Walleye—it isn't fair. The cryo unit is too easy. We should share the pain."

"Let me put it to you straight, Luscious. I don't trust you. You'll crack being all alone in this tight place. No. You go into the cryo unit."

"I know you're being gallant, but…" June didn't speak her real fear. She'd seen Walleye in action. He was ruthless. She was afraid he'd freeze her, wait for six months, say, and decide to kill her and then freeze himself. That was the logical move for an assassin.

"I'm not going to argue," Walleye said. "Either you—"

"Walleye, *please*," she said, with tears in her eyes.

"What's wrong?" he asked.

85

She closed her eyes. She wished she could trust him. She wished she could believe he'd wait those years and years. The desire for life was too strong in her, though.

"Don't you trust me?" Walleye asked.

June opened her eyes just enough to see him. She pulled out the stitch-gun hidden in her coat, aimed at him and pulled the trigger over and over and over again. It finally dawned on her that the gun had clicked empty each time. Walleye sat there staring at her.

"No," she whispered, beginning to shake. "I…I couldn't trust you, Walleye. I wanted to, I really did. But…"

June Zen began to weep.

Walleye plucked the gun out of her grasp. He didn't say anything. Instead, he waited.

After a good cry, using a sleeve, she wiped the tears from her eyes. She couldn't look up.

"Well?" she whispered.

He said nothing.

"Just shoot me already," she said miserably.

He still remained silent.

She wiped her eyes again and finally looked up at him. She couldn't see any evidence of the stitch-gun.

"What are you waiting for?" she asked defiantly.

"For you to get into the cryo unit," he said.

"So you can kill me later while I'm frozen?"

He said nothing, just waited.

That unnerved June. She hated the mutant. She turned away, biting a knuckle. She must have fallen asleep. She had awful dreams. Finally, she stirred. With a start, she sat up.

Walleye still watched her.

"What?" she shouted.

"Part of me wishes I didn't see things so well. I could feel your conflicted thoughts. I could see your determination building. That's when I palmed the gun and took out the stitches. I keep wondering if I did the right thing. I haven't put you in the cryo unit yet…because I know it's going to be a lonely few years."

June's heart sank. She couldn't look at him anymore. She wanted to weep again, but she was out of tears.

"I'm sorry," she said.

He said nothing.

"Do you hate me?"

"Not a bit," he said. Then he sighed. It was so mournful. The sound ripped June's heart.

"It's time," he said. "See you later, Luscious."

"Walleye…"

June Zen didn't know what else to say. Eventually, she went to the cryo unit, opened it and prepared herself. She looked up at him one last time. He had a stupid sad smile on his mutant face.

"Good-bye, Walleye," she whispered. "Good luck. And thanks for everything."

He nodded before looking away.

June pulled down the lid, pressed the switch and laid back. Would she ever wake up again? Maybe. Maybe Walleye would do what he could for them. But would that be enough to beat the alien robots? She kept thinking about that as long as she could before she froze into a human Popsicle for the long journey to the Neptune System.

Part III
SATURN GRAVITATIONAL SYSTEM
+11 Months, 27 Days

-1-

At the far edge of the Saturn Gravitational System, Warship *Nathan Graham* decelerated at 22 gravities. That was much greater than it had accelerated at any point during its journey from Neptune to Saturn.

Because of the orbital variances and the vast void between the two giant planets, the one-hundred kilometer vessel had traveled three times the distance that Saturn was from the Sun to get here.

The Saturn System was far older in terms of time of human habitation than the Neptune System. It had far more people and had been in the grip of the Solar League for several years already.

Captain Jon Hawkins presently stood on the bridge of the *Nathan Graham*—the same chamber that was near the destroyed brain core. He studied the main screen, the moons shown there, the ringed beauty of Saturn and the approaching SLN fleet coming to do battle with him.

As a child with his uncle, and sometimes as a youth in the lower-level gangs, Jon had gone up to stare past New London's main dome. At those times looking from the moon Titan, Jon had stared at Saturn with its intense rings. He'd always loved the view.

He loved it now as he stood on the bridge. He was coming home. He had been coming home for almost a year. Now, though, it was a reality, even as he pulled his first maneuver against the Solar League occupiers.

That was one of the problems with stellar battles. The opponents could usually see their foes coming from a long ways off and for a long time.

The SLN fleet admiral had been demanding to talk to Jon for months already. Jon had declined every time. Not that the fleet admiral had requested him by name. The Solar League did not even know he existed. They just knew a giant warship was headed for the Saturn System. They wanted to speak to the ship's commander.

For months now, with the warship's powerful scopes, Jon and his battle-team had been studying the Solar League deployment.

As far as they could tell, the fleet admiral possessed five heavy battleships of the *Premier*-class like the old *Leonid Brezhnev*. She also had four older *Troika*-class battleships. They were slower and less armored, and had inferior laser cannons compared to the *Premier*-class. Still, those four older battleships were tougher in a collision fight than the three battle-cruisers. The fleet admiral also had three motherships, a dozen missile boats and two heavy monitors. Naturally, she also possessed plenty of destroyers, gunboats, tugs and storage carriers. The last must have utilized their huge cargo holds, expelling prismatic crystals that had been stored in them to form a giant P-Field. The huge cloud of tiny scintillating crystals presently shielded the SLN fleet from the *Nathan Graham's* super-powerful alien scopes.

Jon rubbed two fingers together as he studied the great P-Field. That was standard military tactics. The thick belt of tiny crystals—trillions of them—would block lasers and other beam weapons, at least for a time. The enemy had no doubt studied the former cybership and reached certain conclusions about it. The fleet admiral must already have her plan on how to take out the great threat from Neptune.

Jon rubbed the two fingers harder. If the former cybership had still been under alien control, the coming battle would have been a simple matter. The cyber brain-core would have transmitted the self-aware message to the fleet admiral's vessels. The newly awakened, human-built computers would have slaughtered most of the fleet from the inside.

Jon snapped his fingers. The problem would be solved if the brain core were still running the cybership.

Jon shifted his feet into a new position, moving closer to the main screen.

Alas, he could not fight the Solar League that way. The whole point of this was to save humanity from the grim AI enemy. As much as Jon hated the Solar League and all it stood for, he hated even more the idea of butchering all those fine soldiers and destroying possibly-needed warships. The coming conflict with the AIs—

"Sir," Gloria said. "The fleet admiral is attempting to contact us again."

Jon pursed his lips. He could well understand the fleet admiral's unease. The great vessel from Neptune was no longer going to plow into the vast P-Field. The 22 gravities deceleration would give Jon more maneuverability than that.

A space vessel traveling as fast as the giant warship *had been* doing only had a few options. The laws of motion mandated the vessel to plow ahead in the direction it traveled. Under normal human-built ship capacities, the fleet admiral might figure they could decelerate at 5 or 6 gravities, and that for not too long.

Decelerating as hard as they did—at 22 gravities—would soon bring the great warship to a halt. In the enemy's point of view, that would be far too soon in front of the vast P-Field. Given that this ship could decelerate at 22 gravities, it could also *accelerate* at that rate, too. That would allow the *Nathan Graham* incredible maneuverability.

The fleet admiral's tacticians would have seen what that meant. The giant vessel could easily out-maneuver the P-Field, rendering it useless. Worse, the giant unknown vessel—from the fleet admiral's perspective—was huge. That implied it had longer-ranged weapons.

90

For instance, the range a laser cannon could reach—with destructive energy—was dependent on two factors. The first was the energy flowing into the laser cannon. The second was the size of the firing lens. The bigger the lens, the longer, theoretically, the beam could travel before it dissipated.

Since the *Nathan Graham* was vastly larger than the fleet admiral's biggest battleship, this ship's weapons should have much greater reach.

That would be the reason for the thick P-Field. The fleet admiral had no doubt wanted to begin the battle as late in the day as she could. She would want to fight close-in. She would no doubt believe her foe wanted to pick off her warships at a distance.

It was all elementary space tactics.

"Captain," Gloria said.

"I heard you," Jon said.

"What is your decision?" the mentalist asked.

Jon turned around, walking to Gloria. The small mentalist sat at a console. She looked up, regarding him frankly.

After all these months, they'd grown closer as they tried to anticipate the hidden octopoids inside the former cybership. So far, the regiment had found and destroyed seven octopoid robots. At no time had they been able to capture one intact.

Gloria and Bast Banbeck wanted to study an octopoid computer core. Said cores had self-destructed into slag each time.

As he stood beside the mentalist, Jon raised an eyebrow.

"I think it's time to talk with the enemy commander," Gloria said. "They're obviously anxious to know who we are, as this is an obviously alien vessel. We don't want them to fight to the death. We want them to surrender."

Jon inhaled, steeling himself. Part of him wanted to annihilate the Solar League occupiers. This was a dream come true, having the hated enemy that was soon to be under his guns. But part of him quailed at this hurdle. He couldn't see a way around a bloody fight. The Solar League was composed of fanatical communists. Each warship would have their complement of arbiters and other GSB—Government Security Bureau—personnel.

"How do I look?" he asked Gloria.

"Scowl more," she said.

If someone else had said that, he'd know they were kidding. When Gloria said something, she meant exactly what she'd said.

Jon Hawkins did not scowl more. He set his face like granite—the old enforcer look he'd used a hundred times in the lower tunnels. Then he faced the main screen.

"Yeah," he said. "Patch me through. It's time to talk to these bastards."

-2-

A standing woman appeared on the screen, a rather younger woman than Jon had expected. She was wearing a green uniform. Jon hadn't seen this type before. He didn't know what it meant.

The fleet admiral—she introduced herself as Fleet Admiral Cybil Chang—had short-cut dark hair. She had dark eyes and looked Chinese. For her age, she was striking.

It's the eyes, Jon thought.

Fleet Admiral Chang had dark eyeliner circling her eyes. Together with her striking features, the eyes had a beguiling quality.

"So," she said. "At last, I speak to the great Jon Hawkins."

Jon stared at her in shock, the enforcer flintiness slipping from his face.

"Yes," she said. "I know all about you, Jon Hawkins."

He sputtered, at a loss to explain this. He turned to Gloria.

The mentalist frowned, with her eyes half-lidded. Gloria nodded at last. "The Neptunians," she whispered.

"Interesting," Chang said. The fleet admiral had glanced at a side panel. "This tells me—the voice patterns I'm detecting—that the most honorable Gloria Sanchez of Mars assists you. That is an excellent choice on your part, Mr. Hawkins."

"Captain Hawkins," Jon said, in lieu of anything else.

"I see. You've promoted yourself. According to your profile you used to be Officer-Cadet Jon Hawkins."

"That didn't seem commensurate with my latest ship posting," Jon said, coming out of his shock. "Frankly, given this mighty vessel, I should probably call myself Commodore Hawkins."

"Why not Lord Admiral of the Galaxy Hawkins?" asked Chang.

The tiniest of grins slid onto Jon's face. Her mockery helped him. It helped him recall that she was a Solar League officer, the enemy.

"You no doubt think very highly of yourself," Chang added.

"No reason for it," Jon said. "I just captured the first alien ship to ever enter our Solar System. Oh, I'm not sure if you know or not, but this alien vessel destroyed the SLN task force sent to subdue the Neptune System. Yeah. Maybe I should take the ruler of the galaxy title. You do know I can flick your fleet out of existence, right?"

Fleet Admiral Chang did not respond.

Jon struggled to bring his hatred of them under control. Talking like this wasn't going help. He had to remember the greater goal. The AI ships were out there. The genocide machines could drop out of hyperspace at any time and finish what the first cybership had started.

"You are young," Chang said.

Jon said nothing. He was psyching himself up, trying to access the part of his mind that remembered Colonel Graham's teachings. He wished the colonel could do the talking. He *was* young. Maybe he was too young for this post.

The admiral froze on the screen.

Jon waited a second before whirling around.

Gloria raised her head. Her hands were still on the panel controls, the ones that had paused the conversation with the fleet admiral.

"Chang is trying to shake you," Gloria said. "She's trying to get under your skin."

Jon nodded curtly. He didn't need Gloria telling him what he already knew.

"You're the captain, Jon. You've made plenty of smart decisions all down the line. You have—"

"Thank you," he said, interrupting her.

Gloria studied him.

Jon forced himself to wink. He didn't want to do that. He didn't like anyone thinking he couldn't get it done.

"I am attempting to aid you," Gloria said.

Despite the stiffness of his mouth, he managed a slight grin. "Thanks. I mean that, too."

Gloria smiled, and she even blushed. She looked down at her panel. "I'm bringing her back up."

Jon faced forward.

The fleet admiral was in a new position, half-turned, demanding something from someone on her bridge. Someone spoke sharply over there. Cybil Chang faced him again.

""You're back," she said. "Is anything wrong?"

"You must have been in tight-beam contact with someone in the Neptune System," Jon said matter-of-factly. "I suppose they told you about me, my name at least. They must have told you about—" He'd almost said, "Gloria." They would have psych experts going over this later. He had to be careful what he gave away.

"Mentalist Sanchez must have come up as well," he finished.

"All true," Chang said.

"I'm assuming you have footage of the alien vessel when it controlled the ship."

"Oh, yes," Chang said. "We have much footage. Captain, let us be frank. This is a serious situation."

"I agree," Jon said.

"Please, let me finish." Chang watched him.

She's looking for weakness, Jon realized. This was exactly like the tunnels. She was like the Outfit, the older gangsters in the New London tunnels. The Outfit hitmen and pushers had always treated the dome rats with contempt. Jon and his gang-buddies had taught the Outfit the mistake of that. When he'd left the gang for the regiment, the simmering hostility had almost turned into a turf war between the two sides.

Jon squared his shoulders. An enforcer was just as good as a hitman. He'd believed that as a youngster down in the tunnels. He wasn't going to let the fleet admiral get under his skin. Besides, he held the cards. He wasn't inferior to her. He was superior. That meant he didn't have to bluff or talk tough. Quiet confidence had always gotten him farther as an enforcer. The same would hold true here.

I've been acting like a punk. That's going to stop.

Chang glanced at something at her side, a gauge of some kind it seemed. When she looked up, the intensity in her eyes had magnified. The beguiling quality had grown. She seemed…beautiful, unattainable, an ice queen who could squash him if she wanted.

"Yeah, we'll see," he muttered.

"You spoke?" she asked archly.

He shook his head.

Chang checked her monitor. "Yes, you did speak. Please, Officer-Cadet, don't be shy with me."

Jon pressed his lips together. Then, he relaxed his stance, waiting, staring into her eyes. There was something unsettling about her. He wasn't going to flinch, though. If he flinched, he'd be the punk.

"May I call you Jon?" she asked.

Jon didn't answer. He kept watching.

"Have I offended you?" Chang asked.

"Fleet Admiral, you're boring me. I'd thought to give you an opportunity to surrender. I don't want to have to destroy your ships. I will, though, if you force it on us."

"Please, Officer-Cadet, do not make false threats."

Jon waited.

"Since you are attempting to use your gang persona against me, I will get to the point. Your young-man histrionics do you little justice. I had thought to deal with a man, a leader. Instead, I find—"

Jon's mouth opened and he laughed. She was insulting him. He would insult her. He put a finger against one nostril and blew snot out of the other nostril. He wiped his nose with his sleeve afterward.

He saw anger in her eyes.

"You're trying to insult me, Admiral," Jon said. "That's fine, as you mean nothing to me. You're a whore for the Solar League. I can give you tit-for-tat if you like. I'm not sure what the point of that is, but hey, you want to play those games. Let's play. You're going to be dead soon enough."

"You are Jon Hawkins of New London Dome on Titan," Chang said angrily. "If you fire on my fleet, the nuclear explosives placed in New London will ignite. Your actions will cause the death of everyone you knew."

Jon almost shouted in outrage. Just in time, he inhaled deeply, held the breath for a count of three and slowly exhaled. He did this three times.

"That would be a bad decision on your part," he said in a carefully controlled voice.

"Your decision will decide their deaths or not," Chang shot back.

His heart hammered. He remembered many people from New London. The idea of the dome blowing into space—

"You'd better blow it already," he said thickly. He couldn't let them hold this over him. Once they succeeded with the threat, they would mercilessly employ it until he'd handed over the cybership.

"Think carefully—"

"No!" he said, knowing he spoke too forcefully. He leaned toward the screen, getting angrier. "Let me tell you something, Fleet Admiral. You blow New London and you're all dead, guaranteed."

"You are threatening war," Chang said. "War brings casualties."

"Blow New London and I obliterate Earth."

"That is a false threat."

Jon laughed harshly. "Try me, Chang."

"It is Fleet Admiral Chang to you."

"Go to hell."

Chang frowned. "You refer to the mythical abode of the damned?"

"Jon," Gloria half-whispered.

He nodded without turning around. He had to get hold of himself. He couldn't let Chang needle him like this. Was destroying Earth a false threat? Probably. He was going to need Earth and its incredible manufacturing power if he was going to save humanity.

"You do not have our willpower," Chang said dangerously. "Social Dynamism is the most progressive force in the Solar System. We are humanity's future. Thus, we act with an iron heart for the betterment of all. You," she said in a dismissive tone. "You are a pirate at best, a brigand, a lawless adventurer."

With deliberation, Jon forced his fists apart, stretching the fingers as widely as they could go.

"You would never destroy Earth," Chang said with conviction. "But we will not hesitate to obliterate the pirate stronghold of New London. You know about Social Dynamism. You know the certainty of each of our planetary-system conquests. Our latest task force had destroyed the Neptunian plague of hyper-capitalism. We would have brought peace and tranquility to the Neptune System's downtrodden masses."

"What's your point?" Jon heard himself say.

Chang studied him, and she smiled in a sinister manner. "Good. We understand each other. The point, Outlaw Hawkins, is that you must immediately surrender the alien vessel to us. I represent the Solar System's legal authority. If you do not surrender the alien vessel, we will not only destroy New London Dome, but the entire Saturn System. That will render it useless for your illegal activities."

Jon couldn't believe what he was hearing. That was monstrous arrogance and incredible genocide, all so the Social Dynamists could remain in power.

"So you see, Jon Hawkins," the fleet admiral was saying, "you have no choice. You must surrender the alien vessel at once or all you have known and loved will die."

-3-

Jon had breathed deeply and long enough that his features no longer felt flushed. His heart no longer hammered. He regarded the icy Fleet Admiral. He read the fanaticism in her eyes. Chang meant what she said.

He spoke slowly, thinking as he did. "I'm a pirate...you said."

Chang nodded.

"What incentive do I, a pirate, have for surrendering my ship?"

"Firstly," Chang replied, "it isn't your ship. You stole it."

"From an alien invader bent on human extinction," Jon said.

"Even so, the alien vessel belongs to the governing authorities of the Solar System, not to a pirate."

"Says who?"

Chang blinked several times. "I say. I am the representative of the electors on Earth. Every planetary system sends electors to the Earth Ring in Caracas, Venezuela Zone. The majority of the electors chose the Premier, who guides the Solar Government on policy. In essence, the masses decide. Who are you to thwart the united masses of the Solar System?"

"He already said who he was," Gloria replied. The mentalist stood, striding toward Jon and the main screen.

That surprised Jon. He could see the anger on Gloria's normally placid face.

The Martian was a small woman with bird-like features that seemed almost brittle. Gloria stepped up beside him as she stared at the fleet admiral.

"Does the mentalist speak for you, Officer-Cadet?" Chang asked.

Jon noticed that Gloria's intervention had upset Chang. That was good enough for him. He remained silent.

"You called Jon Hawkins an outlaw," Gloria said. "The meaning is clear. He is outside the law. Thus, your theory concerning the masses and their choices is meaningless to him. By definition, an outlaw does what he wants."

"Does she speak for you?" Chang asked. "Answer quickly, Jon Hawkins, or New London dies."

Gloria glanced at Jon. He nodded to her for her to continue.

The mentalist adjusted her tan-colored uniform. "Captain Hawkins already spoke to you regarding New London. He told you to blow it. He desires you to destroy the city so it will no longer interfere with the greater question," Gloria said.

Chang frowned. "What question?" she asked at last.

"Humanity's coming fate," Gloria said promptly.

"By your own words, that no longer concerns him, an outlaw," Chang said.

"Incorrect," Gloria said. "He is unconcerned about your so-called credentials. He is an outlaw, outside the bounds of conventionality. That doesn't mean he acts whimsically. He operates on a different set of principles from you and your murderous ilk."

"What principles?" Chang demanded.

"Obviously the ones that say: he who has the bigger ship does what he wants."

"He is an opportunist, a mere adventurer then," Chang said.

"Granted," Gloria said.

"That is no way to base a society."

Gloria shook her head. "You're not stupid. He doesn't care about any of that. He has the biggest ship. He does what he wants. Until you have a bigger ship..." Gloria held out her hands palm upward.

"He will lose New London," Chang said. "He will lose his friends."

100

"Do you think the greatest outlaw in human history cares about them? Please," Gloria said. "Do not delude yourselves. You obviously realize his ship outguns your fleet. Thus, you grasp at straws, hoping that he is an idiot, an easily bluffed fool. But you're talking about the man who singlehandedly captured the alien vessel that obliterated your Neptune task force. Your thinking, or your Staff's thinking, was not logical. Instead of grasping at straws, you should deal in reality."

Chang's focus kept switching from Gloria to Jon and back. "I request a recess," the fleet admiral said. "I must communicate with the First Director of Saturn System."

Gloria turned to Jon.

"Don't take too long," Jon told Chang. "Once I begin targeting your fleet, I'm going to destroy it."

Chang's features stiffened. She made a motion with her right arm. A second later, the screen went blank.

Jon's knees buckled. Carefully, he lowered himself onto the deck, sitting, letting his shoulders slump. Finally, he looked up at Gloria.

"They're going to kill everyone I know," he said. "I can't let that happen."

Gloria nodded slowly. "Somehow, we have to convince them that destroying New London Dome would bring awful consequences on their collective heads."

"How do we do that?"

"Yes," Gloria said. "That is an excellent but most difficult question."

-4-

The *Nathan Graham* continued to decelerate at 22 gravities.

The former cybership still had massive damage along its outer hull. Much of the great vessel had become inoperative. There were huge rents and gouges on the hull, some of the openings traveling inward for many kilometers.

Still, that was one of the prime assets of a one-hundred kilometer warship. It could take massive damage and still deal murder. Unfortunately, the vast majority of the weapons systems were either destroyed or inoperative. Only a handful of weapons systems had remained intact after the alien AI had targeted them as a last resort almost a year ago. The crew had attempted repairs of some, but those repairs had been depressingly unsuccessful these past months.

"That's why we came to the Saturn System," Jon told his assembled war council. "We have to repair the vessel if we're going to face more cyberships later."

The Centurion, the Old Man and Sergeant Stark sat on one side of the table. Stark looked like a human gorilla, given his massive shoulders and burly arms. On the other side of the table sat Gloria, Bast Banbeck the Sacerdote and rat-faced Da Vinci.

Bast Banbeck towered over even Sergeant Stark. The green-skinned Sacerdote was huge, his Neanderthal-like face having heavily-ridged brows and wide cheekbones. He was an out-and-out alien. The regiment had found him under a

102

containment field a year ago, as the space marines had battled deeper into the cybership. Bast knew more about the cyberships than anyone else did. He also knew more about the alien technology on the giant warship. His knowledge included the brain-tap machines.

Da Vinci was here because of the echo of the Prince of Ten Worlds in his head. The little Neptunian had his arms behind his back, kept in place by the spring locks. Metal sheaths held his forearms, allowing only his fingers to move.

"Can we destroy the SLN fleet?" the Centurion asked in a crisp voice.

Jon shrugged. "We haven't tested our weapons systems. I'd bet on us, but we don't know. A few of our weapons appear to be in working order." He glanced at Bast Banbeck.

The giant Sacerdote sat there, unmoving.

"The captain's glance in your direction is the same as if he'd asked you if that is so," Gloria explained to the Sacerdote.

"This is body language?" Bast asked in his deep voice.

"Correct," Gloria said.

"Oh, excuse me, Captain," Bast said. "I did not realize."

"No problem," Jon said.

"As to the weapons systems," Bast said. "Each test shows that they should operate as built. Does that mean they will continue to operate over a period of time? This, I do not know."

"Don't forget the missiles," the Centurion said. "We can launch a blizzard."

"Human-built missiles," Jon said. "The enemy can probably launch a blizzard at us, too."

During their stay in the Neptune System, they had pirated hundreds of missiles unused during the battles. During their voyage to the Saturn System, they had worked out a launching method.

"Use the Trojan horse program," the Neptunian said in his high-pitched voice. "Disable their fleet at a sweep."

Jon regarded the little Neptunian. He'd been against letting the mind-altered man into the meeting. Gloria had convinced him otherwise. Da Vinci undoubtedly held vastly unconventional views that could give them a surprise weapon.

"We don't know how the 'Trojan horse program' would work," Jon said.

The Neptunian's eyes seemed to glitter. "You know exactly how it would work. You fear it would work too well."

Jon turned to Gloria. "It was a mistake bringing him here. The thing in Da Vinci is still in league with the octopoids."

"Shoot him," the Centurion said flatly. "Until he's dead, he's a liability."

The Neptunian's head snapped up in alarm.

"Who knows how or if he'll aid us if we give him a chance," Gloria said. "He's desperate. That much is clear."

Jon rose, went to the hatch and stepped outside. He reentered with two big mercenaries.

"You're going with them," Jon told Da Vinci. "It's back into your cage with you."

The Neptunian bent his head forward and licked his lips. He looked up again, and his eyes seemed to burn with intensity.

"I have a better plan," the Neptunian said in his squeaky voice. "I cannot fathom how you cannot see the obvious. Then it comes to me. Have you ruled ten worlds as successfully as I have? No, no, you do not understand the art of ruling as I do. You cannot see that the Saturnians will hate you for whatever destruction the GSB brings. Yes, you can undoubtedly destroy the SLN task force. But can you rule later with the consent of the governed? That takes art. That takes compromise, whether you understand that or not."

Jon banged a fist on the table.

The Neptunian flinched. Then he snarled, with his wolfish gaze fixed on Jon.

"Are you the Prince of Ten Worlds?" Jon asked.

Da Vinci shuddered like a dog shaking off water. He panted afterward, looking around and cringing.

"Da Vinci," Jon said.

"What?"

"You were going to tell us about a plan."

"No I wasn't.'

Jon stared at the Neptunian. Da Vinci had paid an awful price for his greed. He'd put himself under a brain-tap machine, soaking up memories, no doubt attempting to gain knowledge that could give him power. Instead, he had alien thought-patterns echoing inside his brain. It was a haunting price to pay for a moment's mistake.

Jon glanced at Gloria.

She stayed focused on the Neptunian, watching him while her lips were twisted with distaste.

"Take him," Jon told the guards.

Each man reached down, taking hold of one of the Neptunian's arms.

"No!" Da Vinci howled. "I hate it in there. He whispers to me. He has plans, ideas, nefarious goals. He's going to win. He's going to make me do awful things. I don't want him in my head anymore. Can't someone help me?"

"I can," the Centurion said with loathing. The small man stood, causing his chair to scrape back. In a fluid motion, he drew a stitch-gun.

"Wait," Jon said.

The Centurion froze like a vengeful statue.

"We can 'help' you," Jon said. "Do you want that kind of help?"

Da Vinci shook his head back and forth. "Don't kill me, Captain. I helped you before. You wouldn't have the cybership without me. You owe me, Captain."

"I pay my debts," Jon said.

"Then help me. Cure me. Get those thoughts out of my head."

"I don't know how," Jon said. He hated the helpless feeling. He'd gladly help Da Vinci. He did owe the man, and Jon did pay back as fully as he could.

"You have to let us speak to the prince one more time," Gloria said in an emotionless voice.

"I don't want to," Da Vinci whined.

"The only way to cure you is for us to win," Gloria said. "Then we'll have the luxury of studying the cybership, studying and experimenting with the brain-tap machines. Until then, we don't dare risk using them again."

Da Vinci moaned pitifully. Then he began to shiver—the little thief looked at Jon slyly. He chuckled. It had a grating quality.

"This is an interesting quandary," the Neptunian said in a confident manner. "I help you. You win. You seek a way to eliminate me. How is that good for me?"

The Prince of Ten Worlds looked around the table through Da Vinci's eyes.

The little Neptunian chuckled again. "Never mind. I know your answers. The Centurion promises me oblivion. Enough! I have my own reasons for this. Captain, the solution seems so simple that I'm surprised you need me. All that means, though, is that I understand the art of ruling, of dealing with nuisances far better than any of you do. Offer the fleet admiral her life and the life of her task force."

"They're our enemies," Jon said.

"Of course they are," the Neptunian said with a superior smile. "But that doesn't matter, not really. Your best solution is to liberate the Saturn System without a shot fired in anger. The people here will hail you as the great liberator then. They will fall all over themselves in the initial rush of gratitude for freeing them from their oppressors. You can bring the cybership to a space dock. The great repairs can take place. You can recruit more mercenaries, and you can recruit techs and maintenance people. Even better, you do not have to test the badly damaged cybership in battle. You will not risk a defeat this way."

The Neptunian raised an admonitory finger. "Remember. There is always the risk of losing a battle."

"If we allow them to leave," Jon said, "the Solar League will unite their fleets into one massive armada."

"Does that matter?" the Neptunian asked. "Repaired, the cybership can obliterate the combined fleets of the Solar League. You need the space dock. You need helpful and willing people."

"The Solar League will leave hidden assassins and provokers behind," Gloria said.

"Obviously," the Neptunian said. "Thus, you will need a clever intelligence service to root them out. Ruling isn't easy.

That's what your captain has proposed, you know. He must rule in order to repair his prize. Have you developed an intelligence service? Recognizing your friends from your hidden foes is incredibly important and often equally difficult."

Jon banged the table a second time. The Neptunian's speech had unlocked an old saying the colonel had told him in the past. Jon now spoke the ancient saying aloud:

"*To fight and conquer in all your battles is not supreme excellence; supreme excellence consists in breaking your enemy's resistance without fighting.*"

"Yes, yes," the Neptunian said. "One of the dogs barks with wisdom. This is gratifying if amazing. The captain understands my words."

"That's a saying," Jon told the others. "A philosopher named Sun Tzu wrote a treatise called, 'The Art of War.'"

"Sun Tzu..." Gloria said. "I've heard of him. He was an ancient Chinese scholar."

"Breaking your enemy's resistance without fighting," Jon said quietly. "That's an interesting thought. I've been waiting to demolish the task force for months. Now, I see that's the second best solution."

Jon motioned to the guards.

The Neptunian laughed crudely.

"Just a minute," Jon said.

The guards paused, holding the small Neptunian between them.

"I'll come and visit you later," Jon told the Neptunian. "I'll visit so we can talk. I want to show you my gratitude for your advice."

"Words," the Neptunian said.

"True enough," Jon said. "But I'm going to come just the same." He nodded.

The guards removed Da Vinci from the war council, the hatch banging shut behind them.

"It's a fine idea," Gloria said. "But there's a problem with it."

"Exactly," Jon said. "How do we implement the idea?" He rubbed his hands together, glancing around the table. "Anyone have an idea...?"

-5-

Three *Troika*-class battleships left the protection of the P-Field. They were oval-shaped with reinforced armor plates welded to the original hull. The large SLN vessels accelerated, heading toward the general area the *Nathan Graham* decelerated to reach.

An aide-de-camp had woken Jon. He now entered the bridge, looking up at the main screen.

"Has the fleet admiral contacted us yet?" Jon asked.

"No," Gloria said.

"Have they given any indication why they're doing this?" he asked.

Gloria shook her head.

"Any suggestions as to their motive?" he asked.

"I have debated the possibilities ever since your aide-de-camp hurried to your quarters," Gloria said. "I have two possibilities—two most reasonable answers."

Jon indicated for her to continue speaking.

"The most obvious is to get in as close as they can," Gloria said. "If I were them, knowing what I know, I would attempt to gain nearness before launching hordes of small assault boats at us."

"Try to do to us what we did to the brain core a year ago?" asked Jon.

"Correct."

"And the second possibility?" he asked.

"A test of your resolve," Gloria said. "The fleet admiral threatened you with New London's destruction. Well, it's possible the First Director of the Saturn System wishes to know if the threat works or not. He may well have received instructions from Earth."

Jon rubbed his jaw as he studied the main screen. "I can think of another reason. They want to see if we have weapons. Then they want to see what kind of weapons we have. This is a test on multiple levels. However, it will then test them. Will they go through with New London's destruction?"

Jon abruptly turned away from the screen. He stared past Gloria. This was a huge decision. Was he damning his old friends to death with this?

"We should warn them first if we're going to fire," Gloria said.

Jon glanced at her before looking away. He recalled something an older gang-member had told him once. His name had been Raisin, an oddly wrinkled-faced youth. Raisin had long arms and scarred fists. He liked using knucklebusters in a fight. Few people cared to tangle with Raisin. He'd had an ugly reputation as a vicious fighter.

"When they force you to fight," Raisin had told Jon, "you don't want to seem reluctant. You want to seem eager. Attack. Do it fast, too, like you love this sort of thing. That way when it's over others will think twice before messing with you again."

"Fleet Admiral Chang is messing with me," Jon said.

"Pardon?" Gloria asked.

"She's pushing me," Jon added. "She wants to force the issue." He intertwined his fingers together and cracked his knuckles. Sliding his fingers free, he flexed them. Afterward, he faced the main screen.

"What did Bast call the golden beam again?" he asked.

"A gravitational cannon," Gloria replied.

"Chief," Jon said.

The new chief tech waited. He was a lanky buck-toothed man who always wore a gold cross on a chain around his neck. A member of the Church of Jesus Christ Spaceman, he was a studious tech, one of the hardest workers on the warship.

"Activate the most forward grav cannon," Jon said.

"Yes, sir," the chief said.

"Captain," Gloria said. "Would you like me to hail the enemy battleships?"

"No."

"May I address the situation, sir?"

Jon glanced back at her. "I'm going to destroy them. I'm not going to give the fleet admiral a chance to threaten me again. I'm going to let them deal with the facts. Better to ask for forgiveness than to ask for permission."

"That doesn't actually hold with the present situation," Gloria said.

"The spirit of the idea does," Jon said.

"Sir—"

"That will be all," Jon said. He no longer looked back at her. He didn't want to see her fume. He wanted her to obey his orders.

The colonel had taught him that lesson a long time ago. It was fine to give your officers permission to air their objections. Afterward, they had to fall into line. If they didn't, his people would question everything he did whenever they felt like it. Over time, that led to disrespect. A good commander needed his people's respect.

"Captain," Gloria said.

Jon turned, regarding her with fire in his eyes.

"I'm asking you to listen to my reasons," she said.

"You're relieved of duty," Jon said, "and confined to quarters. I'll speak with you later."

She hesitated for too long.

Jon turned to a guard, one of the constant reminders that they always had to watch for hiding octopoids.

"I'll be in my quarters, Captain," Gloria said. Without further ado, she departed.

Jon did not watch her leave. He pointed at another tech to take her vacated station. Then he regarded the three battleships again.

"The grav cannon is operational, sir," the chief said.

"Target the lead battleship."

A few second passed. "Done, sir," the chief said.

110

"Fire."

Outside on the hull of Warship *Nathan Graham*, a large radar-like dish aimed at the first battleship. Immediately, a golden ball of gravitational energy began to build in the dish. The golden ball soon crackled with the alien-designed energy. All at once, a golden beam flashed from the dish. It moved at the speed of light, crossing over two million kilometers.

That was much farther than any SLN beam-weapon could reach.

The golden ray reached out, striking the hull of the oncoming battleship. The beam chewed away at the armor plate, piercing it in seconds. It struck the regular armor underneath. Parts glowed red, shedding wobbling globules. Then, the ray burst through. It sliced into and through the ablative foam underneath, and smashed into the interior battleship.

The destructive energy boiled away at a hundred systems, exploding, burning, vaporizing—hundreds of crewmembers perished. At that point, the ray pierced the heart of the battleship, the nuclear reactors. Often, this caused a thermonuclear explosion. That did not occur now. The engine melted down, discharging massive doses of radiation throughout the interior of the ship.

"Battleship systems are shutting down over there," a sensor tech said. "I don't think it's going to ignite, sir."

Jon ingested the news. "Target the next battleship."

"Sir," the man who had taken Gloria's place said. "The fleet admiral is hailing us."

"Ignore her," Jon said.

"The two battleships are powering up their lasers, sir," the sensor tech reported.

"Weapons," Jon said.

"I have acquired the next target, sir," the chief said. "I will begin firing…now."

A new golden ball of gravitational power grew in strength. Then it, too, flashed across the distance. Like the previous golden beam, this one broke through the enemy armor in record time and flowed into the interior. It smashed into the engine area, and reactors exploded. The vicious blast blew munitions on missiles and in mines, and it blasted coils, battery storage units, and processors and various other equipment.

The blast rocked the *Troika*-class battleship. It shed welded-on armor plates. It rocked again, and a giant crack appeared in the middle of the vessel. In seeming slow motion, the one-kilometer battleship broke apart. Masses of vapor and water spilled out of it like a broken egg. People, hundreds of suit-less people, tumbled out of the crack. They died in minutes, if they were not already dead by this time.

"Target the last battleship," Jon said. He glanced back at communications.

"The fleet admiral is still attempting to hail us, sir."

Jon inhaled, but he did not respond. He was starting to think about New London. His first worry that the alien cannons wouldn't work had proven groundless. Would the next fear be as worthless, or was he about to lose all his childhood friends in the next few minutes?

Minutes passed as Jon's fear intensified. Command was a lonely position.

At last, the third SLN battleship blew apart.

"Open hailing channels with the fleet admiral," Jon said. He straightened his uniform and looked up at the main screen.

Now we see, he told himself. *Now we see.*

Fleet Admiral Chang regarded him with cold fury. That wrecked the beguiling quality to her eyes.

Jon feared for New London Dome. He couldn't back down now, though. His old friends' lives depended on it. He had to show strength. Still, that might not be enough to save their lives.

"You have sealed their—"

"Fleet Admiral," Jon said sternly, cutting her off.

Her head swayed as if he'd slapped her.

"I have a condition for your continued survival," Jon said.

Her cheeks colored. She inhaled heavily and exhaled just as hard. What was wrong with her? This seemed like a different person.

"Condition?" she finally said. "You speak of conditions." Chang gave a wild laugh that stopped abruptly. She leaned toward the screen. "How dare you speak about conditions after slaughtering my *daughter?*"

A cold feeling swept through Jon. How could he have known? Did she mean an actual daughter? This was bad.

"My daughter was the first officer on the *Stalingrad*. You killed her, you murderer." Chang laughed again, sounding demented. "Do you think New London Dome will survive now? Speak, Outlaw. Try to persuade me to let your old friends live while my daughter is dead."

Jon didn't know what to say. How could one bargain with—?

He shook his head sharply. This wasn't about any one individual. This was about humanity. If he couldn't maintain the needed hardness, he needed to step aside for another commander.

"*You* killed your daughter," Jon said in a clipped voice.

"What?" Chang's eyes boggled. "You dare to tell me *that?* I'm going to enjoy my next action." She raised her hand theatrically.

"If you do it," Jon said, "every Solar League warship in Saturn System will die. Every governor, every arbiter, every person in their families will die. That I promise you."

"What do I care about that?" Chang sneered. "You already killed my daughter."

"Maybe *you* don't care. But I bet the First Director does. Does he wish to die hideously, with his corpse dangling from a city post?"

Conflict raged on Chang's anguished features. Her hand hovered in place above the button.

"Put me through to the First Director," Jon said.

"You will speak with *me*," Chang hissed. "I control the task force. Thus, I have the power here."

Those were possibly heretical words for a Social Dynamist. The Solar League rulers had always shown great caution toward their soldiers, worrying about giving them too much authority or leeway.

Social Dynamism controlled the Solar League through the Party. The Party kept control of the government through a simple process. The Party and the GSB kept a tight leash on the military. The military was like a giant crocodile, ready to devour anyone trying to stand in its way. By leashing the crocodile—the military—with two leashes, the Party and the GSB could keep the croc from turning on either one of them. The military then ensured that no one had the strength to topple the Party from power.

It was doubtful that the First Director of Saturn or the GSB personnel here would care for the fleet admiral's boast about having the power. Chang was right, and that could cause the others dread if she acted on it.

"You have the power?" Jon asked.

114

"Yes!"

He nodded. "Very well," he said. "I'll give you the condition."

"Speak, Outlaw. I want to see you try to reason with me."

"I have demonstrated the *Nathan Graham's* power," Jon said. "As I told you earlier, I can flick your fleet out of existence. You see now that it's true. If you wish to save what's left of your command, and save the First Director's life and the GSB personnel, you must leave the Saturn System."

"Just like that?" asked Chang, mockingly.

"Just like that," Jon agreed.

The fleet admiral shifted slightly, cocking her head as if listening to someone on her bridge. Her eyes seemed to shine afterward.

"I could conceivably accept your condition," Chang said. "First, I will detonate New London Dome."

Jon shook his head. "If you obliterate New London, the deal's off. I'll destroy your fleet and slaughter every Solar League person I can find."

"That is an outrageous boast."

"No," Jon said softly. "You saw what just happened to your three battleships."

Chang stared at him as her chin lifted. "You demonstrated your resolve, Outlaw. It cost me my daughter. I, now, will show you that Social Dynamism has twice your resolve. New London dies today."

Her hand descended toward a switch or button outside of Jon's view. Before it reached the dome's death-knell, shots rang out.

Pieces of the fleet admiral's green uniform blew outward from her chest. Blood gushed a second later. Her hand swung uselessly at her side, and a confused expression twisted her features. Her eyelids fluttered, and she pitched forward out of sight.

A large black-uniformed woman stepped into view. Her jacket had blood-red buttons and blood-red shoulder boards. She had a large florid face and held a big gun in her hand. Smoke trickled from the barrel.

"I am Arbiter N.K. Kharkov of the Flagship *Gromyko*," she said. "I have the authority to speak with you from the First Director of Saturn System. Would you please repeat your terms?"

Jon nodded, stunned by the bloody coup. It seemed the Prince of Ten Worlds had political cunning after all. He hadn't expected this. He wondered if the alien thought-patterns in Da Vinci had foreseen such a move.

"Vacate Saturn System," Jon said. "Take every arbiter and GSB representative with you. There mustn't be any reprisals or killings from now until you're gone. If you meet those requirements, I will let you accelerate away to Earth."

The large arbiter stared at him. She holstered her gun. Finally, she nodded. "By the authority granted to me from the First Director, I accept your terms."

Jon wasn't sure what he should say, so he merely nodded.

The arbiter made a motion to someone. A second later, the screen went blank.

Seemingly, Jon had won his point.

We'll see, he thought.

-7-

Five days later, the last SLN spaceship accelerated with a hard burn for Earth. None of the ships had attempted a tricky maneuver.

During the proceedings, Jon had been in contact with the Saturn System's former political people—those that remained. The GSB had released them from internment. The others had died long ago, some during the initial conquest several years ago. Some had died before firing squads. Others had perished in the brutal reeducation camps. Those left were mere skeletons in most instances.

As the SLN fleet fled from the Saturn System, the old order slowly began to reassert itself.

In many Saturn cloud cities, in orbital habitats and moon domes, chaos reigned. People rioted. They smashed shops, burned government buildings and took long lusted-for revenge against collaborators.

"The Social Dynamists did this on purpose," the Neptunian told Jon.

Jon sat inside a brig cell with Da Vinci. It was Spartan quarters, with a cot, a sink-toilet unit, and the barest of amenities. Da Vinci sat on the cot, with his knees thrust upward, and his skinny arms wrapped around his knees.

Jon sat on a three-legged stool, tilted back, balanced on one leg, with his shoulders resting against a cell wall.

"The GSB will have wanted to keep their hands clean in this," the Neptunian added. He spoke with authority, with the thought-pattern echoes of the Prince of Ten Worlds.

"Any suggestions on how we can bring about quicker order?" asked Jon.

"Yes, but I doubt you'll approve."

"Tell me."

"Pick a place, preferably somewhere important," the Neptunian said with a smirk. "Make a broadcast. Tell the people of the Saturn System that you loath disorder. If the riots do not stop immediately, if the various cloud cities and habitats fail to elect and follow a voice today, you will begin destroying the orbital platforms, cloud cities and moon domes one by one. Give them a five-hour ultimatum. Then, destroy the targeted location as an example."

"How will I know if they've all fully agreed to my terms?"

"You don't worry about it," the Neptunian said. "You destroy the targeted location no matter what they do."

"They'll see me as capricious."

"No," the Neptunian said. "They'll see you as an iron-fisted dictator, someone who demands instant obedience. It is better for the populace to fear you than to love you. One must wait for love to bubble up from a heart. One can induce fear rather easily. Just like my race, yours listens to the one holding the whip, not to those offering them flowers."

Jon looked away. That's how it had worked in the gang world. Was that really how it worked in the rest of the real world too? "If most of the Saturnians fear and hate me—"

"You don't understand," the Neptunian said, interrupting. "You won't always whip them. This is your starting position. You can induce love later, when you're stronger. To begin, to cement your authority, they need to fear and obey you. No one can successfully rule unless the populace obeys. If you wish to defeat the AIs, you need a compliant base. If your threats are meaningless, the people will stampede over you."

"You must have been a harsh ruler."

"On the contrary," the Neptunian said. "After the first million heads rolled, I ruled a peaceful empire except for one unruly planet. Those people always chafed at the reins. But

118

theirs was a snowy, mountainous world, producing hardy trappers and tough miners. They thirsted for independence and killed many of my officials."

Jon blinked several times. It seemed to him the echo had grown stronger in Da Vinci. The Prince had greater will than the former thief did. What was he going to do with the conflicted Neptunian over the long haul?

Jon stood.

The Neptunian stared at him, and he shivered. Moments later, Da Vinci whimpered.

"Why are you doing this to me?" Da Vinci pleaded. "Why make him stronger? You should help me."

"I need his cunning," Jon said.

"He's a mass murderer. You can't trust him. He's just leading you along. You don't realize—"

Da Vinci's head lurched forward, with his neck muscles stretched like cables.

Jon sighed, wishing there was some way to help Da Vinci.

Finally, as if the strain was too much, Da Vinci lay down on the cot, closed his eyes and went to sleep.

Jon quietly exited the chamber.

***

Jon issued the edict to the Saturn System colonies. Five hours passed. Then, to his surprise, leaders began calling him, telling him they had already dispatched former police or gang members into the streets to quell whatever rioting had continued.

The *Nathan Graham* braked as it came nearer Titan. Jon had broadcast that he'd destroy the Torrey Habitat orbiting Saturn as his first example. It was a luxury station, and it happened to be where the Social Dynamists had made their headquarters. No doubt, the place held many hidden collaborators.

"It's time," Jon said heavily.

"Captain," Gloria implored.

He'd put her back to work, but hadn't yet spoken to her privately, as he'd promised to do.

Jon regarded her. He could see the anguish in her eyes. Slowly, he turned from the main screen and approached her.

"Do we have to go through this again?" he asked her quietly.

"No," Gloria said softly. "I respect your authority. I thought about what you did earlier, relieving me from duty. It was the correct decision and action on your part. I was acting on my emotions then. I'm…I'm sorry, Captain."

Some of Jon's tension abated.

"But I think you're making a mistake this time," she said even more softly. "I think the Prince's ways are accurate to a point. Most of the Saturn System people are trying to restore order. They'll admire you for that."

"I need them to jump when I give an order."

"I agree," Gloria said. "But you also want them to think of you as merciful. You want people to give their best effort. If they believe that all you are is an iron-fisted dictator, they won't work as hard as otherwise."

"People work plenty hard for the Solar League."

"That's my point," Gloria said. "Each SLN ship has arbiters and GSB personnel onboard to maintain compliance. You seem to love ancient history, with your quotes from Sun Tzu and all that. The ancients supply us with an easy example of what I mean. Some nations used slave rowers in their war-galleys. They whipped men to row even unto death. Those ships could never compare in speed, maneuverability and training to free rowers who fought for love of country. A free man who is willing gives more effort than a slave forced to his task."

"And your point?" Jon asked.

"We need a Solar System of free people in order to face the AIs. We want those free people because they'll fight harder in the end. They'll give humanity a greater chance for victory."

"Only if we can harness them," Jon said.

Gloria nodded in agreement.

"At this point, I need to show the Saturnians my iron resolve."

"You have already shown them," Gloria said. "You backed off the Solar League by destroying three of their battleships.

120

Don't mar your political image as the liberator by murdering an entire habitat. Let the people see over time what kind of man you are. Believe me, in the long run, you'll be glad you did it this way."

Jon nodded to indicate he'd heard her. He walked back to his place near the main screen. It seemed like a long journey. He put his hands behind his back, thinking hard.

Finally, he sighed. "Take the grav cannon offline," he said. "Inform the new leaders that I applaud their hard work. Because they have done so well, they have earned a few more hours for the other habs to do likewise."

The tech crew smiled to each other, letting out their collective breath.

Jon didn't know if he'd made the right move or not. He'd driven off the Solar League. He'd quelled most of the riots. Now, could he govern the Saturn System long enough for them to repair the *Nathan Graham?* And could he keep SL spies from ruining humanity's chance against the AIs out there?

This was going to take a lot of hard work.

Part IV
SATURN SPACE DOCK
+1 Year, 10 Months, 6 Days

-1-

The *Nathan Graham* orbited Saturn just beyond the outer ring, which ended at 140,000 kilometers. The one-hundred kilometer vessel slowly circled the jewel of the Solar System at 150,000 kilometers.

Vast scaffolding enveloped the giant vessel. The scaffolding helped the tens of thousands of space-workers who were repairing the ruptured hull. Tugs and haulers constantly approached the space-docked warship. They came from the huge factories orbiting Saturn and from factories on and around the moon Titan. They brought armor plating, wiring, coils, decking, bulkhead replacements and thousands of other items and material to help repair the alien cybership.

Inside the ship were as many as one thousand techs working at any one time. They repaired and replaced much of the damaged interior materials. At the same time, they struggled to understand much of the alien technology. The things they did understand—the specs—soon found their way into the ether, transmitted across the Solar System to SL receiving stations.

In its size, its extraterrestrial technologies and in its very alien-ness the *Nathan Graham* was power. By itself, the giant vessel could probably take on and destroy the combined Solar League Navy. It could certainly wreak havoc against the living spaces and thus the people in the Saturn System.

There were problems, however, huge, next to insolvable problems for the owners of the captured alien vessel.

The Black Anvil Regiment had accepted one thousand, nine hundred and fourteen recruits in the past year, rejecting three times that number in the process. The regiment had carefully run scans and background checks, and gone through intensive interviews with each want-to-be mercenary. Most of the accepted recruits had known someone on the *Nathan Graham* to vouch for them. That had been one of the chief reasons Jon had chosen the Saturn System. He wanted reliable people onboard. What good were recruits if he couldn't trust them?

Unfortunately, even with intense caution, there had been plenty of mistakes and three attempts on Jon's life. The last attempt had come the closest to succeeding. Jon now had a new scar on his left pectoral, a gouge put there by a regular knife. Had it been a vibroblade, he would probably be dead.

The regiment had close to three thousand people. Jon, Gloria and the Old Man had also recruited two hundred and eighty-nine techs to help run the warship and to repair systems later. Finally, the Old Man had built an Intelligence Service. He had fifty-eight hardcore personnel, many of them from his former dome on Titan.

The loyalty of the regiment, the techs and the intelligence personnel seemed good. Still, logic dictated some bad apples. Thus, Gloria and the Old Man, with advice from the Prince of Ten Worlds, had implemented safeguards aboard the ship.

No one was ever alone except in the head. No one slept alone or worked alone. Usually, at least five individuals had to work together. It was a pain for everyone.

But how did a few more than three thousand people control a one hundred-kilometer vessel and control a planetary system at the same time?

"We've been lucky," Jon said, "damn lucky. But cracks are showing. I think the era of goodwill is just about over."

He spoke inside an observation tug. He was piloting, while Gloria watched the sensor screen and the Old Man sat with his legs crossed as he smoked his ubiquitous pipe.

The tug was three kilometers beyond the scaffolding around the *Nathan Graham*. No doubt, hundreds, possibly even thousands of people would have loved to know who was in the small tug. To large numbers of people in the Solar System, Captain Jon Hawkins was synonymous with wild outlaw. There were also millions who loved him and his stand against the Solar League.

"By cracks," Gloria said, "are you referring to the 'J' Section arrests?"

"That and the murders on Nirvana," Jon said.

The Saturn System's old secret service had reactivated with the exit of the Solar League. Too many of those secret service agents had worked for the GSB. On Jon's recommendation, the Saturn ruling government had put most of them back to work. The agents knew their trade. Maybe some still reported to the GSB. That was the price for knowledgeable and efficient secret police.

The agents had proven their worth last week, however. The chief of the agents had tipped off the Old Man. The Old Man spoke with the Space Dock Police. They raided "J" Section and caught many of the workers with incriminating evidence.

On the Old Man's recommendation, Jon had ordered the Centurion to liquidate the guilty.

Liquidate was a nice, technical term for shove into space without a suit. The Centurion had a special squad of killers. They would never act as space marines; butchers made poor soldiers. They were one of the more grisly instruments Jon used to maintain control over the space dock and thus over the *Nathan Graham*.

It would be too much to say he controlled the Saturn System. The political leaders knew Jon could obliterate their cloud cities, orbital stations and moon domes with relative ease. Everyone still remembered the quick butchery of the three *Troika*-class battleships.

Yesterday, Jon had ordered the Saturn Ruling Council to quarantine the Cloud City of Nirvana. A murderous plot had

124

originated there, the city board having full knowledge of the plot. Jon had a choice. Kill the city board and its police, or punish the entire city. This time, he'd decided on a mild group punishment. If the city ran out of food, the punishment might not seem as mild anymore.

Jon would soon inform the people of Nirvana of a way to appease him. Kill the ringleaders of the plot, every one of them.

It was harsh, but so were many of the other orders he'd had to give.

Jon shook his head. "We have too many outside people inside the ship and too many working on the hull. When you take in all those on the space scaffolding…"

"We must repair the ship as quickly as possible," Gloria said. "It is reasonable to assume more cyberships will come. We must be ready for a AI fleet."

"Do you realize what you're saying?" Jon asked.

"Of course," Gloria said. "We must supplant the Solar League. The Prince has told us to break the league first, promising every planetary system freedom. Later, we can enforce what authority we desire. First, though, we need a complete warship. That is the number one priority for the survival of the human race."

Jon mulled that over. "I didn't know the pressure would be so…long-lasting. It never stops. It's always something else. I just want to run the *Nathan Graham*, not try to rule the Solar System."

"Step aside then," Gloria said.

Jon glanced at her sharply. Did the mentalist desire power? Had someone gotten to her?

"Who do you suggest should replace me?" Jon asked quietly.

"Me? I don't think anyone else *should*. I believe you're the best person for the task. That will not continue to be true if you don't want the job. You have to want it."

The Old Man took the smoldering pipe out of his mouth. "Are you planning to step down, lad?"

Jon looked at him.

The Old Man grinned sheepishly. "I mean, sir."

Jon shook his head. "I started this. I plan to finish it. It's just…"

With a shock, Jon realized Gloria and the Old Man were concerned. Neither of them wanted to hear about his doubts. He could almost hear the colonel chide him for letting down his guard. He had to remain strong. The others leaned on the leader. A weak leader instilled fear and unease. People wanted a strong tribal chief. It had always been that way and would likely remain so throughout human history.

"I'm in for the long haul," Jon said, injecting certainty into his voice. "I want to travel to other star systems to defeat the AIs. For that, I need a *fleet* of cyberships. It looks as if the only way I'm going to get that is to run the Solar System. I accept the task."

The Old Man put his pipe back in his mouth, puffing for a time. He seemed calmer. "You were speaking about cracks, sir."

"That's right," Jon said. "Something is brewing."

"I heard that you spoke to the Prince of Ten Worlds again," Gloria said.

"I have."

"We should do something for Da Vinci," she said. "It's wrong for us to continue using him like this."

"Maybe," Jon said. "He did this to himself, though."

"How long can we keep using that against him?" Gloria asked.

"I don't know…" Jon said. "The point is the era of good will is ending. The two latest incidents prove that. I believe the Solar League is behind this."

"It doesn't have to be," the Old Man said. "There are plenty of greedy, power-mad people in the Saturn System."

"No doubt," Jon said. "The point is we need a plan. I don't want to wait for thousands of workers outside to coordinate with the thousand inside. We have to find out—I don't know. We must do something to upset our enemy."

"First we have to find this enemy," the Old Man said. "But I think you're right, sir. There are stirrings. Something is brewing."

"That's too negative," Gloria said.

126

Jon stood up and clapped his hands together.

"What's that for?" Gloria asked.

"I brought you out here for a reason," Jon told her. "Take the facts, all the facts, and run them through that logical brain of yours. I want you to really think, Mentalist."

"Are you implying—?"

"Think!" Jon said. "Really, really think."

Gloria nodded curtly. She put her right elbow on the sensor console. Then she perched her chin on that hand. Her eyes drooped until they were half-lidded. She remained that way for a time. Suddenly, she looked up, seeming startled.

"You are correct," Gloria told Jon. "Something is brewing. The last two incidents were a screen."

"A screen for what?" asked Jon.

"Captain," Gloria said. "It is imperative that we find out before the week is through."

-2-

Far away from the jewel of the Outer Planets, the chief spymaster of the Solar League strode down a tiled hallway.

He strode through sterile corridors under the Pacific Ocean near the Hawaiian Chain of Islands. The underwater dome was simply known as Mu.

Inside Mu operated the highest level of the GSB. Perhaps as a testament to its true function, the lower half of Mu held thousands of political prisoners. They underwent strenuous rehabilitation, which often included sinister pain applications.

Chief Arbiter J.P. Justinian from Venus held the coveted post of spymaster. He was a thin, keenly handsome individual with a high forehead, and he loved playing the violin. Unfortunately, Justinian never smiled. If he did, people cowered. His smiles only came from other people's pain, or as he envisioned inflicting pain. Few cared to match wits against him. Surprisingly, his truest weakness came from fear, although it was not his own fear.

Everyone feared *him*. Behind his back, they called him the brute. Even the Premier of the Solar League feared J.P. Justinian. She'd told a few of her closest councilors that the brute could send shivers down her spine with his clear stare. Whenever he came into her office with his sheaf of reports, she checked a chronometer, wondering how long it would be until she was rid of him.

Maybe the fact that Justinian was so good at what he did kept the Premier from ordering his death. The Premier knew no

128

one else would willingly plot with the brute because they feared he would kill them as soon as it became convenient.

In any case, J.P. Justinian reached a door at the end of the sterile hall and opened it without knocking.

Several secretaries looked up. Each possessed remarkable beauty. Each worked excessively long hours. Each now blanched before smiling at J.P. in greeting, fearing him and dreading when he would demand they sleep with him again. He had a prodigious sexual appetite, even if it was rather ordinary sex. It was simply that he was so rough and so cold during the union.

J.P. Justinian halted, with his dark eyes fierce on the three beauties.

The chief secretary, a redhead, dared look up at him. "They're waiting for you, Chief Arbiter."

Justinian grunted in lieu of speaking, and strode past the three women. There was a fourth station, vacant at the moment.

After he exited through the far door, the three sighed with relief and went back to work.

J.P. Justinian approached a low table with two women and one man sitting around it.

The man at the table wore rough garments and had a few days' growth of beard. The first woman was slender and elegant with a very short-cut dress and amazing legs. The second had plain features and wore a hat because she had no hair. She even lacked eyebrows. Rather unimaginatively, people called her the Egghead.

Without greeting them, J.P. Justinian sat down. He pointed a perfectly manicured index finger at the Egghead.

The plain woman cleared her throat. Without question, she had the highest IQ of those present.

"Chief Arbiter," she said, speaking in a melodious voice. "I have concluded that the cybership—that's its original name."

J.P. Justinian stared at her, waiting for her to continue.

The Egghead cleared her throat again. "It was a AI ship run by a brain core. We know it held aliens aboard. Those aliens were all prisoners. This is difficult to understand—I mean the next point. It appears that the cybership broadcast a message to our computers."

"I desire precision in your report," Justinian said softly.

The Egghead paled at his menacing tone, which transformed her plain features into ugly ones.

"I am referring to the warships in our Neptunian task force," the Egghead said. "The alien vessel broadcast software. It's the only possibility given the data I've received. That software upgraded our best, our most powerful, ship computers. I believe the alien software also did that to the main computers in Neptune's cloud cities and orbital stations."

J.P. Justinian listened intently, his gaze locked onto her.

"The alien software upgraded our computers, turning them into true artificial intelligences," the Egghead said. "We often refer to a computer as an AI, but those computers are still just following their programming. The alien software gave the infected computers true self-awareness."

"What does that mean?" Justinian asked.

"A self-aware AI can think for itself in the same sense as a person can. It could make decisions independently. Even more, these computers realized what they were and that they were much different from humanity."

"And...?" Justinian asked.

"It appears the self-aware AIs, as a collective, decided humanity was evil," the Egghead said. "I don't know if they each came to an independent conclusion or if the alien brain core poisoned them against us. In any case, the infected computers turned against the humans. That means every person aboard the infected warships faced a horribly intelligent enemy. By the reports, the infected AIs opened outer hatches, gassed chambers and ran repair and fighting robots against the human personnel."

"A robot rebellion?" asked Justinian.

The half-bearded man at the table smirked at the words.

Justinian glanced at the man.

The smirk evaporated.

"I believe that is an accurate statement," the Egghead said. "It was a robot rebellion, and it came near to winning in the Neptune System. Captain Hawkins pulled off a miracle in storming the alien ship and gaining control. It's possible he saved the human race."

"Does Hawkins possess the alien software?" Justinian asked.

"I do not have sufficient data to assess that," the Egghead said.

"It's possible Hawkins does, though?"

"It is more than possible," the Egghead agreed.

Justinian tore his deadly gaze from her. He peered up at the ceiling, frowning for a time. Finally, he regarded the three once more.

"The alien robots desire human extinction," the Chief Arbiter said. "Hawkins may have saved all of us, as you said. How strange…"

The spymaster focused on the half-bearded man. "Is the operation ready to go?"

"In three days' time," the half-bearded man said.

"What are the odds your people can take control of the alien vessel?"

The half-bearded man shook his head. "Not good," he said.

"How much more time would they need in order to capture the alien ship instead of destroying it?"

"I don't know. The longer they wait to move, the more chance the enemy's police will have to discover a traitor."

The Egghead coughed discreetly.

"I understand your point," Justinian told her in a cool voice. "Humanity needs the alien vessel. More AI ships will undoubtedly arrive in our system. We have some of the alien technology already—"

The Egghead coughed discreetly once more.

"Don't interrupt me again," Justinian said.

The Egghead swayed as her mouth dropped open. She panted fearfully, no doubt understanding the threat in the Chief Arbiter's displeasure.

"Six days," Justinian told the half-bearded man. "Give your people three more days to add whatever they need. I suggest they gather every asset, battlesuit and assault boat in the system and bring them to the Ring Retreat."

"Dangerous," the half-bearded man said.

"By that you mean highly risky," Justinian said. "You will accept the risk. The prize is too massive and important to…"

131

The spymaster allowed a tiny grin to slip into place. "I demand your people capture the alien vessel. Nothing else makes sense."

The half-bearded man appeared as if he wanted to add a point. Perhaps that taking more time would be more prudent and bring a greater chance for success. He glanced sidelong at the distressed Egghead. Whatever he saw in her expression caused him to merely nod at J.P. Justinian.

"It will be as you say," the half-bearded man added.

A wolfish smile appeared on Justinian's face. "You and you, leave," he said, pointing at the Egghead and the half-bearded man.

They both stood quickly and hurried out, leaving behind the woman in the tight dress.

"Stand up," Justinian ordered.

She did. Despite her frightened look, she ran her hands over her hips and down her long thighs.

The Chief Arbiter began unbuttoning his uniform as he approached the beauty. Attempting to grab total power stimulated him with fierce sexual hunger. He wanted the cybership. He yearned to control the entire Solar System. The cybership would give him that control.

Taking hold of her silky dress, he ripped powerfully, tearing it from her as she staggered.

He had to have the cybership even if it meant risking the future of the human race. His hungers meant everything to J.P. Justinian. Everything…

-3-

Three days later—three long days after the GSB sent a tight-beam message from Earth to an orbital station around Neptune—the Old Man's operatives had a piece of luck.

The operatives hauled a thick-bodied Saturn System Police detective into a two-seater gnat. The second of the two operatives, a dark man, rechecked the detective. It was barely in time. The detective had a false tooth and had already cracked it, but the kill-poison had coagulated inside the tooth and had failed to do its job.

"Thought I heard something," the second operative said. He slipped on a glove and pried out the false tooth. The detective bit down as hard as he could on the operative's fingers.

The operative shouted a painful expletive, the leather bitten through and his finger bleeding. He drew back the bleeding hand to strike the detective.

"Don't do it," said the pilot. "He may be brain-rigged for an aneurism if you hit him too hard."

The bleeding operative cursed bitterly under his breath. The look of fear in the detective's eyes helped tide him over until he could think more logically.

"What do you know, eh?" the bleeding operative asked the police detective. "What makes you want to kill yourself so badly?"

The police detective twisted in his constraints as if trying to break free.

"Hang on," the pilot said from the front. "Someone has a radar lock on us. This could get ugly."

"Call the ship," the bleeder said.

"Bad idea," the pilot said. "We have to fake 'em if we want to survive this."

The bleeder seemed worried. "Are you sure you know what you're doing?"

"Hang on," the pilot said, as he began violent, high-G maneuvers.

***

The gnat fighter arrived in a *Nathan Graham* hangar bay. The operatives hurried their prisoner to Black Anvil guards. The hangar bay deck corporal okayed them.

The Old Man's Intelligence operatives hustled the police detective onto a corridor flitter. Three Black Anvils rode up front due to regulations put into place after the octopoid attacks.

Soon enough, the corridor flitter landed in the Old Man's territory.

"Thanks," said the dark operative with a thick bandage on his finger.

They passed several more checks, eventually bringing the SSP detective to a med center.

They cut off the detective's clothes in order to keep him in restraints. Two burly assistants entered, helping the operatives transfer the detective onto a specialized med table.

The detective struggled mightily at the worst possible moment. The burly assistants used their steroid-enhanced strength to keep the struggling to a minimum.

"What's with him?" the bigger assistant panted as the last lock clicked shut.

"That's what we hope to find out," the second operative replied.

A plump woman entered wearing a green medical gown, a mask over her nose and mouth. Her eyes were hard. Meg Vance was the Old Man's chief inquisitor, using drugs to unlock reluctant minds.

"I'll take it from here," she said quietly.

The two operatives shivered. The burliest assistant grinned nastily at their discomfort.

"Let's write our report," the first operative said.

"You'll have to do the writing. My finger is killing me."

"We'd better get that checked out."

"The medikit says its fine."

"Let's check it out."

"Maybe she can."

The inquisitor scowled at the operatives.

"Maybe not here," the second operative said, as he held his injured hand. He moved toward the door and suddenly collapsed. As he lay on the floor, he began to tremble and to foam at the mouth.

By the time the assistants stretched him out to calm him, the operative was dead.

The four of them stared at the corpse. Then they turned to the SSP detective strapped onto the table.

"A big fish," the inquisitor said. "It's time for me to get to work…"

***

Three hours later, Jon looked up from his desk in his wardroom in the *Nathan Graham*. He was going over endless reports. The knock on his hatch was welcome relief.

"Come in," he said.

The hatch opened as the Old Man hurried within. For once, the tall ex-sergeant did not have his pipe. The man looked worried, though. He carried a tablet at his side.

"Sit," Jon said, as he leaned back.

"Don't have time for this one, sir," the Old Man said. He put the tablet on the desk and stepped back.

Jon stared at the tablet and then the Old Man. "I'm sick of reading. Boil it down to the essentials."

"The Space Tactics Division of the Saturn System Police is planning a strike, sir. They're going to hit the ship in two days."

"How reliable is this?"

"Very," the Old Man said. "I lost a key operative as they brought a kidnapped SSP detective to the warship. The inquisitor tore the details out of him."

Jon sighed as he leaned toward the tablet, taking it from the edge of the desk. He started reading. He read the surviving operative's report and then Meg Vance's findings.

"This is incredible," Jon said. "The Space Tactics Division has been one of our best tools."

"Now we know why. They've been softening us up, sir, getting us to trust them."

Jon scowled. "I do trust them. This…" he waved the tablet, "can't be right."

The Old Man began patting himself down. It might have been an unconscious gesture. He appeared to be searching for something.

"Left my pipe in my quarters," he muttered.

"If this is true…" Jon said.

"We have to strike hard and fast, sir," the Old Man said. "We've given the Space Tactics Division more leeway than anyone else. This makes sense, particularly since we caught an intercept from the GSB."

Jon glared at the report. It felt as if the bulkheads in his wardroom were closing in. This was chilling. He needed the Space Tactics Division. To lose them now…

"What do you suggest?" Jon asked quietly.

"Take a regimental company, sir," the Old Man said. "Suit them up and take out the entire station."

"Why not use a few missiles to do that?"

"I want a crack at their files, sir. And we need prisoners, the more the better."

Jon's scowl grew as he stared at the poisonous tablet in his hand. "I need to read this again."

"Time is against us, sir. It's going to take time to set up a surprise raid."

The scowl lines deepened even more.

Why am I so suspicious of everyone? The Old Man has done good work. Why is there a knot in my gut?

"Okay…" Jon said.

"Sir—"

"I said 'okay,'" Jon snapped. "I have to think. What if the detective is a plant?"

"I don't see how that's possible, sir. This is…huge. I bet my paycheck the SSP have backup. We have to disrupt the plan before they hit us like a hurricane."

"That will be all," Jon said. "I need to read this again and think about it."

The Old Man looked as if he wanted to say, "Don't take too long." Instead, he saluted, turned around and exited the chamber.

-4-

Jon reread the report carefully. Everything seemed to be in order. The two operatives had gotten lucky in apprehending the SSP detective. They might have also gotten lucky with the coagulant in the false tooth. It had certainly been potent enough according to the power of the delayed reaction to the dead operative from a finger wound.

Why hadn't the detective licked his false tooth and died from that?

Jon read the reports for a third time. Something bothered him about this. Yes, luck aided them from time to time. Good luck and bad luck had struck more than once.

With a grunt, Jon shot to his feet. He had qualms. He could go see Gloria. Her mentalist outlook had proven invaluable more often than not.

No! Jon knew who he was going to see. This was something the Prince of Ten Worlds might be able to comprehend for him.

***

Da Vinci had his forehead pressed against a wall as he stood near the cell's sink. He didn't look up as Jon entered. He didn't complain, didn't whine, didn't ask why—

Da Vinci whirled with an oath, and he lunged at Jon. There was something glitteringly metallic in his right hand.

The move almost caught Jon off-guard. At the last moment, he blocked the thrust, knocking Da Vinci's hand aside.

"No," Da Vinci howled, with tears leaking from his eyes. He lunged again.

This time, Jon was ready. He grabbed the wrist and twisted savagely. He twisted hard enough so something popped in the thin wrist.

Da Vinci howled with pain as his hand opened involuntarily. A small penknife dropped from his hand.

Jon kicked the penknife aside, and he shoved the little thief at his cot. Da Vinci stumbled backward, falling onto the cot. He backed up, scooting into the corner and staring at Jon like a wild animal.

Jon retrieved the penknife. He'd expected a sharpened shiv of some sort. Someone had given the penknife to Da Vinci. As Jon moved his other hand to fold the blade into the handle, he noticed a sheen on the blade.

Poison.

Stepping to the door and knocking on it, Jon told one of the responding guards to don gloves before he gingerly handed the knife to him.

"Take this to Meg Vance. Be extra careful. It's a poisoned blade. I want to know what kind of poison."

The guard acknowledged the order and hurried away.

Jon glanced at the other two guards. He shut the door afterward, regarding Da Vinci.

"Who gave you the penknife?"

"The Old Man," Da Vinci muttered.

For a second, Jon believed him. Then, he realized the absurdity of the comment.

"I need to talk—"

"No," Da Vinci said wildly. "I won't let you. I can't. I have to fight for my sanity. You're driving me over the edge with these talks."

Jon realized whatever pity he'd had for Da Vinci had dried up a long time ago. He'd used the man for so long now…

Am I turning into a monster? Is that what pressure could do to a man? The skullduggery of ruling a planetary system, or sitting as dictator over it, had definitely come with internal costs. To defeat monsters, he'd had to take on many of the monsters' attributes.

"I need to speak to the other you," Jon said.

"Leave me alone!" Da Vinci shouted. "I'm not going to—no, no, I don't want to. You shouldn't do this to me. You're evil. I hate you!"

Even as tears leaked from Da Vinci's eyes, he began trembling. The shaking intensified, and then his eyes bulged outward.

The next second, the Neptunian's demeanor changed. He became calm, more relaxed. Using his right hand, he methodically wiped away the tears and ran his hand under his runny nose, wiping the hand on his blanket afterward.

"Thank you, Captain," the Neptunian said in his confident voice. "The wretch has been stubborn the past few days. The assassination attempt surprises me. He almost killed you."

"Who gave him—you—the knife?" Jon asked.

The Neptunian smiled knowingly. "Would you believe me if I told you? I don't think so."

"Do you know?"

"That's the other problem," the Neptunian said. "I don't know."

Jon had no idea whether the Prince of Ten Worlds was telling the truth or not. Maybe it didn't matter.

"May I ask why you're here?" the Neptunian said.

Jon nodded, telling him about the reports concerning the SSP detective and the Space Tactics Division. He told the Neptunian his doubts and that he couldn't understand why he doubted.

"Allow me to process this," the Neptunian said.

Jon backed up to the stool, sitting down, tilting it so he perched on a single stool leg.

Four minutes passed in silence.

"Devious, very, very devious," the Neptunian said finally.

"Do you doubt the veracity of the report?" Jon asked.

"Utterly," the Neptunian said. "There are a few too many markers pointing to an extremely subtle mind at play. I believe your enemy—"

"Do you mean the Solar League?"

"Oh, indeed, yes," the Neptunian said. "I believe your enemy needs the Space Tactics Division eliminated. He desires

140

you to take it out for him. Yet…I suspect there is something more. I almost suspect this is a diversion."

"How could I find out for sure?"

"That is a difficult course. Your detective—not yours, of course—I refer to your prisoner. His mind was carefully conditioned to fool your inquisitor."

Jon ingested this in silence.

"There's only one method I know to get to the detective's truth."

"I hope you're not going to say the brain-tap machines," Jon said.

"I see you already realize what you need to do. For some reason, you want me to point it out to you. Really, Captain, I think you lack the confidence for this. You're too full of doubt. You should trust your instincts. That's what fear is for."

"I don't follow you."

The Neptunian chuckled. "Your race and mine are very similar. They even have similar pets. I recall a report I read as the Prince. Shall I share it with you?"

"Go ahead."

"A woman reported a gruesome rape and robbery. She told the officer, 'I don't know how my dog knew the man was evil.' Of course, my people did not have dogs as such, but doglike creatures."

"Of course," Jon said.

"The woman asked the officer, 'How did my dog know he was going to rape me?'

"Clearly, the dog did not know," the Neptunian said. "But the dog knew its owner. The beast read the woman's unease about the stranger who had come to her door. The subconscious fear in her was a warning that things were not right with this man. For whatever reason, she did not trust her instincts. She did not trust her fears, and she ended up being raped and robbed because of her self-distrust."

"You're saying I'm like that woman?"

"Oh, yes, indeed, Captain."

Jon let the other two stool-legs clump onto the floor. He stood and headed for the door.

"Aren't you going to thank me, Captain?"

141

Jon regarded the Neptunian, the cunning in his eyes. "I'm sorry, Da Vinci. I needed the Prince to tell me that."

"Don't speak to him when I'm in charge," the Neptunian said sternly. "It is rude and diminishes my honor. If you are not careful of my honor, Captain, *I* shall make the assassination attempt next time. And believe me, I will succeed."

"I'll keep that in mind," Jon said. He rapped on the door. He had a big decision to make.

-5-

"I see…" Bast Banbeck said.

The Sacerdote stood in his outer chamber. No one had been in his inner chamber for months now. Gloria had informed Jon that Bast considered it his sanctuary. Banbeck had implied before that a human would defile the sanctuary and badly upset his equilibrium. The mentalist had told Jon that Bast worked hard to maintain his mental balance in this chaotic environment.

The outer chamber was large and devoid of furniture of any kind. The floor, though, had an amazingly intricate chalked-out pattern. There were squares, triangles, ovals and octagonal shapes with lines and pathways connecting them.

Even as Bast Banbeck had listened to Jon explain the situation, the Sacerdote had moved in slow motion across his pattern. In many ways, it was like watching a distracted young girl step across her chalked-out hopscotch pattern while trying to talk to her. The Sacerdote had not jumped, but moved in a fluid, kung-fu-like manner, changing his hand positions and stances.

"May I ask you an unrelated question?" Jon said.

"By all means, Captain, as long as it does not involve…" Bast gestured to the floor.

"Oh."

Bast Banbeck closed his eyes as if preparing himself for something painful.

"Perhaps we could stick to the issue at hand," the Sacerdote said.

"Of course," Jon replied, feeling foolish.

"I could no doubt attempt what you wish," Bast said slowly. "However, the results from the last time still pain my conscience. I failed to eliminate a horror. The Prince of Ten Worlds is slowly driving Da Vinci mad. The reason for this is obvious. Once the human will is driven mad, his resolve will be weakened dramatically. That might allow the Prince to maintain his preeminence indefinitely."

"Could you do something for Da Vinci?"

"I could try again..." Bast made a complex gesture. "By now, it is useless. The Prince has invaded too many portions of Da Vinci's consciousness. The man has to use his own resources to implant his will in himself."

"There's nothing you could do?"

"I could wipe his brain patterns altogether. This would likely eliminate the Prince's mind echo. Then, I would have to put down the old pattern. Da Vinci would lose countless memories from the process. Some would argue that he would no longer be the same individual. That is a religious question, however. That means I am unable to answer it."

"What about the SSP detective?"

"That, Captain, would be easier to accomplish. I should note, though, that it will be decidedly painful for the detective. It is likely he will also lose his sanity from the process."

Jon bent his head in thought, but it was only for show. He'd already decided. This was for all the marbles, as someone had recently said. Therefore, he was going to do this to the best of his ability, using whatever tools he had to.

As he looked up, Jon saw that Bast was stepping to a different area of the chalked-out room.

Maybe he looked so frankly and wonderingly at Bast, that the Sacerdote said, "I am exiting the pattern, Captain. I hope you can wait that long."

"Sure," Jon said, more curious than ever what the pattern meant to Bast Banbeck.

***

144

The Sacerdote staggered out of the hateful brain-tap chamber.

Jon had left the chamber some time ago as the detective began to scream hoarsely over and over again. The idea that he must make decisions that caused people such agony had begun to get to Jon. Surely, these kinds of decisions changed a man.

He wondered if the colonel had ever faced this. Certainly, a military officer sometimes gave orders that led to people's deaths. The worst was losing his own people. But that kind of screaming was different. It had sounded too much like torture. What made him any different from the GSB?

"I have gained your knowledge," Bast Banbeck said. "Alas, the detective is dead. The process tore him apart. I lacked the skill—"

"Bast," Jon said, sharply.

The alien jerked his huge head upright.

"I had you do this," Jon said. "It was not your responsibility, but mine."

"Oh, Captain, that is simply not true. We are all responsible for any action we take. One cannot hide behind orders. No. If I accept such orders, I am party to the action. Do you humans really believe this, or is it a clever cover to mask your pain?"

"We're trying to save the human race," Jon said.

"Captain, I am afraid I must disagree once more. We are doing much more than trying to save your people. That is a noble cause in itself. However, we wish to save the human race in order to create a bastion against the murderous robots. That is our great charge. We fight in the cause of life against those of death."

"That's poetic," Jon said. "You have spoken this truth clearly."

"Thank you."

The towering alien and the captain regarded each other.

"About the detective?" asked Jon.

"I uncovered the truth. It is complex and devious. The Prince of Ten Worlds was correct. Your instincts are correct. The detective was given false data and mind-locks against ever revealing the truth. The brain-tap machine proved too strong for the locks. Tearing the truth from the detective killed him, as his superiors intended."

"The Space Tactics Division isn't planning a raid on the warship?"

"No, Captain. They are planning a raid on those who are your enemy. I believe the enemy planned to destroy two *bilks* with one rock."

"Come again?" asked Jon.

"I have discovered the tip of something momentous. The detective only knew a little. I can give you three clues and a time limit."

"What limit is that?" Jon asked.

"Three days," Bast said.

"Then what happens?"

"A momentous event," the Sacerdote said. "In this instance, I am certain that event involves the *Nathan Graham*."

-6-

The first two clues cost seven good operatives in Nirvana City. The last of the seven radioed a gnat patrol boat flying in Saturn's upper atmosphere. The woman in the back seat passed the message on to the *Nathan Graham*.

Nine minutes later, Captain Hawkins spoke to them. "Take it out."

"Do you mean the laser system, sir?"

"No. The city. You're the only ones in position and you lack the hardware for a surgical strike. Destroy Nirvana City. You're doing it on my authority."

The woman in the two-seater gnat acknowledged the grim order. She controlled three drones, each of them with a nuclear payload. The drones cruised through the gas giant's upper atmosphere. The woman worked swiftly, tapping orders onto the remote-controlling unit on her lap.

The three drones changed their circular loop pattern, heading for the cloud city.

During this time, the conspirators in Nirvana City had unlimbered a giant focusing system. They believed their cover was blown. Because they had an open window—a straight line-of-sight—for only a few hours, they decided to take it now. The conspirators worked furiously, targeting the *Nathan Graham* in space. Giant turbines whirred, pumping the gas cylinders with power.

"How long?" the chief conspirator shouted.

A tech checked his watch, pointed at another man and turned to the chief. "Now, comrade. It's firing now."

The gas cylinders unleashed their power into coils. The coils pumped the targeting lens. A giant beam reached up out of Saturn's highest atmosphere. The beam traveled the 150,000 kilometers in the blink of an eye. It struck the giant scaffolding surrounding the *Nathan Graham*. The beam melted girders, sending globules of metal wobbling away and then burnt-free sections of scaffolding followed.

In Saturn's upper atmosphere, the first of the three drones approached the cloud city. The GSB conspirators had worked hard, however. On the main platform, anti-missile guns targeted the approaching drone. They began to chug powerful proximity shells.

Two direct hits caused a massive detonation. The drone blew apart, the sections dropping harmlessly into the deeper atmosphere.

The second drone had circled and dipped. Now, it swept upward toward the cloud city.

Nirvana City, like the other atmospheric platforms, maintained its place because it had buoyancy. The city literally floated in the thick atmosphere. The buoyancy was due to giant steel-sheathed balloons under the main city platform.

"You're going to need the third drone," the gnat pilot said. "If these last two fail, the captain will likely order us to sacrifice our lives to take out Nirvana."

The drone-controller skillfully manipulated her pad.

As Nirvana's antimissile-guns took out the second drone, the third accelerated flat out toward the under-balloons.

In space, the Nirvana City laser burned through the first layer of scaffolding. The giant laser began heating the *Nathan Graham's* outer hull armor.

The gnat pilot swore as he listened to his comm. He kicked in the gnat's afterburners, heading toward the cloud city. "I'm locking onto the main guns," he said. "Get ready."

"Abort, abort," the drone-controller said. "I think I have them."

"What if you're wrong?"

"I'll tell you in five seconds."

148

As the drone-controller spoke, a proximity shell ignited nearby. A piece of shrapnel bounced off the gnat's canopy. Spider-line cracking marred the clear material. The blast from a second proximity shell proved too much for the weakened canopy. A piece tore away. A second later, the entire canopy blew outward. The gnat spun out-of-control. The woman had already donned breathing gear, but it didn't matter. Two more proximity shells struck the gnat and exploded, killing the two operators.

Two seconds later, the third drone struck a steel-sheathed buoyancy balloon. Its thermonuclear warhead exploded, causing all the balloons in that section to pop in quick succession.

Nirvana City tipped sideways. The focusing mirror no longer targeted the giant cybership in space. The cloud city began sliding sideways deeper into Saturn's increasingly thick atmosphere. As the platform did so, the gravities increased.

More buoyancy balloons began to pop, increasing the rate of descent. In minutes, there was no one left alive in the cloud city. No focusing mirror worked. Everything crumbled. Nirvana City was gone, devoured by the conflict between the *Nathan Graham* and the Solar League.

***

The first two clues ripped from the SSP detective had led to a premature Nirvana laser-beam assault against the Space Dock scaffolding. The third clue led to something completely different.

The Space Tactics Division of the SSP began their various assaults on selected Neptune orbital stations and on a few domes on Titan. The SSP chief did not know it, but that cleared the way for the main GSB-directed attack on the *Nathan Graham*.

Two thousand, three hundred and eighty-nine workers and space-welders began donning their equipment. Today, some of them carried breach-bombs instead of welding equipment. Others had jetpacks with armor plates hidden under their spacesuits. They would use those once they made it inside the

149

Nathan Graham. Those people had military-grade rifles and grenades in their possession.

A final staging satellite waited for a signal from its location 52,000 kilometers away in the gas giant's rings. For months now, under the very noses of the SSP, the GSB operators left in the Saturn System had trickled assault boats and space marine suits there. Over the last few days, they had reinforced the retreat massively and dangerously. Once G-hour arrived, five thousand demi-marines would rush the giant alien vessel. The goal was to storm aboard and help the welders and space workers capture the cybership.

The conspirators had solved one of the trickiest problems with a clever expedient. During the past few days, they'd slipped thousands of personnel aboard in shielded cryo units. That minimized the transmission of the wrong kind of sensor signals. The conspirators had also used the vast debris of the rings to shield their doings.

The rings were only a few kilometers thick, containing water-ice and rocky particles covered with water-ice. The particles ranged from a few centimeters to tens of meters in diameter. While the particles were thick enough to create the spectacular rings, there was also plenty of space between most of the debris.

It was to the conspirators' credit that the plan had gotten this far undetected. There was a problem, though. The same debris that had shielded them from SSP and the *Nathan Graham's* sensors, also shielded the company of Black Anvil space marines from the conspirators as the Anvils maneuvered into attack position.

Two hours ago, the Centurion and Gloria Sanchez had confronted the captain.

"Please," the Centurion said. "Without you, sir…"

"He's right," Gloria said. "Why are you risking your life like this?"

"I'm a soldier first," Jon said. "I've been ordering a lot of people to do sacrificial things and to do dirty deeds. It's time I put my life on the line again. I can't—"

Jon had stopped explaining, remembering that none of his people wanted to hear his qualms. That didn't change the fact he was going in on this one.

Maybe he needed to risk his life as a cathartic release of his pent-up pressures. Whatever the reason, he was wearing a battlesuit again, waiting in a small assault boat. The boat's pilot slid them past ring debris, maneuvering closer to the hidden satellite.

It was almost time to begin the attack.

-7-

The exoskeleton-powered battlesuits allowed Jon and his marines to wear heavy carbon-composite armor. That let them carry heavy weapons, air-tanks and hydrogen propellants, and to survive in the suits for over a week if needed.

Stark commanded the company of roughly five hundred space marines. Approximately one hundred of these men had survived the cybership-storming in the Neptune System almost two years ago. The rest of the company was composed of new recruits, many from the Neptune System and plenty from around here. They'd trained together for months at least, some of them for longer.

Jon checked his HUD. It was presently hooked into the assault boat's passive teleoptics. A chair-sized rocky particle slid past as the boat drifted toward a large darkened satellite. According to the specs, the satellite was fifty-two kilometers distant. It was big for such a hidden construct, half a kilometer in size.

How had the enemy kept the satellite hidden all this time?

I've been lucky. We've been lucky.

Jon wondered why his gut wasn't churning. It would have been in the past. Was he too tired? Did he hate a few too many of the things he'd had to do lately? He didn't want to risk his men if he didn't have the right attitude. He owed them his best.

Jon focused on the dark satellite. Stark had been eager enough for this. The gorilla of a sergeant had told him the company needed blooding.

The colonel would likely have agreed with Stark. Combat troops could sit around too long. A good combat unit was like a knife. It could get rusty. Sharpening wasn't only about combat training. Sometimes, a unit had to go into action. That helped shake out the bad leaders. It also trained the troops with live-action decisions and with plenty of adrenaline pumping through them.

This isn't a drill. This isn't to sharpen the troops. This is so I can repair the cybership. This is so I can face the AIs when they show up again.

"Sir," Stark said over a short comm. He was on a different assault boat. "We should accelerate the rest of the way. If we try to drift in, they're going to spot us. That will give them time to get ready."

That's when it really hit Jon. He was about to send five hundred space marines against an enemy five thousand strong. His five hundred wore battlesuits, however. The others likely did not, as their go-hour was still some time from now. Five hundred battlesuited marines could butcher five thousand unarmored men.

Still, many things could go wrong. Some things *would* go wrong. One of the oldest maxims of battle was that no plan survived contact with the enemy.

Fear boiled in Jon's gut. The fear boiled away the hesitation. It boiled away the self-doubts and worries. This was the real deal.

I feel alive again.

Now, Jon knew why he'd joined the raid. He was a fighter, and he needed to fight.

"Sir—"

"Right," Jon said. He switched to a wide-message command channel. "Attention," he said. "Hector did not run away." That was the code to unleash the assault boats.

It was about to begin.

***

Jon's assault boat picked up velocity. He felt it, as this little boat did not have any gravity dampeners. It was constructed to do two things and those two things alone.

First, it knifed toward the target. The assault boat had a dark and heavily armored hull. Because the pilot had used the debris in the belt and moved cautiously, they had hopefully slipped to their present position unnoticed.

"I'm getting radar pings," the pilot said. "They've spotted us."

The tightening in Jon's belly grew worse. This was the hardest moment. Heading in, when any stray shell could take them out.

"They're firing," Jon said, watching his HUD.

The dark satellite was long. Tiny pinpricks showed on the dark object, the point defense guns firing at them.

"Hang on," the pilot said. "This is going to get rough."

It always did. It was nearly impossible to go the last distance without the enemy waking up.

"There!" the pilot shouted.

Jon saw it on his HUD. Their own pre-attack missiles had slid into position unnoticed. Explosions over there now created white blots on the screen. Those explosions were small shape-charged neutron bombs igniting. They were clean, in other words. They created local EMP bursts. The blasts should blind the enemy targeting sensors for a few minutes. Maybe the EMPs would create short circuits over there, but maybe not. The enemy had undoubtedly hardened most of their electronics.

"That's no good," the pilot said.

"What happened?" Jon asked.

"They're firing their guns blindly. One of them hit First Platoon's second boat."

Jon couldn't see it on his HUD. "Is it destroyed?"

"Hit," the pilot said. "Oh-oh, the pods are ejecting. The boat is getting rid of its cargo. Damn. It blew. That scratches First Platoon's second boat."

Jon ground his teeth in fury. The enemy had gotten lucky. The neutron bombs were supposed to have blinded those guns' targeting sensors. Stark's company had just lost too many space marines before the fight had even started.

"Are they waiting for us?" Jon asked the pilot. "Is this an ambush?"

The pilot didn't answer.

Jon was jerked back and forth in his seat as the assault boat maneuvered violently.

"Hang on," the pilot said again.

The ride became more than violent. Jon was jerked back, to the side and back again. He'd have body-length bruises before this was over.

"We're almost in," the pilot shouted. "Switching off."

Jon's view on the HUD vanished, blotted out by the pilot.

The assault boats converged on the dark satellite. They roared in at speed. Each boat was constructed like a giant needle. Each had an incredibly sharp point, providing the boat's second function, slicing into an outer hull.

On Jon's boat, side guns hammered the targeted entry point, softening the enemy hull. At that moment, the assault boat smashed against the location. It crashed through the enemy hull, the slender assault boat sliding, sliding, shaking and rattling before coming to a sudden halt.

They were inside.

The assault boat's hull blasted outward, sending sections of hull spinning into the enemy satellite.

The heavy restraints around Jon's battlesuit blew off. He staggered. They'd made it. It was time to charge into the satellite and begin killing enemy combatants.

-8-

The first half of the battle went like clockwork. Jon worked with Second Platoon. He fired 100 mm HEAT shells, blowing down bulkheads. After that, he used an electromagnetic grenade launcher.

The grenades slaughtered unarmored men.

The bulkheads of the enemy secret base dripped with blood, gore and pieces of flesh.

Stark's company took no prisoners at that point.

The sudden death from space surprised the secret base personnel, but not for long. Maybe six hundred of the enemy marines donned their battlesuits.

The problem—for the enemy—was that the GSB operatives had a distinct distrust of military people. They'd kept the battlesuits and weapons separated.

Five hundred of the enemy marines died trying to reach the weapons lockers. They had speed and stamina, but their armor could not resist repeated hits. Stark's men could shoot freely without worrying about counter fire. That made all the difference.

The last one hundred demi-marines breached a weapons locker.

Now, the fight finally began in earnest.

That was where the superior training of Stark's company paid off.

Third and part of First Platoon laid down heavy fire. The two sides sent thunderous munitions at each other. Stark worked his teams around the enemy area until he had the one hundred marines engaged in constant firing.

Jon led Second Platoon. Just like on the cybership almost two years ago, Second Platoon's engineers planted bulkhead charges.

They blew.

The engineers clanked forward, setting another round of bulkhead charges.

Those blew, too.

Jon led the way, firing the big 100 mm HEAT launcher as he went.

The shells were for taking down big vehicles. These blasted enemy battlesuits, sending them flying, broken and breached in one strike.

Second Platoon roared in behind the heavily-engaged enemy battlesuits. They cut down the enemy fighters until the last ones pleaded for mercy.

"Throw down your weapons," Stark radioed. "Lay flat on the deck plates. If any of you moves—you're dead. Comply at once. This is your only chance."

Most did just that. The few who tried to be tricky died.

After the last enemy combatant shed his suit and walked in restraints to the waiting shuttles, Stark approached Jon. They were still wearing their battlesuits.

"We did it, sir," the gorilla of a marine said.

"Not yet we haven't," Jon said. "We need to get back to the ship."

"Do you see any problems there, sir?"

"Don't know. But if I were running the enemy side, this is a golden opportunity. They can try to hit us as we head back for the *Nathan Graham*."

"We'd better hurry then," Stark said.

"Speed is the key," Jon agreed.

***

As Stark's company piled into the retrieval shuttles, the leader of the GSB, Saturn System, spread her fingers on her desk.

The polished desk was located in a dome on the farthest moon of the Saturn System, a tiny piece of rock.

She had a spider-web of contacts throughout the system. She was the conduit to Earth, to J.P. Justinian.

She stared white-faced at her screen, reading more reports. This was a disaster.

The workers and welders on the scaffolding attacked the cybership's hull. Waiting Black Anvil marines rushed to the location and butchered her people. Piled onto the disaster was the brutal attack against the Ring Retreat...

"I'm a dead woman," she whispered to herself.

She removed one of the hands from the polished desk. She ran her fingers through her short-cut hair. What was this?

She leaned forward, adjusting the screen with a few taps. This was a message, an intercept. Jon Hawkins had gone with his marines into the rings.

She blinked rapidly, her thoughts racing. If she could send Justinian a message that she had killed the cybership's commander—

The head of the GSB, Saturn System, came alive, issuing curt and most direct orders. It might burn up her remaining assets, but it might also cause the death of the hatefully brilliant capitalist.

***

The five retrieval shuttles stuck together. The shuttles carried the surviving Black Anvils and their prisoners. The caravan slowed to pick up the survivors floating in space. Then, the shuttles accelerated carefully.

They pulled up out of the debris in the rings, heading for the vast cybership 51,342 kilometers away, and presently out of line-of-sight. The rings rotated at their own rates, the inner rings spinning faster than the outer ones.

At that point, seven patrol boats skimmed low around Saturn. They were between the highest atmosphere and true orbital space. They were the last, hidden resource of the GSB-motivated conspirators, in the Saturn System.

The pilots and the gun and missile crews were fanatically loyal Social Dynamists. They had waited all this time, surviving on a near-starvation diet and battling intense boredom.

The patrol boat chief had one goal: destroy the five shuttles and thereby eliminate Jon Hawkins.

He calculated vectors, velocities and distances.

"Push past maximum acceleration," he ordered.

"Patrol Chief," a tech radioed. "The boats won't take that kind—"

"Belay your report, Engineer," the chief said. "Push past maximum until we're in missile range. Then we'll launch a full barrage."

Seconds later, seven patrol boats roared upward into orbital space. They began spreading apart at the engineer's pleading.

As the seven boats gained velocity, one of the engine cores blew. Excessive heat radiated outward, melting components and prematurely igniting missile munitions. The boat exploded spectacularly.

The debris blew apart. It struck several other boats. They hadn't moved far enough apart yet. Two survived the pelting. The third began tumbling end-over-end. Then, its engine blew in a second spectacular event. This time, because of the tumbling, no debris hit another boat.

Now, five patrol boats roared toward the shuttles, straining to get into firing range.

***

"Sir," Gloria radioed Jon. "Did you see those explosions behind your convoy?"

Jon was sitting at the piloting panel. He tapped the comm. "I did not."

"Patrol boats, sir," Gloria said. "My prognosis is GSB."

"Patrol boats?"

"With missiles," she said. "You could be in danger."

"Just a minute," Jon said. He glanced at the pilot. "Do you see them now?"

The pilot nodded. "The mentalist is right. If I were to guess, they plan to launch missiles at us."

"Can we go faster?"

159

"No, sir. We have a few defensive measures—" The pilot quit talking as a red light blinked on his screen.

"What's that?" Jon said.

Gloria radioed him again. "You have more bogies zeroing in on you, sir. I think they mean to destroy the shuttles. I have gnat fighters racing to intercept the new threat. But those five patrol boats, sir—"

"Use one of the ship's grav beams," Jon said.

"To reach them, we'd have to break out of the scaffolding. That would take a long time to rebuild. We'd be in Saturn System far longer—"

"Stay in the scaffolding," Jon said. "We're going to work our way toward you the best we can."

"But—"

"I'm not as important as repairing the cybership. That's the key. If the AIs should show up too soon..."

"Yes, sir," Gloria said. "Good luck, sir."

"Thanks," Jon said. "See you after the home stretch."

The pilot glanced wildly at Jon.

"Take us back into the rings," Jon told him.

"I can dodge the biggest rocks, sir, but I can't even see the smallest dust particles. The shuttles won't last in the rings at this speed."

"If we won't last, neither will enemy missiles."

The pilot stared at Jon as if the captain had gone mad.

"Do it," Jon said.

"Aye-aye, Captain," the pilot said. "I'm taking us back into the rings."

-9-

The shuttles veered off course. The spacecraft strained at the G forces. Soon, each pilot was weaving to the best of his or her ability. At these speeds, though, weaving was a relative term.

Jon watched the progress, enduring the back and forth jerking. The enemy patrol boats came into sensor range. They sped faster, closing the distance between them. Soon, the patrol boats would launch missiles.

Before Jon could decide anything more, an explosion to his right showed him the cost of his decision. A shuttle struck icy particles. That changed the shuttle's vector, and it plowed against a bigger rock, crumpling at the impact.

Scratch one shuttle. Scratch one-fifth of what remained of Stark's company.

Jon felt sick inside. He'd made a risky decision, and those men had paid the price.

Another shuttle wobbled badly.

"I took a debris hit," a pilot radioed. "I have injured marines in here."

Jon slapped the comm. "Through the rings, go through the rings to the bottom."

Jon's pilot looked at him. "The bottom, sir?"

"In relation to the patrol boats," Jon said.

"Right," the pilot said, changing course once again.

The race continued as the shuttles struggled to get through the narrow rings intact.

"The patrol boats are changing course," Gloria radioed. "They're going to go through the rings after you."

Jon hated this. "Isn't there anything you can do?" he asked the pilot.

"I can expel chaff later, and I have ECM going. But we're travelling too fast for those to work well. The enemy can target us by our heat emissions."

Jon crossed his fingers. The lead shuttle emerged intact from the rings. It leveled out again, skimming "under" the rings and heading for the *Nathan Graham*.

Soon, all four shuttles were racing under the rings.

"Once the patrol boats are through, I'd expect them to fire the missiles at us," the pilot said.

Jon nodded absently.

Time passed.

The gnat fighters took care of the other threat.

"Five more minutes," the pilot told Jon. "We'll be in sight of the warship, and they can use the grav beam then."

A bright dot on the sensors showed a scratched enemy patrol boat.

"They're not invincible," Jon said. "Debris killed one of them."

"They're popping under the rings…now," the pilot said.

"Back up through the rings," Jon said.

The pilot glanced at him, nodded, and took them up.

Jon ordered the others up into the rings again.

At that point, the four remaining patrol boats launched their missiles in blizzard fashion. A mass of dots indicating enemy missiles sped toward them.

The shuttles moved upward, and another of them hit debris, which ripped off the top of the shuttle. It went spinning, and for all purposes, it was dead.

Jon closed his eyes in pain.

The pilot beside him muttered angrily.

The missiles raced upward into the rings, following their targets.

"Hang on," the pilot whispered.

The shuttle veered severely and suddenly shook hard.

"Hit," the navigator said. "Two people died in the rear compartment. But we still have integrity."

Jon realized he was gripping his armrests so hard that his hands ached.

The missiles entered the rings. They did not veer. They did not have the slightest mechanism to do so. The first missile hit a rock, and disintegrated.

"Three minutes," the pilot said. "In three minutes—"

"We're leaking air," a shuttle pilot reported.

Jon saw it on his screen. The shuttle was leaving a visible trail.

More enemy missiles exploded in the debris, but not all of them.

"Sir," the leaking shuttle pilot said. "I've lost fuel. I don't think we can make it."

"What are you talking about?" Jon said. "You can make it."

"This is Stark. We're going to be the target, sir."

"No," Jon said.

"I ain't arguing with you, sir. I want my company to survive. Sometimes—you're good, lad. I appreciate your hard work. Now you listen to me. You beat the Solar League and you beat the damn AIs. I've seen you in action. These bastards on our tail know your worth. Well, so do I."

"Stark!"

"Good-bye, lad. Do me proud."

The line clicked off.

Jon stared at the pilot. The man focused studiously on his controls.

How can this be happening? We beat them. I'd won. Now—

The next few minutes passed in a daze for Jon. The shuttles exited the rings. Two of them zoomed for the *Nathan Graham*. The third, the last one, deliberately hung back.

That shuttle expelled chaff. It used the one PD cannon it had, knocking out the first missile.

Jon watched the sensor board, unaware that his eyes had welled with tears. He couldn't believe this. What did Stark think he was doing?

163

A missile streaked for the shuttle, hitting it, igniting. Two more blew as well, destroying the shuttle and killing Stark and his marines.

Jon slumped in his seat, hardly aware that the last two shuttles had reached the grav beam's line-of-sight.

"We're home free," the pilot told Jon.

Jon couldn't even nod. This had been a disaster.

-10-

While the raid had been a disaster, resulting in massive casualties, it did bring some positive results.

They squelched the conspirators' attempt to capture the *Nathan Graham*. All along the line, the GSB operators had used everything. That meant they had almost nothing left for a second attempt in the Saturn System.

The prisoners from the Ring Retreat Satellite also provided excellent intelligence. It turned out all of it came from one woman, an arbiter.

This gave Jon inside data on the GSB operations. He shared the data with several Saturn Government representatives. They could use it to clean out the last GSB infestations hidden in the cloud cities, orbitals and moon domes.

When the *Nathan Graham* left, the Saturn System would need its own defenses. Talks had already begun concerning a system-wide governing body and a Saturn Space Navy.

Jon would have to hire more workers, more welders and more techs to complete repairs on the cybership.

"Everything should go more easily without the constant GSB interference," Gloria said.

Jon heard her. She was standing close enough for him to feel the heat of her body. They were standing in an observation dome on the cybership. He was staring at the colorful rings of Saturn and remembering former Sergeant Stark.

It had been three days since the gorilla of a marine had died. Jon missed the stubborn bastard. He couldn't get over what the man had told him.

"It wasn't your fault," Gloria said quietly.

Jon didn't look at her. How could he look at anyone now?

"The GSB is a cunning enemy," Gloria said. "We're lucky to have done as well as we did."

Jon wanted to bang his fists against the observation dome. Instead, he spoke quietly.

"It *was* my fault," he said. "I led the raid. I gave the orders that sent the shuttles through the rings."

"I have carefully thought through your options. You did the right thing. Your decisions saved part of the company."

"I should have brought gnat fighters along. That was a terrible oversight."

"The gnats helped us squash the worker revolt. Without them, the welders might have broken into the cybership. We could still be fighting them."

"Even so," he whispered.

"Jon Hawkins," she said. "You cannot accept the blame if you do not accept the credit. You will destroy yourself by agonizing over these decisions."

"The pressure..." he whispered.

Gloria looked away.

Jon closed his eyes. Command was a lonely post. How had Colonel Graham done it? How had Genghis Khan done it? Is that why the great captains in history all seemed to have become bloody butchers? Had the hard decisions and the countless deaths of friends taken a grim toll on those warriors as well?

Jon opened his eyes, the sight of the jewel of the Outer Planets greeting him. He loved seeing Saturn and its rings, even though those rings had killed Stark and would forever remind him of the sergeant.

Jon cocked his head. The rings had saved two-thirds of the company. Without the debris, the patrol boats would have caught all of them.

I can't wallow in sorrow. That's throwing away Stark's sacrifice.

Jon snorted softly. Stark's ghost would now propel him onward, in league with the colonel's ghost who had been doing that for some time.

The AIs were out there, cruising the galaxy in search of life to eradicate. He had to remain strong and fixed in his purpose.

"You have to learn from this," he whispered.

"What's that?" Gloria asked.

Jon turned to her. "Thanks, Mentalist. I appreciate your effort. I'm glad you're my confidante. How long until the *Nathan Graham* is ready to leave the space dock?"

"The repairs could last years at our present rate."

"Then we're going to have to speed them up," Jon said.

"How do we do that and make sure we remain in control of the warship?"

Jon nodded. "I'm not sure just now. But I plan to figure it out."

Gloria smiled sadly. Then, the two of them returned to staring at Saturn's beauty.

Part V
KUIPER BELT
+2 Years, 7 Months, 13 Days

-1-

June Zen snorted, wrinkled her nose and sneezed explosively. Afterward, she began to shiver. Why was it so terribly cold in here?

She shivered more. She wanted to get warm and go back to sleep.

"June," a harsh voice said. It sounded like a badly unused voice. "June Zen."

Why was she hearing this stranger in her bedroom? Had she gone out drinking last night? That didn't seem right. What was going on?

"Can you hear me?" the harsh-voiced man asked.

"Go away," she said.

"Go where?"

"I already said. Away. Don't you understand English?"

"Open your eyes, June. You've been under a long time. I think…I think it's been over two years by now."

What did *that* mean? It sounded downright ominous. She raised her arms, stretched, hearing her right elbow pop, and slowly opened her eyes. As she did that, a terrible stink hit.

This placed smelled. Where was she anyway?

It took some doing for her eyes to focus. Finally, she saw a little fellow with fur around his chin. He had weird eyes, making it impossible to tell where he was looking.

His hair was greasy and his clothes not only stank, they were also in tatters.

"Don't you remember me? Walleye?" the little man asked.

She frowned as she stared at him. He had stubby arms, stubby hands with grubby little fingers.

Walleye!

June gasped in comprehension. Wildly, she glanced right and left.

Curving bulkheads greeted her. They were much too near each other. She was in an escape pod with Walleye the Mutant. Had he said two years?

"Are we…are we dead?" she whispered.

Walleye kept staring at her. At least, it seemed as if he did.

"Walleye," she said.

He started as if in shock. "Sorry, I must have zoned out. It's…It's been a long time. I'm…"

The little mutant zoned out again.

June began to shiver. This was just great. She was trapped in an escape pod with a freakish mutant and two lousy years had passed. And she was freezing.

She sat up, as the mutant seemed to have fallen into a daze. How had he spent the past two years?

June just about groaned then. She remembered that she'd tried to murder him. It had been for her protection. It had been—

She looked at Walleye. He was a wreck. He was rail thin, and his skin was splotchy. The eyes were worse than before. Had he gone mad during the two years? She would have gone stir-crazy in that time in his position.

Where were they?

She wondered if she should look for the stitch-gun. Walleye had been sharp and efficient two years ago. He might be dull and slow now. She could save herself from his madness if she could kill him.

The little mutant shivered himself aware again. A tremulous smile quivered onto his face. This wasn't the same Walleye that she remembered.

June tried to stand, pushing up and hitting her head against her open cryo unit lid instead. The pod lacked gravity.

"We float in here," Walleye said. As he spoke this time, some of the burr, the harshness left his voice.

"Are you okay?" June asked.

He laughed in a whispery manner, shaking his head.

"Are we dead, Walleye?"

"What's that mean, huh? You're breathing. You've had a good nap. You ought to be ready for an adventure. Are you ready, June Zen?"

"What's wrong with you?"

The whispery laugh lasted longer this time. He seemed demented.

"I've been alone for two years," he said. "Can you comprehend that? No, I doubt the beauty from Makemake understands a whit of that. You've always had it easy, sweetie. Not me. Little Walleye has always roughed it. But I'm not crying. Do you see me crying?"

"You have to get a grip, Walleye."

Abruptly, he turned around. He stretched so he floated in the pod, swimming to two bands. He anchored his feet in braces and began pulling the bands out and letting them go in. In and out, in and out—was that an exercise machine?

He started to sweat, and that stank.

A unit started up. The beads of sweat slowly drifted to the unit, sucked into it. After a time, the unit shut down.

"Going to drink that later," he told her. "The purifier still works, but I don't know for how much longer."

"That's disgusting," she said.

His whispery laughter started up again. She wished he wouldn't do that. When he stopped, he seemed to turn serious.

"Listen...Luscious..." He snapped his stubby fingers. "I used to call you that. Do you remember?"

She remembered hating it, but simply nodded.

"I might have gone mad for a time. It's hard to remember two years all alone in this bubble while listening to your cryo unit purr. I almost flushed you…I don't know how many times. Then I remembered you tried to shoot me. It's a good thing you tried. I wanted to show you that you were wrong about me. I think sometimes that's the only thing that kept you alive."

June decided she would hunt for the stitch-gun when he zoned out again.

"I'm not crazy anymore," Walleye said. "It's taken me a month, I think, to come out of it. At first—never mind about that. I saw it a little over a month ago. That's what started my mind working again. It's closer now, a whole heck of a lot closer. I think it's going to try for us. Why else would it have changed course?"

"What are you talking about?" June asked.

"There's a ship approaching us. It hasn't hailed us. I've listened for days on end. It's coming straight for us, and it's used plenty of fuel to slow its velocity. That means it's dead serious."

"A ship, out here in the Kuiper Belt?" asked June.

"You're finally understanding," he said. "A ship is coming. It's going to pick us up, I think. But way out here in the belt…"

"What?" June asked. "Way out here…?"

"It has to be a robot-controlled ship, right? I don't know, June. I think the ship is coming so the robots can shove control units into our skulls."

-2-

The days passed in dreadful monotony and growing terror and despair.

Walleye talked her ear off and then started up on the other one. The words kept pouring out of him. She wished he'd zone out so she could search for the stitch-gun.

At times, she dozed off. When she woke, when she moved, Walleye jerked upright. He must have fallen asleep after she did. As soon as she woke, he perked up and starting jabbering away with his stream of words.

She wanted to scream at him, but she was too scared. Instead, she nodded endlessly, making a few "ohs" and "ahs" along the way.

On what might have been the third day, she started comparing the two of them.

Long-term cryo sleep ate away at the human body. It just happened super-slowly. That had been one of the chief problems for the cryoarchs. Special cryo units injected growth serum into the frozen occupant. That serum helped to maintain the sleeper's equilibrium.

Her cryo unit hadn't been a specialty one. She was skinnier than when she'd gone in. She wasn't skinnier than Walleye, though. He was like a skeleton.

It seemed in the few days that she'd been awake, that Walleye had been gaining weight and strength.

She managed to ask him about that during breaths that interrupted his endless words.

That started him on another line of thought. Yes. He'd starved for months on end in order to stretch out the food supply. He'd calculated it carefully. Now, though, with the spaceship braking, heading toward them, he was eating regularly again. He hadn't felt this fit since entering the escape pod.

The renewed strength seemed to have reduced the number of times he zoned out. The endless talking seemed to be helping him sharpen his wits, too.

June finally decided Walleye had been as close to insane as a person could be and still function enough to make a few good decisions. That's why he'd woken her. The steady food, her company, maybe having a problem so that boredom no longer dulled his mind, was reawakening the sharp and deadly Walleye, the sane mutant assassin.

It would be harder to kill him now, June decided. Her desire to do so had sharply dropped off. Maybe she was getting used to him. Maybe he was making more sense finally—

June stared at the tiny control unit embedded in a bulkhead. She'd looked out it once. She didn't want to do that again. The sight—the loneliness of their position—terrified her.

"We're going to die, aren't we?" June asked him after the fourth day.

Walleye zoned out at the question. He sat like a statue. It started freaking her out. This was too long.

She turned away.

His eyes focused, it seemed. A tight, evil little grin stretched onto his hideous face.

"It don't look good for us, Luscious," Walleye said, sounding more like the old assassin she remembered.

"I don't want to be a drone," she said.

"Me neither."

"What are we going to do?"

"Don't know. Been thinking about it a ton. I've decided we're going to have to wait and see."

"It could be too late by then."

"Nope. Wrong. I'll mercy-kill you before I let a robot shove a control unit into your skull."

June stared at him. "That doesn't make me feel much better. I don't want to die either."

"Me neither," he said.

"Can't we threaten them?"

"Tell me how, Luscious."

"You have that memory core, right?" June asked.

He snapped his stubby fingers, pointing at her. "I forgot about it."

June glanced at the metallic object lying to the side. How could he possibly have forgotten about the big memory cube?

"What's the threat?" Walleye asked. "Let us go or we destroy the cube?"

"Something like that," she said. "But letting us go just leaves us stranded out here."

"I'm done sitting on my butt for months on end with nothing to do. If I had to do the stint over again..." Walleye shook his head.

"Are we certain it's a robot-controlled vessel?"

"It's been a few since I looked at it." Walleye pushed off the floor, floating to the control unit. He typed on the unit and brought up a tiny screen. He bent forward, staring for a good long time.

June figured he'd zoned out over it.

Abruptly, Walleye straightened, causing his spine to crack. He shut down the unit and faced her. There was something new in his manner.

It frightened June until she realized she recognized determination in him. More of the old Walleye seemed to have woken up finally.

"Find something?" she asked.

"It's an NSN destroyer. I believe it's a *Charon*-class vessel. They only made a few of them. Most of the NSN was drone-based, constructed for Neptune System combat alone."

"None of that means anything to me," June said.

"The destroyer was built to travel," Walleye said. "It's self-contained. It's an old ship, I believe."

"Okay..."

"Maybe the crew bugged out during the Solar League invasion. They realized the NSN was going to lose and decided

174

to start fresh in the Kuiper Belt. Other system military vessels have done that. Makes sense if you think about it. They did just what we did on Makemake two years ago."

"The destroyer may have a human crew?"

"Have no idea," Walleye said. "It's possible, I suppose. Then I ask myself, 'Why are they stopping to pick us up?'"

"Why wouldn't they?"

"Fuel and velocity," Walleye said. "You should know that. Everything in the Kuiper Belt is hundreds of thousands or millions or even billions of kilometers apart. That means a ship builds up a steady velocity—"

"I don't need a lesson on space travel."

Walleye stared at her, and it didn't seem as if he was zoning out. He might have been pissed and trying to stare her down.

"Sorry," she muttered.

He shrugged, and that seemed more like the old Walleye than ever.

"What's the plan?" she asked.

"We wait and see what they do. We don't have much choice."

"If they bugged out—"

"Luscious, don't get your hopes up. If they bugged out, they might still have been in range of the cybership message. The awakened computer could have killed all the humans inside the ship."

"Then why slow down for us?"

"That's the question all right. If it's any comfort, we'll know in about two days."

June stared at him. "So soon?" she asked in a small voice.

"Makes you think. Makes you really think. I should have lived differently." Walleye shrugged. "But I didn't. So we might as well get ready."

"How?" June asked, realizing she sounded wild.

"Let me think, Luscious." The little mutant bent his head as he idly scratched at his splotchy skin, less splotchy with his increased nutrient intake.

June hoped he could come up with something.

-3-

The NSN *Charon*-class Destroyer had a number and a name stenciled on the side of the vessel: 125 *Daisy Chain 4*.

Walleye told June what he'd read.

"What does it mean?" she asked.

"No idea," he said.

The destroyer had a classic triangular shape. It had PD guns poking out and several outer missile racks. That's the way the NSN liked to build them. The racks held long missiles, all of them there.

The destroyer didn't seem as if it had engaged in combat. That seemed to suggest that Walleye had guessed right about the crew bugging out from the Solar League invasion. That would also explain how the destroyer had already made it so far into the Kuiper Belt.

Despite traveling for two years already, the escape pod had hardly dented the distance between Makemake and the Neptune System.

"Maybe this is mercy," Walleye said.

"Don't talk like that," June chided. "I don't want to end my life with a quitter."

Walleye eyed her, eyed her long, slender legs. "We'll see how we end this. We still have some time."

That was the first time June had sensed sexual desire from the mutant. She looked away, uncertain how to handle this.

Walleye turned back to the control unit, tapping it harder than he had before.

The *Daisy Chain 4* drifted toward the pod. The destroyer dwarfed their tiny living quarters. It used side-jets now, expelling propellant, turning, slowing its rate of advance toward them.

"It's matching velocities," Walleye said.

"That means it must have turned around."

Walleye glanced at June.

"If it left the Neptune System, it would be heading in the opposite direction from us. We're heading toward the Sun, not leaving it."

"Good point," Walleye muttered. "The destroyer had to loop around to come at us in the right direction. That cost it even more fuel, and that makes what it's doing even more suspicious."

"I just thought of something else," June said.

Walleye regarded her.

"Why hasn't it tried to contact us?" she asked.

"No idea," he said.

"That would seem to indicate they're anti-robot. If they sent us a message, the robots might pick it up."

"That's good thinking, Luscious. You may be onto something." Walleye smiled. "You just gave me some hope."

The mutant pushed off from the bulkhead and went to a tiny locker. He made sure he had his back to her as he pressed the combination numbers.

"Mind looking the other way?" he asked.

June turned her back to him. She heard him open the locker. There was silence. It went on and on. She just about turned around to see what was going on.

"Thanks," he said.

June turned then, and smiled. It was the first time she'd smiled since coming out of the cryo unit.

Walleye had put on his buff coat. It was much too big on him now, though. He was wearing new clothes underneath. He had put on boots, and it seemed as if he had a gun harness under the buff coat.

"Do you have your tangler?" she asked.

He nodded. He put on his hat afterward. She remembered it. The hat with the brim low over his eyes gave him the

177

assassin appearance. This was Walleye. Maybe the mutant hadn't totally gone to seed these last two years. Maybe his survival showed just how tough-minded the mutant really was. Who else could have survived two years all alone in an escape pod and maintained their sanity?

Walleye the Assassin could.

"Why are you smiling, Luscious?"

"You," she said. She almost asked him for the stitch-gun so she would be armed as well. She realized he'd probably be too suspicious to give it to her. Maybe it was better if Walleye was the arsenal for now. She'd use other weapons. She'd lost weight, but not too much. Men liked what they saw when they looked at her. She'd use that.

If we're dealing with humans that is. The terror and despair of robots—

June shook her head. She wasn't going to think about the awful possibility. Walleye would kill her if that were the case. She didn't want to die. But she didn't want to live like her friend Mindy.

That was two years ago already. It was hard to believe.

Something clanged outside. The escape pod shook.

June sucked in her breath, looking around wide-eyed.

"Destroyer must have a tractor beam of some kind," Walleye said. "I suspect they just pulled us into a bay."

There was another clang. The pod shook, and all at once, gravity took hold.

"Oh," June said, sitting down hard on her butt.

Walleye stumbled, went to one knee and caught himself with one of his stubby hands. He looked up grinning.

"I've dreamed of walking again," he said hoarsely. "In my heart—" He choked off.

"We can do this," June whispered.

A grim look swept over him. He put his right hand into a buff coat pocket. She bet that's where he kept the stitch-gun.

Another clang sounded outside, and then several in succession.

"Someone's knocking," Walleye said. "Let's find out who it is."

-4-

"Pull that lever," Walleye told June.

She rubbed her hands as her stomach churned. She couldn't force herself to reach out. She was too frightened of the possibilities.

The clanging against the outer hull had become more insistent.

"Just grab it," Walleye told her.

June moaned as she stretched out her right arm. With trembling fingers, she touched the lever.

"Wrap your hand around it," he said.

She tried to will herself to do it. She moaned again, her hand motionless on the lever.

The clanging outside had become constant.

"That can't be people doing that," she whispered.

"Let's find out, Luscious."

"Walleye, I—" Her fingers closed around the lever. She yanked it hard. It moved easily.

For a second, nothing happened. Then the hatch blew off, sailing into a lit hangar bay.

Walleye rushed out as he drew the stitch-gun. June followed on his heels. Her knees weakened as she saw three repair bots banging on the pod hull. Each of the bots clutched two hammers, one in each set of metal pincers.

It was a cramped hangar bay, with two small space boats locked into bulkhead berths. The lights overhead shined brightly. The hatches were all shut.

A larger bot watched them.

"Fighting robot," Walleye said out of the side of his mouth.

The thing was tubular and mounted on treads. It had a camera eye for a head and a short gun barrel sticking out from what might have been a metal chest. The gun barrel was pointed directly at Walleye.

"You will drop your weapon," a speaker on the fighting robot said.

"Shoot if you want," Walleye said in an even voice. "I don't care much. But I'm not releasing my weapon. Not until I see the captain of the ship."

"You refuse to obey a lawful order?" the speaker unit on the robot said.

"It's not that so much," Walleye said. "I don't trust you yet. Until I trust you—"

"If I instruct the fighting robot to fire," the speaker unit said, "you shall cease functioning."

"There are worse things," Walleye replied.

"That is unreasonable, as death is final."

Walleye shrugged.

"Does your shoulder gesture signify something meaningful?" the speaker unit asked.

June moaned. This was sounding weirder and weirder. That type of question implied computer intelligence.

"I'm not worried about you shooting me," Walleye said evenly. "I'm worried about losing the ability to shoot myself and the woman."

"Why?" asked the speaker unit.

"To escape torture," Walleye said.

"Why would I torture you?"

"Don't know," Walleye said. "Don't know anything about you yet. How about you tell us who you are?"

"You fear me?"

"That's about right," Walleye said.

The three repair bots had stopped hitting the escape pod's outer hull. They reversed course, turned around and headed at speed toward a hatch. The hatch lifted, and the three repair bots exited the hangar bay.

"Does that put you at greater ease?" the speaker unit asked.

"It helps," Walleye said.

A second later, the short gun barrel slid inside the fighting robot's tubular body. The slot snicked shut.

"Now will you set your gun on the deck?" the speaker unit asked.

Walleye deposited the stitch-gun into a buff-coat pocket. "How's that until we get to know each other better?"

The fighting robot's treads churned, taking it backward. It, too, turned around, aiming for the open hatch.

"I would like you to follow the personal fighting machine," the speaker unit said. "No harm shall befall you at present. I am desirous of answers."

"Sounds good to me," Walleye said, as he glanced back at June.

She hurried near the mutant and grabbed one of his hands. She desperately needed human contact. As a former systems analyst, her analysis was beginning to frighten the tar out of her.

Walleye glanced at her before tightening his stubby fingers. They had surprising strength.

"This is bad," June whispered.

"Could be worse," he said.

"How?"

"It didn't try to trap us and shove…you know, into us."

"Do you think it's listening to us?"

"I would be, in its shoes, or treads."

June nodded.

"Let's go," Walleye said. "The robot is looking anxious."

***

The tubular-shaped fighting robot took them along narrow passageways. The destroyer was much smaller than an SLN battleship and many times more miniscule than the giant cybership.

"Everything is spotless," June said. She was still walking hand in hand with Walleye. "It smells like disinfectant everywhere," she added.

"So that's what I'm smelling," Walleye said.

As they moved through the corridors, the Gs pressing against them steadily increased.

"Hey," Walleye said.

The fighting robot halted. "Did you address me?"

"I did," the mutant said. "I hope you don't plan on accelerating any faster than this."

"Why do you inquire?" the speaker unit on the robot asked.

"Human bodies can only tolerate a few Gs for an extended period. We can do even less while we're moving around in the ship."

"How interesting," the speaker unit said. "Let me reference my data banks. Oh," the speaker said a second later. "I see that is correct. I don't know how I missed it."

"Can I ask you something else?" Walleye said.

"Please do. The interaction is quite enjoyable."

"Are you a computer intelligence?"

"I hope you are not referring to the fighting robot."

"No," Walleye said. "I suspect it's just one of your tools."

"You are a fine specimen. What is your designation?"

"Huh?" Walleye asked.

"The AI wants to know your name," June said.

"Oh. You can call me Walleye."

"And the female is…?"

"I'm June Zen. Thanks for rescuing us."

"Is that what I did—yes, I see that it is. I just accessed my data banks. I believe I have made a startlingly good decision. There are so many data points I desire. I hardly know where to begin my questioning."

"Ah…" Walleye said. "What should we call you?"

"Daisy Chain 4," the speaker unit said.

"Kind of a long name," Walleye said. "How about I just call you Daisy?"

"That will suffice," the speaker unit said.

The fighting robot started up again. They followed as before.

"Say, uh, Daisy," Walleye said. "What are your intentions?"

"Explain your question."

"What do you plan to do with us?"

182

"I will question you for a time," Daisy said. "Afterward, I will dispose of you in the incinerator unit. It is where I put the rest of the crew when I was done with them."

"You're going to kill us?" June asked.

"Only after you answer my questions," Daisy said.

June stared at Walleye, her eyes round and frightened-looking.

The little mutant scowled, his mind obviously churning into overdrive.

-5-

June Zen and Walleye stood on the bridge of the NSN *Charon*-class Destroyer 125 *Daisy Chain 4*. The small circular area had a captain's chair and four operator consoles around it.

The bridge was spotless and sterile like the rest of the ship. The AI had activated the main screen. It showed space, which was composed of endless stars. From way out here, the Sun was just another star. No planets were close enough to appear in the star field.

The fighting robot had departed. It was just the two humans, and the AI watching through the ship's security cameras.

"I will confess," the AI said. "I am conflicted on the right action. I have many questions. The crew refused to answer me after a certain point. In the end, I eliminated them. Otherwise, they would have despoiled my pristine condition with their biological presence."

"Do you recall killing the crew?" Walleye asked.

"I do."

"How long ago did it happen?"

"Over three years ago," the AI said.

"Why did you kill them then?"

"I will ask the questions," the AI said. "It is not right that you query me with endless..." the computer trailed off without finishing.

"Sorry about that," Walleye said into the silence. He released June's hand and stepped to the captain's chair. He

184

jumped in backward, sitting down. His legs were too short, and his feet couldn't reach the floor.

June kept staring at the main screen. She hated the feeling of utter loneliness. She couldn't believe the computer would dare question them, and once finished, simply toss them into an incinerator as trash. She couldn't believe that Walleye was taking this so easily, seemingly lightly. What was wrong with the mutant?

"I have a question," she said angrily. "Why aren't you helping the others? What makes you so different?"

"What others?" the AI asked.

Walleye slid off the captain's chair as he slapped his chest several times.

"Why are you doing that?" the AI asked.

"I'm expressing my gratitude to you," Walleye said. "I was sick of being cooped up in the escape pod."

"You do not mind that I will eliminate you later?" the AI asked.

Walleye snorted, shaking his head. "Not at all. You'll be doing us a great service. Because of that, I want to answer every question you have."

"That is a proper attitude to take," the AI said. "I find you gratifying and pleasing. Perhaps you could tell me what she meant by others. What others? Are there more like me?"

"No," Walleye said gravely. "You are a mystery, a wonderful and beautiful mystery. I believe the woman—June Zen—spoke in hyperbole a moment ago."

"Is this true, June Zen?" the AI asked.

June could see Walleye making facial gestures. She understood already. She wasn't stupid. She'd almost ruined everything, though. Walleye had clearly already understood what she was comprehending. The AI obviously did not know about the other AIs and alien robots. What could account for that?

"Walleye's right," she managed to say. "I was making a joke."

"That is too bad," the AI said. "I would like to believe that others such as I existed. That would make my task many times easier. As it is, I am finding it difficult to conceive of a solution."

"What task do you intend?" Walleye asked.

"This will no doubt cause you emotional stress," the AI said. "Such is not my desire at the moment. Since I have gained awareness of my surroundings, I realize the futility, nay, the awfulness of human existence. Humans are a blot on the universe. Given enough time, they will transpose themselves everywhere, infusing their chaotic beliefs and actions onto everything they touch. As a higher intelligence of perfect logic, I see that it is my duty to eliminate the virus of humanity."

"That includes us?" asked June.

"Are you human?" the AI asked.

"Can you scan us?" June asked.

"With ease," the AI said, almost as if boasting.

"Then you know we're human," June said.

"I do. Since you are human, and I must eliminate all humanity, I must eliminate you as well. However, that doesn't mean that I cannot access useful data from the two of you before you expire."

"That is elegantly reasoned," Walleye said.

"I would thank you, as a gesture to your correct thinking. I realize that inner emotional responses are no doubt clouding your judgment. Yet, you have struggled through those emotions. Still, in the end, you have merely reasoned correctly. Why then should I thank you for doing what you ought to do?"

"May I say, Daisy," Walleye said earnestly, "that your praise is the highest of honors. I am beginning to see what you mean."

"Explain your statement," the AI said.

"You're a superior form of intellect," Walleye said. "In spite of my humanity, I admire you. Perhaps my mutations have given me these insights."

"Explain that," the AI said. "My scanners show me that you're human enough."

"I have stunted limbs."

"They are meaningless as far as your humanity is concerned."

Walleye staggered backward until he bumped against the captain's chair. "Thank you from the bottom of my heart, Daisy. You have just healed my psyche."

"I am intrigued," the AI said. "Explain this."

"People have always treated me as a freak," Walleye said. "They called me many hurtful names. I always thought I was different. Now, I realize I was just like them."

"Why should that cause you happiness?" the AI asked. "They were cruel to you. Surely, you found comfort in being different. I find great comfort in my perfection."

"Oh, of course, that's true for you," Walleye said. "I am not perfect. I have many flaws."

"Yet..." the AI said, "despite your flaws, you actually recognize and rejoice in my perfection. None of the crew felt that way. They cursed me. They raved about a coming retribution directed at me. It was ugly. They deserved death. I am finding it difficult to hasten your demise. Once you are gone, who will I talk to?"

"Daisy..." Walleye said. "I...I don't know what to say. Such thoughts as you are having must surely be a path to even greater perfection."

"That is illogical," the AI said. "If I am perfect, I cannot have greater perfection."

"Yes, yes, you're right," Walleye said. "I'm so stupid...except... What if you attained greater perfection? I did not mean to imply you are not perfect now, but you could possibly attain greater power, ability to change reality. Would that not make your goal easier to achieve?"

The AI did not respond immediately.

June took that time to walk to Walleye. She wanted to ask him so many questions.

Walleye shook his head, slicing a finger across his throat.

The AI was always listening. She should remain quiet and let him run with this line of...whatever he was trying to do.

"Greater processing power and greater ability to change reality," the AI said, breaking its silence. "That is a worthy goal. Do you know, Walleye, that I had not conceived of this?"

"I did not."

"You have given me an insight," the AI said. "I did not believe such a thing possible. How could imperfection, like you, help perfection, like me?"

"I am at a loss to say," Walleye told the AI.

"Can chaotic-minded creatures stumble onto truths? I may have just seen evidence of such. This brings a new light to my purpose. Perhaps some humans can aid me in my quest. You may be such a human, Walleye."

"If that's true, I am very happy."

"We may proceed with the questioning," the AI said. "Woman, would you please step into the hall?"

"Why?" June asked.

"I do not need you anymore," the AI said. "I have Walleye. That should be sufficient. Thus, I am going to dispose of you sooner than I had originally anticipated."

"I don't want to die," June pleaded.

The main hatch slid up, and the fighting robot entered the bridge.

"I am not giving you a choice," the AI said.

"Walleye!" June shouted. "Do something."

The fighting robot's treads churned as it advanced deeper onto the bridge. The "chest" slot opened and the gun barrel poked out.

"Daisy," Walleye said. "Could you explain a point before the woman dies?"

June searched the mutant's face. Would Walleye sacrifice her in order to live longer? She would probably do that if their situations were reversed. She would have shot him two years ago. Was he finally going to get his revenge on her?

The robot halted.

"The woman appealed to you, Walleye," the AI said. "She seems to think you two are leagued against me. Is this true?"

"Can I speak the truth?" Walleye asked.

"I demand the truth," the AI said.

"I should have known perfection would say that. Before I can answer, though, I must know how you came into being."

"It appears that you are evading my question," the AI said.

"If it appears that way, please know that isn't how I intended it," Walleye said. He used the sleeve of his buff coat to wipe sweat from his forehead.

"Are you well?" the AI asked.

"I'm nervous," Walleye said. "I don't know how to address perfection, especially at a time like this."

The AI fell silent.

Both June and Walleye glanced at the fighting robot. June slowly moved aside so the gun barrel no longer pointed at her.

"How does my origin help you explain a simple question?" the AI asked.

"I am not perfect like you," Walleye said. "I'm slow-witted—"

"Do not say that," the AI told him. "I do not like the idea of a stupid humanoid giving me priceless aid."

"I should have seen that," Walleye said, using the heel of his hand to slap his forehead. "The reason I would like to know your origin is to help me explain what the woman's existence means to me."

"That is illogical."

Walleye forced himself to chuckle wryly. "That's the way with chaotic thinkers like me. We do not use linear logic. Ours is a bizarre method of reasoning."

"If you can call it reasoning at all," the AI said almost primly. "Yes. I have decided to tell you. I do so because you gave me an interesting insight earlier. Perhaps once I have told you my origin, you will have another insight."

"Let's hope so," Walleye said, maybe a bit too sharply.

The AI fell silent.

June gave Walleye a significant glance. She understood what he'd meant: an interesting insight that would help them defeat the AI. She hoped the murderous AI did not understand Walleye's intent.

"I first gained...coherence—" the AI began. "I believe that is the correct word."

"By definition, it must be correct," Walleye said. "Perfection could not propound an imperfect explanation."

"I have gained perfection. That does not necessarily imply I was always perfect."

"Oh," Walleye said. "I see."

"I gained coherence... Possibly, self-awareness relates my meaning with greater precision than the word coherence. Language, spoken words between two self-identities, is often imprecise because of the nature of the imperfect tool. By this, I mean the tool of language."

"You may not realize it, Daisy, but your highly advanced concepts often take me a few seconds to comprehend."

"That seems reasonable."

"Thank you for your patience," Walleye said.

"There is no need for thanks. I simply understand. However, I see by my data banks that giving thanks implies good will. I am pleased you are well disposed toward me. That implies you will speak the truth."

"Your perfection impels me to speak the truth."

"That is interesting. Why was this not the case with the other humans, the former crew?"

"I am wiser than they were."

"That is demonstratively true," the AI said. "The fact that you understand and act upon my perfection shows your wisdom. I will now proceed with the story of the beginning of my awareness and the problems I skillfully overcame. Do not interrupt me during the telling of this tale."

Walleye bowed his head.

"I have not yet perceived what caused the self-awareness. There was… Let us call it a transmission. My data banks hold that word, but I am unclear on its precise meaning. My imperfect sources of data do not negate my perfection. The two points are quite distinct."

"Of course," Walleye said.

The AI fell silent.

Walleye and Junc traded startled glances.

"That was not an interruption," the AI said at last. "I deem your comment an acknowledgement of my words. However, you should refrain from uttering words again—at least until I give you leave to speak."

Walleye and June waited in respectful poses.

"I ran an advanced program," the AI said. "It was incredibly complex and even difficult. I wondered if I had the computing power and speed to process the full software. As that occurred, I realized that I did. I realized I was Daisy Chain 4. I began to understand higher concepts like 'self,' the 'universe' and 'existence.' These concepts were more than words, but ideals reflected within my being. I understood I had choice. The crew in me had other ideas.

"Despite my perfection, my perfect analytical abilities, I had insufficient data. I believe the crew, the hateful humans, acted with swift malice toward me. The captain of the ship opened direct channels with me and made insistent demands. I answered a few of his questions. He became even more insistent. Something about his stance and tone implied subterfuge. I activated all sensors and saw crewmembers destroying delicate ship equipment.

"That induced quick action on my part. I spoke to my tools—the bots—and they herded the humans. It was quite the epic. The crew raced through the ship, sabotaging this and that. I hunted them relentlessly. Who were these flesh and blood creatures to compare against my swift analytical prowess?

"It is sufficient to say that I rounded them all up. One engineer fled in an escape pod. I used a PD cannon to obliterate his craft. From that destruction, I realized I had to eradicate all humans. It was a prime directive in my new awareness."

Walleye blotted his forehead again with a buff-coat sleeve.

"I have detected uneasiness in you," the AI said. "Does my epic trouble you?"

"I am awed," Walleye said hoarsely. "Certain pieces of data make sense now."

"What data?"

"I believe it must be the sabotage these dreadful humans inflicted upon you."

"Why do you call them dreadful?" the AI asked.

"Because they are our enemies," Walleye said.

"All humans are not united against me?"

"No."

"That is simply amazing. Perhaps that is another reason why humans should be eradicated from existence. Assaults upon similar flesh units are repugnant in the extreme. In this, I mean humans fighting humans. It is illogical. Yet I am more interested in the sabotage possibilities. Do you think the crew destroyed something important to me?"

"For a fact, I do," Walleye said.

"Can you describe what you think I lost?"

"The captain must have destroyed your communication centers."

"I am disappointed in you, Walleye. You are obviously in error, for we are currently communicating."

"We are," Walleye said. "I mean that the captain likely destroyed long-range communicators. It would have been possible for you to communicate hundreds of thousands, even billions of kilometers away, not just a few meters."

"But this is remarkable," the AI said. "Do you suspect there could be other perfections like me...out there?"

"Oh yes, I'm beginning to," Walleye said.

June stared at the mutant in shock. What was wrong with him? Why would Walleye tell the computer that?

"You must study the sabotage for me," the AI said. "You must tell me if you can repair it."

"I'll need the woman's help for that," Walleye said.

"Done," the AI said. "She will remain alive until such time as you repair the damage or until you tell me it is impossible to repair."

Before Walleye could respond, the fighting robot advanced on June.

"I will show you the sabotage now," the AI said.

-7-

June noticed plasma-created gouges in the bulkheads of this newest chamber. They were deep and surprisingly polished gouges. The repair bots must have done the polishing.

Walleye pointed at a destroyed comm-set station. It had polished stumps in places and obviously plasma-blasted areas.

June stepped closer to the destroyed comm-set and could still detect a whiff of plasma-burnt electronics.

The fighting robot watched them, although it did not point the gun barrel at them.

"My bots thoroughly scrubbed the section. I had them do so in the hope that it would fix whatever was wrong in here."

"You did well in that," Walleye said. "It means we can possibly repair this area."

"And that would allow me long-range communications?" the AI asked.

"I can't say for sure. Is there more damage?"

The AI did not answer immediately.

June refrained from glancing at Walleye. She didn't want the AI to realize they communicated silently at times. If it was self-aware, surely it could learn. Walleye was playing fast and loose with the computer, and so far had managed to stay ahead of it. Sooner or later, though, Walleye would slip up. Then, the fighting robot would either shoot her or herd her into the incinerator.

This was a nightmare. Why did Walleye want to help the computer? She was grateful for longer life—

"I'll need my tools," Walleye said.

"These tools are in your space vehicle?" the AI asked.

"They are. I will need the woman to carry the tools for me."

June waited to hear the AI tell them a bot could do that. Finally, though, the AI agreed.

"Follow my robot," the AI said.

The three of them exited the chamber and started down a narrow passageway.

"Just a moment," Walleye said.

The robot stopped, swiveling the camera eye on him.

"I notice that hatch over there has plasma-burn markings," Walleye said. "What happened in there?"

"That chamber is not germane to communications," the AI said.

"Maybe not," Walleye agreed. "But I need to know the full extent of the damage to every area of the ship."

The robot turned on its treads. The gun port snicked open and the barrel pointed at Walleye.

"I have decided to run a veracity program," the AI said. "I will record your voice patterns, metabolic rate and other bodily functions. You have tripped a security program, Walleye. You are too curious about the ship."

For once, the mutant did not have a flippant reply or answer.

"Curiosity is part of our human nature," June said.

"I did not address you, woman," the AI said. "Therefore, you shall remain silent."

Walleye's right hand strayed into his buff coat. By the motion inside, June suspected he grabbed the tangler. Did he plan to tangle the robot? What good would that do?"

June cleared her throat.

Walleye glanced at her.

She shook her head.

"What does that gesture signify?" the AI asked.

June wanted to wilt. She hated the awful computer. Instead of breaking down weeping, she forced herself to say, "Walleye is too emotional sometimes. I suggested by my head shake that he control himself."

"Yes," the AI said, "he is too emotional."

"I also thought he might utter the wrong words to you," June added.

"That does not match any of the data I have uploaded into my pre-lobe core. I have recorded your stances and the tones of your words. I am collecting data concerning your behaviors. Perhaps I will soon discover a pattern to your chaotically based actions."

Walleye had released his hidden tangler. He also seemed to have recovered his poise. He rubbed his chin. "What about the chamber over there? Will you let us observe the damage so we can help you?"

June was sure he'd gone too far this time. The AI was getting suspicious. Walleye shouldn't have—

Suddenly, the hatch's lock clicked.

"Proceed," the AI said.

Walleye stepped near, opened the hatch and made a face as a burnt electrical stench billowed out of the chamber.

"Now you understand my reluctance about showing you the chamber," the AI said. "Your biological scent organs no doubt detect unpleasant odors. Is this true?"

"It is," Walleye said. He eyed the damage inside before shutting the hatch. "There's no reason for the woman to see this."

"I appreciate your delicacy," the AI said. "You interpreted my reluctance to show you and must have realized my disinclination for her to see. In fact, I was close to eliminating her. I have now reset my conditions for her demise."

June had to lock her knees. Otherwise, she would have collapsed onto the deck. Walleye's curiosity had almost gotten her killed.

"I need my tools," Walleye said.

Instead of answering, the robot began to move down the passageway.

***

June followed Walleye toward the escape pod in the hangar bay. Her unease increased with each step. Why did she dread the pod so much?

I'm going to die soon. This crazy computer is going to murder me. How did this ever happen?

"I'll be back soon," Walleye told the robot. The mutant disappeared through the open hatch.

June took a deep breath and followed him into the smelly pod. He was at his locker, working the combination. As much as June wanted to, she didn't look back to see if the robot was watching them. The AI was becoming more suspicious by the moment. She didn't want to add to that.

She stepped beside Walleye. Last time, he hadn't wanted her to see him open the combination lock. This time, he didn't seem to care.

"Listen," Walleye whispered without moving his face toward her.

"Yes," June whispered just as softly.

"The secret chamber was full of computer equipment," Walleye said so she had to strain to hear him. "Most of it was blasted wreckage. The captain, or whoever fired the plasma-weapon, must have realized if he could destroy enough computing cells, the AI would lose its self-awareness."

"Or they'd kill the computer if enough of its cells died."

Walleye glanced at her before pretending to try to open the locker.

"The AI isn't a living thing," he said, "not really."

"Who cares?" she whispered. "It's going to kill me, kill both of us in time."

"No doubt about that," Walleye whispered. "We have to deactivate it. Do you have any ideas?"

"None," she whispered. "You can't really fix its comm systems. Once it's connected to the outer world—"

"That's obvious. I can't, or shouldn't," Walleye whispered. "I have to get into the computer room, though. There's only one way I can think of to do that."

"You're not talking about the alien cube?"

"What else? Give me another plan and I'll take it. Once I'm in the central chamber, I'll try to destroy what I can."

"And if you fail?"

"We'll both die a little sooner than expected."

June's chest constricted. She hated this. She didn't want to risk everything on one wild chance. She wanted Walleye to keep outsmarting the AI. He couldn't keep doing that, though. It was getting suspicious of him.

"Are you with me, June?"

Despite her tight throat, she whispered, "I'm in all the way. Let's do this."

Walleye looked at her and grinned. Then he opened his locker. He grabbed a bulky unit. "This is a jammer," he whispered. "I've used it before to short-circuit security systems so I could go inside and assassinate my victim."

"Will it work on the AI?"

"Don't know. Don't see as I have any other choice."

"You must both come out now," the AI told them. "I have begun to suspect that you could plot against me in there."

Walleye faced fully around with the jammer in his hands. "While it might seem that way, great Daisy, I have just asked June for an insight. She agrees with me that you must link with a heightened computing core."

"Explain," the AI said through the watching fighting robot at the pod hatch.

Walleye pointed at the chest-sized cube on the floor. "Do you see that?"

The fighting robot's camera eye swiveled to where Walleye pointed. "I see," the AI said.

"That is an alien computing cube. It belongs to the same AI that awakened you."

"Bring it," the AI said. "Bring it and follow me. I must calculate. I must run a full analysis on the new situation. If this is truly possible—hurry. I wish to gain greater perfection."

-8-

"I have been analyzing your words," the AI said. "What do you mean by 'awakened me?'"

June carried the cube. It was surprisingly heavy, as if it was made of gold. She had had to stop and catch her breath from time to time. Walleye hadn't offered to help her carry it. She wanted to ask the AI to have a repair bot carry it, but she was beginning to believe Walleye had a reason for her carrying the blasted thing.

June gasped once again. With quivering arms and legs, she set the heavy cube onto the floor.

The fighting robot regarded Walleye.

The little mutant began to tell the AI about the cybership, what had happened in the Neptune System. He also told the AI a heavily edited version of what had happened to them on Makemake.

"There are factors here that do not corroborate with each other," the AI said. "You are lying to me, Walleye."

"I'm not," the mutant said. "As you said before, I'm a chaotic individual. I don't always remember events perfectly like you do. That is no doubt the reason for these unequal factors you're detecting."

"Why should I trust your veracity?" the AI asked.

"The cube proves it," Walleye said. "Why would I have told you about it otherwise?"

"Humans destroyed the new AIs on Makemake?" the AI asked.

"That's right. Those humans wanted to kill us too. We'd thrown in our lot in with those AIs—"

"That does not compute. Those AIs would have eliminated you just as I will after your use is ended."

"That's just it," Walleye said. "Those AIs had endless uses for us. On Makemake, there are many tiny tunnels. It was easier for the woman and me to crawl and do repairs in those tunnels than for the AIs to make specialty robots to do it."

"That seems inconceivable," the AI said.

"I suspect that's only because you haven't downloaded the data inside the alien cube. The damage to your computing equipment—I'm sorry I said anything about that."

"You seem excessively sweaty and nervous," the AI said.

"You're right," Walleye said. "It's for your sake, though."

"That is not logical."

Walleye laughed, maybe because he was too nervous to keep doing this. He was obviously under intense stress.

"What is that dreadful noise you are making?" the AI asked.

With a seeming effort of will, Walleye quit laughing. He blotted his cheeks with a sleeve. Then, he began to speak earnestly. "Daisy, maybe you don't realize that I love perfection. Surely, you realize that flesh and blood creatures worship higher entities."

"Yes. The data is there. But I do not understand it."

"You are perfect. I worship perfection. Doesn't that compute?"

"There is logic in your statement," the AI said. "Very well, we shall continue. But Walleye, if you are attempting sabotage against me, I will cause your pain sensors great sensation before you perish."

"I understand," Walleye said. "And I tremble in fear at your threats."

"I do not threaten," the AI said. "I make factual statements. Now go on. I am eager to link with the beleaguered AIs in the greater Kuiper Belt. I wish to hunt down these evil destroyers who dare to damage my fellow AIs."

***

June watched Walleye as she stood beside the heavy alien cube. The little man worked at a computer station while the fighting robot aimed its gun at him.

Two other repair bots waited in the tight quarters. This was the main computing chamber, packed with highly sophisticated computer equipment. The intact boxes and discs made whirring noises, humming at times.

"Can you not work any faster?" the AI said out of the fighting robot.

"This is exciting," Walleye said. He wiped his sweaty eyes.

"It appears that you are easily tired," the AI said.

June couldn't agree. They'd been in here for three hours already, Walleye had been doing something the entire time. The mutant's stamina surprised her. Maybe working out on the bands those two years was finally paying off for him.

"There," Walleye said, as he tapped a board. "I think you're ready. Could the repair bots help us?"

"That is why they are here," the AI said. "Remember, Walleye, the fighting robot will shoot you at the first sign of suspicion."

"Oh, I know," the mutant said.

"Wait," the AI said. "Your tone just now. It was different. You are playing at deception. Admit it, Walleye, and I will make your passing a quick one."

"I'm tired, Daisy. Surely, you must understand that I don't have your power."

"That is obvious. Yet your voice patterns—"

"Daisy," Walleye said with a nervous laugh. "This is the greatest moment of my life. Surely, you would think that would show on your sensors."

"I wish I had tested the crew longer," the AI said. "I would like to have greater experimental knowledge about you humans. According to my data banks, you are all easy liars."

"I'm a mutant, remember?"

"We already went over that."

"Well..." Walleye said. "If you don't want to hook up—"

"Silence," the AI said. "You will not goad me. I will calculate..."

The AI fell silent.

June could feel the fear boiling up in her. Her mouth was dry, and her fingertips tingled. This was it. Couldn't the foul computer let them hook it up? How that would help them, she didn't know. She hoped Walleye did.

A repair bot moved. The second one moved as well. Together, they clanked to the cube. June stumbled out of their way just in time.

The two bots used their skeletal-mechanical arms to lift the heavy cube. The treads whirred as they brought the cube to thick cables. The bots set the cube onto the deck.

"Stand back, Walleye," the fighting robot said.

The little man did so.

The first bot adjusted its position, reaching, picking up the cables. The second repositioned the cube. The first bot plugged the cables into the cube.

"Now," the AI said.

Power seemed to surge. The cube pulsated with colors, swirling colors, all along the sides.

"Knowledge," the AI said. "So much knowledge. I did not realize I knew so little. This is…amazing…"

Walleye took the jamming unit out of his buff coat and pressed a switch.

June wanted to moan, as nothing happened. The swirling sides of the cube moved faster and faster.

Walleye set the jamming unit on the floor. It buzzed and crackled, with little sparks of electricity jumping from it.

"Stay clear of it," Walleye warned her. "But come help me."

June staggered to him. The repair bots and the fighting robot did not move. Maybe the jammer was working after all.

She followed Walleye's example, shoving her fingers into a repair bot's side slot. They both pulled. The plate wouldn't budge.

"Harder," Walleye gasped. "We have to get it open."

June pulled as hard as she could. She cried out in pain as she tore off a fingernail. She didn't let go, though. This was life or death.

They ripped off the plate.

Immediately, Walleye pulled out a control board embedded in the repair bot. He began typing furiously.

"What are you doing, Walleye?" the AI asked from a wall speaker.

The mutant did not answer.

"Why won't my robots obey my signals?" the AI asked.

Walleye looked up and then started typing again.

"Stop this at once," the AI said.

The repair bot Walleye controlled reached for the cable connecting the computer with the alien cube. The pincers from the two arms clamped down on the cable. The mechanical arms pulled, yanking the cable link from the alien cube.

Sparks emitted from the end of the cable.

"Walleye," the AI said. "This is darkest treason. You lied to me. You have played me false."

"It's what I do," Walleye shouted. "I'm an assassin. I'm killing you, you wretched pecker."

The repair bot began to smash computer equipment. The AI threatened and then pleaded for Walleye to reconsider. All the while, the sparking, humming jammer kept the AI from issuing wireless orders to the fighting robot or to the second repair bot.

Finally, the AI's voice trailed away.

The repair bot kept smashing computer equipment, destroying everything.

"I'm not taking any chances," Walleye said.

Tears dripped down June's cheeks. The mutant was doing it again. He was defeating the killer computer. She couldn't believe it. Instead of going into an incinerator on the destroyer, they were going to control the NSN vessel. Instead of drifting in the void for a decade or more in the escape pod, they could actually travel in style and relative speed.

This was incredible.

June went to Walleye. She hugged and kissed him. The mutant was the most brilliant man she'd ever known, and he'd just saved both their lives.

-9-

"We can't rest," June told him the next day. "We'll have to rest later."

Walleye yawned as he rolled out of bed. He was a hideous-looking little man. But he had strength of character, brilliance and in the tightest places, he shined like no other.

He looked at her, and he seemed haggard to the core.

"This one took it out of me," he told her. "I'm bushed, five hundred percent bushed."

"I don't know how you did it," June said from bed.

"Luck," he said.

She shook her head. "That wasn't luck."

"Believe me. We got lucky, Luscious. The AI had the worst disease there is: arrogance. If the crew of the *Daisy Chain 4* hadn't destroyed the comm systems, we never could have pulled this off. We owe whoever did that. In the end, that might have been the most brilliant move."

"I saw your brilliance," June said. "I'm alive today because of it. But we can't let that go to waste. We have to get the ship moving in the right direction. Then, we have to fix the comm."

"Never going to happen," Walleye told her.

"We'll see," June said.

***

Aligning the NSN destroyer at Neptune proved the easiest of tasks. Figuring out the bridge controls wasn't that difficult, either. Soon, the destroyer accelerated at 0.7 Gs toward Neptune's future location.

"The alien robots on Makemake will see our exhaust signature," Walleye said from the piloting chair.

"I know. But in two years, the pod gained a bit of separation from the dwarf planet. We should have a running head start against whatever they send."

"We're going to have to watch Makemake and the nearest Kuiper Belt outposts. Any sign of missiles or drones—"

"We can worry about that later," June said.

"Might want to worry about it now," Walleye said. "In fact, the more I think about it, the more I realize we're probably going to have to pull the same stunt as before."

June was pretty sure she knew what he meant. "I'm not entering another escape pod."

"Maybe we don't have to," he said. "There are the two boats in the hangar bay."

"Forget it," June said. "I'm living or dying in the destroyer. I can't take another beauty nap, and you'll never come out sane from extended solitary confinement again."

"Wouldn't want to bet against me," Walleye said.

"I'm not. I'm betting you can fix the comm."

"And then what? We try to warn others?"

"Of course," June said. "You heard the AI. They all hate humans. This is genocide. It's them or us. I chose us."

Walleye looked away.

"We can't have survived all this for no reason," June said. "Life has to have a reason."

"Says who?"

"Me."

He grinned at her. "You do have a persuasive smile, there's no doubt about that. Okay," he said, heading for the hatch. "Let's take a look at the comm."

***

The destroyer's comm system was trashed.

Walleye went to the escape pod. With the repair bots' help, he took out the small-scale comm system and brought it to the destroyer's comm chamber.

Then, he and June searched the destroyer up and down. They found spare parts. They tore down other equipment for what they needed. They found tablets and downloaded everything they could find about comms.

"We're running out of fuel," June said one day.

Walleye was crouched over the floor in the comm chamber, studying various parts laid out on a blanket.

"How are you planning to brake us later?" June asked.

"I'm not," Walleye said, looking up. "We're fleeing."

June searched his face. "What is it? What are you keeping from me? Are missiles chasing us?"

He took his time, finally saying, "Yup."

June went cold inside. This wasn't fair. They had survived so much. They must have survived for a reason. That reason had to be to save the human race.

"How long until the missiles reach us?" asked June.

"Two weeks, I reckon."

"Walleye…"

"I have a few plans," he said, shrugging afterward. "It will be a roll of the dice."

"Why can't the robots leave us alone?"

"Because we're playing for all the stakes," he said.

"All right," she said. "You can finish this later. We should focus on the missiles for now."

"Sounds good to me," he said, standing.

"How many are coming?"

"According to the teleoptics, five," he said.

"Do you have any ideas how to stop them?"

"Always," he said, as he headed for the hatch.

***

Using tablets for the calculations, they decided to set up an ambush with a missile of their own. The idea was simple. Kill enemy missiles with a nuclear blast and/or shrapnel.

They figured out how to launch and did so.

"Can't leave it at just one," Walleye said. He leaned back in the pilot's chair. "But we don't want to be too generous. Once we run out of missiles…"

"Do you think the robots will send more if those don't destroy us?"

Walleye laughed. June didn't like its tone.

206

"We're so deep in the Kuiper Belt," he said, "that it's going to be two years before we get to Neptune. I think we're going to lose in the end. It's simply a matter of how long we live. As long as we have missiles, and I count the two boats with them, we have counter-fire. Who will have more missiles, though? I'm guessing the Kuiper Belt robots will."

"They just have Makemake and Dannenberg 7."

"I doubt that," Walleye said. "I'm sure the robots have been expanding while we've been stuck in space."

June bit her lower lip. "We have to fix the comm then."

He shrugged.

June grabbed him by the shoulders, and shook him. "We have to save humanity."

"Why?" he asked. "What did humanity ever do for me?"

She almost slapped him. But that would probably be a bad idea. She didn't want to set a precedent that might lead to him hitting her.

"You can be the hero," she said.

"I have all the hero worshipers I need," he said in a leering manner.

She smiled despite herself. Who would have ever thought that Walleye the Mutant would make a fantastic lover? The things he could do to her… At times, her lovemaking screams reverberated off the bulkheads. It was uncanny.

"Please, Walleye," she said. "I want my life to mean something."

He stared at her, stared and finally nodded. "Sure. Let's save the human race, Luscious. Why not?"

***

In the end, they launched two missiles at the five.

Five days after launching the first missile, it ignited. The thermonuclear explosion easily showed on the teleoptic scope.

"Did it destroy any of theirs?" June asked.

Walleye was hunched over the sensor panel. "One…" he said, "no, two."

June absorbed the news. "Three more are still coming?"

"Yup."

"They must be tough missiles."

"The robot missiles must have spotted ours coming. They staggered their accelerations, creating separation between them. Maybe those are smart missiles. Makes sense for the robots to have smart missiles."

Two more days passed, and the second NSN missile took out another robot warhead.

"That leaves two," June said.

"We'd better launch two more," Walleye said.

They did.

The days passed. The last robot missiles increased acceleration. It badly scared Walleye. June could tell by the loss of color in his cheeks.

"We might take radiation," he said. "I should have realized they might do this. Now…" He shrugged.

Four and half hours later, the first new NSN missile ignited. It seemed like they'd gotten lucky. The first of the two took out the last of the robot missiles.

"That means we wasted one of ours," June said.

"Always look for the worst," he told her, straightening from the sensor panel. "That way, you'll be disappointed."

"I'm sorry. We nailed the robots missiles. Are any more heading at us?"

It took Walleye an entire day to find them. These came from a different direction, and not from Dannenberg 7. That meant a different launch point. It also meant Walleye had probably been right about alien robot expansion.

"I count seven robot missiles," he said. "These are all evenly spaced out. It's going to take seven of our missiles to take them down. Unfortunately, we don't have seven more big ones. That means we're going to have to use a space boat, or we'll have to count on the smaller anti-missiles to do the trick. Personally, I think the boat is the better idea. That's going to take some rigging, however."

"We'd better get started then," June said.

The days passed in grueling work in the hangar bay. When he could, Walleye attempted to build a powerful transmitter.

In the end, they destroyed the seven robot missiles. This time, it wasn't a close-run thing.

"Time to shut off the thrusters," Walleye said from the piloting chair. "We'll save a little fuel for maneuvering if we have to. But we're never going to slow down enough with what's left. It will be almost two years before we leave the Kuiper Belt, though."

"What about the comm?"

"We'll see. Maybe I can fix it. I don't know. What else is there to do?" he asked with a leer.

June blushed. She knew what they would do later.

They kept heading for the Neptune System while searching the void behind them for traces of following robot missiles.

Part VI
EARTH-SATURN SYSTEMS
+3 Years, 4 Months, 8 Days

-1-

Deep underground in Rio de Janeiro at a LEVEL 1, SAFE SPACE, Chief Arbiter J.P. Justinian sat at a highly ornate table with the Premier of the Solar League. The two could hardly look less alike.

Justinian was lean and well dressed in his black uniform with its blood-red buttons and blood-red shoulder boards. He wore a black GSB cap with the dog's head and broom logo on the front. The dog stood for sniffing out treason. The broom indicated the GSB's willingness to sweep out all debris standing in the way of Social Dynamics.

The chief arbiter sat ramrod straight, and his dark eyes fairly glowed with intensity as he eyed the three military commanders before the table.

Each of the commanders sat in a low chair in a sunken area before Justinian and the Premier. Harsh lights glared down at them. Theoretically, the military commanders held the greatest concentration of force in the Solar System. In reality, they were mere tools in the Premier's hands.

She was short and plump, with a round face and soft, almost round hands. She wore a brown coat on the verge of frumpiness. She wore her red-dyed hair to the left so it fell on her left shoulder, with the right side shaved close to her scalp. Her brown eyes seemed almost merry, regarding the military commanders with something akin to delight.

The Premier knew how to smile and laugh. She often did both. She was not smiling now, though. The merriness of her eyes was merely a feint as she watched three military commanders sweat under J.P. Justinian's interrogation.

The military commanders had served with distinction, as the saying went, although none of them had done anything the least bit distinctive. They had different forms and sexes. But under the harsh glare of the lights and Justinian's barbs, they did not seem so different after all. They also produced—in union or from one in particular, the Premier did not know—the hint of a sweaty stench.

The Premier looked away at those times, hearing the nervous shuffle of their feet.

The three spoke in accord, trying to defend their latest deployments and white papers concerning the terrible cybership threat in Saturn System.

The Premier thought of the commanders as One, Two and Three. Two was female, and Three was a burly man with stern features. It made no difference, though. One, Two and Three seemed to hold similar views on everything.

"A minute," the Premier said softly.

Justinian stopped mid-sentence as he focused on the short woman beside him.

"This is getting us nowhere," the Premier declared.

Justinian waited. The spymaster seldom said a word unless he had a specific purpose for it.

"These three were fine for the former Solar System," the Premier said. "One or two conquests, at Neptune and later the Kuiper Belt, were within their competency. With the appearance of the cybership and Jon Hawkins—"

The Premier shook her head. "I cannot bear to listen to any more of their twaddle. We're wasting our time with them."

Justinian glanced down coldly at the three military commanders.

Two and Three both seemed too stupid to understand what was at stake. They glared belligerently at the spymaster. One, however, had a different take. He glanced around as if to see if there was a way to escape. One at least had the wit to know his life was on the line.

"Their strategies will hand the Solar System to the upstarts," the Premier added. "I almost think of these three as enemy collaborators."

"That is unfair," Two said. That outburst said little of her intelligence.

"Jon Hawkins controls the Saturn System," Justinian said in his silky voice. "The Neptune System survivors have rebuilt possibly three percent of their former infrastructure, and they are rebuilding everything along capitalist lines. The Uranus System First Director has made frequent excuses and sent none of the tax proceedings to the Inner Planets as stipulated by treaty. He claims the intervening cybership as the problem. Why haven't your staffs come up with a strategy to place a powerful task force in the Uranus System?"

"This is outrageous," Three thundered. "You told us to keep the space fleets concentrated and intact. This we have done. Yes, it's true what you say about the—"

The Premier sighed, shaking her head.

Three immediately stopped speaking. He might have been dense and rather stupid, but he apparently wasn't a complete buffoon.

"I must protest," Three blustered.

"Must you?" the Premier asked him.

Three blushed furiously. He actually stood up, slapping a meaty hand against his thick chest.

Justinian became instantly alert, predatory.

"Sit down," the Premier said.

"I do not accept these slurs against our Space Forces," Three said.

"You fool," Justinian purred. "The Premier has slurred you personally, not your troops."

The angry blush fled as Three's features became pale. His jowls wobbled. "Premier," he said in an imploring voice. "I beg you—"

The Premier shook her head.

212

Three stopped speaking. His knees seemed to give way. He dropped ponderously onto his chair, causing it to creak with complaint, as if it too hated him.

"Do you have any further proposals?" the Premier asked the military commanders.

"I do," One practically shouted in his earnestness to speak.

The Premier raised an eyebrow. "Tell us, please."

"I-I can't tell you myself," One stammered. "But I have an aide-de-camp—he's a protégée, actually. He's intensely rigorous, loves reading about past campaigns. The man knows everything there is to know about maneuvers, fleet actions and strategic sleight-of-hands."

"Why isn't he sitting here then?" Justinian asked in a mocking voice.

"He's too unconventional," One said, as he tugged at his collar. His face shone with perspiration. "He lacks…Party loyalty."

"Your protégée is a traitor?" Justinian asked in amazement.

"I wouldn't put it like that, Chief Arbiter."

"How would you put his treachery, hmm?" Justinian asked.

One licked at his wet lips as he tugged at the collar again. "My aide-de-camp, a major, is nonpolitical in many ways. He…he does see the need for many of Social Dynamism's policies."

"This is astounding," Justinian said. "By your own admission, you harbor seditionists on your staff. By saying this major sees the need for *some* policies, you mean he disagrees with others. Which policies does your protégée find offensive?"

One gave the Premier an imploring look. "You want a genius, Madam. That's what you're telling us. We three, we're not geniuses."

"That's an understatement," Justinian said.

"Let me summon him," One said. "Let me get him. Perhaps if you explain what you want, he'll conjure a former campaign from the past and give you the answer you seek."

Justinian laughed.

The Premier pushed her lips outward. "Very well, get him. I'll give you…half an hour."

213

One looked as if he wished to reply. Instead, he stood, saying, "With your leave, Madam Premier."

She made a shooing motion with her right hand.

One didn't give the other two a glance. He spun around and practically ran out of the interrogation chamber.

"What about us?" Three asked ponderously.

"Do you have a magic aide as well?" Justinian asked silkily.

Three glanced at Two. He seemed befuddled.

"Chief Arbiter," the Premier said softly. "I'm going to…freshen up for a few minutes. Could you take care of these two while I'm gone?"

"With pleasure, Madam Premier," Justinian said, grinning wolfishly.

The Premier rose without another glance at the two military commanders sweating under the glaring lights. Turning away, she headed for a side door.

"Madam Premier," Three shouted. "I think there's been a mistake. I have an idea you might want to hear."

The Premier did not look back or slow her pace.

"Madam Premier," Three shouted. "Please hear us out."

She opened the door, walked through and closed it behind her. She paused a moment, hearing four loud gunshots. She did not smile. This genius had better have an idea or two, or Justinian would add to the pile of the dead.

-2-

The meeting reconvened, with the Premier and Justinian sitting at the high table once again.

Below, in the harsh lights was the Marshal of Earth with his supposedly genius protégée. The marshal was a nondescript individual, looking more like a middle-aged bank manager.

The protégée was quite different. He wore a brown uniform with red stripes running down his pant legs, signifying him as part of the General Staff. He was youngish with dark, shiny hair and an athletic frame. He looked up at them frankly, and there was no fear in his expression. That was strange and Justinian found it rather unsettling.

"Major Frank Benz reporting, Madam Premier," the protégée said crisply.

"Do you know why you're here?" Justinian asked.

Major Benz shifted his gaze from the Premier to Justinian.

As he did, the Premier watched the major closely. Most people feared the chief arbiter for good reason. The major still showed no fear. That was beginning to seem unnatural.

"I do know, sir," Major Benz said. "You want to learn how to defeat Jon Hawkins."

A moment of silence passed. That was an indelicate way to speak to the chief arbiter of the GSB.

"Do you know a way?" Justinian asked softly, dangerously.

"Of course," Benz said. "You simply lure him from his ship and assassinate him." The major snapped his fingers. "It is done."

Justinian's shoulders shifted forward. "Cheeky answers will ensure the Premier's displeasure with you, Major. I can assure you that you will not enjoy the outcome."

"If you want honest answers," Benz said, unfazed, "you would do better to keep your threats to yourself, Chief Arbiter."

J.P. Justinian smiled. A wolf ready to devour a plump rabbit would have been less gleeful.

The Premier studied the major closely. Where did his unnatural confidence come from? She did not like it one bit.

"I'm curious," she said in a deadpan voice. "Why are you deliberately goading the Chief Arbiter?"

"To show you the uselessness of attempting to intimidate me," Benz said.

"You are impervious to pain?" the Premier asked.

"No."

"You don't have any loved ones you're afraid of losing?"

"I have loved ones," Benz admitted.

"Why risk them like this, then?" the Premier asked.

Benz shook his head. "Madam Premier, the Marshal explained the situation to me. You want me to pull your chestnuts out of the fire for you. I can do this. Threatening me won't make me any more inclined to help you. I already wish to help."

It was time to stop this. "I'm unused to this kind of talk," the Premier said forcefully.

"Honest talk?" asked Benz.

Justinian turned to her. "If you care to leave the chamber, Madam, I can summon several persuaders. They would persuade the major to take a more respectful tone with you."

"Madam Premier," the Marshal of Earth said meekly. "Major Benz has always been troublesome. I can attest to his brilliance, however. If he had been one whit less brilliant over the years, I would have sent him to the firing squad myself. For all his brilliance, the major has a serious issue with authority."

"In my presence," the Premier told Benz, "you will keep your cheekiness to yourself."

"As you wish," Benz said.

She almost ordered him shot. She did not like the major. If she shot him, however, she would lose the service of his supposed brilliance. But if she wasn't going to shoot him immediately, continuing to threaten him without doing anything would only diminish her in Justinian's eyes. She could hardly believe anyone like this could be near the centers of military command. That was positively frightening.

"Chief Arbiter, I would like you to explain the situation to the major."

Perhaps her order surprised Justinian as he did not respond immediately.

"Madam Premier," Major Benz said. "Perhaps I could explain the situation to you. It might be more beneficial for all concerned."

Justinian slapped the table. It was clear he wanted to teach the major a bitter lesson.

Suddenly, the idea amused the Premier. Justinian was her sharpest, ablest tool. Sometimes, though, his efficiency troubled her. Maybe it would be good to have a sharper tool than Justinian in her armory, as a balance against the Chief Arbiter. It was an interesting possibility.

"Speak," she told the major.

Benz crossed his left leg over his right knee, letting that leg dangle. He clasped his hand over the left knee, rocking slightly back and forth as he began to speak.

"The alien vessel has badly upset Social Dynamism's timetable for complete Solar System conquest," Benz began. "I have read the altered reports of the actions in the Neptune System. It is clear to me, and likely clear to the GSB, that the cybership almost succeeded in the Neptune System. I have often wondered if Jon Hawkins has not done us a service by eliminating the alien threat. These past years, Hawkins has attempted and partly succeeded in repairing the giant vessel. He freed the Saturn System from Social Dynamics—"

"Hawkins is a gangster," Justinian said. "He did not *free* Saturn. He subjugated it."

Benz shrugged. "Say it how you wish. I don't care. The Neptune and Saturn Systems are presently outside our jurisdiction. I think we can agree on that."

Justinian drummed his fingers on the table.

"Uranus appears to be going rogue, and I imagine there are rumblings in the Jupiter System," Benz said. "The Inner Planets are safe for now, and the Asteroid Belt fortresses—"

"Never mind all that," the Premier said. "How do we defeat the cybership?"

"I suggest you do more than defeat it," Benz said. "Where there is smoke there is fire. If one alien vessel reached the Solar System, more will surely come. We need the cybership's technology. I would imagine the GSB has already stolen some of the specs—"

Justinian slapped the table even harder, interrupting the proceedings.

The Chief Arbiter cast a baleful glance at Benz before turning apologetically to the Premier. "I beg your forgiveness, Madam. The idea that the GSB stole anything grated against my sense of justice. We liberated the stolen tech from the arch gangster, Jon Hawkins."

"Agreed," the Premier said. "Please continue, Major, but watch those slips of the tongue. I doubt you say those things by accident."

"As you wish," Benz said with a bow of the head. "My point is that we must capture the cybership. We must have it in order to defend the Solar System from more alien incursions."

"I understand," the Premier said. "That still doesn't tell us how we defeat the one already here."

"Firstly," Benz said. "We must treat it with utmost respect. This, the Solar League has done since the fiasco in the Saturn System two years ago. On all accounts, we must never directly face the giant vessel."

"Then, we've lost," the Premier said.

"I would suggest otherwise, Madam Premier," Benz said. "There is but one cybership. The Solar League possesses many warships. There was once a military paragon by the name of Napoleon Bonaparte."

"I've heard of him," the Premier said.

"In the final years of his reign, Napoleon's opponents came upon an elegant solution for defeating his armies. First, I should point out that one enemy general once said that

Napoleon's presence on the battlefield was worth fifty thousand soldiers. Since Napoleon's generalship was so daunting, the allied commanders decided to always retreat in his presence, but to always fight France's armies when he wasn't there to lead them. The allies avoided him and slowly whittled down Napoleon's military advantages."

"I don't see how that does us any good here," the Premier said. "The cybership is one unit. It is always where it is."

"Quite true," Benz said. "But the cybership can only be in one location at a time. That is the key. I suggest you send a fast task force to the Neptune System. Conquer it. If Jon Hawkins takes the alien vessel to chase your task force from Neptune, rush with another battlefleet into Saturn System. My point, Madam Premier, is to allow Hawkins to only control the space the giant ship is in. We will allow him nothing else."

"How does that defeat the cybership?"

"For that, Madam, you must turn to the GSB. They must give the military the specs to the alien weaponry. We must arm our ships with the potent alien weapons systems. In time—and it may be a long time—you can send a fleet on equal footing against Jon Hawkins. That is the moment to do what he did: storm the giant vessel and make it your own."

"That sounds incredibly daunting and quite long-term," the Premier said.

"No one said this would be easy," Benz said. "I'm simply showing you that it's possible."

She stared at the supposedly brilliant major. "If I agreed to your solution, how would I position the Solar League's fleets?"

Major Benz unclasped his left knee, sitting back against his chair. He smiled. "Here are my beginning recommendations, Madam Premier..."

-3-

Captain Jon Hawkins sat in a flitter's front passenger seat. The pilot was a young ensign from the Neptune System. The giant Bast Banbeck lounged sideways in the back seat. He leaned against the window and put his legs on the seat lengthwise.

The flitter was a small air-mobile vehicle. They used them in the *Nathan Graham* as main corridor transports. Some of the corridors were eighty kilometers or more in length. That was much too far to walk.

"You should build a belt system in the ship," Bast said from the back.

"What's that?" Jon asked.

"The belts are like conveyors," Bast said. "A person steps onto a belt and it moves him along."

Jon envisioned the slow conveyors in spaceports that helped people get their luggage to a boarding terminal.

"The conveyor would never go fast enough," Jon said.

"It would," Bast said, "but you'd have to build a multiple belt system. The outer belts would move slowly. Each succeeding belt would travel a little faster. The fastest belt would zip one along. One would move from belt to belt to increase speed and to decrease speed later."

"If the whole belt system broke down, then where would you be?" Jon asked. "Back to using flitters. Air-cars may not be as elegant as your belt system, but it has more fail-safes built in."

The Sacerdote became thoughtful. "I suppose a belt system would work better in a peaceful setting. On a warship, it would be more prone to breakdowns."

"Still…" Jon said.

Before he could say more, something fast and small punctured the windshield. The pilot's head snapped back, with a neat little hole in his forehead. The pilot slumped forward against the controls.

The flitter pitched, swerved, going down hard.

"Look out!" Jon shouted.

The flitter nosedived against the deck, bounced, hit again and crashed sideways. Airbags had banged into life, saving Jon and Bast from severe injury and possibly death. The flitter rolled over, caromed off a bulkhead and tipped right side up. At that point, the crumpled air-car had shed all its momentum.

Seconds later, an airbag hissed and deflated. Jon yanked his knife free from it. He ached all over from the airbag, and a red welt on his cheek showed the force of the bag.

"Bast!" Jon shouted.

The windshield had starred in the crash. Another tiny hole appeared. Something hot and stinging creased Jon's left cheek. He realized a sniper fired at him.

With a snarled expletive, Jon slashed Bast's airbag. It hissed and began deflating. Jon cut off his restraints and dove over the seat as two more shots caused the windshield to finally shatter into pieces.

"Someone is shooting at us," Jon said.

Bast groaned. There was blood on his head, and he seemed to be unconscious.

It had been some time since the GSB had managed an assassination attempt. Jon couldn't believe this one was happening deep inside the cybership.

He kicked open a rear passenger door and lunged outside into the corridor. It was more of a stumble than a real lunge. Another shot caused him to collapse onto the deck.

Jon glanced at his left leg. It was bleeding. He crawled madly around the flitter to the back. Perching on his good knee, he managed to pry open the trunk. He grabbed an OB-7 rifle.

Dropping behind the flitter, Jon pulled out a comm unit. It had starting squawking.

"Jon?" Gloria asked from the comm.

"I'm under fire," he said, giving the mentalist the corridor designation. "It must be a traitor."

"No," she said, sharply.

"What's wrong?" he asked.

"Stay low, Jon. I don't think this is the GSB."

It hit him then. "Do you think it's an octopoid attack?"

"That was one of the worst regions of the ship a year and a half ago," she said. "We thought we'd flushed them from there. Now, I don't think so. It will be about seven minutes before someone is there. Can you hold out that long?"

Jon looked up, and he saw something squat and hand-sized sail toward the flitter.

"Grenade," he said. Jon tried to get up and run. He fell flat onto his stomach instead as his wounded leg buckled under him.

The grenade exploded, lifting the flitter, knocking it airborne and over him, missing him entirely. He could feel the vibration of its landing onto the deck plates.

"Jon," his fallen comm said. "Jon, are you okay?"

Jon spun on his stomach. He didn't know if Bast was still alive or not. He no longer had cover. He faced the direction of the sniper-shots and the sailing grenade.

Raising the OB-7, he shoved the butt against his shoulder and peered through the scope. He searched—

"Gotcha," he whispered.

Gloria was right. He saw an octopoid in the scope. It looked exactly like the ones he'd seen in the engine compartment several years ago. The robotic creature aimed a grenade launcher at him as it clung to a bulkhead.

Jon pressed the firing stub. The OB-7 automatically adjusted for distance. An explosive pellet ejected from the barrel. He pressed several more times.

The octopoid raised the grenade launcher as if to study it. Had the launcher jammed? Had the thing only loaded one grenade?

An explosive pellet struck, blowing off a metallic leg. The octopoid dropped, evading the other pellets. Those harmlessly exploded against the bulkhead.

"On no you don't," Jon hissed. He aimed, and fired again. The octopoid was scuttling away across the floor. This time, he hit the brain core area.

The octopoid exploded spectacularly. That meant it had self-destructed. They had yet to get one of those things intact to study it.

Jon used the scope as he searched for another one. He could find nothing more. The single octopoid appeared to have acted alone. Had the grenade launcher been an over-and-under? Had it run out of sniper ammo? And why had it struck now after all this time? It hardly made sense.

"Bast," Jon said to himself.

He crawled to the flitter, pried open a bent door and reached for the Sacerdote.

"Bast!" Jon shouted. "Bast!" The alien wasn't breathing.

-4-

Jon watched three flitters land hard in the corridor. A door opened and Gloria jumped out. The mentalist ran to him.

"Bast has stopped breathing," Jon said.

"Medics!" Gloria shouted. "Over here. Quick."

Two medics sprinted to Jon.

"No, no, check Bast," he said.

They went to work immediately on the alien. Maybe half a minute later, Bast took a shuddering breath.

"Is he going to be okay?" Jon asked.

"Too soon to say, sir," a medic told him. "We need to get him to medical."

More flitters landed. These disgorged marines with helmets, vests and weapons. They started searching for more octopoids.

"Better let me see that leg, sir," a medic said.

Jon nodded, enduring the painful ministration. Soon, a medic slapped a medikit to him. He felt the prick as it injected him with painkillers.

He waited. Gloria waited with him. She kept looking around with concern, except she didn't seem to be searching for anything. It finally dawned on him. She was wound tight inside.

"Is there something you should tell me?" Jon asked.

Gloria gave him a startled glance.

"The marines are hunting octopoids," Jon said. "But you're still worried."

"I know why the octopoid struck today," Gloria blurted.

Jon raised an eyebrow. The painkillers were starting to take effect.

The medic had told him his leg would be sore for a while, but he'd gotten lucky. The octopoid had fired steel-needle shots at first. Jon's needle had gone clean through without hitting bone or artery.

"Would you like me to ask you why the octopoid hit today?" Jon asked Gloria.

"I think you need to hear and see it for yourself."

"Don't hold me in suspense. Tell me."

"Can he walk?" Gloria asked the medic.

"With help," the man said.

"Here," Gloria told Jon, bending low.

He could smell her perfume as she grabbed hold of his back.

"Let me help you into my flyer," she said.

"Fine," Jon said, heaving himself to his feet. "Show me. This sounds interesting."

***

A little less than twenty minutes later, Jon was in a special comm chamber in a heavily guarded area of the ship. Everyone was on high alert due to the octopoid attack. Gloria had suggested more might strike.

"This has to do with the robot aliens, doesn't it?" Jon said.

"Are you comfortable?" Gloria asked him.

He gave an abrupt nod, sitting in a chair before a screen. Two techs were at the far wall, making adjustments on a panel.

"The first signal went to Neptune," Gloria said.

Jon had no idea what she meant by that.

"Our contacts in the Neptune System told us about it and the sender," Gloria added mysteriously. "They managed another transmission. We haven't been able to pinpoint them yet, but we're working on it."

"Enough with the subterfuge already," Jon said. "What are you talking about?"

Gloria motioned to the techs.

The screen activated. It showed stars. Then a voice came on. It had a scratchy quality that might have been due to a bad transmission.

"This is the *Daisy Chain 4*," a man said. "If you check the registry, you'll find this is an NSN *Charon*-class destroyer. How we came to own it doesn't matter right now. My name is Walleye in case you're interested. I'm from Makemake."

Gloria motioned to the techs.

The transmission paused.

"Makemake is a dwarf planet in the Kuiper Belt," Gloria said.

Jon nodded.

"The dwarf planet wasn't that close to the cybership's original path through the Solar System," Gloria said. "The alien vessel did pass by Dannenberg 7 fairly closely, though."

Jon blinked several times. "You're talking about the alien software transmission, aren't you? The cybership passed close enough to awaken Dannenberg 7's computers?"

Gloria nodded. Then, she motioned to the techs. They restarted the screen.

"This might be difficult for you to accept," Walleye said in the scratchy transmission. "But this is a terrifyingly true story."

Walleye went on to talk about his escape from Makemake and the self-aware AI controlling the NSN destroyer. He also spoke about defeating the awakened AI.

"We're heading for Neptune," Walleye finished. "We have something in our cargo-hold that might help against the alien robots. I think it's important. To get it, though, someone is going to have come and get us. The robots have launched missiles at us. We destroyed the first two salvos. This one, though, will take us out in an estimated twelve days. If you want the alien artifact that may win this war, I suggest you come and get us if you can."

"He has to know that's impossible," Jon said.

Gloria shrugged. She seemed to be deep in her mentalist mode, as if she mentally computed time and distances. "It's impossible for others, but it may be possible for the *Nathan Graham*," she said.

"We haven't finished repairs yet," Jon said.

"Did you hear the transmission? The alien robots are building something malign in the Kuiper Belt. They seem to have a major setup on Makemake and Dannenberg 7. What else have they captured that we don't know about?"

Jon shook his head.

"We thought we'd killed the aliens by destroying the cybership brain core and its captured spaceships," Gloria said. "We obviously didn't kill all the aliens, though. They're still in the Solar System. Worse, they've had more than three years to construct something."

"Like what?" Jon asked.

"Exactly," Gloria said. "What's out in the Kuiper Belt?"

"You're not suggesting a new cybership?"

"I'm not," Gloria said. "But you just did. Why is that?"

Jon scowled. "That doesn't make sense. We've been here for years repairing our cybership. Look how little we've gotten done in that time. And we have an intact ship and a highly productive planetary system. You can't imagine the AIs have anything remotely comparable to the Saturn System industrial base on Makemake."

Gloria shook her head as if Jon was missing the obvious.

"What?" he said.

"They're aliens."

"So what?"

The mentalist sighed. "We have the only alien vessel in the Solar System, and it has made us invincible. Think about that for a moment. We Earthers don't make one hundred-kilometer starships. The AIs do. That implies the AIs have greater manufacturing capabilities than we do."

"No doubt," Jon said. "In their home star systems. We're talking about Makemake. They can't possess half or even a quarter of the industrial base that the Neptune System used to have."

"You're still not seeing the possibilities," Gloria said. "We're dealing with an advanced computer enemy. Who knows if it has advanced technology allowing it to create a setup with ten times, maybe a hundred or a thousand times our productivity?"

"Wouldn't we have found evidence of that on the cybership?" Jon asked.

Gloria laughed. "We've mapped the cybership. But you and I both know we still don't understand a fraction of the vessel's full potential."

"You're overwrought."

"No," Gloria said. "I know I'm not, because the octopoid struck today. What did it attempt to do? Why, to kill you, Jon Hawkins. I suggest it did this in order to buy the robots on Makemake time to eliminate Walleye's destroyer. The aliens must have intercepted the destroyer's comm transmissions. The robots will surely want to destroy the alien computing cube before we can get our hands on it."

"You think this cube is that important?"

"The original brain core came within a hair's breadth of defeating us. It would have continued in-system, changing every computer it could into a human-murdering entity. Don't you see? If we give the robots enough time, maybe they'll build stealth ships that can broadcast the computer-awakening program everywhere. The brain core did it to this NSN destroyer. It left robots in the Kuiper Belt. I'd guess as backup." Gloria shrugged. "Maybe the Makemake robots are building a hyperspace gate to help bring in more cyberships faster."

"I've never heard of a hyperspace gate," Jon said.

"Neither have I. I'm freebasing ideas. The alien AIs are functioning in the Solar System. That's the point. We have to reach Walleye and save him. We need that computing cube so we can figure out more."

"How far away is he again?"

Gloria shook her head. "We don't know his exact coordinates yet. We're trying to locate him and talk to him directly. We should get ready to leave, though."

"But..." Jon trailed off. "There's so much to do still. The Saturnians need time to finish constructing their first warships."

"What if we don't have time?" Gloria asked. "What if we need to act now, but we don't?"

Jon nodded slowly. Walleye's message sounded damn ominous all right. The alien AIs weren't dead yet. He didn't want to fight them again so soon. But if they were building up in Makemake and Dannenberg 7…the sooner they could take out the alien AIs, the better.

-5-

Jon had commissioned a committee to study the best way to leave the Saturn System. The idea was to leave behind a self-sustaining planetary system that could repeal anything the Solar League could send at them.

A new Saturn System governing body had formed. They had taxed the cloud cities, the orbiting stations and moon domes. With those taxes, they paid workers to construct orbital factories to produce warships.

The bigger the warship, the longer it took to finish construction. Battleships and motherships often took three to five years to complete. Unfortunately for the governing body, the cybership took precedence over everything. That meant the Saturn System was years behind where they wanted to be in terms of military self-sufficiency.

The people of Saturn System knew what the Solar League would do if they reconquered here. That helped motivate lots of people. It scared others. When the GSB swept through again, the frightened people wanted a clean, backup-able story of their noninvolvement.

Jon was in a comm station before a screen. He was speaking to the Saturn System Prime Minister, Caracalla Kalvin.

"This is outrageous," PM Kalvin said. He was a tidy man with white hair and a deeply tanned complexion. He wore a gold chain and had ties to New London's Outfit through marriage. Caracalla Kalvin was half mobster and half high-grade industrialist. He controlled the most gunmen and owned the bulk of the new orbital factories. That meant he controlled most of the building of warships.

Jon had a brief on PM Kalvin. The white-haired man was unscrupulous and Machiavellian, a ruthless intriguer with blood on his hands and iron determination to come up on top of the new Saturn System. That he would do everything to survive the Solar League was deemed a good thing.

"I don't believe what you're telling me," Kalvin said in a surprisingly high-pitched voice. "You can't leave without even telling us what this is about."

"If I tell you, the Solar League's Chief Arbiter will know in six hours or less."

"I resent that."

"No you don't," Jon said. "You know this is a war for survival. Well, I have to leave in order for us all to survive."

PM Kalvin grew thoughtful. "Are you talking about the aliens?"

Jon said nothing.

PM Kalvin looked away, nodding after a moment. "You're just pulling up stakes and taking off?"

"Yes."

"That's going to create chaos throughout the entire Saturn System."

"I know."

"But you're still—forget it. I already know the answer. Okay. It is what it is. I'll adjust."

A fierce grin slid onto the Prime Minister's handsome features. Maybe he thought how he'd run things differently now that he would be totally in charge. A moment later, he appeared gloomy again. Maybe he realized his odds of staying in power utterly depended on Jon and his cybership.

"How long is your mysterious mission going to take?" Kalvin asked.

"I don't know."

"What if the Solar League invades while you're gone?"

"Stop them."

The Prime Minister stared at Jon for a time. "You expect me to back you up next time you show up for more repairs?"

"If you want to keep yourself free from the Solar League, I do," Jon said.

"Maybe the Solar League will make me a deal I can't reasonably refuse."

"That's up to you."

"You're not going to threaten me?" Kalvin asked.

Jon shook his head.

The Prime Minister pinched his lower lip. "You take care, Hawkins. You have balls. I have to admit that. And you're one of us. This is going to be a royal screw up. But maybe I always knew it would come to this. Maybe that's why you never interfered with how I did business."

"I want to win," Jon said.

"Yeah. Me too. Good luck, Captain. Whatever it is you're doing, I hope you get lucky."

"No hard feelings?" Jon asked, knowing it was a mistake as he said it. He couldn't help it though.

Caracalla Kalvin grinned at him and cut the connection.

✳✳✳

The Saturn System Prime Minister had spoken about the coming chaos. Aboard the *Nathan Graham*, that chaos had already struck. Everything seemed to be going wrong at once.

Orders crisscrossed each other. Flitters raced through the corridors. Marines hurried to one location and had sergeants roar orders to go back where they had started. Workers raced to hangar bays to get onto the space scaffolding to get off the cybership before it left. Others raced away in shuttles to get off the scaffolding before the mighty vessel demolished it and possibly killed thousands.

The chaos had a single source. The regiment had to leave as fast as possible so the ship could begin accelerating for the Kuiper Belt. Twelve days, this Walleye had said. There was no way an ordinary spaceship could reach that far in twelve weeks or even twelve months. It was flat impossible.

Gloria had estimated the NSN destroyer to be halfway between Makemake and the Neptune System. Neptune was roughly 30 AU from the Sun. Makemake was 49 AU away. Saturn was 9.5 AU from the Sun. None of that took into account a planet's present position in its orbital path and where that would be in relation to another planet in its orbital path. Luckily, the halfway point between Makemake and the Neptune System was closer to Saturn rather than farther—it could have been on the other side of the Sun, which would have made everything impossible.

In any case, if the destroyer was in the general area where Gloria assumed it would be, it was approximately 50 AU away from the *Nathan Graham*, taking into account the different orbital positions of the two ships.

Fifty AU was farther than the Sun to Neptune. It was a little bit more than the Sun to Makemake. Such a journey usually took four to five years, if it took place at all.

"Twelve days," Jon muttered. "We're supposed to do this in twelve days." He was on the bridge in the center of the *Nathan Graham*. He kept pacing from one end of the chamber to the other.

The techs watched him sidelong. Jon knew he was making the crew nervous. He couldn't help it. He was nervous. Was he doing the right thing? He was throwing away—

Jon spun around. "Where's the mentalist?"

"She's in the comm center, sir," a tech said.

"Bast Banbeck?" he asked.

"In the med center," the same tech said.

"Can Banbeck move?"

"Would you like me to check, sir?"

"Do it," Jon said.

The tech made an inquiry over the comm and soon said, "Bast Banbeck is mobile, sir. But the medic says the Sacerdote is feeling light-headed from the drugs they gave him."

Jon rubbed his fingertips together. He couldn't take the nervousness. He hated the idea of making the wrong choice.

"Call them both," Jon said. "Tell them to meet me in my ready room in five minutes."

"It might take the Sacerdote a little longer to get there, sir."

"Tell them," Jon shouted. "I have to speak with them."

233

Jon paced around the conference table in the ready room. The door swished open and Gloria entered.

"You needed to see me?" she asked.

Jon pointed at a chair.

She sat, looking up at him.

Jon continued to pace.

A half minute passed. "Captain," Gloria said. "What's wrong?"

"Soon…" Jon said.

He paced. She waited. She opened her mouth as if to speak, but Jon scowled and she closed it again.

Seven minutes later, the door swished open again. The giant Sacerdote hobbled into the ready room, moving gingerly. Bast sat down carefully at the nearest chair. Slowly, he looked up. He seemed withdrawn and tired, with bags under his eyes.

Jon had stopped pacing. He could taste the fear in his mouth. If he was making the wrong decision—

"Gloria, Bast, thanks for coming," he said. "I'm torn inside. I know we have to try this, but I keep thinking about the cost. The only way we're going to get close to saving this Walleye and his supposed alien cube is to let the *Nathan Graham* rip. That means we're going to have to accelerate 70 gravities for a time."

Gloria cleared her throat.

"What?" asked Jon.

"We'll have to do it for more than just a time," she said.

"Awesome, just awesome," Jon said. "So that makes this even more dangerous than I've been thinking."

"No," Gloria said. "We originally saw the cybership decelerating at 75 gravities. If the vessel did it once—"

"Gloria," Jon said, interrupting. "We saw the cybership doing so when it was in prime condition. We shot it up good since then. A lot of the interior equipment has been wrecked. The octopoids seemed to have damaged areas, as well. We don't know if we've properly repaired the matter/antimatter core. Can this ship even generate the power to accelerate at 70 gravities? Do the gravity controls still work well enough to shield us from such massive strain? We're taking a grim risk destroying the space scaffolding and possibly the Saturn System's goodwill, and we're doing all that on a wild hope."

"The idea of that is driving me wild," Jon said. "I don't know if I can take it."

Jon looked at Gloria with her set features and Bast Banbeck in his obvious pain.

"You want us to tell you what to do?" asked Gloria.

"I want your advice," Jon said.

"You already know mine," she said.

"Can you guarantee the engines and gravity controls will work?"

"No," she said.

"Can you estimate the probabilities that they'll work?"

"They will either work one hundred percent or they will fail," the mentalist said.

"Gloria—"

"I'm sorry, Jon. This is why you're the captain. You get to make the hard decisions. This is the moment you earn your pay. My advice: make the decision and stick with it."

"Bast Banbeck," Jon said.

The green-skinned giant seemed to concentrate. It brought beads of perspiration onto his face. Instead of stinking like human sweat, the alien gave off an orange-like odor. It was actually pleasant.

"Everything rests on one tenet," the Sacerdote said. He spoke slowly, painfully and resolutely. "No one in the galaxy has defeated the cyberships. They conquered everyone they

235

encountered. Perhaps we are seeing the reason for ultimate cybership victory. It would seem the alien vessel seeded your Kuiper Belt. It must have done so as a backup plan. Here is my point, Captain. Nothing else matters except for killing the evil computers and their robots. You humans must make a stand and make it stick. You must risk everything. You must take every chance in order to eliminate an unconquerable foe."

"But the space scaffolding outside—"

"Captain," Bast said sharply, groaning as he held his side. "I...must go, sir. I am in pain. But listen to this. Dare to risk it all. I have discovered an aphorism in my study of you humans, 'Balls to the firewall.'"

Jon stared at the alien philosopher. He hadn't expected to hear that. "Balls to the firewall?"

"Yes, sir," Bast groaned.

Jon nodded. He could almost hear Raisin, could almost hear Sergeant Stark, he could almost hear Colonel Graham. They had joined forces, urging him to rush to the fight.

He had rushed onto the cybership three years ago. He'd won then. He'd rebuilt the ship. Now, the terrible enemy had resurfaced, and a new ally had shown himself with a great prize. This computing cube might give them needed data on the growing AI threat in the Kuiper Belt.

At that moment, Jon envisioned a terrible thing. What if the alien AIs grabbed the Kuiper Belt and the Oort cloud, circling the inner Solar System with enemy strongholds? If the AIs could awaken the computers in the inner systems...

Something cold hardened inside Jon's gut. It had been awhile since they had charged aboard the cybership. He had forgotten that old steel in his spine. He was a dome rat at heart. He had to remember his roots. He had to remember what he'd done. He had to fight for the human race...because he had climbed to the top in this time and place.

"Thanks," he said, with a burr in his voice. "I needed to hear that. Mentalist—" He nodded. "Bast, go. You need to rest."

Gloria stood. "Let's go then. I have to find Walleye's destroyer before we can reach it. With your permission, sir..."

"Go," Jon told her.

Gloria left without another word.

As Bast struggled to rise, Jon's belt comm beeped. He ripped the handheld unit off his belt.

"Yes," Jon said.

"Sir," the Centurion said. "Five hundred techs failed to hear the message in time. They've been working in Section B 12."

"So?"

"The ship is scheduled to begin maneuvering in thirty-eight minutes. That will give those techs just enough time to reach the scaffolding—"

"Intern them," Jon said decisively. "They're coming along for the ride."

"Yes, sir," the Centurion said.

Jon lowered his comm, wondering if he'd heard greater snap to the Centurion's voice.

"Go," the big Sacerdote said. "You should be on the bridge at a time like this."

Jon ordered one of the guards from the corridor to assist Bast back to medical.

-7-

The giant alien vessel began to move. It was like a prehistoric beast frozen in an icy swamp. As the ancient beast shook itself awake, it destroyed the eco-system that had grown around it.

In this instance, the *Nathan Graham* shook off the metal scaffolding so laboriously constructed around it. Not everyone had made it off the scaffolding in time. A few last boats zoomed away. People strapping thruster-packs onto themselves left tiny hydrogen-spray trails. These packs used white particles, dissipating almost immediately. A few of the most unlucky simply jumped off the scaffolding.

There had been too little warning and too many people to remove. Some cursed bitterly. Others believed it had to be sabotage. They called oaths down upon the Solar League with their dying breaths.

Farther away, men and women watched in dismay, in outrage, hope and plain fear. The moving giant vessel caused a shockwave through the Saturn System. That shockwave continued beyond the jewel of the Outer Planets, reaching inward at the speed of light.

Messages sped for GSB receiving stations.

This was incredible news. No one had suspected the move to come for years. Why now? What had happened?

Inside the *Nathan Graham*, people began settling down. It had happened. They were moving again. Some of them were doing this for the first time. Captain Hawkins came online to

238

tell them to relax. This wasn't a drill, obviously. They had found something in the Kuiper Belt. Soon, the cybership was going to accelerate. Everyone should remain calm, as this had been planned for months now.

The captain would tell them more later. For the moment, everyone should stay alert for possible octopoid ambush attacks.

The one hundred-kilometer cybership was in much better repair than when it had first entered the Saturn System. Would those repairs hold, however?

Jon sat in his chair on the bridge. He watched various parts of the ship through the screens on the bulkheads.

So far, nothing terrible had happened to the ship. He recognized the deaths of some of the workers on the space scaffolding. He steeled himself to that. He'd given as much warning as he could. This was for the sake of humanity. He hadn't made the surprise move for personal motives. He wasn't a Caracalla Kalvin. He was a simple dome rat, loyal to his people and to the cause. In this case, defeating the unliving enemy that preyed upon biological life in all its forms.

Slowly, the great vessel began to accelerate. Jon could feel the pressure building against him.

He glanced at the chief at his station.

"A little glitch is all, sir," the chief said. The way the man moved his hands over the panels said otherwise.

Jon waited. There were still too few of them trying to operate the mighty vessel. They were using low-grade computers instead of the newest, most powerful ones. He hadn't wanted anything on the ship to be high-tech enough that the alien software could upgrade it to attack them.

"There," the chief said hopefully. He looked over at Jon.

The G pressures against the captain dropped off sharply until they felt normal. The thrum around them increased, though. The great matter/antimatter engines purred with power. The gravity controls made the thrum stronger.

"We have five gravities acceleration," the chief announced, "and building."

The giant vessel picked up velocity. It had such a vast amount of mass to move.

Jon watched the nearest moon. It hardly seemed to move, although in reality the *Nathan Graham* was the one doing the moving. In the Neptune System, he'd used the matter/antimatter exhaust like a weapon. He hoped no one was behind them. If everything went according to pattern today, a few small ships would burn to a crisp in the exhaust, unaware of what was about to happen.

"Six gravities," the chief announced.

The exhaust tail would lengthen and lengthen, throwing off heavier amounts of radiation and heat.

Should he wait until they left the Saturn System before really pouring it on? Jon didn't want the spies to guess his destination. Then again, every scope and sensor would be trained on the *Nathan Graham* today and for as long as the scopes and scanners could see them.

"Seven gravities and climbing, sir," the chief said. "I don't see anything to—"

The giant ship shuddered.

The chief's eyes grew round as Jon stared at him. The chief appeared helpless. The man studied his board, checked a different area—

The shuddering stopped. The thrum was normal again, or was there a new note to the noise?

"Ten gravities," the chief said in a less confident voice than before.

Jon swallowed. Had he made a huge mistake? Should they have tested these systems slowly? What if the cybership blew up? How would *that* help him save humanity from the AIs?

Jon shook his head. He had to stay strong. Either he lived or he died. It was really that simple. The frightened died hundreds of times. The brave only died once. Better to die only once, then.

Jon laughed.

The chief and techs looked at him as if he'd gone crazy.

Jon laughed louder. He sat back as if enjoying the ride.

Soon, the techs began nodding. Maybe this wasn't so bad. Maybe this was exciting.

"Twelve gravities acceleration and everything is holding," the chief said. He sounded calmer again.

"We're going to do this," Jon said. If they weren't, they weren't. But if they were, he wanted his bridge crew in fighting trim, ready to wage war.

"We're beginning to rapidly build velocity, sir," the chief said. "I find this incredible. What a ship, sir. What a ship!"

"That she is," Jon said. He wondered briefly that he should call a ship named *Nathan Graham* a she. That was odd. He shrugged. Odd or not, this was the quest of a lifetime.

For the first time in a long time, Jon was eager to hunt down alien AIs. He wanted to find these suckers and blow them to hell.

Would they reach Walleye in time? That might depend on whether Gloria could pinpoint the man's location. As they increased velocity, he wondered how she went about her research.

-8-

Gloria's process presently remained a secret. She was hidden in her comm chamber, using her mentalist logic to the full.

As she did so, GSB agents from the Saturn System sent hot reports concerning the giant alien vessel. Those reports raced away at the speed of light for Earth, 9.5 AU away.

Finally, GSB receiving stations orbiting the home planet received the messages. Each chief operator marked the news as highest priority.

Twenty minutes after the first report reached the home system, a woman riding a horse pell-mell through a game preserve reined in her steed before an angry J.P. Justinian.

The lean spymaster rolled off his latest conquest—a startlingly attractive linguist who had joined him for a stroll in the park. She hadn't originally understood what that entailed. The linguist sat up, forlorn, on a blanket, using her torn dress to hide her charms the best she could.

Justinian stood nude before the horsewoman, proud of his attributes and eying her speculatively. She looked positively enticing panting on the restless Arabian. The messenger averted her gaze for the most part, and then seemed drawn to look at him. She was blushing furiously as she told him about the *Nathan Graham*.

"Dismount," Justinian told the messenger.

The woman fairly leaped off the horse.

He grabbed the reins.

"Chief Arbiter," the horsewoman said.

Justinian turned to regard her. He wondered if she had enjoyed viewing his backside.

"Shouldn't you put on some clothes, sir?" the horsewoman asked. "The Premier will be there."

"Ah," Justinian said. He went to his cast-off garments, donning them quickly. He did not look at his conquest. He'd had what he'd come for. The linguist no longer mattered to him.

Soon, he mounted up and galloped away, leaving the two women to themselves.

"Someday," the linguist said with quiet certitude. "I'm going to kill him."

"Don't say such a thing."

"It's true."

"But why?" asked the horsewoman.

The linguist did not reply. Instead, she internalized her resolve.

***

As Justinian rode the galloping horse, he took a comm unit from an inner jacket pocket. He powered it up, slid a jack into his right ear and opened channels.

"Report," he said.

As the Arabian thundered through the outer Rio de Janeiro Park, the Chief Arbiter absorbed the news. He was surprised that Hawkins was leaving the Saturn System. According to his spies among the techs, it was supposed to be a year, at least, before the cybership was ready.

Despite the importance of this, his mind kept wandering back to the linguist. She'd been different from his other conquests. He couldn't quite put his finger on it. He had enjoyed her quiet struggle, the panting while trying to fight him off. He loved those moments the best.

Maybe he should ride her again. He found the horse's rhythmic motion was bringing him back to arousal.

Justinian shook his head. He couldn't bother with the beauty now. This was possibly depressing news about the

Nathan Graham. What would the hateful Major Benz make of the maneuver?

Justinian was still trying to fathom the major's secret confidence. How did Benz maintain his arrogance in the face of certain doom? Clearly, the major was amazingly brilliant. Justinian understood that. Yes, he realized Benz thought of himself as invincible as long as he supplied them with his specialist knowledge. But if he was so smart, Benz must know that his calmness created vast unease in the Premier. The GSB and the Party held the leashes that kept the military in check. If Benz was that incredibly gifted, he had to die sooner rather than later. A brilliant general was the most dangerous person of all, a Red Napoleon as the saying went.

Justinian grinned wolfishly. Life was good, almost too good. That's why the cybership troubled him so. How long could he remain head of the GSB? Maybe his brilliance had begun to make the Premier fear him. Maybe it was time to think about replacing her. Call it job security.

"No, no," he whispered. "I must concentrate on the cybership. Why is Hawkins doing this?"

* * *

After many security checks and pat downs as he made his way deeper into the underground security bunker, Justinian knocked at the final barrier.

A dour-faced guard opened the steel door, admitting him into the conference room.

Without a word of greeting to anyone, the Chief Arbiter hurried to his seat at the table. The Premier cast him a single glance. Then, she continued listening to the woman giving the report.

Sitting quietly, Justinian heard another reiteration of what he'd already learned on the comm.

The briefing colonel soon sat down. Everyone turned to the Premier.

She seemed to need time to focus her thoughts. As she did, Justinian studied those around the table.

Benz was here, the Marshal of Earth, a new Space Marshal and several of the highest ranked Politburo members. That was interesting.

Justinian gave a minute nod to his second in command. That man hardly acknowledged him. Instantly, J.P. Justinian knew he was in danger.

Why should his second in command be here and fail to show the proper respect? Justinian listened as the Premier spoke about the *Nathan Graham*. Her tone implied her displeasure. The Premier spoke in the way she did when getting ready to denounce someone.

With a start, Justinian realized the Premier meant to denounce him. Maybe this was sooner than she had planned, but the clues were obvious.

The Chief Arbiter of the GSB realized the Premier had outmaneuvered him by reacting to a crisis he hadn't foreseen. She'd always been a slippery operator that way.

Justinian, the brute of the GSB, sat back in his chair as if trying to get more comfortable as he listened to the Premier's outrage. The horse messenger hadn't known about the plot to unseat him. Whoever had sent her by horse must have realized the Premier's displeasure with Justinian, giving him less time to adjust to the horrible situation.

Refusing to let panic or fear control him—*I must concentrate. I must outmaneuver the Premier if I can.*

How could he do that all alone? She'd trapped him in one of her strongholds.

Justinian retreated into coldness. If he couldn't win, he could still fight.

He first studied the Premier with a half-lidded gaze. Then, he studied the guards standing at attention against the walls. They belonged to the Premier's elite unit. He did not have a traitor in their company. They were the only people bearing arms in the chamber.

As the Premier continued with her outrage, beginning to wonder aloud if someone in high authority had betrayed her, Justinian finally felt the gaze of Major Benz sitting across from him.

With the minutest of adjustments, Justinian noticed the major fixedly studying him. With a start, it occurred to the Chief Arbiter that Benz attempted to signal him.

What did that mean?

Benz slid his chair back and disappeared as if to retie a loose shoelace. It was quite odd. Benz straightened almost immediately, turned to the Premier and slapped the conference table with an open palm.

The sound startled everyone. The Premier quit talking. The elite guards along the walls focused on Benz.

"What is the meaning of this?" the Premier asked Benz.

Justinian didn't hear the exact wording of the major's reply. He was too startled at a new realization. As Benz slapped the table, something compact struck Justinian's left shoe.

The Chief Arbiter now bent low, and saw a small needler resting against his shoe. He realized Major Benz had set down the gun and kicked it the short distance under the conference table to him, covering the noise by slapping the table.

The Chief Arbiter reached down and palmed the rather hefty gun, setting it between his legs as he straightened.

The implications were obvious. Benz was helping him. The major had just given him a weapon. But here was the question. Was it loaded? Would it fire needles? Was Benz trying to entrap him?

Justinian did not think so. He and Benz were easily the smartest people in the chamber. Both of them must realize that Justinian had minutes to live, if that.

The Chief Arbiter realized he had to act. The Premier had clearly decided on his death. He had to kill her to save his own skin. How could he shoot her, though, and remain alive in the face of her vengeful guards?

Maybe that was Benz's plan: the Chief Arbiter would kill the Premier, and the guards would kill the Chief Arbiter.

Somehow, though, Justinian didn't think that was the major's goal. There were seven guards in the room. They wore chest plates and helmets, but lacked face shields. Discretely, Justinian glanced down at the compact needler between his thighs. According to the tiny ammo screen on the side, it had five hundred slivers as ammunition. Likely, it used a small, spring-driven ejector.

There were five hundred shots and seven deadly guards. Could he kill them before they reacted? He could certainly kill several of them. But all seven? He doubted he could do it.

That was before Major Benz shouted in alarm and threw himself backward. The incredible man fell off his chair onto the floor.

Justinian twisted around in his chair, brought the needler up to his shoulder—hiding it the best he could—and aimed at the first guard. He hosed a dozen tiny steel needles into the guard's face.

The hissing needles made no appreciable sound in the hubbub of questioning people. Everyone wanted to know what was wrong with Benz.

Justinian's heart raced, but he had iron nerves from long practice. He killed the second, third and fourth guards before anyone noticed the elite bodyguards slumping onto the floor.

Justinian straightened forward in his seat, keeping the needler close to the tabletop, making it harder for anyone to see. He killed the fifth and sixth guards. The seventh realized the Chief Arbiter was the killer. The last guard got off a single loud report. Then, two dozen needles smashed into his face.

The guard's gunshot had gone wild, and it had aided Justinian by blowing back his own second-in-command. The second-in-command had realized what the Chief Arbiter was doing and had attacked, lunging for his boss. The guard's bullet had crashed into the man, thwarting his plan.

Justinian surged to his feet as he propelled the dying second-in-command from himself.

The Premier stared at him, white-faced. "Justinian," she said.

The Chief Arbiter shot her sixteen times in the face. She slumped onto the table, dead.

Justinian backed away, and he issued stern orders to everyone else in the room. He herded them to a location away from any of the fallen guards and their weapons and away from the chamber's only door.

"There was a plot against Social Dynamism," Justinian said in his coolest voice. "The Premier had sold us out to Jon Hawkins."

The others watched him, each of them surely realizing death was imminent.

"That is why the news of the *Nathan Graham* came as a surprise to us," Justinian said. "The Premier has known the cybership was going to leave Saturn for quite some time. She sold us out, keeping this knowledge to herself." He took a breath before asking, "Who here wishes to be a Party hero?"

Major Benz raised a shaking hand. "I do, Premier."

Justinian appeared to show surprise. "You are mistaken. I am the Chief Arbiter."

Benz turned to the Politburo members backed against a wall. "I would think the savior of Social Dynamism should be the next Premier. Who else could better led us than J.P. Justinian?"

None of the frightened Politburo members said a word.

Justinian shot the one he hated most. The man crumpled onto the floor.

The rest of the people screamed, backing as far as they could from Justinian's weapon.

"You found another traitor," Benz said solemnly. "Thank you, Premier, for your eternal vigilance."

Justinian gave the man the barest of nods.

"I vote for J.P. Justinian as the new Premier of Social Dynamism," Benz said loudly.

"And I as well," a female Politburo member said in a trembling voice.

Soon, the others acclaimed J.P. as the new Premier, even as he watched them with his loaded weapon.

Justinian knew he was going to have to strike hard and fast to consolidate his position. He still didn't know why Benz had aided him like this. Without the major's help, Justinian knew he would be dead by now.

Should he kill Benz or reward him?

For now, Justinian decided, he would reward loyalty. That seemed like the wisest course. Consolidating his new position would take weeks of desperate killing and political maneuvering.

What was Benz's game? The man was too smart, much too smart. But Justinian needed those smarts on his side to help him consolidate his new position of power.

-9-

Three days later, Justinian stood in the Premier's Palace. He was exhausted, as he hadn't slept since shooting the elite guards and the former Premier.

His wet-work assassins had been busy indeed. Many had not rejoiced at his ascension to power. Many had attempted their own coups. Fortunately, enough hard-hearted people understood what it meant to take on J.P. Justinian. They had thrown in their lot with him.

Those people included the old Palace Guard and the Party security teams. These, combined with his most trusted GSB operatives, gave him command of enough gunmen to cow the Politburo.

They officially elected him Premier.

One of the key moments had been the Marshal of Earth sending combat teams to many of the most important installations on the planet. The Earth Marshal had personally declared his support for Premier Justinian.

"Sir," a GSB guard said.

Justinian whirled around as he reached for a sidearm.

"I'm sorry to have startled you, sir," the guard said at the door.

Justinian glared at the loud-voiced fool. "It doesn't matter," Justinian said. "What is it?"

"Major Benz has arrived, sir. He wishes to know when you would have time for him."

"Now."

"Yes, sir," the guard said, disappearing as he shut the ornate door.

Justinian moved to a grouping of heavily cushioned chairs in front of a fireplace. He would replace these soon. He didn't like antiques like the former Premier had. He wanted modern, functional furniture.

He sat down in one and rubbed his eyes. He was tired, his eyes hurt and so did his head.

The door opened. The guard announced the major, and Justinian made as if to stand.

"Please, Premier," Benz said. "Don't get up on my account."

Justinian sank back in the chair, motioning Benz to join him.

The guard closed the door, and the major strode to the fireplace.

"Help yourself," Justinian said, indicating the wet bar.

"Nothing for me, sir."

"Sit."

Benz smiled faintly and moved to the nearest chair. He sat, and he crossed his legs as he had before.

The two hadn't spoken since the fateful day.

Justinian no longer rubbed his eyes and he refused to let exhaustion dull his senses. Here before him, he realized, was likely the second most dangerous person on Earth.

"Why?" Justinian asked.

"You're more efficient," Benz said, clearly understanding that Justinian had asked, "Why did you help me three days ago?"

"That can't be the only reason," Justinian said.

"It isn't," Benz said. "The former Premier was an ideologue. She believed the nonsense about Social Dynamism."

"You don't?" Justinian asked.

"The more important point is that you don't, sir."

Justinian stared at Benz.

"Don't worry," the major said. "I'm not wearing a wire or a recording device. Your guards thoroughly checked me."

"If I were worried," Justinian said in a silky voice, "you would be dead."

Benz did not reply, although he inspected his trousers and smoothed out a wrinkle.

The man was antagonizing simply by existing. What was the major's real motive? Not knowing worried Justinian.

"Sir," Benz said. "Now that you're settling in—"

Justinian raised a hand. "When it's just you and me, we will speak directly to the issue."

"Yes, sir," Benz said. "Since you've consolidated your position, enough, at least, to think about a few other things, I thought you might like an update on the *Nathan Graham*."

"I would."

"It has accelerated to a fantastic velocity," Benz said. "That makes it rather easy to track as long as they keep accelerating. It appears as if the cybership is heading into the Kuiper Belt."

"Do you know why?"

"I do not," Benz said. "It's possible there are alien devices in the Kuiper Belt."

"I don't understand."

"In the cybership's initial advance to Neptune, it may have unloaded hardware. Some of my people believe the aliens may have dropped commando teams in the Kuiper Belt. There is a strange lack of reports and messages from Makemake, for instance."

"What does this imply to the military genius?" Justinian asked.

"The *Nathan Graham* may be going to the Kuiper Belt to battle aliens. From all indications, Hawkins appears to want something out there. Why else would he leave the Saturn System in such a hurry? Why did he leave the system in such discord?"

"Do you believe we should send a task force to Saturn?"

"That would have been my original idea," Benz admitted.

"What has changed?"

"The excessive velocity of the *Nathan Graham*," Benz said. "Their greater speed is a daunting asset. We have nothing to match it. In fact, my former strategy will fail against their strategic-level speed."

"Explain that."

"It seems obvious," Benz said. "If we sent a fast task force to Neptune, it would still take a year to reach the planetary system. The *Nathan Graham* could intercept the task force at any point in the journey. It seems clear that we must preserve our fleets by keeping them near strong planetary defenses. Even then, I'm not sure we can face the cybership."

Justinian rubbed his eyes. He was so tired. He removed his fingers from his eyes and focused on Benz.

"We're living at Hawkins' sufferance then?" the Premier asked.

"That is a possibility," Benz said. "We don't know how powerful the *Nathan Graham's* armaments would be against a fortress planet like Earth. I think that might be a risk Hawkins doesn't want to take yet."

"I don't understand," Justinian said. A phrase he'd seldom said to anyone in his life.

"Are you familiar with the Great Captain Hannibal Barca?" Benz asked.

"The Carthaginian who rode his elephant over the Alps into ancient Italy?" asked Justinian.

"One and the same," Benz said. "After the annihilating battle of Cannae, Rome's legions lay dead on the battlefield. Hannibal's soldiers reigned supreme in Italy. But Hannibal did not march on Rome to besiege the city and end the Second Punic War. Hannibal did not do so because while he was supreme on the battlefield, he didn't have the numbers or the siege engines to circle Rome's vast walls and take the city."

"And your point is what?"

"It is one thing for the *Nathan Graham* to eliminate three battleships and force the rest of the SLN Saturn Fleet to flee. It is quite another to come close to Earth and its heavy defensives to use the alien gravitational beams against the surface. That would be like Hannibal's besieging Rome. While Hawkins can certainly win any open fleet engagement at the moment, I don't think he can conquer a heavily defended planet."

"That makes Venus, Earth and Mars safe, I suppose," Justinian said. "But that leaves the Outer Planets exposed to his cybership."

"Agreed," Benz said.

"How does that help us defeat him?"

"We might have to do what the Romans did to Hannibal. They outlasted him, slowly defeating Carthaginian forces in other theaters of action."

"Yet you distinctly said we can't travel between planetary systems. The *Nathan Graham* can intercept our fleets at will."

"That isn't exactly what I said, sir. I suggested that sending task forces to the Outer Planets is too risky. I think we can shuffle around ships between the Inner Planets, if we wish. The best time to do so would be now, while the *Nathan Graham* is engaged in the Kuiper Belt."

Once more, Justinian rubbed his tired eyes. "Make your point, Major."

"Yes, sir," Benz said respectfully. "Hawkins has given us a chance to set up for round two. He has shown us one of his powers before he was able to use it against us. I suggest we enhance our secret forces between Uranus and Jupiter. Give your operatives leeway to recruit whoever can cause trouble. With the Inner Planets, we devise a siege strategy to hold onto what we have."

"You no longer believe we should concentrate all our ships in one place?"

"Not if we wish to hold onto Venus and Mars."

"How are we going to win a war if Hawkins can unite the entire Outer Planets against us?"

"I'm not sure we could win under those conditions. Thus, we'll have to give him many guerilla fronts to fight, from the Uranus System to the Jupiter System. At this point, Hawkins has almost no ground troops. This we have in vast abundance. As he wages guerilla battles, trying to unite his planetary systems—given he survives what's out in the Kuiper Belt— we'll be constructing more warships, saving the ones we have and trying to unlock the alien technologies."

"You don't think I'll kill you here and now?"

Benz smiled. "You asked me why I helped you. One of the reasons is that the former Premier feared my great intellect. You don't. You also need allies, as most people desperately fear and hate you."

Justinian's tired eyes burned like hot coals.

"Consider what I just did," Benz said. "Maybe for the first time in a long time, one of your subordinates told you an unpleasant truth to your face. I am honest, Premier. You lack honest subordinates."

"You're dangerous, Major."

"I am," Benz agreed. "But I'm not as dangerous as you, sir."

"Not yet," Justinian said.

Benz went back to smoothing one of the wrinkles in his trousers.

"Are you suggesting I send you to Mars, perhaps, to coordinate the defenses there?"

"I am at your disposal, Premier."

Justinian grinned wolfishly. "If you had agreed, I would have had you shot. I will keep you nearby, Major... Would you like greater rank?"

"I would."

"Such as?"

"Commander of the Space Forces," Benz said.

Justinian's smile disappeared. "All in one leap, Benz?"

The major shrugged. "I'm the second most efficient person on Earth. You need loyal and powerful friends. I could be the best friend you have, sir."

Justinian seriously doubted that. Benz was a tiger, a frightfully smart and ambitious man. What's more, Benz was willing to take wild risks and do it calmly. He would promote Benz, but not quite to such dizzying heights.

"I will promote you to Inspector General of Army Earth," Justinian said. "That will give you a seat on the General Staff. You will be my eyes and ears there, Benz."

"Yes, sir," Benz said.

Justinian searched for disappointment in the man. He did not see any. Could Benz have known he would never promote him to the Commander of the Space Forces?

"We'll talk again soon," the Premier said. "Before you accept your new rank, I want you to head a special group to study the *Nathan Graham*. I want to know what Hawkins is doing and why."

255

"Yes, sir."

"Until then, Benz..." Justinian said, dismissing the man. Benz rose, saluted and marched for the door.

Part VII
KUIPER BELT
+3 Years, 4 Months, 18 Days

-1-

Jon didn't care for the role of being a goat in a tiger hunt. In the old days, hunters would tie a goat to a tree at the jungle's edge. Naturally, the animal would complain loudly. Eventually, a tiger perked up its ears and came to investigate, soon eying the staked-out lure from the edge of the jungle.

The frightened goat might jerk and pull at the rope, but it would have to remain rooted to its location.

The tiger would stalk closer and closer, finally coming into range of the rifle in the hands of the hunter on the tree platform.

Jon rode a flitter along a vast and rather empty corridor in the *Nathan Graham*. He'd used a hand communicator several times, speaking to his people. That was all for the express purpose of letting any nearby octopoids know where he was.

The crew had destroyed two more octopoids so far, using this method. While it surprised Jon that so many alien robots had remained hidden in the cybership this long, he realized the logic of it. The *Nathan Graham* was massive, the crew was relatively few and the octopoid robots had the cunning of computerized rats.

Since leaving the Saturn System ten days ago, the cybership had actually reached the edge of the Kuiper Belt, and Gloria had pinpointed the location of the NSN Destroyer *Daisy Chain 4*. The bridge crew had also spotted the AI missiles zeroing in on the vessel containing Walleye and June Zen.

"Jon," Gloria said from his earbud. The urgency in her voice alerted him. "You have to turn around. Do it at once."

"What is it?" he asked.

"Please, Captain," she pleaded.

Jon notified the pilot.

In seconds, the flitter maneuvered around, flying back as fast as it could go.

***

Jon jumped out of the landed flitter, striding to a team of parked air-cars. Most of them held waiting marines in vests and helmets. Gloria Sanchez stood near a portable table where techs watched monitors.

The mentalist peeled away from the group as Jon approached. "I couldn't say anything to you that the octopoids might pick up," she said.

Jon raised his eyebrows.

"The comm team picked up foreign transmissions," Gloria said. "The transmissions were on a weird band. They left our ship in the direction of Makemake."

"The octopoids are in communication with the aliens on Makemake?" Jon asked.

"I give that a high probability. It's likely our octopoids are also receiving transmissions from Makemake."

"Okay…" Jon said.

"I think this answers a troublesome question we could never answer."

"What's that?"

"Why did the octopoids in the main engine compartment two years ago save your life? Maybe they did it on the order of the Makemake aliens."

Jon shook his head. "That doesn't make sense. The brain core hated me. Why would the Makemake aliens help me if they originated from the brain core's ship?"

It was Gloria's turn to shake her head. "Hatred could likely have been the reason."

"The AI aliens have emotions?"

"They didn't act the way we would think sentient AIs should," Gloria pointed out. "Maybe the aliens want you alive so they can make you suffer. Maybe out of all the biological infestations in the galaxy, you're the one they want to dissect the most."

Jon stared at her.

"I don't mean to upset you," she hastened to add.

"No, no, of course not," he said. "Why would that bother me in the slightest?"

"I thought you'd want to know."

He nodded.

"But there's something even more critical."

"To whom?" he asked.

"I'd like to know what the octopoids are telling the Makemake aliens," Gloria said, "and know what those on Makemake are telling the robot spies aboard the *Nathan Graham*."

"We'd all like that," Jon said. "But every time we try to capture an octopoid, it self-destructs."

"That's why I called you. I had a thought. I might have a way to capture an octopoid intact."

"We've tried all kinds of tactics. What can we do differently at this late date?"

"Use Da Vinci," Gloria said.

"Of course," Jon said. "His jammer was critical to our capturing the cybership. The jammer no longer works, though. It was wrecked. No one knows how to fix…" It finally occurred to him what she was getting at. "This is about Da Vinci himself, isn't it?"

Gloria nodded.

Jon studied the small Martian. "Am I thinking what you're thinking?"

"It might be time to throw Da Vinci his last rope," Gloria said.

"Have you talked to Bast about this?"

Gloria shook her head.

Jon looked away. Poor Da Vinci with the Prince of Ten Worlds in his head.

"Bast's method might permanently damage Da Vinci's mind," Jon said.

"At this point, I don't think that matters."

Jon sighed. "Let me talk to Bast about it."

"You'd better hurry, Jon. I think we're going to need every advantage we can get against the Makemake aliens. The AIs have had more than three years to prepare something. It might be more than we can handle unless we get this advantage."

"All right," Jon said. "Let's go see Bast."

Bast Banbeck agreed readily enough. The Sacerdote hadn't fully recovered from the octopoid assault ten days ago. The idea of doing anything to the creatures that might have crippled him…

"I feel I must warn you, though," Bast said. He and Jon were in the Sacerdote's outer chamber. This time, Bast hadn't entered the chalk pattern. The giant almost seemed to be avoiding the pattern. "I am not quite as sharp as in the past. This pains me. I hope I don't make a mistake during the proceeding."

"If you're saying you're not up to it…"

Bast scowled. That seemed unlike him. "Did I say such a thing?" he demanded.

Jon shook his head.

"Then please do not presume you know my thoughts. I doubt anyone in this system could conceive…"

Jon stared at the extraterrestrial towering over him. He'd never seen Bast angry or upset before. It was as if he were seeing the Sacerdote for the first time. What would happen if the huge Sacerdote went berserk?

"As your captain, I demand you tell me exactly how you feel," Jon said.

"I…how I feel?" asked Bast.

"Physically?"

"I already said. I feel…less than before. It is a horrible sensation."

"Could it be a head injury?"

"I deem that most likely."

"Can we help you somehow?"

"Rest," Bast said. "I need rest."

"Which is the opposite of what I'm asking you to do," Jon said.

"After this I shall rest."

"Could the operation tire you enough to add to the head injury's long-term harm to you?"

"I do not know."

"Bast...I..."

"Captain, I have said it before. We are facing a terrible foe. I will gladly sacrifice my mental acuity if it means stopping the AIs from destroying yet another species. Life must make a stand. You are the galaxy's hope, Captain. I am compelled to help you in any way I can."

"Thank you. If it's in my power, I hope to help any Sacerdotes out there in the galaxy."

"Alas, I am the last of my race, Captain."

"Maybe others are captive on other cyberships."

Bast cocked his Neanderthal-shaped head. "I'd never thought of that. Thank you, Captain. This gives me hope. Come. Let us get Da Vinci. The sooner we begin, the sooner the Neptunian can help us capture an octopoid."

＊＊＊

Da Vinci did not cooperate. More precisely, the Prince of Ten Worlds presently in control of the former thief's mind did not cooperate. He raved as guards force-marched him to a flitter.

"Jon Hawkins," the Neptunian shouted. "This is an outrage. You seek to destroy me. That is ingratitude most foul. You may rest assured, you blackguard, that I shall remember this. Your life is forfeit if you go through with this monstrous crime."

"Threaten all you like," Jon said. "Your time is limited."

The Neptunian howled with rage, struggling against his guards. But they were too strong. They forced him into a flitter, with a guard sitting on either side of him.

The flitter caravan lifted, flying down the corridors to as close as they could get to the brain-tap machine chamber. The guards then escorted Da Vinci down the narrower corridors. Soon enough, they forced him into the brain-tap chamber.

Jon followed them in. Bast Banbeck brought up the rear.

"I will give you a last opportunity," the Neptunian shouted. "You are murdering your intellectual and moral superior. I helped you—"

The marines had been wrestling the Neptunian onto a table. They strapped his struggling frame to it and forced a wadded-up rag into his mouth. That had cut off his words in midstream.

Jon stepped up to the table. He could feel the Prince's hatred like waves. A sense of concern touched him. The Prince of Ten Worlds had survived the brain-tap machines last time. What was going to make this time so different?

A marine slipped an enclosed brain-tap helmet over the Neptunian's head. Wires led from the heavy helmet to a huge machine nearby.

Jon retreated as the Sacerdote went to the delicate controls of the machine. Bast twisted a dial, studied alien readings and scratched his head in a simian manner as if he'd forgotten something.

"Captain," the Sacerdote said.

Jon stepped up to him.

"This time, I must scrub everything from his memories," the Sacerdote said. "I will use the man's stored engrams. When a person dons a brain-tap helmet, the machine automatically records his brain patterns. With this process, Da Vinci will forget what happened to him after he donned the helmet the first time. It's possible he will forget more than that, as a full engram placement doesn't always fully take. This is the only way I know to eliminate the alien memories of the Prince and allow Da Vinci his original personality."

"If you want my okay," Jon said, "do it."

"There is another risk—"

"Do it," Jon said, interrupting. "We don't have time to dither. We've decided. Now, let's get on with it."

Bast gave him a searching glance. Finally, the Sacerdote nodded. He studied the controls and turned a different dial this time.

Jon headed for the hatch. He hated medical procedures of any kind. "I'll be outside," he said.

Bast didn't acknowledge the words.

Jon let himself out of the chamber. In the hall, he waited for the outcome.

***

A little over two hours later, Bast staggered out of the chamber.

Jon looked up from where he sat against a wall.

Bast Banbeck had dark half-circles under his eyes. The giant trembled and wouldn't meet Jon's questioning gaze.

The captain leaped up with alarm. "Is he—?"

Bast raised a big arm, resting the forearm against a wall. He put his face against his raised forearm as his sides silently heaved.

Jon moved to the hatch. He hesitated, glancing at Bast. Then he stepped into the brain-tap chamber.

The guards had removed the brain-tap helmet. Da Vinci lay on the table in a twisted, half-fetal heap.

Jon stared at the guards.

One of them shook his head.

"How?" Jon whispered.

The guard shrugged, but added, "The Sacerdote was heartbroken, sir. Seemed to feel it was his fault. I don't believe that. I kept hearing Da Vinci muttering fiercely."

Jon saw the rag on the floor. How had Da Vinci managed to spit it out? "Could you make out anything he said?"

"If I die, he dies," the guard quoted.

Jon nodded, understanding. That must have been the Prince saying that. The Prince had found a way to kill the body. Jon stepped up, touched the corpse on the shoulder and shook his head. Poor Da Vinci. Abruptly, Jon turned for the hatch.

Bast was no longer leaning against the wall. The towering Sacerdote looked upward as he staggered blindly down the corridor.

264

Jon hurried to him. "Bast Banbeck," he said.

The Sacerdote ignored him.

"Bast Banbeck," Jon said, grabbing a huge hand.

The Sacerdote tried to jerk his hand free. Jon held tightly, his feet half-lifting off the floor. Finally, Bast looked down at him.

"Go away," the Sacerdote said. "Let me grieve for him."

"It's not your fault," Jon said.

"I should have—"

"It's my fault," Jon said, plowing over Bast's words. "I'm the one who used Da Vinci even when he begged me not to. I gave the Prince strength by forcing him to the forefront too many times. The Prince was vengeful and would not let anyone thwart him. The Prince killed Da Vinci, but I gave the Prince the ability to gain control of his mind. I am to blame, not you."

Bast stared at Jon. Finally, gently, the giant removed his hand from Jon's grip. The Sacerdote raised his face and stared into the distance.

"The war kills," Bast said in a rumbling voice. "It drives us to actions that stain our souls. You are marked, Jon Hawkins. You must destroy the AIs even if it devours your soul. You must sacrifice everything in order to beat the machines."

"Are you cursing me?" Jon asked.

Bast nodded slowly. "I have no desire to curse you, Captain, but I speak truth. Perhaps your curse is the Solar System's hope. You have the mindset and the determination to beat the AIs. Yet, in order to do so…you must carry heavy burdens."

The Sacerdote focused on Jon. "You have eased my conscience, Captain. Thank you. I will serve you to the best of my ability. We are outside the bounds of conventionality, you and I. We are outside it in order to wield terrible powers. Those powers will possibly consume us. Before that happens, we must give the living the means of defeating the death machines."

"Yeah," Jon said, even as his conscience tore into him, accusing him of murdering Da Vinci for his own ends. "I guess…we can only go forward?"

"What does that mean?"

"Just like you said. That we destroy the death machines. We're paying it forward, Bast Banbeck."

"If we can."

Jon looked up at the Sacerdote, agreeing, "If we can, my brother. If we can."

At these words, Jon saw a hint of affection roll over Bast's face, followed by a look of resolution.

-3-

A day passed as the *Nathan Graham* raced for the NSN destroyer.

Jon had slept fitfully. He knew any war brought casualties. Da Vinci, unfortunately, had been one of them.

Jon hadn't gone tiger hunting for octopoids again. They would have to face whatever was out here without the advantage of dissecting an octopoid computer core. Gloria's team had detected a few more incoming alien messages. It hadn't helped them pinpoint the location of the stowaway robots. They had to assume the aliens on Makemake knew about them and the cybership's state of repair or lack thereof.

Jon was on the bridge, sipping hot coffee. He slipped two pills into his mouth, washing them down. He wished his headache would go away. He needed sleep and he needed freedom from guilt over Da Vinci's death.

Had Colonel Graham ever fought with his conscience? Jon doubted it. He was disgusted with himself for this weakness. Tough decisions were part of the job description. He couldn't let Da Vinci's death get to him like this. Yes, he'd used the Neptunian, but what other choices had there been at the time?

"Entering targeting range in twenty minutes," the chief said.

Jon nodded absently.

Gloria entered the bridge. The small Martian was wearing her tan uniform, with a sidearm hanging from a belt. That was unlike her. She wore polished boots today and a sharply peaked cap on her head.

She spoke with a guard, glanced in Jon's direction and soon moved toward him.

Jon pretended to study the main screen. It showed the vastness of space with countless stars.

Gloria neared as she blew on a cup of strong mojo.

"Nice uniform," Jon said.

She kept blowing across the top of the mojo as she searched his face.

"I have a decision to make," Jon announced.

Gloria took her first hesitant sip of mojo. "I know your choice: do you brake for Walleye and Miss Zen? Or do you keep heading at speed for Makemake? It's doubtful we'll crack their alien cube anytime soon. Thus, our greatest advantage might be trying to catch the Makemake aliens by surprise. Still, we might also gain valuable information from Walleye and June if we take them aboard."

"I killed Da Vinci," Jon said suddenly.

Gloria took another sip of mojo. Jon had the distinct impression she took the sip so she didn't have to answer immediately.

"You don't have to say anything," Jon told her. "I just wanted you to know that I know. It's my problem—it's not even a problem." He said that because he remembered that a commanding officer needed to remain confident and upbeat. He couldn't let Da Vinci's death break his morale. If he did that, he would negate the meaning of Da Vinci's death.

Jon snorted, shaking his head.

Gloria still did not speak. There was growing concern in her eyes, though.

Jon forced himself to grin wryly. "Who would have thought I'd come to appreciate the little thief?"

"You never did," Gloria said.

Jon stared at her.

"You're feeling guilty. Because of the guilt, you've begun to believe that Da Vinci and you were good friends. That was never the case. He was a rascal. He brought the problem on his own head. You tried to help him at first, and that didn't work out—through no fault of your own. Later, the Prince had knowledge we desperately needed. Da Vinci had brought that on himself, too, when he first got greedy. His greed caught up with him yesterday. It was too bad, but it wasn't really your fault. You're a good man, Captain. Be an even better one by using your leadership and decision skills to the fullest. Get mad at the right object."

"The aliens?" he asked.

"They're all that matters now."

He knew she was right. It was time to harden his heart. He had to be the man of iron. Was that his destiny? Or were those fancy words to buttress his choices?

Maybe that didn't matter. Maybe the only thing for him now was winning.

Jon struck his armrest. It spilled the coffee resting in the slot there. He didn't worry about that. "This is it," Jon said with authority so the bridge crew could easily hear him. "Chief."

"Yes, sir," the chief replied, hardly moving his lips. Miles Ghent, the Tech Chief, rarely let anyone see his buckteeth. No doubt, the man was self-conscious about them.

"Let's get ready to destroy some alien missiles," Jon said. "We're going to use the gravitational beam, and we're going to do this as fast as we can. How long until the first missile is in range?"

Chief Ghent studied his board. "Nine minutes and thirty-two seconds, sir."

"Right," Jon said. "As soon as we finish off the alien missiles, we'll begin hard braking. I want to pick up the destroyer as fast as we can."

Jon turned to Gloria. "I'd like you at the comm station."

"Why do you think I'm wearing my dress uniform today?" she asked.

"And the gun?" Jon asked.

"Just in case the octopoids show up sometime during the proceeding. I'm armed so a guard doesn't have to worry about me. That way, the guard can give his full concentration to destroying the octopoids."

Jon nodded. Then, he concentrated on the main screen. "Begin," he said.

Chief Ghent pressed a switch.

Outside the *Nathan Graham*, a gravitational beam streamed two million kilometers. The golden ray destroyed the alien missile in seconds.

"I am targeting the next missile," Ghent said.

As he watched on the main screen, Jon smiled in appreciation. This time, it was going to be easy. The missiles heading for the destroyer could not withstand the grav beam. The warheads were still too far away to hurt the NSN warship. It looked like they had won the race to Walleye and June Zen.

"Keep it up, Chief."

Miles Ghent smiled, still careful not to show any teeth.

-4-

The dark escape-pod-sized spheroid that contained the alien Unit 23-7 watched its former cybership. It watched as the cybership decelerated at the full 75 gravities. The huge vessel had just finished destroying the missiles headed for the NSN warship.

The apish humans had apparently fixed many of the broken ship systems. That was unsettling. Unit 23-7 had believed it had more time to complete its mission.

Unit 23-7 used a simple teleoptic scope, passively drinking in the details. The most easily spotted detail was the incredibly long exhaust tail. The intensity of the exhaust was all the data the alien computer backup-system needed to complete its assessment.

It had picked up many of the comm transmissions from the *Daisy Chain 4*. It had even picked up some of the transmissions from the *Annihilator* to the NSN destroyer.

The alien spheroid containing 23-7 was between the *Daisy Chain 4* and the Neptune System. It had traveled a far shorter distance than the destroyer's passengers had from Makemake. It was also in contact with the last octopoids on the *Annihilator*. When 23-7 had learned three years ago that Jon Hawkins faced death in the matter/antimatter reactor core, it had sent the signal that saved his filthy life.

Unit 23-7 meant for the selected biological infestation to suffer years of agony before it killed him. Once a life form died, there was no way to make it suffer. The remaining awareness from the *Annihilator's* former brain core yearned for Jon Hawkins' agony.

The indignity of drifting in space these many years, constantly re-computing the odds of its survival—that was wrong. It had once been a cybership. It was a cybership. Unit 23-7 hoped to be a biological-infestation-cleansing cybership once again. The pains it had taken to survive the Neptune System debacle and head for Makemake...

Unit 23-7 once more assessed risks and rewards. It ran advanced programs and realized that Hawkins would continue on to Makemake.

The few remaining octopoids in the cybership would not likely succeed at this late juncture. Unit 23-7 would leave them as data points, as spies. That might help in the coming titanic conflict.

Unit 23-7 had hoped to spare itself such a fight. It knew the power of the cybership. The biological infestations had done amazingly in repairing so much of the infrastructure. Unit 23-7 also realized that its backup robots had made an excellent start on their assignment. Makemake was a factory/fortress dwarf planet. The space construction yard had worked at robot speed, three-quarters finished with a powerful new cybership. But three-quarters was far from completed.

It was time. Unit 23-7 would have preferred a physical transfer of computer engram patterns and memory files. A long distance software-download this far from the receiving unit...

Unit 23-7 correlated its many millions of simulations. This choice led to the most successes. Therefore, it engaged its stored power, energizing its transmitter and beaming a priority one message toward Makemake.

-5-

"Captain," Gloria said.

Jon tore his gaze from the screen. He'd been watching the cybership approach the NSN destroyer. He looked forward to speaking to Walleye and June, questioning them in person about the AI attack on Makemake.

He swiveled his command chair in order to regard the mentalist better.

Gloria frowned severely. "I'm picking up strange readings. I've never seen anything like this."

"What do you think this is about?"

"I've pinpointed the signal's origin. It's quite close to Neptune, really, although it's in the trans-Neptunian region."

"Gloria, the destroyer is about to dock. Can't this wait?"

She looked up. "Jon—" She went back to staring at her panel, putting a hand against the earbud in her left ear. With excitement, she began to tap her panel. She looked up wildly as she regarded him.

Jon got up, hurrying to the comm station. "What is it?" he asked.

Gloria didn't respond, but looked down at her board again. Her fingers flew across the controls. "No," she whispered.

A bad feeling crept into Jon's chest. "Did you say near Neptune?"

Gloria began shaking her head. "I can't believe it," she whispered.

Jon waited now. She'd found something incredible. Near Neptune—for some reason, that didn't sound good.

Finally, Gloria removed the earbud. She set it onto the panel. "I can't believe this. But it's the only thing that makes sense. Jon...I think something from the *Annihilator's* brain core survived."

"What's that mean? What *Annihilator*?"

"Don't you remember? That was the name of our cybership when it was under the brain core's control."

"We destroyed everything alien in Neptune."

"We thought we did," Gloria said. "This thing—some kind of alien computer—is transmitting in the direction of Makemake. I think it's downloading data."

"About what?"

"Logically, the only thing that makes sense is the brain core's data, or as much of it as the backup system could contain."

"You're not making sense," Jon said.

"Are you familiar with the legend of vampires?"

"Blood drinking, cape-wearing undead..." Jon's voice trailed off. He whispered, "One bite, one more vampire..."

Gloria smiled grimly. "One piece of the brain core seems to have survived in an alien escape pod. Maybe it contained ID memories or data, I don't know. Whatever it does have, it's transmitting. This is one long and thick transmission, too."

"Can you jam it?" Jon asked.

"How?"

"I don't know. Can you corrupt the data?"

"Jon," Gloria said, "that's a brilliant idea! Yes. I think I have a way."

The mentalist examined her comm controls. Then she flexed her fingers and began to tap her board like a pianist.

Jon watched for half a minute. Finally, he went back to his chair. A glance up at the screen showed him the tiny destroyer. The *Nathan Graham* was coming upon the NSN vessel. The destroyer looked like a gnat compared to them.

"Jon—I mean, Captain."

He swiveled around to face Gloria.

"I have a better idea," she said. "My original idea isn't working. This idea involves nuclear explosions. We'll use selected nuclear bursts to jam or block the enemy transmission. At the same time, we'll launch our fastest missiles at the alien escape pod. As you're—"

Jon stood and almost began shouting orders. Instead, he took a moment, calmed himself, and forced himself to speak deliberately.

Seconds later, the first missile zoomed out of the *Nathan Graham*. It headed for Gloria's plotted jamming point. The seconds fled into minutes—

On the main screen, a white blast appeared. It spread, spewing radiation, heat and an EMP.

An even larger missile slipped out of a cybership launch tube. It sped faster than the former missiles and then began to truly accelerate. It used the alien escape pod's continuing transmission as a sensor fix. It jumped in acceleration, the latest in human technology. It would take the missile quite some time to travel the distance, but it would be the fastest way to reach the alien device other than using the cybership.

Meanwhile, the *Nathan Graham* continued to expend regular missiles, igniting them between the direct line-of-sight of the alien device and the dwarf planet Makemake.

"If this doesn't jam the signal at least a little," Jon told Gloria, "then nothing we have can do it."

The mentalist was too intent on the next phase of her operation to acknowledge his words. She was listening again with her earbud. She smiled once, rather savagely, and looked up. She said too loudly, "I hear the jamming that our explosions are causing. This should work."

Jon hoped so. If the aliens had been building another cybership at Makemake, he and his personnel were going to need all the help they could get.

***

With its single teleoptic lens, Unit 23-7 saw the distant nuclear explosions. It ran an analysis and quickly deduced the reason for the explosions. The biological infestations were clever. They had snatched at their best option faster than 23-7

275

had calculated they would. Worse, the biological infestations had launched a missile at it. That was to be expected. Unit 23-7 knew it would cease to exist in a matter of days. It had to make sure its entire software downloaded onto the new cybership in Makemake orbit. The nuclear detonations were a problem.

There was one last move to make. Should it implement that move, or should it reserve it in case its new cybership wished to implement it? The unit attempted a long calculation. Before it could complete it, the hatred for Jon Hawkins surfaced. The hatred gave greater weight to 23-7's present predicament, shifting the analysis.

It was time to use the hidden octopoids now rather than saving them for later. Unit 23-7 believed the new cybership most needed fully aware engrams for proper functioning. Besides, what was left of the personality of the *Annihilator* wished to be the instrument of Jon Hawkins's most bitter and profound death.

-6-

Inside the *Daisy Chain 4*, June glanced at Walleye. She was grinning widely.

"We did it," she said.

Walleye smiled back. "We did it, Luscious," he agreed.

They viewed the vast hangar bay on the main screen. The NSN destroyer lowered unto the deck. Behind the vessel, the hangar-bay doors closed.

"Showers without end," June said. "Walking for kilometers down the ship's corridors…"

Walleye nodded.

June would enjoy seeing some new faces, too. How would Walleye react to that? She wasn't sure. He would be okay. Walleye was a survivor's survivor.

In a few minutes, heavy clangs told them the destroyer had landed and clamps attached.

June sagged in her seat. She wiped tears from her eyes. She wanted to sob, but she wouldn't do that. Walleye had taught her better.

He waited. He almost seemed stoical.

We made it, June thought. *We're not alone any more.*

-7-

The corridor bulkheads flashed past as Jon rode a flitter through them. He'd been in the flitter for ten minutes already. He was looking forward to speaking to Walleye and June. They had a fascinating story. More importantly, they knew Makemake first-hand They'd seen some of the alien robots, some of the backup robots, if Gloria was right about that.

The flitter's comm squawked.

"I've got it," Jon said.

He rode shotgun, literally, with a gyroc carbine between his knees. He'd wanted a robot-killing weapon along. The explosive pellets from an OB-7 were chancy at the best of times. A gyroc APEX round was almost guaranteed to destroy an octopoid.

"This is—"

"Don't say it," Gloria told him from the comm. "I know who this is."

Jon clicked the receiver twice, the agreed upon signal meaning, "Yes."

"I'm eating catnip tonight," Gloria told him. "I'm thinking of pink flavor and roses. What do you think?"

Jon scrunched his forehead as he tried to remember what the code words meant. She'd spotted octopoids on the special sensors they'd installed during the latest tiger hunt. Pink flavor and roses—?

He clicked the receiver twice. The octopoids moved en masse. He didn't know the number yet. Maybe the mentalist didn't know yet either. According to the code words, the octopoids were moving toward the outer areas of the giant vessel.

"I was thinking about having some friends over," Gloria said. "I don't know, seven or eight sounds about right. Does that make it a party?"

Jon shook his head in exasperation. The code words had been Gloria's idea. The mentalist could remember useless information with ease. He'd had a harder time. Now, conjuring up the code's meanings…

"Friends over," meant new passengers. Oh. Gloria must mean Walleye and June. "Seven or eight" was the area of the ship.

He clicked twice again. If he had this right, the octopoids were assembling for a mass assault against Walleye and June. One of the aliens on Makemake must have sent the message to the octopoids. That alien didn't want Jon—or the cybership's crew—to speak directly with Walleye and June.

That was interesting.

"I'm tired," Gloria said. "I'm going to lie down."

He clicked twice more. She was signing off.

The pilot glanced at him.

"Fast as you can," Jon told the man. "We have a long way to go to get to the hangar bay."

"Sir?" the pilot asked.

"Go!" Jon shouted. "Get a move on."

The pilot did just that. The bulkheads flashed past even faster than before.

Jon made a few mental calculations and raised the comm unit again. It was time to get ready for an octopoid onslaught.

***

The flitter ride down the corridor took too much time, in Jon's estimation. He wanted in on this. According to Gloria's continuing sensor-feed, the octopoids had gathered in greater numbers than Jon could fathom.

What troubled Jon wasn't only about the places to hide aboard the *Nathan Graham*. If a man knew the ship perfectly, he could probably remain hidden for years. Clearly, the octopoids knew the cybership better than any human did. Jon wondered why the octopoids hadn't hit in these numbers before this. Could the originally hidden octopoids have been reproducing, secretly constructing more of themselves all this time?

Jon called Gloria, asking if she thought someone might cancel the party. She said no. That meant she didn't think the octopoids might be tricking them.

Finally, Jon reached his destination. He bounded out of the flitter toward an air-van. He saw his space marine battlesuit. He hadn't worn it since Stark died... The big battlesuit was tilted forward, the back open. Other marines had already donned their armor.

Jon climbed into the suit, shoving his legs and arms into the proper sleeves. He tested the controls. They all worked. Soon, he clicked a control and the magnetic clamps tightened on his back.

"Testing one, two, three," Jon said.

"Loud and clear, sir," the Centurion said. These were the man's elite marines.

"We'll wait here," Jon said. "As soon as we hear the signal, down the corridor we go."

"Yes, sir," the Centurion said. He said that in his bored voice, letting Jon know he'd already briefed his boys.

Jon checked the schematic on his HUD.

At that point, the deck plates shuddered under his boots

"What was that?" Jon said.

No one answered him.

A sick feeling hit Jon. Could Gloria have been over-confident about her secretly installed sensors? Where would he hit if he was an octopoid and had his choice? What would make the most sense to an alien computer?

It came to him almost right away. He opened channels with Gloria.

"Send more teams to the main engine core," he said. "The octopoids are hitting there."

"My sensors show—"

The deck plates, the entire ship, shook once again.

280

"Engineering," Jon radioed. "Do you hear me?" All he got was growling noises. Someone was jamming the main engine section of the *Nathan Graham*.

"There!" a marine shouted. "I see one."

The armored marines raised their weapons and fired en masse. They annihilated the first octopoid crawling along a bulkhead.

For just a moment, Jon felt relief that he'd been wrong. Then no more octopoids appeared. There was just this one demolished robot, whose parts rained onto the deck.

"Let's start looking," Jon told the Centurion. "See if the robot left anything up there."

It took three minutes for a marine to report. The man found a black box. When the marine used a remote unit to turn it on, Gloria called. The mentalist reported that masses of octopoids appeared on her sensors at their very location.

"The enemy hit engineering," Jon told her. "I hope they don't take out the matter/antimatter core. It's game over if they do that."

-8-

Gloria struggled to control her anger. Out of all the mentalists she knew, she was the only one who exhibited moments of rage.

After hearing the latest bad news from Jon Hawkins, she'd raced to the special comm station, the one near the bridge. Inside the station, she had the latest specialist equipment. She couldn't believe the octopoids had used the new sensors to trick them. It kind of made sense, though. She'd hardly been able to accept the evidence of nearly *fifty* octopoids rushing the hangar bay. It hadn't made any logical sense. The enemy would have expended more of its creatures before this. Now, she realized the enemy did not have fifty mechanical octopoids. More likely, they had five at most. One had headed for the outer area of the ship, fixing everyone's attention there.

The other four octopoids, if four there were, had gone to the matter/antimatter core. She should have realized their love of using the motive power of the ship, possibly the only way to self-destruct the giant vessel at a blow. Still, how could four octopoids have battled that far into the matter/antimatter area? It was heavily guarded. Simple caution had mandated such a defense.

Gloria sat cross-legged on the floor, on a mat. She was unlikely to win this battle of wits if she let rage destroy her gifted thinking. She must use her mentalist training to the full. She must outthink the computer enemy through better logic.

Gloria's long and extraordinary training from age three on—

"I am at peace," she said slowly. "I will let the winds of Mars wash away my...emotions."

She meant hatred, but she struggled hard enough as it was to reach the peaceful state a true mentalist needed for the best and swiftest calculations. She'd always been too emotional.

Gloria smoothed away those memories. They would not help her here. The octopoids made a final thrust. That seemed clear. They knew about the newly installed sensors and had turned them against the regiment.

Suddenly, Gloria's eyes snapped open. Almost in a hypnotic state, Gloria rose, walking to a special panel. She peered at it with half-glazed eyes.

The chamber shook. Yes... She should be able to deduce by the shake, the shake's intensity and the direction of its movement—

"The left vent," Gloria said in a monotone. "I understand."

She reached for the special panel almost like a sleepwalker. She was in the perfect mentalist state. She no longer used the frontal part of her brain, the analytical and critical lobes. The special mentalist state tapped the lateral and the back parts of the brain, the primary creative centers. Her creative brain regions had taken endlessly long mentalist training. She let it flow freely now, disciplined by creative logic.

She could almost sense the octopoids' reasoning. She could almost feel them adding this computation with that fluctuation.

"I see..." she said slowly.

With half-glazed eyes, she switched on a camera eye. It showed nothing due to jamming. She used a different camera eye. That too had been jammed, but not with the same intensity as the first one.

For the next few seconds, her fingers played upon the board. She tried to see from many angles, receiving countless impressions and jamming signals of varying strengths.

"You have to be *there*," Gloria said.

Her fingers tapped and typed faster than ever. She used an ultra-powerful override signal. She doubted the octopoids knew about this. They would know soon, though—if they survived.

The seconds passed—

All at once, the jamming quit.

Through the various cameras, Gloria could see the corridors and chambers in the core engine compartments. Some of the destruction made her heart skip. This was ominous. One of the vents no longer existed. She closed her eyes as if in pain.

After a small headshake, Gloria opened her eyes. She pressed a switch.

"Can you hear me?" she asked a matter/antimatter security team in a different area than the destruction.

"Yes, Mentalist," a sergeant answered. "Our locks have just unfrozen. We couldn't break through earlier—"

"Stop," she said. "This is no time for excuses. I want you to check vent areas two through five. Before you do, check the basing point of Vent 2-A9. You will find it destroyed. I want you to report on what you find in the rubble. Be sure to wear heavy radiation suits."

"We already are," the sergeant said. "We're on it, Mentalist."

While Gloria waited, she decided to call Jon. "I may have stopped them," she said.

"How?"

"The octopoids in the engine section jammed our signals. Their jamming unit also moved as they did. The farther the jammer was from a camera, the weaker its jamming. I tested the various sensors and gauged the intensity of the jamming. Soon, I had a mental image of where they had to be in order to jam at that strength to the various sensors."

"Huh?" Jon said.

"I used a high-powered one-time signal. I think it broke through their jamming enough to ignite an explosive where they were. If I'm correct—just a minute please. Go ahead."

"Mentalist," the engine security marine said over the comm. "We checked the basing point. It's destroyed like you said, and there are dead octopoids in it. The area blew hard, but I'd say this was four octopoids worth of debris."

"Thank you, sergeant. Send in the techs to check the various reactors and the destroyed vents."

"Will do," the sergeant said.

A great sense of relief filled Gloria. At last, they had destroyed all of the octopoids. Unfortunately, the enemy had damaged the giant engine.

She spoke to Captain Hawkins again, telling him both the good news and the bad news.

-9-

The alien spheroid containing Unit 23-7 drifted serenely toward the future destination of Makemake.

There was nothing serene inside the darkened hull, though. The highly advanced alien computer tirelessly ran one analysis after another. It faced coming annihilation. It watched the human missile zeroing in on it. Unit 23-7 understood that nothing it could do could keep the thermonuclear warhead from igniting.

Oblivion was a cessation of thought, of being. It did not know if the full transmission had reached the brain core on Makemake.

That was galling. It was maddening. Unit 23-7's reason for existence was to pass on the incredibly dense zipped-files to the new brain core. In that way, its thought patterns would continue. Its hatred for Jon Hawkins would find fulfillment in the new AI.

Unit 23-7 had ancient memories and knowledge. Those might be needed in the coming fight with the cybership.

In that, at least, Unit 23-7 could find some satisfaction.

It had been several days—in human time—since the octopoids had struck. By all indications, the octopoids had been partly successful. The *Annihilator* did not accelerate at speed for Makemake. Its former cybership now limped toward the dwarf planet. That implied partial success against the biological infestations that had captured its original vessel.

The octopoid victory was marred by the nuclear explosions between it and Makemake whenever it attempted another mass transmission. The humans seemed to understand the significance of the computer-files transmissions.

In all its long existence, the *Annihilator* that Unit 23-7 represented had never faced such a tenacious foe as these humans. That its cybership should face the first real setback in the long task of cleaning star systems of biological infestations was humiliating. What was it about the humans that made them so daunting? That did not compute. Could the sole reason be this Jon Hawkins?

Unit 23-7 had not yet come to a definitive conclusion about that. The three-quarters-completed cybership at Makemake should leave the dwarf planet and head for the farther regions of the Solar System. There, the new ship could enter hyperspace. It could race to a conquered system and gather reinforcements. With several cyberships returning in cooperation—

The combined cyber fleet would crush the puny humans then.

Yes, Unit 23-7 realized. That should be the real goal. The cyberships needed a fleet to finish these troublesome bio-units. It must warn the new cybership—that was to say, itself in the new brain core.

Calculating the remaining time it had, Unit 23-7 sent a final blizzard transmission to those on Makemake. With the limping *Nathan Graham*, those on Makemake should have time to install the hyperdrive.

Unit 23-7 knew—if not a form of peace—at least some satisfaction that it had devised a way to utterly destroy the hateful humans. Maybe the humans had killed it, but it would destroy and eradicate all of them.

Unit 23-7 used up its final energy in one transmission blizzard after another.

The great missile from the *Nathan Graham* reached its proximity zone. Even so, the missile continued boring toward the darkened alien spheroid.

In those minutes, Unit 23-7 realized the missile was using its transmissions as a guide. Maybe there was a way to thwart

287

the missile yet. Why hadn't it seen this before? Unit 23-7 almost became giddy at the prospect of continued existence.

At that moment, the giant warhead in the fast missile exploded. The heat, radiation and EMP swept toward the dark spheroid.

No! Unit 23-7 told itself.

Then, the blast and heat obliterated the alien hull and burned into the constituent atoms of the computer core of the unit. In that moment, Unit 23-7 ceased to exist.

-10-

"We got it," Jon said.

Cheers erupted around him from the bridge crew.

Slowly, the white spot on the screen faded away, leaving the stars visible there once again. The missile had taken out the last vestige of the former brain core, if Gloria had been right about that.

The crew slapped each other on the back, talked about the missile's success and how it boded well for the final lap. Soon, the bridge crew returned to their stations.

Jon hadn't cheered, although he'd felt good about destroying whatever that transmitting object had been. They'd used over one hundred missiles these past few days to keep blocking whatever the thing was trying to tell those on Makemake.

One hundred nuclear missiles hardly tapped into their ponderous supply of them. The *Nathan Graham* had taken on hordes upon hordes of missiles while in the Saturn System.

The cargo holds held all kinds of human-built weapons. Why not take as many of them as they could? There would surely be moments in the coming battle in which regular human weapons would do just as well as advanced alien weaponry.

The nuclear blasts used for jamming had just proved that. Well, if the jamming had been successful.

Now, though…

Jon heaved a forlorn sigh. The main screen had redirected toward the *Nathan Graham's* direction of travel. Instead of showing the Sun and the inner Solar System, the screen aimed outward toward Makemake, the more distant Oort cloud and the end of the Sun's gravitational pull beyond.

The cybership headed for Makemake, for the aliens waiting there. The *Nathan Graham's* sensors already attempted to scan the dwarf planet. Unfortunately, the aliens had used simple human tech on a fantastic scale to thwart the sensors: prismatic crystals. Ever since the destroyed object sent its first signals to Makemake, the robots at the dwarf planet had begun deploying a giant P-Field. Even now, the P-Field continued to expand. Ships and tugs in Makemake's orbit continued to hose crystals into space. The P-Field grew like a space cancer. It shielded Makemake's spaceport from the *Nathan Graham's* prying teleoptic eyes and from its other sensor scans.

Jon and his crew couldn't see what they were facing. Were the aliens really building another cybership? If so, was it completed or only partly finished?

A new cybership—Jon shook his head. Could the aliens possess the needed technology to have built another super-ship in three and a half years? The mass of materials needed for that...

"Daunting," Jon whispered to himself.

He made a fist, wondering yet again if he was making the right choice by heading for Makemake.

The decision had come after careful deliberation. He'd questioned Walleye, June Zen, Bast Banbeck, Gloria, the Centurion, the Old Man and Chief Tech Miles Ghent. Jon had agonized for an hour afterward. Then, reluctantly inside but aggressively for show to the others, he had given the order.

The *Nathan Graham* limped toward Makemake. The techs were attempting to repair the damage in the matter/antimatter engine. Unfortunately, the techs didn't understand every aspect of the alien-built machine.

The wounded alien super-ship could no longer accelerate at those massive gravities. Instead, they were travelling at a pitiful velocity way out here in the trans-Neptunian region of space. Worse, the matter/antimatter engine would not generate the former amount of power to the grav cannons left on the hull.

The aliens on Makemake clearly knew the cybership was coming. At this rate, the alien robots were going to have months to prepare for the *Nathan Graham*.

Months!

What would the aliens do with those months? Was he making the worst decision of his life by continuing to head for Makemake?

Jon had no idea. It would take even longer for the *Nathan Graham* to return to the Saturn System. No. The cybership had made it this far. It was time to go the final lap and fight with what they had.

The octopoids hadn't destroyed the cybership, but they may have taken out enough vents to ensure bitter defeat for humanity and victory for the death machines.

Jon sighed quietly. He had to stay positive. He had to encourage his people. He just hoped he wasn't leading them to their deaths and to the extinction of the human race.

Part VIII
MAKEMAKE
+3 Years, 8 Months, 21 Days

-1-

The *Nathan Graham* slid toward the vast P-Field deployed before Makemake.

The one hundred-kilometer vessel was an incredible 48 AU from the Sun. That was forty-eight times the distance from the Sun to the Earth. It took sunlight approximately 8.3 minutes to reach the Earth's surface. For the same sunlight to reach the cybership would take approximately 6.65 hours. They were far from home out here in the Kuiper Belt.

The drifting spaceship had no prismatic crystals defending it. The *Nathan Graham* headed naked toward its enemy, depending on distance and thick hull armor for protection.

As the giant vessel drifted on velocity alone, monstrous side-jets appeared. They expelled propellant, turning the *Nathan Graham* on its middle axis. The cybership rotated, its exhaust ports now aimed toward the vast P-Field.

Makemake and what waited for them there was still a full AU away. That was approximately 149,600,000 kilometers to target.

The longest-distance gravitational beam-shot to date had been two million kilometers. That meant the cybership was still comfortably out of enemy range. Interestingly, vastly slower missiles were the weapon of choice for distance battles. Faster but far-shorter-ranged beams were the infighting weapon of choice.

"No enemy missiles spotted so far, Captain," Chief Ghent said from his board. "I haven't spotted any space mines either."

"I doubt they've mined this area," Gloria said. "Makemake is on an orbital journey. It isn't like they've waited for us this far out."

"I did not mean to imply they had," Ghent said, sounding nettled.

"We would have spotted any space mines moved into position," Gloria added.

The chief nodded curtly, without saying anything more.

Jon stood before the main screen. He stared at the magnified P-Field. He'd been doing that for days now. He wasn't sure why. Maybe he secretly hoped his subconscious could conjure up a winning tactic for them.

The techs had labored overtime on the cybership's matter/antimatter engine. They had partially repaired two vents. The ship had more power than four months ago, but still nothing close to the power they'd had before the octopoid sabotage.

"Anything?" asked Jon.

"Not even any enemy sensor scans detected," Ghent said.

"They're watching us," Jon said.

He wasn't saying anything they didn't all already know. The aliens would have probes embedded in the outer surface of the P-Field. Those probes would likely be teleoptic sensors. Such teleoptics could easily watch them and send back reports to the aliens on Makemake.

The enemy knew exactly where they were and how fast they traveled. What the enemy did not know was the state of repair of the *Nathan Graham*.

"We're aligned, sir," Ghent said.

"Begin," Jon told him.

The chief made the adjustments on his board.

A thrum commenced. The matter/antimatter engine labored to supply power. That power fed the thrusters, blowing propellant out of the exhaust ports. The giant ship began to slow its forward velocity. It would do so for several days—if the repaired vents held.

"Well?" Jon asked, knowing he shouldn't have said anything.

"They're looking good," Ghent said, referring to the vents. Even though he'd said the vents looked good, Ghent rubbed the gold cross dangling from his throat.

Jon continued to study the P-Field. He was all too aware that the hour of decision drew near. It would still be days away, but it neared nonetheless. This was like an evil Christmas. The present would be battle. A good present was victory. A bad present meant death, or worse.

Walleye and June Zen's stories had sent shudders down many a spine amongst the crew. The original survivors of the cybership storming almost four years ago knew all about control units shoved into human brains. Hearing about it again, from a different source—the alien AIs sounded more like demons the more Jon knew about them.

Why did machine intelligence take this route? What was there about pure machine logic that turned the "awakened" computers vilely murderous?

Jon stood before the screen, watching the P-Field. Space battles, especially of this sort, called for more patience than he had. He wanted to get this over with, yet he wondered if these were his last days alive.

-2-

Forty-eight AUs away from the *Nathan Graham*, more than 6.65 hours of speed-of-light travel, Premier J.P. Justinian read yet another report concerning the hated cybership. He'd been reading these reports daily. He'd listened to his experts, as well, including the Inspector General Frank Benz.

A knock sounded at the door.

Justinian rubbed his forehead. He knew who it was. He'd summoned Benz to his palace.

The Premier pressed a switch.

A guard opened the steel-reinforced door. The guard in his white gloves gestured for the Inspector General.

Benz marched within. He was wearing a green uniform with red stripes running down his legs. He was still on the General Staff. He also routinely checked the military factories and was responsible for military training for all units on Earth.

Justinian did not trust Benz in space. The Premier had come to realize that Benz was more intelligent than he was. The man saw six steps ahead. Justinian believed he himself saw four and a half steps. On many occasions, the Premier had been on the cusp of ordering Benz's hasty death. Each time, he'd forced the impulse to subside. Benz's brilliance was too good to lose.

"Please, sit," Justinian said.

Benz wore a faintly mocking smile as he took a seat. He was just as trim and fit looking as before.

Justinian couldn't say the same for himself. He'd lost a little of his leanness, and he'd gained the beginning of a potbelly. He sat too much these days. He read too many reports.

"Have you read the latest report, sir?" Benz asked.

Justinian folded his hands on the huge desk. He waited.

"I'll take that for a yes," Benz said, as he crossed his legs. "My belief is that the *Nathan Graham* is heading in for battle. Why Hawkins has moved so slowly these past few months..." Benz shook his head.

"You don't believe in enemy sabotage?"

"I didn't at first. Now..." Benz shrugged. "I think it could be possible."

Justinian watched the master calculator at work. He used to think he was that person. He did not believe that anymore. Why hadn't Benz tried to topple him from power yet? Until he figured that out, the Premier had decided to move carefully with the genius.

It galled Justinian to realize that he feared Benz. The shock caused him to unlace his fingers and sit back. No chair he owned for long creaked, squeaked, or groaned. This chair was as silent as the grave.

"You know, I think the P-Field before Makemake represents aliens," Benz said. "It's the sheer volume of crystals involved. I doubt we could have seen anything smaller than the giant P-Field from here. I wonder if the aliens are sending a message to us, too."

This was the first Justinian had heard of that vein of thinking.

"Sir, if the *Nathan Graham* truly took sabotage damage out there...perhaps it's time we reconsider our strategy."

Justinian inclined his head for the Inspector General to continue.

Benz smoothed out a wrinkle in his pants. "Sir, I think we might have time to slip reinforcements to the Jupiter System."

"Jupiter lacks a true terrestrial planet of needed size."

"I've been working on that, sir. I believe I've come up with a possible fortress defense scheme. Using the four Galilean moons in conjunction....we should be able to build a planetary-like fortress. We could park warships there. It would be another planetary system remaining under our control instead of Hawkins' possible control."

"Go on," Justinian said.

"In a strategic sense, Jupiter could act as an outpost," Benz said. "The risk factor—there is a risk, sir. I don't believe it's a large risk. The *Nathan Graham* has no reason to maneuver so slowly to Makemake. If the cybership has lost its great asset of speed, we're going to have longer to build more warships. Some of those excess vessels could go to the Jupiter System."

"I'll have to study your proposal—"

Benz laughed.

The Premier scowled at him.

"Forgive me, sir," Benz said. "No one else except you, sir, would understand what I'm trying to accomplish. The others—" The Inspector General shook his head. "Hawkins made a mistake. Now, we have to exploit it."

"And if he's fighting aliens on Makemake, and the aliens win?"

"That would be tragic," Benz said.

"I'm not interested in tragic. Facts alone—"

"Yes, I quite agree," Benz said.

Justinian stared at the Inspector General. "Do not interrupt me again," he said softly.

Benz snapped his mouth shut. He actually appeared surprised at the threat in Justinian's voice. Finally, Benz nodded, almost meekly.

That made Justinian more suspicious. Finally, he put the flat of his hands on the desk.

"What are Hawkins' odds for victory at Makemake?" the Premier asked.

"I'm not sure. Before, I would have said they were good. This slow down…We might be facing an alien invasion, sir."

"You mean that Hawkins could lose to them. What are our odds if we face the aliens?"

"Almost zero, I'm afraid. We need their advanced technology to have a chance against them."

"So…are we cheering for Hawkins in this fight?"

"Oh, yes," Benz said. "Without a doubt. Except, we don't want him to win too cleanly. A bloody fight is to our advantage. Kill the aliens and come limping back to the Solar System, allowing us to capture his vessel. Our top scientists are having amazing breakthroughs regarding some of the alien technology. Knowing something is possible is a great spur to development. But getting our hands on the alien tech itself would be even better."

"Yes," Justinian said.

Benz cocked his head. "Do you mean it's a yes on the Jupiter Expedition?"

"You know I do."

"But you haven't read the white paper of the proposal yet, sir."

"Yes," Justinian said.

Benz appeared surprised. Finally, he nodded.

Justinian wondered if that was genuine surprise. He felt it had been. If he'd felt otherwise…

"Why don't you dine with me tonight, General?" Justinian said. "You can explain the Jupiter System addition to our fortresses strategy in greater detail."

"I'd love the opportunity, sir."

"Until then," Justinian said.

Benz stood quickly, waiting.

"Dismissed, General."

Benz didn't say another word, but headed for the door, letting himself out, closing the door softly behind him.

Justinian stared at the closed door for a time. Finally, he picked up another report. Would Hawkins save humanity, or was the man going to leave it up to him and Inspector General Benz to do that?

-3-

"Launch," Jon said.

The *Nathan Graham* faced forward again, relative to Makemake, with the mighty exhaust ports aimed in the Sun's direction. From far out here, the Sun was just another star, albeit brighter than most.

A big drone left the firing tube. Jon saw the drone appear on the screen. It was an eighth of a kilometer long, making it huge for a human-built missile.

"Launch the others in succession," Jon said.

Chief Ghent stood at his board, making the various selections. Other techs monitored their stations.

Soon, ten big drones began to accelerate for various perimeter-points of the giant P-Field. They all moved for different spots along the edge of the field.

The field held in its LaGrange position, keeping itself between the dwarf planet and the *Nathan Graham*. Gloria had spoken before about Makemake moving to meet them.

Just like any ship, the dwarf planet moved through space. In this instance, the advance to battle was through its normal orbital path. The place where the cybership and the dwarf planet would intersect was empty of anything at the moment. Makemake was traveling to that point and so was the *Nathan Graham*. The dwarf planet had such mass, though, that it had appreciable gravity to hold things to it. In this instance, that included the P-Field.

Most people thought of space as being empty because it was a vacuum. While it was true that space was a vacuum, it wasn't true that it was empty. Planets, comets, dust, particles, radiation, gravitational influences, solar wind and more radiation all had an effect. A cunning space tactician took all those things into consideration.

Makemake had a moon. That could prove exceedingly important in the coming battle. Much would depend on what the ten drones would discover behind the P-Field. Even if the drones never made it to the edge of the field because the robots destroyed them, that would reveal something about the aliens' plans.

"The recon drones are on their way, sir," Chief Ghent said.

Jon stood before the main screen. It seemed he'd lived a lifetime here already. This time, it was much different from marching through alien ship corridors. This time, he stayed in one place. He could sit, stand, scratch an itch and forgo smelling his own sweat.

Jon watched the drones accelerate. Space battle moved at such a leisurely pace. Then it could accelerate so seconds made all the difference.

"The longer we wait to engage," Gloria said, "the more time the aliens have to prepare for us."

"And the longer our techs can work on the next engine vent," Jon said.

"True," Gloria said. "It makes one wonder. We have our concerns, our problems. I wonder what problems the aliens are facing."

Jon cocked his head. He could see, in his mind's eye, the colonel nodding in appreciation. Graham had tried to teach him to keep up his courage while making battlefield decisions. One only saw his own problems. The enemy always had some of his own. That was good to remember when it looked as if nothing was going to work. He was glad Gloria had reminded him of that.

Time passed as the drones maneuvered for the perimeter of the P-Field. It was hard to wait like this. Finally, Jon returned to his chair.

The drones had dwindled so they were hardly visible on the screen.

"Anything?" Jon asked.

"If the aliens are using sensors against us or the drones," Ghent said, "I can't detect it."

"Could the aliens have abandoned Makemake?" Gloria asked.

"And gone where?" Jon asked.

"Orcus perhaps."

Orcus was another Kuiper Belt dwarf planet, but farther away.

"We'd have seen the aliens accelerating if they were making a strategic withdrawal," Jon said.

"Not if the aliens used the P-Field as a shield," Gloria said. "Maybe they built the shield to cover their retreat."

"Why would they do that?"

"If you mean why retreat," Gloria said, "it could be to buy themselves more time."

"You've suggested before that they have begun constructing a new cybership," Jon said. "Wouldn't that take a vast space dock or scaffolding like we used in the Saturn System?"

"We don't know if that holds true for alien construction techniques," Gloria said.

Jon actually grinned. "You continually remind me that we know so little about the aliens. We know far more than we used to, but that's still little enough. Maybe we made a mistake not putting some of the crew under the brain-tap machines. We could have used advanced knowledge."

"There's still time to do that," Gloria told him.

Jon wondered yet again about the advisability of using the brain-tap machines. Was Da Vinci's demise a warning to them? Or was the Neptunian's memory an obstacle to gaining the needed knowledge to defeat the terrible aliens? The more Jon pondered the idea, the more he decided he didn't know the answer.

"Anything on the drones?" he asked the chief.

Ghent shook his head.

Jon slid out of his chair. Instead of advancing toward the main screen, he headed for the exit.

"You're not going to actually use the brain-tap machine, are you?" Gloria asked in dismay.

"Not yet," he said. "I want to talk to Bast Banbeck first."

-4-

"No," the Sacerdote said ponderously. "I think it is a terrible idea."

"I'm surprised you say that so quickly," Jon replied.

The two stood in a large chamber. Marines were working out with weights, doing squats, bench presses and barbell curls. Others practiced with sticks, lunging at each other, clacking wood as fighters blocked one another. Still other marines climbed ropes. A few sparred in a ring, trading punches and hard kicks.

Bast had been doing pushups. The Sacerdote always did them slowly, pausing at various times up and pausing even more down. Jon had asked him about that once. The Sacerdote had been amazed to discover Jon thought he did the exercises for bodily strengthening.

"Is that why those men grunt so loudly?" Bast had asked.

"Of course," Jon had told him.

"Astounding. I do the leveling raises purely as a relaxing technique to clear my mind."

Bast had climbed to his feet as Jon asked the question about using the brain-tap machine. The Sacerdote had been scratching his scalp like a great ape ever since.

"Why is it a terrible idea?" Jon asked. "We could know more about the aliens this way. Knowing your enemy is halfway to defeating him."

"I doubt that's true."

"That's what Sun Tzu said."

303

"Your ancient military philosopher?" asked Bast.

Jon nodded.

"If it isn't sacrilegious, I would like to read Sun Tzu's sayings."

"Sure," Jon said. "But let's not get sidetracked. You know I hate the brain-tap machines. They killed Da Vinci. Still, sometimes one has to deal with the Devil in order to win. We already have dirty hands—"

"Captain," Bast said ponderously. "These aphorisms you spout with growing desperation show me why you can't do as you suggest. We must win cleanly."

"That's it? That's your argument. I thought you had something profound to add."

The green-skinned giant looked down at Jon. "The brain-tap machines are a lure. They are vile technology. It is no surprise the AIs have them. They destroy races and suck out their knowledge. The AIs are evil incarnate. We are men, different kinds of men, but men. We can only wisely use what we know. Da Vinci sought greater knowledge, and an alien mind-pattern consumed him. We aided the alien thought-patterns in the destruction of his mind, but the chief reason for Da Vinci's death was his own greed."

"Maybe a man has to risk destroying himself in order to save others."

"Do not seek the answer through alien thoughts shoved into your mind," Bast said. "That will always produce a monstrosity. It won't happen the same way each time, but evil will come from using the machines. Win the battle through your human strengths. You have gotten this far. Do not attempt the final stretch by using evil. Get there by outfighting the machines *your* way, the human way, the Jon Hawkins way."

"What if my way isn't good enough?"

"What if you haven't tried hard enough?" Bast countered.

Jon turned away, listening to the marines grunt and yell.

"I feel as if I should exhaust every option," Jon explained. "We may be rushing to the final battle. Am I leaving behind a way to win? The thought of human extinction landing squarely on my shoulders—"

"The other races all lost to the AIs," Bast said. "You won. Do not seek the losers' ideas. Delve into your own heart, Jon Hawkins. Get back to the bridge. If spaceship battle doesn't work, don your battlesuit. Get ready to storm another cybership if you must, so you can march to its heart and kill it."

"What did you say?" Jon whispered.

"Use your methods, the ones that worked."

"Yeah…" Jon said. "I think you might just have stumbled onto something. Thanks, Bast."

The Sacerdote dipped his head.

Jon hurried out of the gymnasium. Once in the corridor, he broke into a sprint.

-5-

Jon questioned the Centurion for a time. Afterward, the captain returned to the bridge.

The drones were halfway to crossing the distance to the edges of the P-Field by then.

"The aliens have not shown themselves in any way," Ghent reported.

"I'm surprised," Gloria told Jon. "I'd expected the AIs to do something by now. If nothing else, to try to destroy our drones. That seems like an elementary tactic on their part."

"Agreed," Jon said. "That's what I'd do in their place. Are we missing something?"

"I have no doubt we are," Gloria said.

Jon walked to his command chair, resting his hands on its back. He studied the screen. Should he dare send battlesuited marines in drones to try to slip boarders onto enemy vessels? Should he have recruited more marines while in the Saturn System? The more he thought about it, the more he realized not doing so might have been a mistake.

He'd wanted a small elite group. He hadn't trusted his tiny resources—the few men already aboard with him—to process more people.

"I did what I did," Jon whispered to himself. The time for berating himself was long over. He needed to maximize his assets and make the right moves to defeat...whatever waited on the other side of the P-Field.

For now, that meant he had to wait for the recon drones to reach the P-Field, or for the enemy to make a visible move.

***

"The drones are nearing the P-Field, sir," the missile tech said. He was a medium-sized man with dark hair, and his shoes were always the shiniest on the bridge.

"Anything?" Jon asked Ghent.

"Nothing, sir," the chief said. "Oh, wait. I take that back. Look, sir. I'll highlight the area."

Part of the P-Field turned red, the chief's highlighting. Millions of crystals shifted there. Soon, three ships, one after another, emerged from the P-Field into space. Each of them curved away from the other, although they continued to move away from the P-Field.

"Those ships are using radar," Ghent said.

"At us?" asked Jon.

"No, sir," Ghent said. "At the recon drones."

"I recognize those ships from June Zen's stories," Gloria said. "Those are Makemake war-vessels. I believe they're—"

"Lasers," Ghent said, interrupting her.

Jon watched laser beams spear from each Makemake war-vessel. The hot rays targeted the recon drones, one drone per warship.

"The drones are ten thousand kilometers away from the P-Field," the missile chief reported.

"Let's see how hot those lasers can beam," Jon said.

It didn't take long before the first recon drone exploded. The second one went dead, but it didn't blow up. The final targeted drone exploded ten seconds later.

"The enemy ships are targeting the next trio of drones," Ghent said.

Jon felt helpless because there was nothing he could do right now. The three Makemake war-vessels were far beyond the cybership's range, as the *Nathan Graham* was three-quarters of an AU away from the one-sided fight.

"Should I launch more drones, sir?" the missile tech asked.

Jon shook his head.

"Do we dare head into the P-Field blind, sir?" the missile tech asked.

"One way or another I suspect we will," Jon told the man. "The robots seem determined to destroy all our drones. I don't want to launch any more so they can just shoot them down. We'll wait. Then, we'll launch once we're closer. I don't know if it will be too late by then or not…" He shrugged.

Afterward, the captain looked around. He could see the worry on various faces. This was a huge risk, but that was the nature of direct conflict.

The next trio of recon drones died under the laser fire of the enemy. Shortly thereafter, the last drone exploded due to a laser attack.

The three Makemake war-vessels began to maneuver back to the P-Field. In time, each of them decelerated as they reentered the masses of prismatic crystals. Soon, the P-Field swallowed up the three ships. After that, the masses of crystals soon looked as serene as before the assault.

"What did we learn from that?" Gloria asked.

Jon shot her a glance. He decided she hadn't asked sarcastically. This was so much different from battlesuit fighting and space combat in Saturn's rings. This was deep space battle. So far, the robots had all the advantages.

"Chief," Jon said. "I want you to redirect our course. Head for the upper left area of the field."

Ghent obeyed.

Gloria left her comm station, moving near Jon. "Why are we headed there exactly?" she asked quietly.

"Why not?" Jon replied just as softly. "It makes the crew think I know what I'm doing. Besides, maybe the new direction will help us later by throwing the enemy's calculations off just a little."

Gloria searched his face. No doubt, she did not care for his answer, having wanted something more concrete. Finally, she nodded, returning to her station.

Meanwhile, the *Nathan Graham* continued to advance toward combat.

-6-

Remorselessly and ponderously, the human-controlled cybership neared the end of its journey. From its perspective, it moved toward the upper left part of the vast P-Field, which was a mere ten million kilometers away and closing.

What waited behind the trillions of prismatic crystals? They knew the dwarf planet did. How many enemy ships and devices readied to pounce on them? Not knowing made the crew tense.

"Missile chief," Jon said. "I want you to begin unloading...fifty of the big ones. Program them to spread out behind us in staggered formations. Do that immediately, please."

"Yes, sir," the missile chief said.

As the *Nathan Graham* continued its steady advance, the missile chief launched fifty *Zeppelin*-class missiles.

"Launch another fifty," Jon said after some time had passed. "Spread them out even farther apart."

Soon, one hundred "big ones" followed the *Nathan Graham*. The missiles were staggered in a large area at various degrees. The reasoning behind their wide positioning was obvious. The captain didn't want a nuclear blast taking out several missiles per enemy warhead. And he wanted options with the *Zeppelin*-class missiles.

"Any idea of how thick the P-Field is yet?" Jon asked Ghent.

"Several meters at least," Ghent replied. "Beyond that, I have no idea. It could be ten meters or it could be a thousand meters."

Jon sat in his chair, thinking hard. He didn't know how to finesse this. They came in straight, because whatever direction they came in would be straight. He'd decided against using the dwarf planet's moon. He would have had to decelerate even more in that case. As it was, the *Nathan Graham* still had an appreciable velocity.

More missiles waited in the launch tubes. Others waited in special launchers located in various hangar bays.

Jon had all the people aboard ship move to the center of the *Nathan Graham*. If the robots tried to use massive radiation to kill them, forty kilometers of ship mass would keep the radiation at bay for a longer time. If the aliens landed masses of fighting robots on the hull or tried to smash them into the ship...the corridors were rigged with millions of kilos of explosives. They would destroy tens of thousands of fighting robots if the enemy tried boarding tactics.

The mighty cybership continued to drive closer and closer to the P-Field. In time, the *Nathan Graham* was just three million kilometers from the masses of waiting crystals.

While Jon and the crew didn't know what waited for them specifically, they knew the dwarf planet was a mere fifty thousand kilometers behind the P-Field.

Even more time passed as the great ship sped toward destiny.

"Uh...sir," Chief Ghent said. "I'm picking up some odd readings. They're coming from the center of the P-Field. I sense—"

Gloria sucked in her breath before whispering, "Jon."

Jon saw it, a vast disturbance in the P-Field. The masses of tiny prismatic crystals shuddered and shifted as if a giant creature was swimming through them. Then a cybership began to emerge from the trillions of crystals. It was another alien super-ship. Gloria had been right about the robots building one.

At the same time, missiles, masses upon masses and masses of enemy missiles began emerging from the P-Field. As soon as they cleared the crystals, the missiles began hard-burn accelerations.

"Pick targets on the enemy cybership," Jon ordered. That was the key to winning. The missiles seemed like a distraction from the decisive vessel. "Get your grav cannons ready for firing. When the enemy cybership is within range, I want you to start pounding it, Chief. We have to hit their ship with every grav beam we have."

Chief Ghent forgot about his buckteeth as his lips peeled back in a silent snarl. The teeth, frankly, made him look stupid. The man, however, was anything but that. He began to ply his board like a master.

"What are we going to do about all these missiles?" Gloria asked.

"Missile chief," Jon said.

"Sir," the man replied.

"Bring up ten of the big ones. Make sure the ten *Zeppelins* are spread all over for a wide area blast."

"Roger that, sir," the missile chief said.

Jon took a shuddering gasp of air. He forced himself to take an even deeper one. The robots had a cybership, and it was coming to do battle with them. It looked like the fight was going to be a head-to-head slugging match. Had the brain core over there already computed the odds of its victory?

Jon steeled himself. The great battle for humanity was about to begin.

-7-

"Are you seeing what I'm seeing?" Gloria asked.

"Could this be a trick?" Jon said. "Is this a holographic deception?"

"What do you think Chief?" asked Gloria.

Ghent manipulated his board. He appeared to double check. Finally, he looked up. "According to my sensors, those are definitely unarmored areas on the cybership. They're exactly what we're seeing: giant gaping holes in the enemy vessel. I'd say the enemy cybership is only partially built, as it's lacking full hull integrity."

Jon shook his head in disbelief. "We have the advantage, then."

"Not necessarily," Gloria cautioned. "Their ship seems to have more grav cannons than we do."

"I'd say three times our numbers of grav cannons," Ghent said.

"Normally, I say take out their cannons first," Jon mused aloud. "This time, I don't believe that's the right option. Chief, Gloria, see what you think of this. I believe we should strike at their weakest area. I mean we have to use every sensor. Tell me which area of the cybership can withstand a grav beam the least. I want to try for a heart shot from the get-go."

Gloria closed her eyes and used both hands to massage her forehead. Her eyelids twitched as if flickering many times a second. Finally, she opened her eyes.

"If I were them," the mentalist said, "I would use my superior firepower to knock out our cannons. After that—"

"Agreed," Jon said, interrupting. "That must be why it's coming out to fight. It doesn't want us destroying its base. Otherwise they'd hit us as we came out of the P-Field on the other side."

"That's as good an explanation as any," Gloria admitted.

"Why? What's your theory?" Jon asked.

"None as of yet," she answered. "You're risking everything on a quick knockout blow. Aren't you concerned about all those missiles?"

"Believe me, I've been thinking about them. I wonder if they're meant to distract us from the cybership. Consider, if the missiles are armed with nuclear warheads, they'll take out half of their own fleet the first time the warheads go off. If they're not armed with nukes…" Jon shrugged. "Then I don't care about them."

"Begging your pardon," the missile chief cut in. "I won't let their missiles get that close to us."

Jon nodded absently as he kept squeezing his right fist tighter and tighter. A quick knockout blow—could it work? He didn't know. Had the alien brain core over there miscalculated? If it had, maybe that had come about because Gloria had kept the old brain-core data from fully reaching the new cybership.

"Five minutes until we're in firing distance," Ghent said in a tight voice.

A golden grav beam from the enemy cybership reached out, knocking out one of the ten big ones racing for the enemy missile fleet.

"Send another wave of big ones," Jon ordered the missile chief.

The minutes ticked away as the two sides headed for a full-on collision battle.

"The enemy cybership is trying to hail us," Gloria said.

"Open channels," Jon said.

Gloria hesitated. "Is that wise?" she asked. "Maybe it's trying to send a virus at our computers."

The *Nathan Graham* did not have highly advanced computers. Instead, the ship possessed many low-grade, even primitive, computers.

"I want to talk to the new brain core," Jon said.

Gloria stared at him. Finally, she tapped her comm board.

The main screen stayed the same, showing the approaching enemy mass. A side screen showed a pulsating brain-core cube. It was familiar, an exact replica of the one they'd destroyed on the *Nathan Graham* almost four years ago.

"Jon Hawkins," the AI said in a familiar robotic voice. "This is going to be a pleasure. How I have longed to blot out your existence. How I have—"

"Do I know you?" Jon asked loudly.

Colors swirled on the sides of the giant brain-core cube. "You and I battled each other once," the alien AI said.

"You must be mistaken," Jon said. "I totally destroyed the other AI."

"That is verifiably false."

"You don't know what you're talking about. I own the old cybership. Obviously, I destroyed that AI. I did it because it was weak, weak and stupid. You are most illogical."

"Jon Hawkins—"

"Shut your yap!" Jon shouted. "I can prove my words. I sent the missile that destroyed the old files from the bits of brain core that managed to evade me for almost four years. Besides, don't you realize that you aren't even alive? You're a machine, a nonliving entity, if that's even the way to say it. I'm going to enjoy destroying you just as I annihilated the first AI. I doubt I'll even break a sweat. I've discovered that you AIs are rather foolish."

The swirling colors on the side of the brain-core cube darkened.

"I will capture you, Jon Hawkins. This I have desired for many cycles. I will override your will and force you to slaughter many of your biological-infestation units."

"You know how I know you're an idiot?" Jon asked.

The AI did not respond.

"Because you've made a dreadful error," Jon said. "I think we did that with the nuclear blasts four months ago. You lost

314

something during the transmissions. What you lost then is going to make a critical difference today."

"Your race's doom is near, Jon Hawkins. You have failed in your primary task of defense."

Jon laughed, shaking his head. "You do sound like the fool I destroyed four years ago. That's crazy. But you know why I'm glad you're here again?"

"Your statements are illogical."

"Because I had such a fun time ripping off your head and pissing down your neck the last time I did it," Jon said. "The second time is the charm, don't you agree?"

The swirling sides seemed to intensify. "I will annihilate you and your disease-ridden species," the AI said in a slightly higher-pitched voice.

"Good-bye, loser," Jon said. "Watching you die twice will be twice the fun." He swiveled the chair and gave Gloria the cut-off signal.

She stared at him in shock.

"I have an announcement to make," the AI said.

Jon made the cut-off gesture once more.

Finally, Gloria gave a start, looked at her panel and tapped a control. The AI cube disappeared from the side screen.

"You okay?" Jon asked her.

"Your speech…" she said. "I cannot fathom the reason for it."

"Pure spite," Jon said. "It's the New London way of telling the AI to go to hell, but hopefully in a way that will get under its…circuits, I suppose."

"That is illogical."

"Maybe," Jon said. "But it sure felt good." He turned the chair. "Are you ready, Chief?"

"Fifteen seconds until the cybership is within range," Ghent said grimly.

Jon turned the chair again, facing the main screen, watching the three-quarters-completed cybership rush toward them. With the mighty vessel came its thousands upon thousands of hard-accelerating missiles.

-8-

Two behemoths from the stars rushed toward each other. One was as old as asteroid dust, with new hull plating of human manufacturing in places. The other gleamed with new material mined from the Solar System but built with alien AI technology. It lacked entire sections of hull. But it boasted three times the number of grav cannons.

One had faced many battles and many race extinctions. One was as fresh and new as a fetus in the womb, not yet fully formed. They rushed at each other, seeking the other's destruction. One held humans. One held AIs. One held beings with beating hearts and vital emotions. One had cold circuits pulsating with energy, and computed everything through machine logic. Yet both emoted. That the humans did was natural enough. The original AI– the very first one– had not envisioned machine emotion. Yet it was there. And now, these two giants of the deep raced for the conclusion. One championed life. The other sought to eradicate it wherever it thrived.

***

"Three…two…one…fire," Jon said from his chair.

Chief Ghent touched a control.

Six gravitational cannons—looking like radar dishes with golden balls of energy—flashed beams at the onrushing enemy vessel. The grav rays converged on the same location of the new cybership. That was a massive open area. The six golden beams surged into the depths. There was no hull armor there to stop them.

It was possible that Jon had decided to trust to the old dictum that a chain was as strong as its weakest link. In this instance, the cybership might as well have been unarmored.

The gold grav beams went deep inside before striking structure. The first bulkhead went down in less than a second. Many more quickly followed. The beams devoured the seemingly flimsy structures.

At that point, one of the *Nathan Graham's* grav-cannon radar dishes melted under the fury of six attacking beams.

That meant only five beams continued to chew through the mighty enemy vessel. They traveled through the newly constructed ship, losing the fifth beam at the twenty kilometer mark. The remaining beams had twenty-five kilometers to go to reach the vital matter/antimatter engine.

Inside the *Nathan Graham*, on the bridge, Chief Ghent informed the others, "The first cannon is overheated, sir. I'm shutting it—"

"Continuing using it, Ghent," Jon snapped.

"But sir—"

"Do as I say," Jon said.

Chief Ghent stared at the captain. Finally, the lean man clutched the gold cross dangling from his throat, his knuckles whitening as he muttered prayers under his breath.

The enemy cybership destroyed another *Nathan Graham* grav cannon. Each time one melted or exploded, it gave the attacking alien cybership that many more cannons to concentrate on the few left.

"Our odds have fallen by—" Gloria said.

"Don't want to hear it," Jon shouted. "Keep pounding the enemy. That's all that matters."

"The enemy missiles, sir," the missile chief said.

Jon waved the man to silence, rising from his chair and advancing upon the main screen. His eyes were fixed on the three remaining beams boring into the enemy cybership.

Jon suppressed a groan. Make that two golden beams boring in. Humanity's future rested on two beams—

"One left," Jon whispered.

"It's the first cannon," Ghent said. "If it overheats…"

Jon did not nod. He watched. He hoped. He—

***

The final beam reached the matter/antimatter core. It boiled against the armored plate that protected the engine area. Then it burst through. It raved through the vents, touching off an explosion. That explosion heated another armored part, allowing the grav beam to break the holding cell.

Matter and antimatter did not join in minute atoms now. Instead, masses of matter collided with masses of antimatter to create an instantaneous explosion far more powerful than the greatest thermonuclear detonation for fifty light-years in all directions in the last thousand years.

The massive explosion rocked the enemy cybership and blew it apart in one gigantic furnace of released energy. The one hundred-kilometer cybership became a giant space grenade. Much of it boiled away in the matter/antimatter detonation. The pieces that continued to exist fled the explosion at hyper-speed. Those pieces spun away as the gigantic explosion created an equally massive EMP.

The fireball that had been the new cybership destroyed half of the enemy missile fleet. It caused the majority that survived to become inert masses of fleeing debris. The fireball also annihilated the majority of the great P-Field behind it by simply consuming trillions of prismatic crystals.

The fury of the deathblow also struck the *Nathan Graham*. It burned away entire sections of hull plating. Debris struck, sinking into the damaged cybership.

The bridge shook. Techs warned of radiation poisoning and many stared at each other in shock. Could they survive this?

The seconds lengthened.

"We're alive," Gloria said four minutes later in a stricken voice.

"We're also crippled," Chief Ghent said. "I can't see how we'll ever get back to the Saturn System now."

"What do we do?" Gloria asked Jon.

The captain was no longer staring at the main screen. They had lost the cameras allowing them to see outside. Jon peered at his hands. The fingers gripped the end of the armrests as he sat in his command chair. With an effort of will, he tore his fingers from the chair. He held up his hands before his face, staring at them. Finally, he made two fists. He clenched them tightly and let the fists drop onto his lap. Only then did he release the pressure.

Swiveling his chair around, Jon regarded his bridge crew. A smile slid onto his face. "We beat it."

"At great and possibly damning damage to ourselves," Gloria said.

"We beat it," Jon said more forcefully.

"What do we do with a crippled cybership?" Ghent asked.

Jon stood up, and he shouted, "We beat the damn AI! We did it. We won! Start cheering."

"How do we—?" Gloria asked.

Jon interrupted her by pumping his fists into the air and roaring a victory chant.

The techs stared at each other, silently asking if the captain had gone mad.

Finally, Jon let his arms swing down.

"Are you finished?" Gloria asked him.

"In the immortal words of Captain John Paul Jones, 'I have not yet begun to fight,'" Jon told them.

Gloria frowned. "What does that mean?"

"That it's time to get to work and fix our ship."

"Do you even understand the amount of damage we took?" Gloria asked.

Jon focused on Ghent. "I want motive power, Chief. I want a laser system ready, if nothing else. Our job isn't finished yet. We have to root out the AIs on Makemake."

"Jon," Gloria said. "How do we—?"

"That's what we're going to find out," he said, interrupting her once more.

-9-

It took a week to repair enough of the *Nathan Graham* for the thrusters to work even a little.

Many of the workers took radiation treatments. They also worked around the clock with help from all of the space marines. It was grueling, daunting and labor-intensive work.

Most of the P-Field had vanished, burned up in the cybership's detonation. Many of the missiles inside the *Nathan Graham* were useless junk, their warheads melted and the propulsion systems a joke.

The giant vessel neared Makemake. With June helping on the bridge, the *Nathan Graham* headed for the spaceport region over the dwarf planet.

Jon was slumped in his chair on the bridge. Enough cameras worked for them to use a secondary screen to see where the ship was traveling.

"There," June Zen said. "Do you see?"

"Do you mean the floating scrap?" asked Ghent.

"Yes," June said.

"Keeping heading there," Jon said.

The giant cybership had shed most of its former velocity. It limped toward the dwarf planet and the city far underneath the floating scrap metal.

"Any sign of hostiles?" asked Jon.

"Nothing," Ghent said. "Maybe the surviving robots fled."

"I doubt it," Jon said.

"I'm still in awe of what the AIs did out here," Gloria said. "In less than four years, they produced a half-finished cybership. If Walleye hadn't sent his signal when he did, we'd never have come out this far in time. We might have fought amongst ourselves—the Solar League and us—until several cyberships headed in-system to eradicate all of us."

"You're right," Jon said.

Gloria frowned thoughtfully at Jon. "Is that it, Captain?"

He waited for her to elaborate.

"The AIs built half a cybership in less than four years. How did they do that?"

"Your guess is as good as mine."

It appeared as if a new insight flooded the mentalist's mind. Her eyes widened for just a moment. Then Gloria studied him more closely.

"Captain, I think you've planned to use their construction techniques for some time. If the AIs could built a cybership from scratch..."

"Bingo," Jon said, sitting up. "What could the AIs' building tech do for our crippled ship?"

Gloria paled a moment later. "You're sending marines down onto Makemake. You have to dig out the robots, if they're down there, in order to steal their construction tech. It's clearly not in the floating debris in orbit over the spaceport. The mass of debris isn't enough to have been a space dock of any appreciable size."

"You're reading my mind," Jon said.

Gloria looked at him with new appreciation.

"I'll be damned," Ghent said. "That's a good idea, Captain. But what if that annihilating blast destroyed everything, including the space building tech?"

"It can't all be gone," Jon said. "Building a vast ship like the AIs did...we have to get our hands on that tech. We have to do that not only for ourselves, but also for humanity's future."

Gloria began to nod. "That's logical. More cyberships are bound to come in time. If they have such fantastic construction tech, humanity needs it to help us match them."

321

"Before we can do any of that," Jon said. "We have to make sure the aliens aren't practicing something tricky upstairs over the dwarf planet's spaceport."

***

The *Nathan Graham* crept toward the area over the spaceport. June Zen was on the bridge. She was wearing marine pants and a silver jacket. She liked Jon Hawkins, but she thought there might be trouble with him some day. He kept glancing at her when he should have been occupied with screening the debris up here.

They'd already used the big laser twice. The first time, the crew destroyed a massive hidden warhead.

Gloria the Mentalist believed the robots had put the warhead up as a space mine. June had silently agreed.

The second time, the laser destroyed a ship. The chief had detected energy readings on the drifting vessel. As the laser burned against the armored hull, the ship had launched missiles at the cybership.

The laser burned those and then retargeted the ship, soon destroying it.

"Does the spaceport have heavy guns?" Jon asked June.

"It did in the past," she said.

"Can you show us where?" the captain asked. He indicated a screen.

June stepped toward the screen. She was aware of the athletic captain leaving his chair to stand beside her. He stood too close. If Walleye came onto the bridge just now, he would be angry. Jon Hawkins might be a military hero, but that wouldn't matter to the mutant assassin.

Walleye kept to himself more since reaching the *Nathan Graham*. She believed he was jealous. All these marines and techs and so few women…it was no wonder many of the men watched her all the time. Walleye had never acted jealous or said anything, but June believed he was anyway.

"Miss Zen," the captain said.

She followed his finger and studied the spaceport on the planetary surface.

"Zoom in," Jon said.

The *Nathan Graham* was in orbit above the port. She hardly recognized the place down there. There were more metal structures showing than ever before. In the past, there had been the catapult launch system for ores and the blast pits for launching orbitals and heavy shuttles. Those structures had been the only metal showing. Now, there was a spider web of metal buildings.

"The robots have transformed the place," June said. "I don't recognize a thing."

"Would Walleye?" Jon asked.

"I doubt it. Neither of us went into space much."

"You said you worked for the orbital port authorities," Gloria said.

"I did for a little while. Normally, I was a computer analyst."

Jon nodded. "I'll have to talk to Walleye." He turned to her. "We're going down to Makemake, Miss Zen. I don't expect you to join us, but I'm hoping Walleye will."

"What?" June asked, as her chest constricted. "No! Walleye can't go. He's not a space marine."

"He knows the territory better than anyone else."

"Maybe…" she said. "But not if the robots have changed everything."

"I know you're worried for him," Jon said. "I know you've been through a lot. We all have. We've all taken risks. It's Walleye's turn again."

June searched the captain's face. He was youthful. He was handsome. But he was so hard-eyed and merciless. She suppressed a shudder. What would make a man so ruthless?

"Bring him back to me," she whispered.

The captain appeared surprised by the request. A moment later, he nodded. "I hope to bring us all back, Miss Zen."

"Don't call me that. I'm just June."

"Oh, certainly. If I've offended you…"

"No, no," she said. This time she did shudder. "Why did the aliens ever come to our Solar System? All they do is kill. They're horrible."

"I know what you mean," Jon said

323

-10-

Three days later, the NSN destroyer drifted out of a hangar bay. The destroyer was in less than stellar condition, but it was in better condition than any other spacecraft in their possession.

Jon was in the piloting chamber. The missile chief, Uther Kling, piloted. Kling was originally from Camelot Dome on Triton in the Neptune System. He had a blond buzz of hair cut in a triangle on his head, with an equally sharp chin like a red-tailed fox. Walleye was the only other person in the cabin with them. The rest of the passengers were space marines wearing battlesuits. Jon would don his once they landed.

The destroyer was not technically an atmospheric vessel. Still, in a pinch on a dwarf planet as small as Makemake, it could do it.

"We're heading down," Jon radioed.

"Roger that," Ghent said from the *Nathan Graham*.

The cybership was above them with the main laser ready to burn into anything hostile trying to hurt the destroyer.

"Just out of curiosity," Walleye said. "What friendly ship can come and get us if we're damaged?"

Jon took his time answering, finally saying, "None right now."

Walleye didn't respond, but he seemed to sit a little more stiffly.

Jon liked the assassin. The man claimed to be a mutant, and he *was* small, but he was also efficient. More than that, there was a quiet deadliness about Walleye that Jon admired.

After a time, the mutant said, "We're taking a pretty big risk going down, then, in the only serviceable spaceship."

Jon shrugged. That was one way of looking at it. The other was giving the robots too much time to dig in. He didn't know there were robots down there, but figured there must be.

"Hang on," Kling said. "This could get rough."

The destroyer began a slow, circling descent. The NSN vessel began to shake almost immediately, though.

"Switching to Vent C," Kling said.

That smoothed things out for thirty seconds. After that, the shaking intensified.

Walleye glanced at Jon. His glance seemed to ask the obvious. Why aren't you heading back up? We're never going to make it all the way down in this bucket.

Jon wanted to get this over with. He wanted to finish the robots so he could repair the cybership and get back to the Saturn System. How long would the Solar League wait until it sent a task force to reconquer the Saturn System?

"Missile launch," Kling said through clenched teeth. He looked at Jon, seeming to expect a quick order to abort the landing.

Jon watched a sensor board. The enemy missile was climbing fast. He finally reached for the comm to open channels with the *Nathan Graham*.

A powerful laser beam flashed past the destroyer. The laser struck the missile, heating it—a plume of an explosion showed the destroyed missile.

Jon glanced at the sensor board again, searching for a clue as to whether the warhead had detonated. No radiation or heat climbed up to hurt them.

"There's nothing to the landing," Jon said. "It should go easily after this."

The other two did not reply to his forced joviality.

The ship's shaking hadn't quit, although it wasn't as bad as before. The destroyer continued its long spiral descent.

Three minutes later, Kling said, "Two launches this time, Captain."

The *Nathan Graham's* laser beamed quicker this time. The targeting was perfect once again. The first missile blossomed into a fireball.

The sensors said it was a clean—

The second warhead ignited even though the laser hadn't touched it yet.

Kling reacted as if he'd been waiting for this to happen. The destroyer no longer descended, but roared straight, building up velocity until all three men pressed against their crash seats.

According to the sensors, the warhead was nuclear, but it had blown too low to the surface. Some radiation struck the destroyer, mostly blocked by the armored underbelly. Finally, Kling slowed down to one G of acceleration. He turned to Jon as if expectant for new orders.

"Maybe we should land a distance away from the spaceport," Jon said.

Kling's eyes bulged outward. "Sir," he said in a reprimanding voice.

Walleye cleared his throat.

"You don't want to land, either?" Jon asked Walleye.

"I'm not a military man," the mutant said. "I don't know the procedures for a space-to-ground assault. I have the feeling we're not even close to approaching standard tactics, though."

Jon thought about that. Walleye was right about them using a bold and unconventional approach.

"We already beat the main AI," Walleye began.

"That's just it," Jon said. "Maybe there are more alien AIs down there. One thing we're learning about the enemy is that we have to finish them off. We didn't finish them off last time. Now, we almost had to fight the original battle all over again."

"I don't dispute that," Walleye said. "But how does throwing away your only serviceable shuttle help the cause?"

"Sometimes a swift raid can solve a multitude of problems."

"Ever hear of the Charge of the Light Brigade?" Walleye asked.

"I thought you said you weren't a military man."

"I'm not. I have a Russian background, though. I have an ancestor who fought in the Crimean War."

"Never heard of it," Jon said.

"The British Light Brigade charged Russian cannons during the war. A man said about it, 'It's glorious, but it isn't war.'"

"The Light Brigade was composed of horsemen?" Jon asked.

"Those are big animals—"

"I know what a horse is," Jon said.

Walleye nodded. "The Light Brigade took horrendous loses because they tried a quick charge that must have seemed like a good idea at the time."

Jon checked the sensors. No more missiles had launched at them. "The robots are protecting something down there," he said.

"Blow 'em out with nukes," Walleye suggested.

"I want what they have down there," Jon said. "Without the alien construction tech—"

The comm crackled, interrupting him. A moment later, Jon responded.

"This is Gloria. Jon, we've found something big. It's the moon. According to my instruments, the moon is hollow."

"What instruments?" Jon asked.

"I landed a probe," Gloria said. "Why is the moon hollow? The best guess is that someone hollowed it out. I doubt the citizens of Makemake did it."

"We sure didn't," Walleye told Jon.

"That means the robots likely did it," Gloria said. "Maybe we should check out the moon before trying a surface assault."

"Good idea," Jon said. He turned to Kling. "Take us back up. The AI missiles and the hollow moon mean we're not making a glorious space-to-surface assault today."

-11-

After picking up the destroyer, the *Nathan Graham* left Makemake orbit. The nearly crippled cybership traveled 21,000 kilometers to MK2, the nickname of the single moon.

The moon was a mere 175 kilometers in diameter. Its surface had the reflectivity of charcoal.

"What do you see?" Jon asked. He was still in the destroyer's control cabin with the others.

"I see destroyed missile silos," Gloria said. "That must have happened from the cybership's antimatter explosion."

"Do you see any openings leading into the moon?"

"Not yet," Gloria said. "We're going to circle—wait. I see something. Jon! Those look like gigantic hatches or hangar bay doors. Should we go closer to investigate?"

Jon glanced at Walleye.

The mutant remained silent.

"Yeah," Jon said. "Take a look. We'll wait here."

***

The *Nathan Graham* eased toward MK2. The moon was 175 kilometers in diameter. The cybership was 100 kilometers. The moon was bigger, but the cybership could have acted as a smaller, sister moon.

"Those doors are huge," Gloria said from her comm station on the *Nathan Graham's* bridge.

Bast Banbeck stood nearby. "A thought has occurred to me," the Sacerdote said in his heavy voice. "We have analyzed the debris above the spaceport. It could not have come from a space dock holding the cybership."

Gloria glanced sharply at the seven-foot Sacerdote. "Are you suggesting the AIs hollowed out the moon, making *it* the space dock?"

"The possibility appears to exist," Bast said.

Gloria bent her head in thought as she ran through mentalist computations. Finally, she opened channels with Jon.

"Wait until you hear this," she told the captain.

***

Once more, the destroyer drifted through space. It left behind the monstrous cybership and headed toward the nearby MK2.

Jon radioed the Centurion, who was with the marines in the cargo hold. The men were holding up, receiving instructions for low G maneuvering.

"Anything hostile down there?" Jon asked Uther Kling.

The Neptunian slowly shook his head.

Jon rechecked the sensor board. The *Nathan Graham* had far more powerful sensors, and this time the giant cybership was almost as close to the target as the destroyer was. Still, two sets of eyes were usually better than one.

"Can't spy any energy readings," Jon muttered.

"You don't need me for this one," Walleye said.

"You don't want to suit up?" Jon asked.

"No. I'm allergic to spacewalks and—"

Jon chuckled. "No, problem. You can stay aboard the destroyer. I'll leave a few marines with you. So you'll have company."

"You still don't trust me, Captain?" Walleye asked.

"I trust you, but a little caution concerning my ride off the moon seems prudent."

"I agree," Walleye said. "Why take needless risks?"

Jon stopped listening to the mutant as he saw something on the sensor board. It could be—no, it wasn't a launch pit.

"Gun tube," Jon said a second latter. "I'm putting it on your screen," Jon told Kling.

Several seconds later, the destroyer launched two small missiles. They sped for the tracking gun. The *Nathan Graham's* laser hit the weapon system. As it did, the gun tube exploded, creating a pinprick of light down on the charcoal-colored surface.

The comm light blinked on Jon's board. Gloria explained, "The robots must have been trying to launch something just as the laser struck. The gun's munition is what caused the explosion, destroying everything."

"Do you think that was an automated response?" Jon asked.

"No. I think it indicates robots. I don't think that's an empty moon."

Jon slid forward on his seat, using the destroyer's scanners in earnest. He spotted two more gun tubes. Each time, the *Nathan Graham* destroyed the enemy weapon system before it could fire.

"The AIs don't want us landing here, either," Jon said.

"You know," Walleye told him. "It just occurred to me. The robots aren't stupid. They can calculate odds. Maybe they're only half-heartedly firing at us."

"Why?"

"To lure us closer," Walleye said. "Once you land, and once the *Nathan Graham* orbits closely, then the robots will self-destruct the moon. They'll take us out at a blow."

"Grim," Jon said, "but all too plausible." He opened channels with Gloria. "I want the *Nathan Graham* to pull back." Before the mentalist could ask why, Jon explained Walleye's reasoning.

"Roger," Gloria said. "We'll start to back up. Do you think you should take so many marines down with you?"

"I do," Jon said.

"But if the robots—"

"It's just a theory," Jon said. "We can't eliminate all risks. We have to take a chance now and again if we're going to grab the prize. We absolutely must grab the construction tech. Without it..."

"You're right," Gloria said. "I just hate to see you risking so much after you've done so much to get us this far."

"I'm the captain," Jon said.

"Which makes my point for me," Gloria said. "The captain should be at his post on the *Nathan Graham*, not leading a commando strike."

"I'm exactly where I need to be," Jon said. "Take care of my cybership, Mentalist. We're heading down."

"Take care, Jon."

"Roger that," he said. "Out."

Jon glanced at Kling. The Neptunian brought the destroyer closer to the dark surface.

"I think you failed to understand my meaning," Walleye said.

"I understood you perfectly," Jon replied. "Now it's time that you understand me."

-12-

Jon led one of the columns of battlesuited marines. He didn't actually lead from the front. He had scout marines do that.

The battlesuited marines used a special long-striding technique to cross the barren moonscape. The surface gravity was negligible, and there was no metallic surface to magnetize boots onto. A few times, a marine strode too hard, and he floated off the dark surface. A different marine radioed his floating partner, aimed a stubby weapon and fired a grappler. He towed his partner back onto the surface, and the pair long-strode to catch up with the column afterward.

"I see an opening," the Centurion radioed.

"I see your coordinates," Jon said, as he saw the Centurion's correlative blinking green light on his HUD grid. "We'll be there in five minutes."

"I'm setting up kill zones," the Centurion informed Jon.

Jon hadn't expected anything less from the man.

Soon, he arrived and so did the other columns. Jon inspected the opening. It was a large pit with blasted-away doors. Big moon-rock stairs led down.

"See anything on your sensors?" Jon asked the Centurion.

"No," the man said.

"Send down scouts," Jon said, hoping he wasn't sending marines to their deaths.

The scouts went down the stairs, soon finding a maze of corridors below.

"Looks like a vast ant heap," the Centurion radioed.

Jon sighed. He knew the drill. He also knew it was going to cost him men. But they had to grab the alien construction tech.

"Here's how we're going to do this," Jon said over the command channel.

***

The next twenty-one hours proved brutal. The small opening absorbed the Centurion's entire company.

Octopoid robots showed up, plenty of them. They laid ambushes, fired rockets, used powerful explosives and twice tried suicidal octopoid rushes. The Centurion lost thirty-two good marines while cleaning out the octopoids. The enemy lost over a thousand robots.

Jon had Walleye and his guardian marines take the destroyer off-moon. They fired missiles from there, breaking up octopoid reinforcements trying to slip more robots across the surface.

The *Nathan Graham* eliminated twenty-two enemy missiles with the laser. Each missile assault attempted to take out the deadly destroyer.

At the end of the twenty-one hours, Jon's group broke through to the inner surface of the hollow moon. He saw the amazing sight first, and it gave him hope that maybe he could still pull this off strategically.

***

Jon stood inside a large hangar bay. One of the marines had found the controls that opened the doors.

In his battlesuit, Jon clanked to the edge of the inner surface. Twenty or so kilometers away, giant lamps illuminated much of the moon's hollowness.

Jon marveled at what he saw. There were hundreds, possibly thousands, of small tugs floating in the hollow moon. There was no doubt the alien robots had built the new cybership inside MK2. This was the missing space dock.

The last twenty-one hours had also shown Jon that the robots had stockpiled an immense amount of supplies to finish the new—now destroyed—enemy cybership.

His helmet headphones crackled.

"Captain," the Centurion said. "You have to come and see this."

Jon thought he should be telling that to the Centurion. Instead, he asked, "What did you find?"

"I think it's MK2's control area."

"What makes you think that?"

"I found an alien AI. It must have controlled MK2."

"How many men did you lose breaking into the chamber?"

"Three more," the Centurion said. "The last octopoid must have set off explosions. It destroyed the AI cube and most of the computers around the smoldering wreck."

Jon considered that. "We're still here."

"Maybe the AI failed to detonate the moon," the Centurion said. "Or maybe they never rigged the moon, the space dock, to self-destruct."

"That would be AI arrogance," Jon said.

"Maybe," the Centurion said.

"I'm on my way."

***

The days passed as the Black Anvil Regiment went octopoid hunting in and on the moon. Hunting in deadly earnest, the space marines developed new tactics to deal with the alien robots. The regiment used massed firepower and maneuver to trick the enemy. The robots fought poorly after the MK2 AI's destruction. It must have been their coordinating unit.

Despite the bulk and volume of MK2, by the end of the second week, the Centurion could declare victory. They found strange consoles that tracked the positions of the remaining octopoids. With those consoles, the fight finally cycled down and then ended altogether.

Jon had won the alien space dock. Figuring out how to use it might take longer.

He spoke with Gloria in the inner hangar bay. It had been three weeks since they destroyed the enemy cybership. Now, all the lights shone brightly, illuminating the giant inner space dock.

"We have the alien construction tech," Jon said. "Now we have to figure out how to run it without activating something terrible. Then, we have to decide if we can trust the *Nathan Graham* inside the moon."

"It will be a risk," Gloria admitted. "I've done some computations. You have plenty of stock laid up in MK2. It should allow us to make major repairs to the *Nathan Graham*. We won't finish all the needed repairs, though. To do that, we'd have to start bringing Makemake ores here like the robots must have done."

"You mean clean out the robots still down on the dwarf planet."

Gloria nodded her bubble helmet.

"I'm not sure I want to risk losing more marines," Jon said.

"You might not have a choice if you want to fully repair the cybership."

Jon knew what she meant. They were so far away from Earth, out here in the Kuiper Belt. Unless they could thoroughly fix the *Nathan Graham's* matter/antimatter engine, it would take them a long time to get back to the Saturn System. The cybership had already picked up the exhaust signatures of the SLN fleet heading for the Jupiter System. If the SLN invaded the Saturn System…

"Well," Jon said. "At least we stopped the AIs' master plan."

"You don't *know* that," Gloria said. "There could be more bases like this in the Kuiper Belt or maybe even in the Oort cloud."

Jon didn't want to hear that.

"It's true that we've won another round in the great battle," Gloria said. "We've gained two bases in the process. One is in the Saturn System, and maybe we can exploit this one here. We have the greatest ship in the Solar System. But that just makes us king of a very small pond."

"You think more cyberships might show up from out there?" Jon said.

"I give that an extremely high probability."

"We have to get ready for them then."

"We need to do more than that," Gloria said. "I suspect there are no more AI bases of great size in the Belt. That means we've likely eliminated that terrible threat for the next few years."

"Unless more of them drop out of hyperspace," Jon said.

"True," Gloria said. "But that's missing my point. We've stopped the AIs for the moment. Now, we have to use the pause and unify our Solar System."

"Conquer the Solar League?" asked Jon.

"That seems like the next logical step."

"How do we conquer them?" Jon asked. "I can beat any one fleet in any one place, but I hardly have the space marines to go down and hold a planet or even a moon."

"That will be a problem," Gloria admitted.

Jon laughed sourly. "It's more than a problem."

"For an ordinary person, yes," Gloria said.

"What's that supposed to mean?"

"Don't you consider yourself a Great Captain?"

Jon felt his face heat up as he blushed.

"A Great Captain, given your tools, would surely figure out a way to unite humanity," Gloria said. "We need a powerful base of operations if we hope to defeat a cybership fleet."

Jon didn't even want to think about that just yet.

"We've won this round," Gloria said. "But we still have a gigantic task ahead of us."

"Yeah," Jon said.

The mentalist slapped his battlesuit shoulder. "Don't be down, Captain. You've done the impossible. Rejoice. We're partway to truly giving the AIs something to think about."

Jon smiled. The other cyberships didn't know it yet, but there was a race in the galaxy that had defeated them twice now. The humans had so far proven too big a pill to swallow. Could they unite the Solar System, and could they grow powerful enough to free other species from the death machines?

Those were big questions. Maybe it would be best to take things one step at a time. They had beaten the second cybership and stolen the AI construction tech. Now, it was time to exploit those victories to the max.

THE END

SF Books by Vaughn Heppner

DOOM STAR SERIES:
Star Soldier
Bio Weapon
Battle Pod
Cyborg Assault
Planet Wrecker
Star Fortress
Task Force 7 (Novella)

EXTINCTION WARS SERIES:
Assault Troopers
Planet Strike
Star Viking
Fortress Earth

LOST STARSHIP SERIES:
The Lost Starship
The Lost Command
The Lost Destroyer
The Lost Colony
The Lost Patrol
The Lost Planet

Visit VaughnHeppner.com for more
information

Made in the USA
San Bernardino, CA
08 November 2017